A House of Fangs & Deceit

Lunaria Realms
Book 1

Alex Frost

GREYMALKIN

Published by Greymalkin Press
www.greymalkinpress.com

Dev & Line Editing by Proofs by Polly
Copy-editing and Proofreading by Ashley Olivier
Cover Design by Cover by Jules

Ebook ISBN - 979-8-9881893-4-3
Paperback ISBN - 979-8-9881893-5-0

The Lunaria Realms Series

A House of Fangs & Deceit

A Court of Bones & Sorrow

A Throne of Blood & Vengeance

Note From Author

A gentle reminder that this is a why choose romantasy, which means there are going to be multiple love interests. And our dear, sweet Samara will not be choosing between any of them.

You can still pick a favorite though. I won't tell.

Let's chat real quick about what to expect in this book. This is a fantasy novel that contains adult content and situations. If it was a movie, it would probably be rated "R" for violence, language, and sexual content. If you want to go into this book completely blind and prefer not to read content warnings, you can skip on ahead, my friend.

If there are certain topics that you need to avoid for the sake of your own mental health, or that you simply don't like, please take a look at the list below for some things you will find in this book.

- Explicit consensual sex scenes (there is no dub-con or non-con)
- Blood drinking
- References to parental death
- Cheating but **not** between love interests

Also… quick little note on language. I am a strange, strange person, and I've lived a bit of an odd life. I was born and raised in California, but was mostly raised by my Canadian grandmother and was then unofficially adopted by an Irish family in my late teens. You might be wondering why I'm mentioning this, and the reason is that I have a bit of a magpie approach when it comes to the English language.

Sometimes I like the American English spelling… sometimes I'm really attached to that extra "u" and go for the non-American version. Variety is the spice of life y'all.

Bless the soul of my copy-editor because she just sighs heavily at the start of each manuscript and deals with my eccentricities. So if you're an American and looking at a word and thinking it's not spelt right… it is most likely the non-American version of the word.

LUN
Lake Sp
Alph
A
VELE
Lake Turoth
ORDER OF
FERVIS TERRITORY
Lake Aridesh
FURIE
REALM
Fae Temp
Ruins
The
Badlands
Furie Stronghold
N
W
E
S

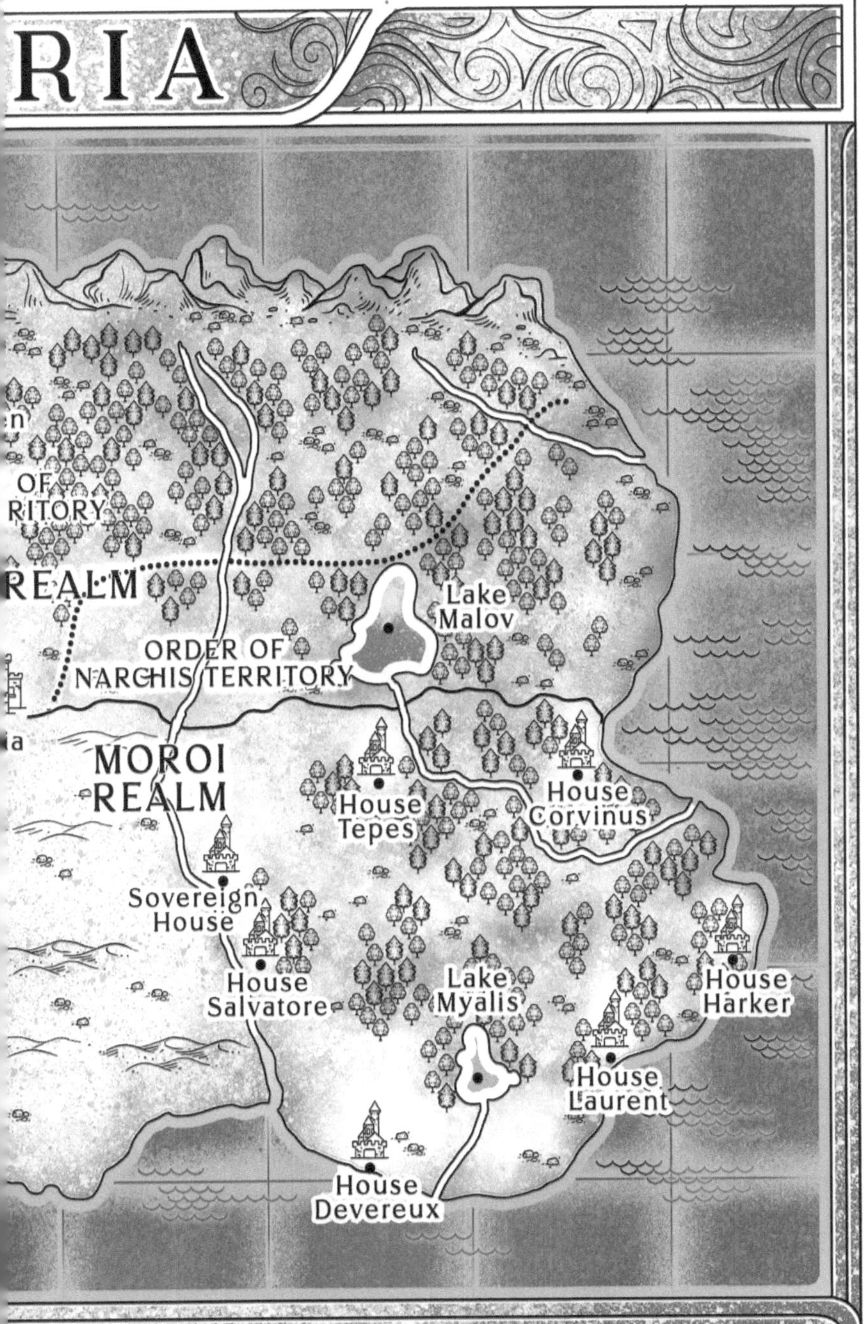
RIA
OF
RITORY
REALM
ORDER OF
NARCHIS TERRITORY
Lake Malov
MOROI REALM
House Tepes
House Corvinus
Sovereign House
House Salvatore
Lake Myalis
House Harker
House Laurent
House Devereux

To Ash, for encouraging me to get my smut on.

Prologue

WE WALKED single file to our deaths. The cool night air seeped through my thin cloak, but I didn't mind.

Being cold was the least of my concerns. Whatever happened on this night, we would not live to see the morning.

Not as humans.

What remained of the village elders walked in front of us. A few more years and I would have been considered one of them.

I was Rosalyn Harker, and my family had been part of this village for generations. Our name passed down through the maternal line. The women of our family were strong. Resilient. Natural-born leaders.

But that was a different future, one that I couldn't even imagine anymore.

A few sobs escaped those trailing behind me, but nobody turned back. There was nothing to return to. We'd fortified the village as best we could over the last few months, but nothing kept the monsters out.

When the elders had first suggested this idea, they were

met with harsh denial, then silence, and finally, reluctant agreement.

In the end, we all knew it was clear the future only held death for us now.

So, we might as well do it on our terms.

When we finally reached our destination, the elders formed a small circle around three flat stones, each bearing a carefully carved symbol within its face. The shiny black surface of the stones perfectly reflected the light of the moon.

The elders gestured for me to join them and then instructed everyone else to form circles.

We'd already practiced this, so everyone fell into place quickly, and soon we had six circles expanding from the one I stood in with the elders.

I spared a look over my shoulder and met the even gaze of my daughter.

The barest hint of sorrow flickered deep within my chest. She was almost twenty years old, but she would always be my sweet little girl.

When my sleep wasn't plagued by nightmares, I had dreams of summers spent in flowery fields with her laughing as she raced along, chased by her twin sister, while they plucked purple and blue flowers to wind into crowns later.

She hasn't laughed since the monsters tore apart her sister.

I twisted back around to stare at the carved-up stone at my feet. It would be our death, but it also might be our salvation.

The Fae had vanished, leaving us defenseless against the cruel beasts that prowled these lands. They may not have been the kindest of rulers, but they had kept the worst of the horrors at bay.

Now they were gone, leaving us not only at the mercy of the monsters of old but new ones made of nothing but shadows.

The elders suspected that the Unseelie had done something, performed some spell, perhaps against the Seelie, and lost control of it.

After all, it couldn't be a coincidence that the Unseelie, who could send their shadows off to spy or shape them into vicious guardians, had disappeared without a trace, and now creatures of darkness roamed our lands at night. They'd likely killed all the Seelie in the process of whatever wicked magic they had worked.

The clouds above us parted, revealing the bright, full moon. We'd been waiting for this night for weeks, and there were times when, admittedly, I thought we wouldn't make it.

Six months ago, there had been hundreds of thousands of us living across these lands. Now there were less than ten thousand humans left. Our village had fared better than others. Almost five hundred of us remained of the twelve hundred who had once called this place home.

My mind wandered bleakly to the graveyard not too far from here. My parents were buried there, as well as my grandparents. Generations of Harkers had lived and died here.

I hadn't been able to bury my daughter or my husband. There had been nothing left of them to bury.

The lack of feeling that had become my constant companion since their deaths lifted for a moment, and in its place, I felt unimaginable pain.

I swallowed and begged the numbness to return. For the pain to abate, if only just for now.

I needed it to get through these next few moments.

We all knew what we were giving up with this spell, not only our humanity but our identities as well. Who we were would die tonight.

It had started as a plan for survival.

We couldn't live as humans anymore, not in a world ruled by monsters.

We had to become monsters as well.

The elders believed that we might remember bits of our humanity if we survived long enough. That we could claw it back from the darkness.

But I didn't want it. Fuck humanity.

No, what I wanted was far simpler. I wanted to race away from this village tonight and tear into the beasts that had torn into my daughter. Who had snatched away the man I'd loved since I was sixteen years old.

I wanted to make the monsters afraid.

"It's time," Irina said from where she stood opposite me on the other side of the stones.

I could remember her sitting in our house sipping coffee when I was a little girl. My mother would braid my hair while they discussed potential new hunting grounds. She had a slight curve to her back, and her chestnut hair was mostly grey now, but she still had a will of iron. The Laurent family had been in this village even longer than the Harkers.

The whispers and shuffling died down as the elders started chanting, keeping their words slow and carefully enunciated.

Irina turned towards her right, and the woman standing there bared her neck. Tali, our neighbor. Her dark brown eyes used to be so warm and inviting. Now they were cold and hollow. She was the only surviving member of her family.

Neither hesitated nor flinched as Irina carved a symbol into her neck from a blade made from the same type of stone at the center of our circle. Once Irina was finished, she passed the blade to Tali, who did the same to the man standing at her right.

One by one, the elders marked each other until it was my turn.

I barely felt the blade dig into my neck. When the cool stone knife was placed in my hand, I turned around to face my daughter. My hand hesitated, but Nysa wrapped her fingers around mine and guided the knife to her neck.

Our bloodline was strong. And Nysa was owed vengeance too. I would not deny her this. The sharpened stone cut into her skin. The magic guided my fingers as I etched a crescent moon into the left side of her neck.

Choosing that particular symbol hadn't been a conscious decision on my part.

The elders had convened for weeks to settle on what beasts we would turn into. It was impossible to know which ones would fare best against the monsters of our world, but if too many were chosen, we risked the spell being watered down and failing entirely. In the end, these were the three that were selected. Each bearing different strengths to better our odds of surviving.

The blood trickling down my neck started to burn, but I kept saying the words over and over, only vaguely aware of their meaning.

Across all of Lunaria, what remained of the humans had gathered to conduct the same ritual as we asked the moon to bless us.

A haze filled my mind, and I felt myself unravel. But I welcomed the feeling and begged it to take me faster, only wavering when I felt my daughter's hand slip into mine. I turned towards her and watched as her light sky-blue eyes darkened until they were almost black.

She smiled at me for the first time in ages as the magic took her, the chant never faltering from her lips. I gave her a vicious grin in return as the last of the words rang into the night sky, their meaning revealed.

"We will give our lives for the blood."
"We will yield our fates in the wild."
"We will lose our souls to the fury."

CHAPTER ONE

—

Samara

200 Years Later

"Is that what you're wearing?"

I glanced away from the mirror outside my closet to the bed, where a man with auburn hair and light brown eyes lounged. Demetri's lips twisted in a concerned frown as he gestured towards the dress I'd just put on.

"What's wrong with it?" I turned my attention back to the mirror. The deep royal-blue color complemented my golden-hued brown skin. Twisting around so I could see it from the side and back, I peered over my shoulder at him. "Everything is covered up, and it's not *that* formfitting. Not a hint of cleavage to be seen," I teased.

My husband of three years rolled his eyes. "I think you look perfect, but you know how things are around here."

Boring. That's how things were at House Laurent. *Fucking boring.*

I plastered a pleasant smile onto my face and sauntered over to the bed. Demetri's eyes lit up as he watched me approach, but he didn't bother getting up.

"I'll see what else I can find in the closet," I told him. "I'm meeting with your mother and her council today, so it's probably for the best that I don't *offend* anyone by reminding them that I have curves."

He snorted a laugh as I placed my hand on my chest dramatically. Demetri wasn't nearly as conservative as the others of House Laurent, but he also wasn't the type to push for change.

But it was easy for him to follow the unspoken fashion rules of this place, unlike myself. Unless I donned a shapeless sack, anything I wore would be obscene by their standards. Even then, I'm pretty sure my large chest, wide hips, and luscious ass would still make whatever I wore too scandalous for my husband's House.

"I'm sure you'll find something." Demetri's gaze went a little distant, his mind clearly already moved on from our conversation.

I held in a sigh as he rolled out of bed and gave me a chaste kiss on the lips.

He murmured, "A friend of mine is visiting from one of the other Houses today. I'm going to catch up with them and probably plan a trip to go to their House and a few others this month."

"You're going to leave again?" My hand froze on the dress I'd been about to shove aside. "But you just got back."

"You know how the life of an Heir is," he reminded me, already walking away. A moment later, I heard the door to our suite open and shut.

I knew *exactly* what the life of an Heir was like. I'd grown up as the Heir of House Harker and had only given up that title to marry into House Laurent... where I was supposed to be an Heir alongside Demetri.

Every time I suggested that I should travel with Demetri to other Houses, I was shot down for one reason or another.

For a long time, I'd been determined that I could make this work, that eventually Demetri and, more importantly, his mother, would realize they were wasting my potential.

But now I was starting to wonder if I'd made a serious mistake coming here.

"Are you happy?"

Those three damn words had been bouncing around in my mind since Rynn, one of my best friends, had asked the question during our weekly check-in.

I was the daughter and former Heir of House Harker, and now I was the wife of the Heir of House Laurent. Both Houses were made up of some of the strongest Moroi bloodlines, and I now represented them both.

This marriage arrangement might have been my aunt's suggestion, but I'd not only agreed with her idea, I'd been *excited* about it. The marriage between our two Houses was an important alliance for House Harker. I was happy to serve my House in such a way and had worked hard my entire life to be the perfect wife and partner.

But in the decade I'd spent studying and training for my fated role in life, I never thought to question if it would be something I'd actually enjoy.

In the three years that I'd been married to Demetri and living in House Laurent, I'd never really thought about whether I was happy or not. This was my life, and it was important for me to be successful. My happiness shouldn't matter. It was as simple as that.

Yet that moon-damned question was all I could think about. Fucking Rynn and her pointed questions. She knew I wasn't exactly happy, but had she said that, I would have denied it. By phrasing it as a question, she was forcing me to answer. It was one of her more aggravating tactics of getting me to face the truth.

Cali would never have asked such a thing. No, she just

noted every time my eyes were red-rimmed from crying over my loneliness at House Laurent or from the constant slights and barely disguised insults that greeted me almost every day. I'd gotten the distinct feeling over the years that she was very much considering killing Demetri for not protecting me in his own House. I'd had to make her swear to me that she wouldn't harm a hair on his head.

It wasn't out of love for my husband, as we didn't have that kind of relationship. But as Heir of House Laurent, Demetri's death wouldn't exactly go unnoticed. Besides, I could fight my own battles and didn't need Cali sweeping in to save me.

My two best friends were the opposites of each other in so many ways, but they loved me as much as I loved them. Even when they asked questions that sent me down an emotional spiral.

I chucked the dress I'd chosen off and put the new one on, frowning as I looked at myself in the mirror. Demetri's mother would likely hate this one too, but there wasn't much I could do about it.

Hopefully, I'd be able to impress her enough with my trade proposition that she'd overlook my appearance.

Thoughts about the conversation with Rynn and Cali and my time at House Laurent clouded my mind as I absently made my way down the long hallway outside our suite. Servants scurried by with their eyes firmly on the floor.

When I had first come to this place, the opulent decor and meek servants had thrown me off. It was so different from the understated elegance of my own family home and the humble furnishings of Drudonia where I'd studied in my teenage years.

Happiness was something I could seek later.

At least, that's why I told myself these past few mornings when Demetri gave me a dutiful kiss and a charming smile before disappearing for his various House responsibilities.

It was what I repeated throughout the day as I sought out knowledge of what was happening outside these fortified walls.

"Do you need anything, my lady?"

I tore my gaze away from the painting of some distant relative of Demetri's great uncle, perhaps, and looked at the girl before me.

Despite my attempts to befriend the household staff—because as a good friend had taught me, the servants always held the best gossip—they treated me the same as all the Laurent family.

I wasn't used to failing at anything, so I kept at it, hoping I would one day win them over.

The servant girl's blonde hair was neatly tucked away in a braid, and her eyes were firmly fixed on the tips of my toes, her expression submissive, albeit slightly nervous. The latter struck me as odd, something I'd noticed around the premises on occasion.

"I'm fine, Rose. Thank you," I said kindly. Her pretty green eyes peeked at me before hastily looking away. "My mind is just a little adrift this morning. Perhaps I'll swing by the kitchen for a second cup of tea."

"I can bring you some," she said quickly. "Black tea with honey."

"That would be lovely," I lied.

While the tea sounded fantastic, I'd really been wanting to get it myself as I so often did in the morning.

The kitchen was one of the few places the staff relaxed enough to talk, and I'd been hoping to maybe overhear some gossip, but it was probably for the best. I should be preparing for the meeting later today anyway.

"Would you mind bringing it to the study on the third floor?" I asked. "I have some paperwork I'd like to review."

She nodded once and hurried away.

I frowned after her departure. Demetri and Marvina, his

mother, had always treated the staff fairly. They may not be kind in their orders, but I'd never seen anything to explain why there was such an undercurrent of fear amongst them.

Shaking my head, I continued on to the study that I had taken over as an office of sorts.

I hadn't been lying about feeling off-kilter today. Rynn's simple question had hit me when I was already in a weird mental state, and I hadn't been able to snap out of it since.

After years of being shoved to the sidelines and playing the role of the smiling bride, I was finally making headway in getting involved in House politics. Demetri's mother ruled House Laurent with an iron fist and was pleased that her son held zero interest in taking over one day. She was less pleased about my interests in ruling, or at least co-ruling.

Though, for the last six months, she had allowed me to sit in on meetings with her advisors. I wasn't entirely sure why she had offered this, but I suspected it was my Aunt Carmilla's doing.

Being that she oversaw House Harker and was close friends with the Sovereigns who ruled over all the Moroi, she wasn't shy about flexing her political power when she needed to. If she had stepped in on my behalf, I was grateful... but also a little annoyed that I'd needed her help, which was probably why she hadn't told me about her interference.

I'd been working on a trade proposal for the last week with some of the Velesian packs, mostly of the Narchis Order. It wouldn't bring us in any great riches, but it would help the tension that had been growing between the Moroi and Velesians for the last decade.

I just had to present it in the right way. It had taken some time, but I was beginning to learn how to manage Marvina. Now, if only I could figure out the same with my dear husband.

Maybe then I could get a damn orgasm once in a while.

I didn't count the one I gave myself every morning before I rose from bed after Demetri had already gotten up and left.

I laughed softly to myself, earning a few wayward glances from a servant girl as she hurried by. Cali had quickly pointed out my rather lackluster sex life after Rynn had asked about my happiness, which summed up my two besties rather accurately.

We might come from different species and backgrounds, but we each knew each other well. Far better than anyone else could claim.

"Give her a break, Rynn," Cali had said. *"Her husband might be easy on the eyes, but he's clearly as boring in bed as he is in conversation."*

"He really doesn't have a lot going on upstairs." Rynn's voice sparked with the mischief that she hid from everyone but us.

"Not a lot going on downstairs either," I'd drawled wryly, prompting a laugh out of them.

It'd been a bit mean of me, but I knew that they'd never share anything we talked about, so I tended to let my inner catty self out around them.

I needed the break from having to constantly measure out my words and watch my tone every day. Besides, they knew I was joking.

During one of our many chats via shadow magic, Demetri had walked in from the washroom completely naked, unaware that I was talking with Rynn and Cali, and gave them both an eyeful.

Truthfully, there wasn't anything wrong with Demetri. He was a perfect specimen of a Moroi male in every way.

Every way.

Unfortunately, he was rather uninspired in how he used that perfection.

There'd never been any kind of passion between us, but at least we didn't outright hate each other like some of the other married couples I knew.

Maybe once I got Marvina to take me seriously, I could

spend more time with Demetri, and we could figure out how to get some spark in our relationship. Give my poor fingers a break.

I breezed into my study, pleased to see that everything was exactly as I left it. Chaotic.

I knew it made the servants nervous to leave the room in such a state, but *I* knew where everything was, and that was all that mattered. Settling into my favorite chair by the window, I picked up the thick tome from where I'd left it on the windowsill and plucked out several papers.

The musky smell from the pages made my nose twitch as I carefully unfolded the map and stretched it out on the low table in front of me.

House Laurent was located on the coast and had the most mines out of any of the Moroi Houses. At least half a dozen deposits of gold, silver, and iron wound their way under the House itself before stretching far out, and the coastline that was less than an hour's walk from where I was sitting was lined with basalt.

It was these metals and minerals that allowed us to safeguard our territories against the monsters that roamed these lands, but there was one crucial resource that House Laurent didn't have. Malachite.

The Velesian packs in Narchis territory had plenty of it, though.

I wasn't able to get the exact numbers, but I was reasonably sure that our stock of malachite was running low. Likely to run out within the next year, in fact.

In the past, House Laurent had gotten the resource from other Moroi Houses, but it made far more sense to go to the Velesians because they had so much of it, and the few Moroi Houses that had it would demand far more in trade.

The wards that were used by the Houses to keep out the wraiths were created with blood magic and various metals like gold or silver, but minerals were required to keep them powered up, and malachite was the best. Other minerals like quartz could be used, but they had to be replaced every few weeks, whereas malachite could be powered up to last for almost a year.

Footsteps sounded from the hallway, and a moment later Rose entered with a steaming cup of tea in one hand and a plate of pastries in the other.

"Thank you," I murmured as she set everything down on the table, taking care not to disturb the map or the teetering stacks of scrolls and books.

"Can I get you anything else, my lady?" She studied the map curiously but didn't ask about it. When she felt my attention on her, she quickly cast her eyes to the floor and hunched in her shoulders.

"I realize that telling someone you can trust them doesn't mean much. Trust is something that can only be earned through actions and time." I reached over and broke a piece off one of the pastries. "But if there is ever something... amiss about how you or any of the staff are treated here, please find a way to let me know, and I will help."

A slight tremble ran through her, and she opened her mouth, only to snap it shut.

"All is well," she said finally before turning to leave the room. As she arrived at the doorway, she slowed and rotated her head slightly, not completely turning towards me. "Thank you for your concern."

Disappointment weighed heavily on me, but she was gone before I could respond. I popped the pastry morsel into my mouth and chewed thoughtfully. Rose seemed like a naturally shy person, so it was hard for me to get a read on her. The servants here were much more reserved and timid than the ones at House Harker, but that didn't necessarily mean anything was wrong.

Maybe I was just looking for something that wasn't there, and they were all intense introverts who wanted to retreat to their rooms and read. Perhaps my being nosy all the time was what set Rose on edge.

A smile tugged at my lips. If only I had Kieran's charm. My childhood friend could talk to anyone and put them at ease.

I sipped my tea for another hour, the floral blend my favorite because it was good even after it had cooled. My argument for why we needed to improve our trading with the Velesians was sound and my proposals perfectly reasonable.

Confidence firmly in place, I rose ten minutes before the meeting was due to start and made my way to the second floor.

There was a large room dedicated to assemblies, but that was mostly used when representatives from other Houses or from the Velesian packs visited. I strode past that room and instead headed to Marvina's study where she ran all the meetings with her advisors. It was easily four times the size of the cozy one I preferred to work in.

Almost everyone was seated when I entered. There were six chairs with thick cushions and tall regal backs spaced out in a half-moon shape, all facing a massive desk with a single chair behind it.

I strode over to the desk with my chin held high and placed my proposal on it.

Hestia and Gaelin, who were the closest to my age and also originally from other Houses, nodded to me in greeting, but the others dismissed me. They took their cues from Marvina, and until she took me seriously, they didn't consider me worth their time.

Rather than take a seat and wait in awkward silence as everyone tried to pretend I didn't exist, I did the same thing I always did—toyed with them.

I aimlessly walked around the room, studying the various

paintings on the wall as if I hadn't already looked at them a hundred times. Although, I did pause with genuine interest when I reached the large map that took up almost a quarter of the wall space. It was beautifully painted, displaying not only Moroi territory but also that of the Velesian's and Furies' as well. Every city and stronghold was carefully placed on the map, along with all existing trade routes.

As I studied the map, I felt several of the male advisors' eyes on me as they hungrily took in my flesh, and my lips curled in satisfaction.

House Laurent was different from the House I'd been born into. House Harker was well-respected both because of our age and because my aunt was close friends with the ruling Moroi queen and her consort, known collectively as the Sovereigns. But my birth House still retained a bit of our wild side, and I'd grown up amongst Moroi who dressed with most of their flesh on display.

We thought bodies were things to be worshipped and celebrated. It'd been quite a shock when I'd visited House Laurent for the first time, shortly before I'd married Demetri, and seen everyone wearing conservative clothing that played down their curves rather than enhanced them.

Marvina had arranged for an entirely new wardrobe to be made for me, and it had awaited me in my suite when I'd visited for a second time. The message of how I was expected to dress while in the walls of her House was quite clear. I'd added different pieces to my wardrobe over the years that were slightly more risqué than what most wore here, but nothing too daring.

I hated my new wardrobe, but I tried to be respectful of House Laurent's customs... most of the time.

Everyone in this House pretended to be so uptight, but it wasn't like they didn't have dirty thoughts spiraling around in their minds like the rest of us heathens.

We were Moroi for fuck's sake. We craved sex almost as much as we craved blood.

Absently, I trailed my fingers down my soft belly and then rested my hands on my hips. One corner of my mouth tugged up in a smirk as Gaelin caught the movement and gawked openly before Cazimir cleared his throat and Gaelin quickly looked away.

Cali always teased me that I had a body for sin, and it was a waste for me not to use it to my advantage. I always rolled my eyes when she said it, but I had to admit that it was fun to mess with Marvina's advisors and see how close I could get them to outright drool over me.

It was petty, sure, but things around here could be dreadfully boring, and I had to take my fun where I could get it.

Before I could think of more ways to torture some of the advisors, Marvina swept into the room and took a seat in her chair. With its wide back made of rich dark wood and grooves inlaid with obsidian and silver, I always thought it was more throne than chair.

I calmly took a seat in the remaining empty chair and folded my hands across my lap, then swept my gaze over her while the rest of the council settled further into their seats.

Demetri had taken after her, sharing the same dark auburn hair and beautiful light brown eyes. I didn't know what his father looked like, as he died over a decade ago, and his portrait was oddly absent from all the walls. When I'd asked Demetri about it, he'd just shrugged and said he had no idea. Marvina's skin was a few shades lighter than Demetri's lightly tanned hue, and the sharp features that were charming on my husband always gave off a haughtier expression on Marvina.

I gave her a polite smile when her piercing eyes fell on me before she flicked her fingers towards my proposal. Then she plucked the pages up and skimmed through them, her face unreadable. I forced myself to remain calm and fixed my features into a neutral expression.

My proposal was sound and made both financial and political sense. Rynn was technically supposed to join the Alpha Pack, who belonged to the Order of Avala, but she'd been born into the Order of Narchis, which meant she had experience with both Orders.

Like me, she had been training her entire life to serve in an elevated position, and she'd been an excellent resource to help smooth things out from the Velesian standpoint.

I was confident in my proposal and hopefully, Marvina would finally see me as the asset I was.

"Well, Samara, I have to say that it's fascinating to me that in the three years you've been residing in my House, you never once displayed such an interesting sense of humor," she said in a light, airy voice.

My breath caught in my throat as several of the advisors snickered in their seats. "I'm sorry," I said tightly with a false smile. "I'm afraid I don't understand."

"You want us"—she placed a hand ordained with rings of gold and glittering jewels on her chest—"to trade with the mongrels? What could they possibly want with gold and silver? They spend half their lives in fur."

Anger flashed through me then, vibrant and hot. For a second, I felt my bloodlust rise.

I should have known that Marvina belonged to the group of Moroi who thought they were better than the Velesians. She'd never been so obvious about it in the past, but she'd made little comments here and there. It was one of the reasons why I'd never invited Rynn here, despite her hinting that she would like to come and see me.

We were all Moon Blessed. Our human ancestors had performed a ritual to make themselves better able to survive in a world full of monsters. The Moroi, Velesians, and Furies had just as much in common as we had our differences, but some refused to see it that way.

"While they have no need of gaudy jewelry,"—my eyes flicked to the rings on her finger—"gold and silver are used to lay enchantments on weapons so that they can fight against the wraiths. We need malachite. Everyone wins in this trade." I said straight in my chair, refusing to give up under the weight of her glower.

The advisors who had been snickering at my expense earlier were now completely silent as their eyes darted back and forth between me and Marvina. Tension filled the room as everyone waited to see how Marvina would respond to my refusal to back down.

"House Laurent is one of the oldest Houses in existence," she said coldly. "I agreed to the marriage between you and Demetri because it was in the best interest of our House at the time. I have made sure you remained in these walls because I refuse to allow you to represent us to the other Houses. Not with the way you are and the way you dress. You should have been grateful that I've allowed you to sit in on these meetings but instead, you bring me this ridiculous trade proposal."

I bristled as rage and humiliation warred within me. House Laurent might be one of the oldest Houses, but House Harker *was* the oldest. My ancestors had been the first of the Moroi to claw back their humanity.

As much as I wanted to rub that into Marvina's face, it wouldn't help anything, and it would only cause a problem for my aunt and House Harker. I knew Marvina thought poorly of the Velesians, but I thought she'd been smart enough to at least see the value of this trade.

I had miscalculated badly, and I was furious at myself for such a misstep.

A persistent ache flared in my gums as my bloodlust stirred

thanks to my spiraling emotions. I wrestled it back, but it still felt like my blood was burning through my veins.

"My apologies," I said tightly as I rose from my chair, barely managing to keep my emotions off my face. "I will work on a different trade proposal that is more befitting for House Laurent." *You stuck-up, arrogant bitch.*

"That's not necessary. I have my advisors to help me with such endeavors. Your only job here is to make my son happy, and you can't even manage that." She gave me a cutting look. "I suggest you spend your time trying to rectify that situation."

CHAPTER TWO

—

Samara

Pain shot through my gums as my fangs started to extend further. Heat burned behind my eyes, and all I could do was jerk my head in a nod before fleeing the room.

Amused snorts and chuckles followed in my wake as I clenched my fists until my nails bit into flesh and blood dripped from my knuckles. I used the sharp pain to help ground me as my feet carried me through the halls and stairwells until I found myself in the main garden located in the center of the fortress that was House Laurent.

I sucked in a breath as I wiped the blood from my hands onto my dress. The crescent cuts across my palms stung from where my nails had dug in. At least they hadn't shifted into claws and done more damage.

After a few moments of steady breathing, my fangs receded to their normal length of being only slightly longer than the rest of my teeth.

It'd been a while since I'd drunk from Demetri, and I was overdue for some blood. He tended to treat our feeding sessions like an unavoidable duty, if not a nuisance, so I only did it when I had to, which usually led to me putting it off for longer than I should. My bloodlust had come dangerously close to rising in that room, and Marvina likely would have had me chained in the dungeon if that had happened, even though I wouldn't have actually attacked anyone.

Probably not… unless one of them tried to run. I hissed as my fangs once again lengthened at the thought of chasing down prey. Screw it. They could stay out for a bit. They would naturally recede once I calmed down.

Since I was a Harker, it was unlikely I'd completely lose control of my bloodlust and be unable to come back from it.

When that happened to a Moroi, we referred to them as Strigoi. To my knowledge, no one had ever come back after earning that title. All Moroi had to contend with bloodlust, but some were more likely than others to completely lose their grasp on humanity and devolve into beasts driven by nothing but hunger and survival.

Our bloodlust gave us an edge in a world full of monsters. Not only did we grow fangs and claws, but our instincts also went into overdrive.

Truthfully, I found it a little intoxicating, but mostly because I never feared losing myself to it. My bloodline was strong; even our ancestors who originally turned Moroi had retained some of their humanity.

Most of the Houses, including Laurent, could boast the same. The strength of our bloodlines was the foundation for the ruling Moroi Houses.

We had yet to discover why certain bloodlines were so resilient against turning into Strigoi. There were many reasons I was thankful to be born a Harker, but not having to fear losing my humanity every time I got thoroughly and completely pissed off was definitely at the top of the list.

But even without the risk of turning Strigoi, it was still not a good look to lose control of your bloodlust. It was bound to happen, and Carmilla was forgiving about it, but Marvina would no doubt view it as *unbecoming*. She was bothered enough by my appearance and bold demeanor as it was.

I wanted nothing more than to scream at the top of my lungs and kick something. Repeatedly.

But while that would feel fucking glorious, it would also no doubt get back to Marvina, and I refused to give her the satisfaction of knowing just how much she had hurt me.

A few courtiers walked through the garden, glancing at me sideways while whispering furiously amongst themselves.

Great. Marvina and her lackeys were likely already telling everyone about what happened in her study. Now I was a spectacle for all of House Laurent. It wasn't even lunchtime yet, and this was already shaping up to be a spectacularly bad day. On the plus side, it was unlikely things could get worse from being laughed out of Marvina's study.

When yet another group of whispering courtiers passed me, I gritted my teeth and headed for the structure on the other side of the garden.

The three-story building continued the House Laurent trend of being ridiculously opulent. Gold and silver accents bordered the windows and shone brightly in the late morning sunshine. Those materials would have been better served on weapons in the hands of Velesians than on a fucking building.

This was exactly why so many Velesians hated the Moroi. I'd hoped to start mending that rift with the trade agreement I'd put together, but it was clear that wouldn't be happening.

"Your only job here is to make my son happy, and you can't even manage that." Marvina's insult rang through my mind, and I had to shove the bloodlust down again.

Demetri and I might lack passion, but I desperately needed to blow off some steam and get my blood fix.

When he was home, Demetri tended to have a wide-open schedule because he was content to let his mother rule over everything. It was one of the many things he had never understood about me, my desire to want more in life.

But right now, I just wanted to bury my fangs in his neck while he buried himself inside me.

I entered the guesthouse and made a left down the long hallway that led to the main set of guest suites. Demetri had mentioned that some courtiers he was friends with were currently in residence and that he'd be visiting with them today. I was pretty sure Demetri spent most of his time in the guesthouse when he wasn't traveling to other Houses.

Despite being the Heir to House Laurent, he lived his life more like that of a courtier, spending all of his time socializing and none of it ruling.

A low, throaty moan carried down the hallway followed by a deep, masculine laugh, and my pace slowed. I knew that laugh.

A peculiar, numb feeling crept over me as I slipped forward, quiet as a ghost.

The door at the last suite was left ajar, and there were pieces of clothing strewn about as if someone had pulled them off in haste. I froze in the doorway with Demetri's back to me, all of his lovely flesh on display as he pounded into the woman stretched out on the bed. She moaned as he thrusted harder and faster. Her legs were over his shoulders, and I watched as his fingers dug into her thighs, pulling her closer.

Either she was one hell of an actress or Demetri had some skills that he'd just never bothered using on me.

I should be angry about this, I thought as I watched with an odd sort of detachment about his betrayal. I'd been loyal to him and him alone since we'd signed the marriage contract. I should be fucking pissed, and I definitely was. Nestled between the shock and the disjointed numbness was definitely rage, but not just because he was cheating on me. That was almost secondary to the other reason my blood felt like it was boiling.

No. I was pissed because she was enjoying the hell out of getting screwed by my husband, and I'd never *once* found pleasure in it.

Are you happy?

I was goddamn brilliant, my mind was sharp as hell, and I was a fucking asset to any House. I spoke two dead languages, was well-versed in the political machinations of all the Moon Blessed, knew the strengths and weakness of every single Moroi House. The elders I studied under for the years I was at Drudonia had said they'd never had a student with such a sharp mind for political negotiations.

And yet Marvina and everyone here treated me like I was fucking beneath them when I was made to rule a House.

Are. You. Happy?

When I walked into a room, every being looked my way because I was hot as fucking sin. The same people who looked down on me couldn't keep their eyes off of every flash of skin I showed and every rise and dip of my body.

Demetri should have been on his knees crawling to me, *begging* for the privilege of touching me, because I was made to be worshipped.

ARE. YOU. HAPPY?

"No," I spat out.

The woman yelped as Demetri whirled in surprise, grabbing a pillow off the floor to cover himself as he stepped towards me. I laughed. Modesty? Really?

"Fuck. This." I spun on my heel and stalked back down the hall.

"Samara!" Demetri called frantically after me. "Wait!"

I stopped halfway to the exit and spun to face him.

His steps faltered as he quickly buttoned the pants he'd pulled on and brushed his dark auburn hair away from his face.

My eyes ran over his body, taking in his well-muscled chest

that was slicked with sweat and the flushed color in his lightly tanned face. He really had put in more effort into fucking whoever the hell that was than he ever had me.

My lips curled, putting my fangs fully on display. Demetri's gaze widened at the sight.

"Let's discuss this," he started, holding out his hands in a placating manner as if he were trying to calm down an unruly horse.

A humorless laugh poured out of me, and whatever he saw in my face made him flinch and take a step back, still holding his hands up, but now it felt more defensive on his part.

"There is nothing to discuss," I said coldly. "My life here is a joke. I should have realized it sooner, but the events of today have made it very clear. I'm fucking *done*."

"What does that mean?" His eyes widened, and he reached for me, but I stepped back.

I needed to get the hell away from him. From Marvina. From this House. There was only one place I could go to regroup and figure all of this out.

"I'm going home."

CHAPTER THREE

—

Samara

"You can't be serious," Demetri said for what felt like the hundredth time. That seemed to be all he was capable of saying at this point, and it was really getting on my nerves.

Exactly how the hell was I supposed to react to walking in on my husband fucking someone else? Our marriage might have been arranged for political purposes, but I'd been loyal to him all these years.

Clearly, I'd been an idiot for thinking he would be the same.

"It's in your best interest to let me leave and cool down," I said evenly as I scoured my room for what to pack.

The numbness had crept back in after my outburst, and I was embracing it wholeheartedly so that I didn't rip out Demetri's throat and enjoy the feeling of his hot blood on my face as he bled out at my feet.

Right. The bloodlust was still there.

I pulled in a deep breath and let the rage settle back a bit, then focused on the task at hand. I needed to get out of here and put some distance between me and my piece of shit husband and his domineering bitch of a mother.

If I left within the next hour, I could easily make it to House Harker before nightfall.

I looked around the room, eyeing all of my things. Most of my possessions here meant little to me and could be easily replaced.

My eyes fell on a stack of scrolls and notebooks that I'd piled haphazardly on top of a dresser. All my notes about things I'd learned about House Laurent while I was here plus several ideas for trade alliances between the Houses and Velesians.

I snatched them up and shoved them into my pack. Otherwise, there was nothing else I cared about here.

My eyes met Demetri's and while I felt hurt and betrayed, I was surprised to find cunning calculation in his eyes. I blinked and whatever I saw was gone, replaced by a chagrined expression that had me briefly doubting what I thought I saw seconds before.

"I'm so sorry, Samara." He closed the distance between us and clasped my hands in his. "It was never my intention for you to walk in on us like that, but I assumed you knew that I had other partners on the side, given the nature of our marriage. Let's talk this out. I'm sure we can come to an understanding."

I stared at him in disbelief. Was he seriously apologizing for *how* I found out about him fucking other people behind my back and not the actual fucking?

He took my silence as an opening and gave me a beautiful yet apologetic smile.

Yep. He really was.

"The only *understanding* I'm capable of coming to in the next five minutes is one that involves your cock flopping around on the floor and you bleeding out at my feet." He blanched and dropped my hands as he quickly staggered away from me. "I'm going back to House Harker where I will consider my future and decide if you will continue to be a part of it or not. I strongly advise you to get out of my sight."

Demetri's mouth gaped open, and I found satisfaction in the fear that shone clearly from his eyes. He snapped his mouth shut and fled without another word.

I snorted. Such a coward.

Once he was gone, I quickly changed out of my gown and into a soft, long-sleeved shirt and a stretchy pair of riding pants that I kept hidden in one of my bottom drawers. Marvina didn't approve of a lady of my stature wearing such attire, and I knew she told the servants to confiscate the clothes whenever they saw them. Speaking of…

I dropped to my knees at the foot of my bed and stretched my hand underneath, grasping around until I finally felt the bundle of fabric I'd tucked up between the boards that supported the mattress.

I withdrew my prize and shook it free as I rose. The matte black cloak fell to the floor, not a single wrinkle in the fabric despite being wadded up into a ball for the past three years. Only the symbol of House Harker, two crossed axes over a crescent moon, adorned the cloak. I ran my fingers over the symbol before throwing the garment over my shoulders and securing it in place.

After one last sweep of the room, I headed towards the kitchen to grab a snack on my way out.

"My lady!" Rose squeaked as I swept into the room. The other two servant girls sitting with her froze, their eyes darting to the exit. They'd have to walk past me to get to it.

"Don't worry yourself, Rose. I'm just grabbing some food for the trip." I plucked a couple of freshly baked rolls from a basket and wrapped them in a cloth napkin. Some shiny red apples caught my attention, and I added them to my pack as well.

"Your trip?" Rose asked in confusion as she watched me pack up the food.

"I'm leaving," I said hesitantly, unsure how much of my personal business I wanted to share. "Things haven't gone the way I'd hoped they would here, and I just need a break to collect my thoughts."

"Surely, you're not planning on going out on your own?" one of the other girls blurted. When I looked at her, she paled and shook her head violently. "Apologies, my lady! I didn't mean to question you! I just—I wasn't—"

She looked at Rose for help as she started to hyperventilate.

"Don't worry yourself, Catrina," I said gently. She blinked at hearing her name come from my lips.

Rose was the one who waited on me the most, but I'd been working on learning the names of all the staff members while I'd been here. Some of them I rarely interacted with though, such as the girl sitting with Rose and Catrina. She might be new, or she worked somewhere in the large fortress I didn't frequent often.

I calmly explained, "The road to House Harker runs along the coast, and there are rarely attacks there. Besides, I'll arrive well before dark."

If it'd been even a couple of hours later, I wouldn't have considered making this ride today despite how desperately I wanted to get out of this House. The world outside the thick walls of our fortresses was a dangerous one during daylight hours, but the dark belonged to the wraiths and other monsters.

I shivered at the thought of being out at night. I'd only experienced it a couple of times in my life, but the memories were forever etched into my mind.

Rose bit her bottom lip as she looked at me, clearly not liking this plan, but also knowing she couldn't stop me.

"Here, take these too." She quickly packed together some dried meat and more fruit, which she handed to me, and I tucked them away in my bag. When she passed me a couple squares of chocolate, my eyebrows crept up in surprise.

It was a delicacy and usually saved for special occasions. I couldn't even remember the last time I'd had some. Maybe my birthday two years ago?

When she noticed my expression, she gave me a sheepish shrug. "Lady Marvina requested some for a meeting last week, but they barely ate half of it, so we stashed it in here."

I smiled as I pulled one square out and placed it in my pack with the rest of the food. "The three of you should enjoy it." Rose tried to refuse, but I grabbed her hand and somewhat forcibly placed the chocolate in her palm. "You deserve it far more than me, and chocolate is one of those things that should be enjoyed whenever you have the chance."

Catrina and the other servant girl shyly smiled at me before breaking off a piece and popping it into their mouths. Then they both let out twin moans of pleasure before staring at each other and bursting into giggles. I huffed a laugh at their antics before I shifted the pack further onto my shoulder.

"I need to get going," I said. "I suspect my dear husband is crying in his mother's lap right now, and I don't want to be around for any further drama."

Rose barked out a laugh, and the other two girls covered their mouths while they tried to hold in their chuckles.

I winked at Rose. "If you ever need help, don't hesitate to reach out. I mean it, Rose."

"Do you think you'll be coming back?" I felt a little guilty at the sadness that touched her eyes, but I didn't want to lie.

"I can't say for sure, but I'd say it's unlikely."

She nodded in understanding. "Safe travels, Lady Samara."

With that, I took my leave and headed towards the stables. I hoped that Rose would reach out to me if she or any of the other staff needed help, but I wasn't holding my breath. If I ended up truly never returning here, I'd have to figure out a way to check in on them.

Thankfully, I didn't encounter anyone else on the way to the stables. I was a little surprised to find them empty but decided to count my blessings. I was perfectly capable of saddling my own horse.

"Hello, my love," I crooned at the dapple grey mare who stuck her head out at my arrival.

Most of the horses were used by the rangers to patrol the surrounding area, but one of my only requests upon arriving at House Laurent was a horse of my own.

Zosa had been a wedding gift to me from Demetri. At the time, I thought it was very sweet, and I gave him a very enthusiastic thank you that night, but now I knew that he'd likely had nothing to do with choosing Zosa. He'd just put in the request to someone else, and they'd done it.

I set my bag by her stall and quickly went about collecting her tack and readying her for the journey. She snorted and nudged me in the shoulder as I led her out of the stall.

"We'll be out of here soon, sweetheart," I murmured.

I tied my bag to the back of the saddle and did a final check to make sure everything was secure.

Zosa thought it was fun to hold her breath and puff up her belly so that the saddle came loose after someone climbed onto her, but I'd grown up riding far trickier mounts, so none of her shenanigans got by me.

The sun shone brightly above us as I led her out of the stables. It was nearing noon, which meant I now had less than seven hours to make it to House Harker. The single guard on duty at the gate leading out of House Laurent spotted me from his perch, and his eyes widened. I chuckled under my breath as he desperately swung his head back and forth, probably looking for someone of higher rank than him to deal with this.

Usually, when I went out for rides, I had at least two rangers with me, but there was currently not a ranger in sight.

Somehow, I didn't think asking Marvina to spare a couple rangers to escort me the hell out of her House would go over well. But I was more than capable of getting myself home, at least during daylight hours.

"Open the gate, please," I said in a pleasant tone that was still clearly an order.

I'd been perfecting both the tone and facial expression over the years, and I found that it worked very well. When the guard saw no one else in the vicinity who could override me, he nodded in a jerky motion and pulled on the thick chain next to him.

The portcullis rose, and I led Zosa underneath it.

"HALT!" someone commanded from further behind us. I looked over my shoulder to see Demetri running towards me with half a dozen guards and Marvina striding out onto a balcony to overlook the scene playing out before her.

My heartbeat picked up as I rapidly thought through my options.

I could stay to hear them out and then politely decline whatever they offered before leaving. That was probably the more politically advantageous approach and would help reduce the fallout between House Harker and Laurent.

Despite that, my head whipped towards the open road that beckoned to me beyond the gate.

I didn't want to wait.

I didn't want to hear Demetri's false platitudes and Marvina's thinly veiled threats.

I wanted to get the fuck out of here.

Before the guard who'd opened the gate could stop me, I vaulted onto Zosa and spurred her forward. She didn't need any more encouragement as she leapt into a gallop, kicking up dirt in her wake.

I laughed as we raced away from House Laurent, my raven-black hair intertwining with the cloak as they both whipped behind me.

Demetri's scream for me to return echoed through the trees, but I ignored it. I was done with him and his bloody House, and that thought felt just as freeing as the wind on my face.

Excitement coursed through me as I crouched over Zosa and she only ran faster, her mane flying back to brush against my cheeks. After a few miles, I pulled her back into a ground-eating canter and glanced behind me.

No one was following us, but I suspected they would soon. If we stayed on the main road, our only option was to outrun them.

I looked to my right and left as Zosa continued her steady pace. She was in good shape thanks to our frequent rides, but I couldn't ask her to keep this up forever.

The right led to the coastline, and I knew from experience that the ground would turn sandy very quickly, which would be tiring for Zosa. To the left meant more forest-type setting, where the ground was firmer but uneven.

Choices, choices.

"A little further, girl," I whispered over Zosa's neck. "Then we'll take our chances in the forest."

Once I was confident we'd put a decent amount of distance between us and House Laurent, I slowed Zosa and directed her off the trail.

As long as we stayed close to the main road, we'd be fine. After some trial and error, I found a good path that wasn't too far from the main road but also wasn't overgrown so much that it hindered Zosa from continuing her steady jog. My thighs and core burned from maintaining my seat with the bumpier gait, but I promised myself that I would soak in a bath all night and possibly all day tomorrow.

My bloodlust had all but disappeared now. The physical exertion of riding had helped, but it was mostly the distance between me and House Laurent. I should still feed soon because I was overdue, but at least I didn't have to worry about showing up at House Harker's gates with my fangs on display and a wild look in my eyes.

Now that I had successfully escaped and my mind was more settled, my thoughts turned to the future… which for the first time in almost a decade looked drastically different. If not hopeful.

My parents had jointly ruled House Harker until they died, and then my mother's sister, Carmilla, took over because I was too young. She'd adopted me and I was officially named Heir, but as I grew older and became more involved with the runnings of our House, we'd discussed how I could benefit House Harker the most.

Carmilla was a fourth-generation Moroi, and despite being only a few years away from turning a century old, she was showing no signs of slowing down. House Harker was in good hands with her, so we'd turned our attention to other Houses and what they could do for us.

There were a few contenders, but we'd ultimately decided on House Laurent because they controlled a lot of resources and there was already a strain between them and our House.

Really, between them and most of the other Moroi Houses. I wasn't the only one who had a problem with Marvina; her opposition to the Sovereign House was well-known, although nobody exactly knew why. Even in the three years I'd spent at House Laurent, I'd never been able to uncover the reason Marvina hated the Sovereigns so much.

The marriage proposal between our Houses had been initially suggested when I was fourteen and Demetri was sixteen.

After some back-and-forth negotiation, everyone had

agreed to the marriage that would take place when I turned twenty-one with the understanding that either House could break the arrangement prior to then with no penalties.

From that moment on, I'd spent my life preparing for my marriage and joining House Laurent. I retained my title as Heir to House Harker, but it was more of a courtesy title until another was chosen. I was supposed to eventually rule House Laurent alongside Demetri. Maybe one of our children would have taken the title of House Harker Heir someday.

But after the events of today, I no longer believed my future was with House Laurent. Even if things could be repaired between me and Demetri, it was clear that Marvina had no intentions of allowing me into a more authoritative role, and apparently, Demetri was more interested in finding new women to sink his cock into than learning how to rule a House.

With my background and education, surely I could be of more use to House Harker than playing a minor, powerless role in House Laurent.

I wasn't entirely sure what the current state of my birth House was. While I'd grown up there, I'd moved to Drudonia when I was sixteen to further my education. Scholars from all three types of Moon Blessed lived in the enormous fortress, and almost every piece of knowledge that we had of our history could be found in the libraries of Drudonia. I'd loved it there. Having so much knowledge at my fingertips had been a dream.

Even before I'd left, I'd spent most of my time studying in preparation for going there.

While my aunt and I regularly traded correspondence, that wasn't the same thing as being immersed in the day-to-day dealings of the House.

I knew that my childhood friend, Kieran, and my childhood archnemesis, Alaric, were still there, and to my disappointment, Vail not only remained at House Harker, but he was now the Marshal, which put him in charge of all the rangers. He was definitely going to be a problem.

Alaric, Vail, and I had grown up together, while Kieran didn't move to House Harker until later.

Alaric and I had always been at odds. His parents had served as advisors to Carmilla and had personally trained their son to replace them one day. He thought I was bold and reckless, whereas I thought he was arrogant and boring. But we were both brilliant and ambitious. Our rivalry had been instantaneous.

The history between Vail and I was completely different. He'd also grown up at House Harker but was three years older than Alaric and me.

His parents had been the previous Marshals, and they trained their son to be the same. As different as the three of us were, the one thing we all had in common was that our destiny was not our own. We each had responsibilities set in motion by our parents, or in my case my aunt, that we couldn't sway from.

There was a time that Vail and I had been friends, but that all changed the night our parents died.

Now Vail hated me with every fiber of his being because he held me responsible for their deaths. Despite the fact that my parents had died alongside them, and my actions had saved his ungrateful life. It was possible that hatred had dulled over the years, but I doubted it.

As a ranger, Vail spent most of his time out in the wilds hunting down monsters that were causing problems along supply lines or specifically attacking some of our outposts. With any luck, I wouldn't have to see him anytime soon. I was looking forward to seeing Kieran again, although we hadn't spoken much since I'd been gone. I even missed Alaric and the nearly constant annoyed expression he wore in my presence.

An hour into me plotting out my theoretical future, I heard hoofbeats beating into the ground back on the main road.

I instantly pulled on the reins, and Zosa obediently stopped. She stayed still as a statue as I held my breath. My heart was beating so loud that I had the irrational fear that they would somehow hear it. The sound of a dozen horses running down the road came toward us and then gradually faded as they raced away.

I waited a few minutes before urging Zosa onward. At some point, the search party would be doubling back, so I'd have to listen out for their approach.

They no doubt knew I was heading back to House Harker; there was nowhere else for me to go, and I'd told Demetri I was going home. But I was pretty confident that the rangers wouldn't ride all the way to House Harker because then they'd have to not only explain that I'd left House Laurent, but also why.

Rangers were excellent at fighting monsters and surviving in the wilds when no one else could. But they did not handle delicate political situations. That was something Demetri or Marvina would try to explain while they attempted to convince me of all the reasons I should come back.

Like hell that would happen.

Currently, I couldn't think of any reason why I'd ever want to go back to that House, but maybe after my temper cooled, I'd change my mind. Or at least think of a solution benefiting both Houses.

Zosa and I continued unhindered on our journey throughout the afternoon, and whenever I heard hoofbeats coming from ahead of me, I halted Zosa where we were still tucked away in the woods away from the main road. I could just barely make out the dark green cloaks bearing the symbol of House Laurent that the riders wore.

Once I could no longer hear them, I maneuvered Zosa back onto the main road so that we could travel faster.

Just as the sun dipped dangerously low on the horizon, I glimpsed three silver-capped towers rising towards the sky in the distance.

The tension I'd been carrying since leaving House Laurent eased, and a long sigh slipped from my lips.

I was home.

CHAPTER FOUR

—

Samara

As I ᴀᴘᴘʀᴏᴀᴄʜᴇᴅ the portcullis that was almost identical to the one I had passed through this morning, two guards immediately raised it. Zosa pranced as she walked underneath, apparently feeling the need to show off and make sure everyone appreciated just how beautiful she was.

"Welcome home, Samara." The older of the two guards gave me a warm smile as she took Zosa's reins and stroked the mare's neck.

I slid off the saddle and returned her friendly smile.

"Hello, Denisa. Aren't you supposed to be retired?" I teased. "That's what you claimed you were finally doing when I visited two years ago."

The corners of her eyes crinkled as her smile widened. "I tried the whole retirement thing, but honestly, it was really boring. For a while I helped out in the garden, but the other workers got tired of me killing all the plants, so I volunteered to help train the next generation."

She jerked her head towards the other guard who appeared to be a few years younger than me. He was tall but still in that awkward gangly stage where he hadn't grown into his body yet.

My lips twitched in amusement as he tried very hard not to check me out, but his gaze kept dropping down to my chest. I winked at him when I caught him looking, and the tips of his ears burned red.

Denisa chuckled. "This is Jesper. It's only his second day on the job and he already gets to meet our long-lost Heir."

"I wasn't lost, Denisa," I said dryly before holding my hand out to the young guard in training. "Hello, Jesper."

He grasped my hand and shook it a little too eagerly. Color stained his cheeks when he realized what he was doing, and he quickly released my hand before running his own through his hair as he blustered through an apology.

"It's fine," I said with a laugh and then pointed to my bag. "Would you mind getting that for me?"

Thrilled to have something to do, he leapt at the chance and quickly untied my pack from the saddle, all awkwardness from before forgotten.

I turned to Denisa. "Thank you. Would you mind seeing Zosa to the stable? I'd like to check—"

"Sam?" a deep, masculine voice called out from above me. I looked up towards the balcony across the main courtyard, smiling more broadly than I had in three years.

"Hello, Kieran." I laughed as the golden-haired man leapt off the balcony, landing on his feet like the twenty-foot drop was nothing, and raced towards me. He crushed me in a hug and spun me around, sending my black hair flaring around us. "You're making me dizzy," I complained, and he finally set me down after one more twirl.

"You didn't tell me you were coming for a visit!" He looked over my shoulder toward the gate, eyebrows bunching together as he saw no House Laurent rangers behind me. "Where is your escort?"

"Well…" I started, reaching for my bag that one of the guards still held, but Kieran snatched it from him first.

"Where is your escort, Sam?" He narrowed his eyes at me. I'd spent a significant portion of my childhood lusting after those deep brown eyes that were flecked with gold.

Moroi's had multi-colored eyes. We had one dominant color and then another secondary color that weaved through our irises like thin little cracks. Most of the time, the secondary color was only faint, but the lines would widen whenever our bloodlust rose until it completely dominated our eye color. Strong emotions brought on the color change as well.

Kieran's eyes were currently blazing gold.

Rynn and Cali were my best friends, but Kieran and I were just as close, only in a different way. He'd been my first serious crush, and while we'd always just been friends, there was a part of me that had desperately always wanted more.

I wasn't entirely sure he had felt the same back then because he was a notorious flirt and regularly practiced his skills on me.

We'd also always known that I was going to marry Demetri, so there had been a line we didn't want to cross. Leading up to my marriage, I had few regrets. Not being able to explore things with Kieran had definitely been one of them.

Given how quickly my body came to attention at his presence, my crush clearly hadn't faded over the years.

"My trip was unplanned," I said smoothly.

Kieran was usually pretty easygoing, but he could be obnoxiously protective of me sometimes. I needed to keep my explanation short and simple and then distract him with something else.

I continued, "An escort wasn't a possibility, but it was daytime, and you know it's a relatively short trip between House Laurent and here. Besides, I mostly stuck to the main road."

Shit. I shouldn't have said that last bit.

"Mostly?" His nostrils flared as he kept his gaze trained on me.

I raised my chin and tried my best to look down on him, which was a little hard to do because he had several inches on my five-and-a-half-foot frame. "You're not the boss of me, Kieran."

The annoyance slipped off his face as he gave me a charming grin. That same damn grin was what had the ladies in court taking off their panties and throwing them at him. Or just throwing themselves at him in general. It had driven me insane when we were younger.

Thanks to my marriage agreement, Kieran had always been off-limits to me, so I had to stand by while he flirted with every girl who caught his eye.

"You're right. I'm not the boss of you."

He looped his arm through mine and tugged me inside towards the stairs that led to the upper floors of the main house.

"Kieran," I warned, struggling to keep up with his fast pace.

He didn't say anything as he pulled me through the hall-ways, and I let him because I knew where he was taking me, and it's where I wanted to go anyway.

Although, I would have preferred to walk there at a leisurely pace while I gathered my thoughts instead of being dragged through the House for everyone to see.

"Samara, you're home!" an older Moroi wearing an apron dusted with flour and stains called out in greeting.

"Hi, Leora!" I waved and eyed the empty platter she was holding in her hands. "Are there any more honey cakes left?"

"I'll send some to your suite in a bit!"

Two more servants came around the corner and smoothly slid out of Kieran's way as he continued pulling me along.

"Oh! Hey, Floran! Hi, Nora!" I grinned at both of them.

They were a few years older than me and worked in the gardens.

Two years ago, they'd gotten married, and I'd come back for the ceremony. I'd had to lie to Marvina about my reasons for visiting House Harker because she never would have approved of me coming back here for the wedding of low-ranking servants.

"Hey, Sam!" Floran laughed. "I see nothing has changed between you and Kieran."

"He's still very emotional." I patted Kieran's hand where it rested on my forearm. "He needs to find a nice Moroi to settle down with like you did with Nora."

Kieran let out an exasperated breath before he spun around. Suddenly, my world tilted, and I found myself tossed over his shoulder.

"Ow!" I tried to shift, but his arm clamped around my thighs. "Your bony shoulder is digging into me."

"It's not bony." He swatted my butt. "You can chat with everyone later."

I raised my head and waved at the two love-birds. "Come and find me tomorrow! We can valiantly raid the kitchen and then catch up on the garden!"

"Pretty sure Leora will be baking all morning to celebrate you being back!" Nora snickered. "Have fun managing Kieran and your aunt!"

Kieran carried me up to the third floor with only a few more interruptions. I was kind of impressed; I wasn't exactly light, but he wasn't even winded. Growing up, Kieran had always been on the slender side, but it had been three years since I'd seen him last since he'd been away during Floran and Nora's wedding.

My pondering of Kieran's new physical prowess ended when he dropped me back to the ground in front of a familiar study. The large double doors were open, revealing walls lined with books and scrolls, some well-used couches and chairs, and a large desk at the back of the room.

A woman who looked like an older version of me sat behind the desk, the last rays of sun shining through the floor-to-ceiling windows at her back.

My aunt was wholly focused on the scroll in front of her. Out of nowhere, heat built behind my eyes, and I found myself fighting back tears.

How many times had I sat on one of the comfortable couches complaining about some asinine thing Kieran had done? Or how I vehemently disagreed with one of my instructors over marks I'd received on my work?

She would let me ramble on and on, seeming to not be paying attention as she focused on her own work, only to raise her head when I finally stopped talking to smile at me and say, *"That sounds like quite the problem, my dear. So, what are you going to do about it?"*

I blinked my tears away at the memory and the crushing realization of just how much I had missed my home.

Kieran nudged me further into the study before dropping down onto one of the couches and arching an eyebrow at me. I envisioned grabbing one of the throw pillows and smothering him with it when he smirked and settled further into the thick cushions.

Carmilla Harker finally raised her head. Her dark, ivy-green eyes met my deep purple ones, the color of our eyes only distinguishable because of the last rays of the dying sunlight.

At night, our eyes looked black. It was a trait shared by all those of the Harker bloodline.

"Samara?" She blinked in surprise before rising from her chair and rushing towards me. "What are you doing here? Has something happened?"

The familiar sound of her rich, captivating voice was my

undoing. Tears flowed down my cheeks as I threw myself into her arms.

"Shhh. Shhh, my dear," she said as she stroked my hair. "It'll be alright."

After a moment, I sucked in a rattling breath and pulled myself together. My cheeks were likely stained red with mortification. I was goddamn twenty-four years old. Way too old to be sobbing on Carmilla's shoulder.

Sensing the shift in my mood, Carmilla tutted. "You'll always be my niece, and you need never hide anything from me. Outside of these doors, present a brave, unbreakable front, but not in here." She settled down on one end of the settee and looked pointedly at the other end.

I immediately sat down, wiping the last of my tears from my face with a sniff.

"If you need another shoulder to cry on, you can always use mine." The grin Kieran gave me was truly wicked, but I saw the concern in his eyes. Apparently, he still felt the need to cover up any true emotions with his ridiculous flirty behavior.

"I will smother you in your sleep." I narrowed my eyes at him, but Kieran merely cocked his head to the side and raised an eyebrow.

"So, you still want to climb into my bed then?"

"Children," Carmilla smoothly cut in, "you can continue whatever this conversation is later. For now, I'd like to hear what has brought you home, Samara."

I stared at my folded hands, suddenly feeling small.

Had I made a foolish decision to return here? Maybe I should have stayed and tried to figure things out with Demetri.

My returning home didn't just impact me; it would put everyone in House Harker in an uncomfortable position. I had signed a contract with House Laurent, and I was now in violation of that. My knuckles turned white as I squeezed my fingers tighter together.

"Hey." Carmilla's soft tone broke through my panic, and she leaned forward to wrap her hands around mine. "While you have quite the temper, you're never one to act without reason. I love you, and I will support you in anything."

Releasing the breath I'd been holding, I loosened the death grip I had on my fingers as Carmilla reclined back in her seat. "I think me marrying into House Laurent was a mistake." I proceeded to recount the past three years to her, trying my best to keep things succinct, focusing on my efforts to prove my worth to Marvina and earn a spot on her council, and trying to be a good wife for Demetri.

Kieran offered colorful commentary throughout my story, mostly at the expense of Demetri, and I was thankful for the distraction, otherwise I probably would have gotten super pissed-off again.

I left out the part about walking in on Demetri cheating on me. Carmilla would need to know that, but I couldn't bring myself to say it in front of Kieran. To admit that I hadn't been enough for Demetri. Rationally, I knew it was foolish of me to think of it that way, but I didn't always think logically when it came to Kieran.

Carmilla maintained a neutral expression through it all, which set my nerves on end, even though I knew this was how she typically reacted in these situations. My aunt was always calm and levelheaded, and it was something I hoped to claim as well someday. My damn temper still got the best of me sometimes.

Silence fell over us once I finished catching them up on the events of this morning and basically the last three years of my life.

Carmilla knew some of it because she and I corresponded regularly, but I hadn't told her everything like I had now, and Kieran hadn't known any of it. We hadn't spoken much since I'd left. I didn't know his reasons, but mine were because it hurt too much. I hadn't fully realized just how deep my feelings were for him until I'd left House Harker.

There hadn't been anything I could do about it, and he hadn't reached out, so I assumed he wasn't as affected by my leaving as I was.

So, I'd just packed up that painful realization and tucked it away. Right next to all the other painful memories.

But as I looked at Kieran's tight expression, I realized maybe there were other reasons he hadn't contacted me. He looked pissed enough to grab a horse and ride all the way to House Laurent just to beat the shit out of Demetri.

It helped settle me a little to know that he was still in my corner, even after all these years apart.

Carmilla finally rose and stepped around her desk, grabbed three crystal glasses and a bottle of dark amber liquor, and then returned to where we were sitting. She poured the brandy generously into each of the glasses before nudging them in our directions.

I plucked mine up and inhaled the earthy aroma. I might be biased, but I maintained that House Harker made the best moon brandy.

My aunt raised her glass in the air, with Kieran and I doing the same before we each slammed back the shot.

Heat burned down my throat and filled my center. I'd missed that feeling. The wine at House Laurent was nice, but sometimes you just needed a goddamn shot of liquor.

"Fuck Demetri," Carmilla said loudly with a determined nod.

My hand flew to my mouth as I choked, and Kieran's mouth dropped open as he stared at my aunt. I could count the number of times I'd heard her swear on one hand, and apparently, Kieran felt the same.

"Fuck that bitch, Marvina," she continued. "And fuck House Laurent. They don't deserve you."

I gawked at her, my mouth gaping in what was probably a very unattractive manner as she poured us each more liquor. This one I sipped as I came to terms with my aunt's proclamation.

"We can work with Alaric to draft the marriage dissolution. It was clearly stated in the contract that you would be offered an advisory position once you had proven yourself capable. I have no doubt that you have done so, and we can provide more than enough evidence of this. If Marvina wants a fight, she'll fucking get one."

I lost it and threw myself across the couch, hugging her fiercely. Carmilla laughed as I spilled liquor everywhere.

"Thank you!" I squeezed her once more before pulling back to look her in the eyes. "I promise you that I will be a strong asset for House Harker and will do whatever I can to support our House in the future."

"I know you will." She patted my cheek lovingly. "Now, you've had a long day. Go get settled. Your room has been kept up while you were gone, and all your belongings are still there. We'll speak more tomorrow."

Kieran trailed after me as I found my way back to my old room, and I only half paid attention to everything he was saying. For the first time in years, I had a future in front of me that I was actually excited about.

"Have you been listening to anything I've said?" he asked when we reached the doors to my suite.

"No," I said honestly. He huffed a laugh and moved to follow me inside, but I blocked his entrance with a pointed look. "Nuh-uh. I'm going to have a nice long soak in my tub and call my besties."

"Or,"—he offered me a heated look—"I can join you in the bath and maybe rub some of the tension from your shoulders?"

I leaned against the doorframe and tilted my head while I

gave him a very obvious once-over, noting all the ways he'd changed in the years I'd been gone.

Kieran had never been that tall or big. When he'd first arrived at House Harker, he'd just turned fourteen like me. I'd just gone through a growth spurt and towered over him with my five and a half feet. He'd gradually caught up to me and during my years at Drudonia; every time I came back to the House for a visit, Kier would be just a little taller. I unfortunately never grew any further, so now I was the one always tilting my head back to look up at others.

Even after surpassing me in height, Kieran had been on the slender side back then. That was no longer the case. While I wouldn't describe him as bulky, his lean frame was now corded with muscle. Fuck. Kieran had always been good-looking, but now he was absolutely gorgeous.

"Based on the way you're practically drooling over me," he drawled with a smirk, "I'm assuming the answer is yes to that shoulder rub."

"It's not my shoulders that I'm interested in having rubbed," I said with a shrug, pleased when a spark of surprise lit up his eyes.

Our flirting had always been harmless and mostly one-sided growing up. Kieran was a flirt with everyone, and I'd been promised to Demetri. Part of me had always wanted to flirt back, and sometimes I did, but normally I refrained because it'd felt too dangerous at the time.

Because I *liked* Kieran.

It would have been too easy to cross that line with him, and that would have ended with me nursing a broken heart.

But now, even if I didn't go through with the marriage dissolution… Demetri clearly didn't view our marriage as one based on love and respect. If, and that was a very big if, I decided not to dissolve our marriage and return to House

Laurent, our marriage would be one in name only. I wouldn't deny myself pleasures any longer.

However, I would deny them for this night, because now that I had the conversation with my aunt over with, all I could feel was the sense of grime on my skin. I needed to cleanse myself of the trials of the day and fill Rynn and Cali in on everything that had happened.

I reached out and flicked Kieran on the nose. "See you in the morning." Then I shut the door in his face.

"I'M gonna cut off his balls and make him choke on them!" Cali snarled. Her shadowy form was perched on the edge of the bathtub and was practically vibrating with unrestrained rage.

Rynn waved her hand dismissively, causing the shadows that made up her fingers to swirl through the air from where she was leaning against the wall next to the tub. "Demetri has always been worthless. He's hardly worth the effort. I'm more pissed about his mother. Who the fuck does she think she is?"

"The head of House Laurent," I said dryly as I sunk further into the bath.

As the Heir of House Harker, my suite was comprised of a large sitting area, a bedroom, and a rather lavish en suite. Every time I used the tub, I silently thanked the Fae for being such fans of luxury and leaving this all to us.

Granted, that probably hadn't been their intention, but whatever. Finders, keepers.

Cali snorted and flicked her hand. A dark tendril whipped towards the water, solidifying for just a second, and water splashed against my face. I wiped it off with a laugh. If anyone else saw Cali using her magic so casually they would be terrified.

Shadow magic was feared thanks to the wraiths that roamed the nights, but the Furies excelled at wielding it the same way Moroi were skilled with blood magic and the Velesians had some psychic abilities.

Cali, in particular, was quite talented, well on her way to becoming the strongest Furie in existence. That is, if she didn't lose herself in the process.

At least, that was what her family and the Furie elders feared. The Rayne bloodline was notorious for being incredibly powerful... and going insane. Because of that, the family worked hard to control and tamp down the rage that burned within them.

It required a delicate balance on their part because they needed that rage to fuel their magic the same way Moroi required blood and the Velesians relied on a connection to the earth.

They devoted their lives to walking the line of suppressing their rage without making it disappear completely. That meant they avoided anything that might tip them over the edge.

Like love.

While the Moroi and Velesians used marriage for political jockeying, the Furies never married.

Lust and short pairings were acceptable, but nothing long-term. Even children were raised in a communal sense so that they didn't form too strong a connection to their biological parents.

I thought it was a sad way to exist, but I'd also seen the carnage left behind by a Furie who had lost themselves to the pull of their magic. The Furies had taken longer than the Moroi and Velesians to claw back their humanity, and their grasp on it was tenuous. Perhaps that would improve for future generations.

Cali, however, refused to fall in line. She pushed boundaries constantly and probably would have been shunned by her people if not for her power.

They couldn't afford to lose her because when Cali cut loose, she was a one-woman battalion.

Still, lately, I had noticed something off about her. She was still the wild Furie I'd always known and loved, but there was a distance to her now. She was like that with other Furies, but she'd never been like that around us.

I wasn't sure what was going on with her, and neither was Rynn. We'd discussed it and tried to pry it out of Cali, but she had just laughed us off.

I refused to believe that my friend would ever lose herself, and I didn't love that she was keeping secrets from us when we'd always sworn to be open books to each other, but all I could do was lead by example and hope she came clean with us eventually.

"So, what are you going to do now?" Rynn asked.

"Well, I have some time to figure that out." I lifted my hand and watched the soapy water drip through my fingers. "Right now, I'm leaning towards drafting up that marriage dissolution with Alaric and writing off the last three years, but that feels like a waste, considering my upbringing."

I frowned and sank all the way down until the water covered my face before resurfacing.

"The same skills and knowledge that made you an asset to House Laurent will make you one to House Harker as well," Rynn scoffed. "They were foolish to treat you this way and let you go. Hell, I would snatch you up for whatever Pack I go to if I could."

"Whatever Pack?" Cali spun to face Rynn, causing shadows to swirl around her. "Like you don't know where you're going."

Rynn stuck out her tongue. "It's not completely settled yet."

I rolled my eyes, agreeing with Cali. Rynn was destined for

the Alpha Pack the same way that I had been destined for House Laurent.

Although, I hoped my friend's fate would work out better than mine. But Cali didn't have a set path ahead of her. She'd been just as well educated as me and Rynn, but there was no marriage laid out for her and no high-ranking position within a Pack arranged.

Cali's only goal in life was to not go insane and kill us all.

"So," Cali said mischievously, "how is Kieran looking these days?"

I flicked some bubbles in her direction, which only made her smirk as she let them pass through her shadow, causing it to flicker briefly. "He's fine," I muttered.

Rynn laughed. "That man is more than fine."

A smile tugged at my lips as I recalled his physique from earlier. "Yeah, fine doesn't quite capture his hotness."

"The question is, what are you going to do about it now that you're back?" Cali asked.

Both she and Rynn arched their eyebrows at me as they waited for my answer.

What *was* I going to do about it? My life had radically changed in a day, and I didn't think I could ever go back to how I'd been living these past three years.

Our world was a dangerous one, and while I hoped to live a long and fulfilling life, there were no guarantees. Why should I deny myself pleasure when the opportunity presented itself?

With my mind made up, I gave them a sinful grin. "I'm going to try a new motto in life."

"Oh?" Rynn tilted her head at me in a way that always reminded me of her wolf's side.

"Yeah," I said slowly. "If I see something I want, I'm going to take it."

CHAPTER FIVE

—

Samara

I woke up early the next morning and stared at the intricate design laid out on the ceiling of my bedroom.

All of the Moroi Houses were originally built by the Fae. This fortress must have been built by the Seelie because the mural above me portrayed a bright, sunlit setting of grassy hills.

I loved the painting, but I always thought it was strange because I'd never seen anything like this in Lunaria. Most of the continent was covered by thick forests. The only places the woods retreated were on the coasts and in the badlands, but nowhere were there long stretches of gently rolling hills.

When I was a child, I used to gaze up at my ceiling and wonder why they had chosen to paint this scene.

Had Lunaria changed? Was this what it used to look like once upon a time? Or had the Fae come from somewhere else, and these murals reminded them of a home they had lost?

I never found an answer to my childhood questions. The Fae had loved art, and most of the fortresses that had been repurposed by the Moon Blessed held murals like this in them.

Sometimes they were of scenery that made no sense, but other times they were of places that I recognized.

House Laurent had belonged to the Unseelie, and its murals were always of night skies and dark forests. I loved both sides and wished the Fae hadn't hated each other so much. It would be nice to live somewhere where I had both types of murals to peruse.

My thoughts briefly wandered to Demetri and how he was dealing with my departure. I wondered what had been said to explain my sudden disappearance. Marvina had no doubt spun the story to make me look bad. Did I care?

I chewed my lip as I thought about it and decided that I didn't. Neither Demetri nor House Laurent were worth it. I would prove my worth here, at House Harker, and make them regret how their actions had resulted in losing me.

A distinct, slow three-beat knock sounded on my door, and a grin tugged at my lips. I'd been curious as to how long he'd wait before coming to harass me.

I hopped out of bed and threw a robe over the thin shift I'd slept in before going to open the door. Kieran's hand was raised to knock again, but he reached out to pull on my tangled hair instead.

"Sleeping in?" he tutted. "You've become lazy in your old age."

"We're the same age," I grumped, swatting his hand away from my hair as he peered over my shoulder and into my room. "Something I can help you with, Kier?" I shoved him back a step.

"Just trying to see how you were settling in." His lips twitched as he slowly scanned me from head to toe. "Want me to help you pick out your clothes for the day and brush your hair?"

"No." I slapped his hand away again when he went to teasingly pull on another knot. "I'm perfectly capable of getting myself dressed."

"Just trying to be helpful." He shrugged. "Come get breakfast with me?"

"I can't," I said reluctantly. But lazing around with Kieran all day sounded really tempting… "I promised Carmilla I would have breakfast with her this morning."

"Lunch then?" he asked hopefully.

I bit my lip, not really sure what my schedule for the day was going to be or how I'd feel after talking to Carmilla. "Sure, but no promises. I might get caught up in something else."

"The only thing you'll be getting caught up in later is me giving you all the gossip you've been missing out on." He brushed a kiss against my cheek before strolling down the hallway.

I closed the door and leaned against it, holding a hand to my cheek. It'd been three years since I'd seen Kieran. Despite being a courtier who regularly traveled around to the different Houses, he'd never once visited House Laurent, and the few times I'd returned to House Harker, he'd been away. I'd never been sure if he was avoiding me or if his life was simply busy.

I'd assumed that when I returned here, things would be different between us, but instead, we'd slipped right back into our easy friendship that included some light flirting. Okay, maybe heavy flirting.

The sun rose higher into the sky, and golden light filtered in through the windows of my room, reminding me it was time to get on with it.

I tossed on a deep forest-green dress that was made of a stretchy soft fabric, which meant it hugged all of my curves and was incredibly comfortable. After spending a few minutes detangling my hair and tying it up in a bun, I made my way to Carmilla's study.

Several other Moroi passed me on the way, all flashing

welcoming smiles. I wasn't sure if they knew the exact circum-stances of my return, but it felt so damn nice to be somewhere I was wanted.

"Good morning, dear," Carmilla said warmly as I entered her study. "The tea should be set if you wouldn't mind pouring us some cups."

Shutting the door behind me, I nodded. "Of course."

I noticed several pastries piled up on a plate as I poured our tea, and I quickly snatched the one that had sugary crum-bles along the top. I tore off a chunk and popped it onto my mouth, savoring the flavor while I watched Carmilla furiously scribble something onto a scroll.

When I'd arrived yesterday, I'd been in such a weird state that I hadn't looked that closely at my aunt, but now, as my eyes swept over her, I was happy to see that she looked the same as she always did.

At ninety-five years old, Carmilla didn't look a day over forty. We had similar facial features and the same straight black hair, but Carmilla's skin was several shades lighter than mine. I had my father to thank for my darker complexion. Aside from that, I'd taken strongly after my mother's side of the family, which meant Carmilla and I looked a lot alike. An old pang ran through me as I thought of my parents. I'd lost them over a decade ago, but I still missed them fiercely.

Carmilla sat down on the couch beside me and blew a wayward strand of hair out of her face, drawing me from my melancholy.

I chuckled and passed her a teacup. "Rough morning?"

"Yolanthe is supposed to be working on a trade agreement with House Devereux," she sighed. "Unfortunately, in the midst of negotiations, she learned that the nephew of the ruler of House Devereux had a tryst with her sister, and it ended badly. Nothing terrible happened, just young people getting wrapped up in their passion, but Yolanthe still doesn't like the boy, and it's clouding her judgement."

"Who's leading negotiations on their side?" I asked as I blew on my tea to cool it down.

Carmilla's lips twisted into a frown. "Severen. He's the father of the boy who was involved with Yolanthe's sister."

I did a quick rundown of the Devereux family. The current leader of the House was Thessalia, her brother was Severen, and from my understanding, they were close. Thessalia was old, at least a decade older than Carmilla, and Severen was her baby brother. Their parents died when they were young, and Thessalia basically raised him. She'd be protective of his children.

"Why don't I catch up with Yolanthe this week and see where I can be of assistance?" I suggested. "I would love to get her opinion of the trade agreement I've been working on with one of the Velesian packs. She can look that over while I review the trade agreement with Devereux."

Truthfully, I didn't need Yolanthe to look over my trade agreement. I'd already done all the hard work on the offer because I had Rynn as a resource for the Velesian side of things, but I knew enough about Yolanthe to know that she would be more amicable to me stepping in on her negotiations if I asked for help on mine. She could be stubborn, but she wasn't impossible to work with.

"Are you sure?" Carmilla asked with a gentle tone, studying me carefully. "You don't need to jump back into things right away. Why don't you take this week to think about what you want to do?"

"You mean if I want to walk away from the marriage we spent a decade planning for and was supposed to help our relations with House Laurent? The relationship I just completely and utterly ruined?" I'd meant to play it off as a joke, but my voice cracked on the last word.

Who was I to think I could just come back and help with negotiations and establishing solid alliances with other Houses when I hadn't even been able to keep my political marriage going?

My throat tightened, and I gave Carmilla an apologetic look. "I'm sorry."

"Samara," my aunt said firmly as she peered over the rim of her teacup. "You did nothing wrong. We didn't arrange the marriage with Demetri solely for the benefit of House Harker. I honestly thought the two of you would be happy together. If you had told me earlier about what was going on with Marvina and House Laurent, I would have called you back here and ended the marriage immediately."

I swallowed, blinking back tears. Carmilla's faith in me never wavered, and it helped me brush aside my doubts.

"Now, I want you to take this week to think about what you want to do." When I opened my mouth to argue, she raised a hand to silence me. "I'm not going to stop you from talking to Yolanthe if that's what you want to do, but you do *not* have to do it. You have nothing to prove to me or to House Harker. We're all simply happy to have you home."

"Thank you," I said quietly, trying to wrestle my emotions back under control. "Have we received any messages from House Laurent?"

Carmilla stared at me for a beat before answering, "No."

I popped another piece of pastry into my mouth and chewed slowly. Part of me had expected some type of message from Demetri. He wasn't the type to ride back here heroically and apologize for all of his mistakes, but it wasn't that damned hard to scribble a note together and send it on its way. We were close enough that the message could have easily been delivered overnight.

"I'll take your advice and think things over this week," I said. "But unless new information surfaces,"—*or Demetri stops being a useless asshole*—"I think it's likely that I will move to dissolve my marriage. Marvina might be a problem."

"My dear…" Carmilla gave me a sharp smile. "If Marvina comes looking for a fight, I'm more than happy to give her one."

CARMILLA and I chatted for several hours before I took my leave and aimlessly wandered around the grounds of House Harker.

It was nice to catch up with my aunt. We'd spoken while I'd been at House Laurent, and I'd come home a few times to visit, but I'd always felt this underlying pressure to maintain a positive attitude around her. Now that my marriage had gone down in flames, I didn't have to lie about anything.

Despite Carmilla's reassurances though, I was still determined to prove my worth to House Harker and planned on tracking down Yolanthe tomorrow.

A splash of purple caught my attention, and I wandered over to the delicate flowers of the coastal lavender plants that were in full bloom lining the back of the garden. It was late spring, and a few stocks here and there had been harvested. I ran my fingers along one of the long stems, breathing in the relaxing scent. Further inland, lavender blossoms were larger and held a more earthy scent, but I'd always preferred the coastal variety.

"Thought I'd find you here," an amused voice called out.

I glanced over my shoulder to where Kieran leisurely made his way through the garden. He'd changed since this morning and now wore a turquoise doublet that made his golden hair and lightly tanned skin further stand out.

"Aren't you hot in that thing?" I gestured towards his outfit.

"It's almost summer and you're wearing, like, three layers of clothing."

He raised an eyebrow to match mine. "Is this your round-about way of asking me to take my clothes off?"

I rolled my eyes. "If you pass out from heat exhaustion, I'm leaving you here."

"You would never," he retorted with an easy grin. "I've been down in the cellars all morning catching with Caedmon."

"Were you actually talking, or were you sampling all the wine and ale he's been working on?"

"Both, of course." I laughed and shook my head at him as he gave me a wounded look. He added, "I'll have you know I picked up a lot of useful information."

I crossed my arms. "Do tell."

"He recently met with one of the Velesian brewers to arrange a trade of our grapes and their grain. Apparently, another trade deal broke down between the Narchis and Fervis."

"Interesting. What else did you learn?"

Rynn was my main source of gossip on the Velesians, but it was nice to get other information. Plus, Rynn wasn't exactly social whereas Kieran did his best to be in everybody's business.

"You'll have to join me for lunch to learn more." He held an arm out to me, and I looped mine through it without hesitation.

A few Moroi came out to tend the gardens and waved at us as we passed. Like me, Kieran knew everyone by name and asked after them or their family as we walked by. I recognized most of the names, but I filed away the ones I didn't, along with other bits of information.

Kieran was one of the reasons I always made such an effort to learn everyone's names and about their lives, no matter their position in the House.

Not only was it polite, but servants picked up all kinds of information, so it was always useful to be on their good side.

"I had everything brought to your suite. Is that okay?"

"That's fine." I let out a sigh of relief. "Everyone has been really nice to me, but if I get one more sympathetic look or pity hug, I might scream."

Kieran released my arm so that he could pull me in for a side hug. "I promise to give you no sympathetic looks or pity hugs. Only amused looks and sweaty hugs." He leaned over to wipe some of the sweat that had been dripping down from his forehead onto my cheek.

"Ugh!" I shoved him away from me. "I told you that doublet was too warm for this weather!"

He chuckled as his fingers nimbly worked to undo the front buttons while we hiked up the stairs to my room. By the time we got there, the doublet was slung over his shoulder and Kieran had unlaced the top of his shirt, putting a decent amount of his chest on display.

I fought back the blush that was threatening to creep up my neck as I realized we were about to be alone in my room with Kieran looking absolutely indecent.

My emotions were all over the place, and I really didn't need this right now.

Thank the moon Carmilla had insisted I feed from her earlier when she found out it'd been over a month since I'd last fed. It was a little awkward, since at this point, I was used to having sex with my blood, but that probably wouldn't be happening anytime soon, and I had desperately needed a blood meal.

Even with my thirst being sated I was still nervous about being alone with Kieran right now. I could have blamed my wanting of him on the bloodlust, but that would have been a lie. The desire was always there and had been from the first day I'd met him.

My hand hesitated on the doorknob as I tried to come up with an excuse not to go inside. But the decision was taken away from me when Kieran brushed past me to open the door and waltzed into my suite.

Shit.

Steeling my inner turmoil, I walked in after him, because like hell would I run away from my own damn room.

I froze a few paces in as I took in the feast before me. Honey biscuits, several types of fish sliced up into thin pieces, and an assortment of berries and salted nuts.

Kieran's grin faltered when he saw my expression, then he looked over the food he'd set up on the low table in front of my settee before facing me again. "Is it too much?" he asked, concern lacing his words. "It's too much. I'm sorry. I just… I thought…" He ran a hand through his hair. "I'll go get us something else."

"You remembered," I choked out.

His expression softened then. "Of course I remembered, Sam. I'd never forget anything about you."

The memories of us raiding the kitchen and throwing together this exact meal every time one of us had a bad day paraded through my mind.

The last time we'd done it had been when my wedding date was set. At the time, I hadn't been willing to admit I had any reservations about the marriage itself. Instead, I had mentioned how sad I would be about leaving House Harker.

About leaving him.

He remembered. After all these years. He *remembered.*

To my absolute horror, I burst into tears. Body-racking sobs tore out of me.

I was vaguely aware of Kieran as he swooped me up into his arms and placed me down carefully on the chaise lounge near the table of food before leaving quickly.

I didn't blame him. *What the hell was wrong with me?*

Gradually, the sobbing abated. Unfortunately, hiccups were quick to step into their wake.

I mournfully looked at the food that had set me off. My appetite had fled, and all I wanted to do was curl up in my bed and hide under my covers for the rest of the day. I was working on convincing myself to get up and shove the food in my spelled cold box for keeping when the door to my room opened again.

I peeked over the back of the lounge to see Kieran storming back in with a somewhat panicked look on his face.

"What are you—" My words were cut off when he dumped an armful of sweets into my lap.

"That's my entire stash," he said as he knelt in front of me and started holding up various pieces. "A few different types of chocolate. This one is a caramel. These are different types of hard candies."

I took the carefully wrapped candy out of his hand and unwrapped it before popping it into my mouth.

"Strawberry," I whispered as the sweet flavor exploded across my tongue. Infusing fruit flavors into hard candies was a relatively new technique, so even though the ingredients required were more common than the ones for chocolate, few people knew how to do it. "This is easily one of the best things I've ever tasted."

Kieran's bright hazel eyes looked at me as his features softened. "I'm sorry about lunch. I didn't mean to upset you. Whatever you want, I'll get it for you. Just *please* don't cry, Sam."

Carefully, I moved the ridiculous pile of candies from my lap to the table and patted the seat next to me. Kieran carefully joined me while keeping an eye on me like I would break down again at any moment.

"Lunch is perfect," I told him earnestly. "It is absolutely perfect, and you are perfect."

"Your reaction said otherwise," he said wryly.

"My mind is kind of weird right now," I admitted. "Carmilla advised me to take this week off and give myself time to adjust to everything that has happened. I brushed her off, thinking I could just dive back into my life here, but I think she was right, and I need to give myself some time to adjust to… everything."

"It's almost like your aunt knows what she's talking about since she's been alive for almost a century." He gave me a pointed look.

"Shush, you." I bumped my shoulder into his as a smile tugged at my lips. "I'm going to try to give myself a break this week and think carefully about what happened at House Laurent and what I want to do going forward." I gave Kieran a rueful glance. "Chances are pretty good that I'll be randomly bursting into tears all week. I totally get it if you want to avoid me."

Kieran held my gaze for a moment before he shifted until he was sitting on the floor and leaning against the settee. "This isn't my entire stash of candy. I lied before. I can break out more as needed."

I laughed as I joined him on the floor and leaned my head on his shoulder. "I knew you were lying, you greedy asshole. Now, pass me a dark chocolate."

CHAPTER SIX

—

Samara

I TWISTED from side to side as I studied my reflection in the mirror.

Okay, maybe I was dressed a *little* over the top, but after spending a week in comfy clothes and alternating between lounging in my suite or Carmilla's study, I needed to get back to a normal schedule.

This morning when I walked into my closet, I bypassed my loungewear to where my favorite dresses waited for me.

Aside from keeping my suite clean, nobody had moved anything in the years I'd been gone. I didn't know if that was because Carmilla expected me to visit more often, or if she somehow knew that I'd be back here someday.

I may or may not have cried when I saw my clothing hanging exactly where I had left them. My emotions had continued to be all over the place this week, which was why I'd mostly hidden away in my rooms. Kieran brought me lunch every day, along with a new assortment of candies. When I had random meltdowns, he didn't say anything. He just held me through it and then continued on with the conversation like nothing happened.

I absolutely adored him for it.

My random crying bouts were mostly over now, which I was extremely happy about. I was far from being back to my normal self, but I felt ready to tackle my new life.

Absently, I swayed in front of the mirror, flashing bits of skin with each movement. This dress would have been absolutely scandalous in House Laurent, but here, no one would bat an eye at the amount of skin I had on display. It was the golden threads that wound through the fabric in an ornate design that would draw attention and would have made the dress more reasonable for a fancy dinner instead of a normal day.

But as I pulled the long pieces of fabric through my fingers and let them fall back down to my ankles, I knew I wouldn't be changing into anything else.

Today would be the start of my new future, and I wanted to wear this dress while I set things in motion.

Want. Take.

My simple motto rang through my mind, and I smiled. It's not like it would truly be that easy, but I could still embrace this new outlook for a while and see where it got me.

I didn't bother with any makeup and pulled my hair back into a high ponytail so that it tumbled down my back in a long stream, showing the black outline of the crescent moon shining boldly on the left side of my neck.

It was the symbol that all Moroi were born with, the same as the Velesians and Furies who were born with their own crescent moons. The Velesians bore theirs on the right side of their neck, and the Furies at the base of their necks, with both points facing upwards.

The symbol of House Harker was tattooed on the right side of my neck. Fortunately for me, House Laurent turned up their noses at tattoos, so I didn't have to worry about bearing their mark for the rest of my life. Instead, they bore rings with their sigil stamped onto them. I'd tossed my ring into the drawer where I kept all my miscellaneous jewelry my first night back. I had another tattoo on my bicep that was a mishmash of the three crescent moon symbols.

Cali and Rynn had identical ones on their arms. After spending five years together while we all studied at Drudonia, we rarely saw each other in person anymore, but our bond ran deep, and something so insignificant as distance would never dampen our loyalty to each other.

I bit my lip as I thought back to our conversation last night. Rynn and Cali had been focused on supporting me, but I was still worried about both of them.

Despite Rynn's nonchalant words, I knew she was stressed about serving the Order of Avala. Unlike the Moroi, the Velesians didn't organize around specific bloodlines. The Moroi had seven Houses in our realm, including the Sovereigns, each ruled by a different family. The Velesians only had three Orders: Narchis, Avala, and Fervis. All of their territory was divided up among those three Orders, and leadership changed as new Velesians rose and challenged those above them. It always seemed a little chaotic to me, but it worked well enough for them.

Despite her timid personality, Rynn was brilliant at planning defensive and offensive moves across Lunaria. She knew everything about the monsters that roamed these lands, all their strengths and weaknesses, and when she was in her element, few things rattled her.

She could be staring death in the face and calmly recite all the various points where mortal wounds could be dealt, but she was also terrible at talking to people without sounding like she was talking down to them.

Which, to be fair, she normally was. Not because she was a snob but because Rynn was perfectly aware that she was usually the smartest person in the room, and she didn't understand why people didn't just listen to her. It had been a good source of entertainment for me and Cali over the years.

My frown deepened as I thought about Cali. She was another concern.

I was pretty sure that if something was seriously wrong, Cali would tell us, but I also knew my friend's definition of "seriously wrong" and mine were quite different. Maybe once I got my life figured out, I could plan a trip to visit both of them in person.

Their ability to appear to me in their shadow forms was convenient, but it made it hard to read their facial expressions that way. Plus, I knew that if I pushed Cali on it, she would simply disappear and probably refuse to talk to me for weeks.

I was still lost in my thoughts about Cali and Rynn when I realized I'd walked up to the third floor of the main house, where most of the studies were, but I didn't know which one was Alaric's, and many of the doors were closed.

Carmilla wanted me to work with him on drafting my marriage dissolution, which I personally thought was unnecessary. I was more than capable of writing it myself, but Carmilla had simply smiled at me when I'd voiced that opinion and asked me to work with him as a personal favor to her.

My aunt knew exactly how to manipulate me into doing things her way, and I couldn't even be mad when she did it because it was so annoyingly impressive.

Alaric had still been studying under some of the elders when I'd last lived here and hadn't had his own space yet. I glanced up and down the hallway but wasn't able to find any clues about which way to head.

I supposed I could just go to Carmilla's study and hope she wasn't in the middle of something and ask her.

"I'm assuming you're looking for me," a sardonic voice said from behind me in a tone that made it clear it wasn't a question.

I bit back the insult that tried to leap out of my mouth. While Kieran and I traded barbs with each other in our own weird way of flirting, Alaric and I had never gotten along. I would have been happy to avoid him entirely growing up, but his family had already resided in House Harker instead of one of the outpost towns and, much to my dismay, he became best friends with Kieran.

The two of them were as close as I was to Rynn and Cali, so Alaric and I had to tolerate each other to the best of our abilities once Kieran entered the picture.

It appeared nothing had changed. Great.

I plastered a smile on my face before turning around to face him. "Yes, I was. Carmilla thought it would be best to speak with you about dissolving my marriage agreement."

His always serious light green eyes flittered across my body, lips curling in distaste at my choice of dress.

I sighed inwardly. One of the many reasons Alaric didn't like me was because he thought I was just the spoiled niece of House Harker, flitting about through life without a care in the world. The fact that I had studied my ass off at Drudonia and gone through all kinds of training for my marriage to Demetri meant nothing to him.

Alaric's biggest fault was that once he'd made up his mind about something, nothing could change it. I thought it made him a stubborn ass and had told him as much to his face regularly, which usually caused him to make some sort of cutting remark, and then we'd trade insults until one of us stalked away or Kieran interrupted us.

I liked my dress. If he thought less of me for wearing it, that was his problem.

"Is there something wrong with my outfit?" I asked.

I made a show of looking it over as I tugged on the fabric a little, causing a little more of my cleavage to be on display.

Alaric gave me a flat stare in return, which I returned with a salacious grin. He let out a long-suffering sigh next, which only made me grin wider. He was so easy to mess with.

"Come on." He stepped around me and continued down the hall. "Let's get this over with."

I followed him around the corner and down another long hallway until we entered a door at the very end.

Of course, he would choose a study as far away from others as possible. Aside from Kieran, Alaric preferred to keep his own company as much as possible.

He went directly to his desk and took a seat before gesturing at one of the dark red velvet chairs across from him. I ignored him and walked around slowly, continuing my perusal of his space, partly to annoy him but mostly because I was curious.

Despite Alaric and I disliking each other, we were similar in a lot of ways. We were the same age, both of us had grown up in the shadows of others at House Harker, we both claimed Kieran as a friend, and we were both ambitious and more than willing to be cutthroat when needed. Despite all of that, our ideal workspaces fell under the "different" category and not the "similar" one.

"Are you sure this is your study?" I frowned, glancing around dramatically. "There's nothing in here. Do you just sit at your desk and glare at anyone who dares to enter your domain?"

"You are literally surrounded by floor-to-ceiling book-shelves, all of which are full," he replied evenly. "Now if you'll just—"

"There's nothing on your desk, though." I perched on the corner of his very large, very empty desk and tossed one leg over the other. The movement made the fabric part, leaving most of my right thigh exposed.

A muscle ticked just below Alaric's right eye, and I gave him a lazy smile.

"It's okay." I leaned over and reached out to pet his hand, which was clenched so tightly into a fist that I was surprised there wasn't blood leaking out. The movement gave him a view straight down my dress. "I won't tell anyone that you hide out in here all day just to play pretend advisor."

"Get. Your. Ass. Off. My. Desk," he ground out. "I know what you're doing, and I didn't have time for it when we were kids, and I sure as shit don't have time for it now."

I snickered before sliding off his desk and onto one of the velvet chairs that were every bit as uncomfortable as they looked. While my aunt liked to invite people into her study to discuss things, Alaric made it very clear that people only needed to state their business and get out.

"You make it so easy to push your buttons." I laughed. "Just checking to see if maybe you'd developed a personality over these last few years."

"It's a shame you didn't trade out your personality for one less annoying," he sniped back.

"Looks like that's something you and Marvina agree on," I said dryly.

He snorted, making the sound somehow seem intelligent, and pulled out a stack of papers from a drawer. "I spoke with Carmilla earlier this week and drafted up a dissolution based on the marriage contract between you and Demetri. Even without the recent events, they're in violation of several stipulations. Marvina will likely push back just to avoid looking weak, so I kept it simple for now."

"She will absolutely fight it." I held my hand out, but Alaric just stared at me. Shadows be damned. He was so frustrating.

Keeping my left hand outstretched, I braced my other elbow on the desk and plopped my chin into my palm. If he wanted to be childish, I could play that game too. It's not like I had anywhere else to be.

After a minute, he caved and slapped the papers into my hand, then looked towards the door in clear dismissal.

Nice try.

"Did Carmilla also tell you that I wanted to support House Harker?"

"She might have mentioned it." He leaned back in his chair and gave me an appraising look. "I assumed you'd be assuming the role of the House Harlot."

"That does have a fun ring to it." I let my eyes wander over his face.

Even I had to admit that you'd have to be blind not to find Alaric attractive. His skin was a rich dark brown that seemed to glow against the well-fitted black clothes he always wore.

I'd witnessed more than one courtier openly admire the chiseled jawline, sharp cheekbones, and striking eyes that made up his handsome face. His mouth was wide with lips that I would have dreamed about kissing if they were on literally anyone else.

Those gorgeous lips flattened into a hard line, and one corner of my mouth tugged up into a lopsided grin.

While Kieran knew how gorgeous he was and absolutely loved the attention, Alaric always seemed to be uncomfortable when others checked him out. I was pretty sure that was the reason he always wore nothing but simple black clothes instead of the bright clothing Kieran always donned. Alaric was more than happy to blend into the background and let Kieran attract all the attention.

But those goddamn eyes of his always drew people in. They reminded me of the ocean with their dominant sea-foam green and the turquoise lines that weaved through them.

Truth be told, one of the reasons I loved to annoy him so much was because I loved to see the turquoise color spread, making his already beautiful eyes truly extraordinary. I'd thought about telling him that before but decided that if he knew just how much I adored his eyes, he'd find a way to deny me the pleasure of seeing them in their true glory.

So instead, I always kept my tone teasing. That way I could both annoy him and admire him at the same time.

"With that gorgeous face of yours, I think you'd be better suited to the title of House Harlot," I drawled. "You'd just have to pull that stick out of your ass." Turquoise fractures bled through the light green, and I snickered. So easy to rile. "Look, you know that I'm good at negotiations. The same ones I was working on for House Laurent would work for House Harker. We'll just have to tweak them a little."

"We?" He arched an eyebrow at me.

"I'm not trying to step on your toes or make your life harder," I said quietly. "We had similar instruction, Alaric. You know what I'm capable of. I'm not asking you to be my best friend and dress in matching outfits every day. I'm just asking you to work with me."

I kept silent while he stared at me and thought over my words. His eyes roamed over my dress, and I saw the disapproval in his face, but still, he said nothing. It was just a damn dress and had no bearing on my ability to think. It wasn't any more scandalous than what most of the other Moroi in this House wore.

"You were raised and trained to be a wife. Nothing more. All those years of education were just so you wouldn't make a fool of yourself," he said matter-of-factly. "You were meant to serve House Harker by joining House Laurent and improving our strained relations, and you failed spectacularly."

I stiffened, unable to keep the hurt from flashing across my face. He began pulling out scrolls and papers, setting them in organized little piles on his desk as he barreled on.

"You may have left that House, but they were probably close to throwing you out of it anyway. You still act like a spoiled little brat, Samara."

"Don't hold back." My jaw flexed. "Tell me how you really feel."

"I have no choice but to work with you because Carmilla requested this." He raised his eyes to look at me, his expression cold and full of disdain. "It's a waste of everyone's time and this House's resources, but congrats, you'll get your way. For now. I'm sure you'll fuck it up and even Carmilla will have to admit it was a mistake."

I was practically vibrating with anger and the need to reach across the desk and slam Alaric's head into it repeatedly, but I took a deep breath and swallowed down my rage.

He wanted a reaction out of me, something he could add to the list of why I was unsuited for this task, but I refused to give him that.

"Thank you for drawing up the first draft of the marriage dissolution." I rose from my seat, my head held high. "I'll make the corrections to it this afternoon and run them by you tomorrow morning before we send it off to House Laurent."

"Fine." He waved a hand in casual dismissal.

"Fine," I echoed and left without another word.

I FORCED myself to take calm, measured steps as I left, even though I wanted to stomp out and toss some stuff on the floor for good measure.

But I wouldn't give Alaric the satisfaction of knowing just how much he'd gotten to me.

Fucking prick.

Once I was down the hallway and around the corner, I stopped and leaned against the wall. I'd forgotten just how much Alaric got under my skin when he wanted to.

After a few deep breaths, I was settled enough to acknowledge that I had also behaved badly. I'd started needling him right away and pushing his buttons, which only encouraged him to do the same. It was an old habit that I'd fallen back into instinctively the same way I'd slipped back into my easy friendship with Kieran.

Nevertheless, I was older now, and I needed to do better. I couldn't dictate how Alaric acted, only my own behavior and actions. He might still view me as a spoiled, privileged daughter of House Harker, but I wouldn't make it easy for him.

In fact, I'd make him work for it. A devious smirk slowly spread across my lips. Nothing would annoy Alaric more than me succeeding and proving every insult he'd ever hurled at me wrong.

The game of annoying the hell out of each other would continue. I was just changing the rules.

With a new goal in mind, I continued down the hallway. I needed to find a space to work in.

Technically, my suite was more than big enough and had a large sitting area that I could use as a study, but I always preferred to keep a separate workspace so that my suite could be a place to relax and take a break from the pressures of work.

I walked past the closed doors of Carmilla's study. I couldn't hear any voices from within, so either she was deep in thought over some problem, or she had activated the silencer spell that was standard in all of our studies.

More closed doors lined the halls, and I kept walking.

At least whatever empty space I found would be far away from Alaric.

The hallway eventually ended, and my options were right or left, both of which were dead-ends with only a couple of rooms.

Tentatively, I pivoted left. It seemed unlikely that the room

I thought of would be available because despite it being a small space, it had the best view on this floor.

But when I saw that the door was open, my steps quickened. I peeked inside and, to my delight, the study appeared to be unclaimed. It was almost half the size of Alaric's, with a desk on the right side of the room, angled so that you could see both the door and the window.

My feet carried me to the floor-to-ceiling window of their own accord, and I rested my hands against the glass as I looked out.

From this high up, I could see over the thick stone walls that protected all of House Harker to the sandy beach beyond. The tide rolled in gently over the shore, making it glisten as the waves pulled back before pushing inward again.

When we were growing up, this was where Kieran and I would work on our studies or just hang out. Occasionally, Rynn and Cali would come visit me, and we would use this space as well. It had never officially been mine, but looking back, Carmilla must have told everyone to leave it unoccupied so that we could use it.

Glancing around, I noticed that it was very clean, despite not being in use.

I wasn't surprised by the lack of clutter, but why would the staff bother dusting a room that no one was using? Even the rich wood of the desk shone like it had been polished recently.

"Thought you might claim this one."

I smiled over my shoulder at where Kieran was leaning against the doorframe. His loose blond hair fell around his face in soft curls, and his eyes shone with pleased satisfaction.

"Are you the reason this one is still free?" I tossed the marriage dissolution draft onto the desk as I hopped up onto it.

He shrugged. "No one has ever officially claimed it. It's mostly been used by visiting nobles and representatives from other Houses. One of the studies down the hall was free, so I helped the most recent occupant move to that one this morning."

"Thank you," I said honestly as I leaned back onto my palms and studied my new space.

The wall opposite the desk was mostly filled with bookshelves, but there was still some wall area left. Maybe I could get a miniature version of the map from Marvina's office and hang it there.

Thinking back to my encounter with Alaric, I grimaced. "My morning had a bit of a rough start, so this was a pleasant surprise."

Kieran pushed off the doorframe and took a seat in one of the chairs facing the desk. Then he swung his long legs over the arm of the chair so that he was sitting sideways and let his head hang back. It didn't look comfortable at all, but it was such a Kieran move that it tugged another smile out of me.

Kieran was as good at cheering me up as Alaric was at pissing me off. It was a cruel joke of fate that they were best friends.

"You were in Alaric's office for less than fifteen minutes, and you already pissed him off." He smirked. "Impressive."

"He's the one who pissed me off!" I seethed as flickers of the anger I'd felt at Alaric earlier caused my body to tense up again. "Whatever. Glad to see that you're still taking his side."

"Did you do that thing where you flash unnecessary amounts of skin just to make him uncomfortable?" He looked pointedly at the bare thigh I was now showing. When I glowered at him, he just laughed. "I thought so."

"Fine," I admitted, my shoulders slumping a bit. "I've already acknowledged to myself that I could have behaved better, and I will do so in the future, but we both know it won't make a difference. He's never going to change his mind about me, and I don't care."

"Hmm," Kieran mused but didn't deny my statement.

"Anyway," I drawled, "I'm going to review the draft that he wrote up for dissolving the marriage between me and Demetri. I promised to bring all the changes to his office tomorrow morning."

I leaned over and started flipping through the paperwork. Despite Alaric claiming to have just pulled together the basics, he appeared to have done a thorough job. I chewed on my bottom lip as guilt began to set in. Carmilla had no doubt ordered him to do this, but he still obviously put a lot of effort into it.

"You really going to go through with it?" Kieran's tone was curious with a touch of something else that I couldn't quite place.

"They'd have to work very hard to change my mind," I said simply, already half-focused on a particularly tricky wording I'd stumbled onto in the third paragraph. "I spent the last three years trying to make not only my marriage work but also demonstrate that I was an asset to House Laurent. They put zero effort in. If anything, they worked against me. I realize that this marriage was arranged to better our relations with that house of vipers, but it just wasn't working."

I blinked several times when I realized I'd just been reading the same sentence over and over again. With a sigh, I dropped the document back onto the desk and focused on Kieran once more. He'd repositioned himself so that he was slouching against the back of the chair with his legs stretched out in front of him, giving the impression of languid ease.

"I wasn't happy." I tried to keep my tone even, but a little of the pain I'd felt leaked through, and Kieran's expression hardened.

"What did he do?" His eyes scoured my face as if he would find the answer he sought there.

Seeing Kieran's protectiveness over me helped ease some of the pain left over from my time at House Laurent. I'd been alone there, but here I had the full support of my aunt. And I had Kieran.

"Nothing I shouldn't have expected." I let out a mirthless laugh. "I knew that our marriage was a political one. There was never anything romantic about it. We didn't exchange love letters, we exchanged updates about our Houses. Updates that were carefully reviewed by others because, despite the impending marriage between our Houses, information is still something that should be tightly controlled."

I could still remember walking to Carmilla's office every morning and handing over my drafts. We'd discuss them over tea and make slight adjustments to make sure we weren't giving House Laurent, Marvina in particular, something that could be used against us later.

Demetri had almost certainly done the same. I snorted at that thought because he probably never wrote them to begin with. That was likely either done by Marvina herself or one of her underlings. Never once in our three years of marriage had I ever seen Demetri do any work other than visiting the Houses to "strengthen relations with House Laurent."

I supposed sleeping with various courtiers was one way to strengthen relations.

"Our marriage wasn't something built on love, but I did think it would be one built on respect and loyalty. And monogamy." Understanding dawned on Kieran's face then. "I know," I groaned and slapped my hands across my face. "I was an idiot."

"I wouldn't say that." He winced. "You found out that monogamy wasn't part of the deal, I'm guessing?"

The sounds of moaning and a squeaking mattress replayed painfully in my mind.

"Yeah," I said dryly. "Walked in on Demetri showing a hell of a lot more enthusiasm for his mistress of the week than he ever had in our bed."

"Well, fuck him," Kieran scoffed.

"Nah, I don't think I want to do that anymore," I deadpanned.

He chuckled, and I couldn't help but laugh too. The more I laughed, the more emotions poured out of me from the whole situation. Hurt and rejection from Demetri's betrayal. Humiliation from the meeting in Marvina's study. Rage at both of them for, well, everything.

And guilt because despite all that had happened, I was so fucking happy to be home. My laughter gained a maniacal edge until I was laughing so hard, tears streamed down my cheeks.

Kieran waited until I'd wiped the tears from my eyes and rested my hands on my thighs to say anything.

He murmured, "I'm sorry, Sam."

He leaned forward in the chair and placed his hands on top of mine, giving them a gentle squeeze. Heat burned in my eyes as more tears threatened to fall at the simple gesture, but I blinked them back. I hated crying, and I'd been doing a lot of that lately.

Kieran added, "I know that you did everything you could to make it work. No one has ever doubted your dedication to House Harker."

"Tell that to Alaric," I muttered.

"You should cut him some slack," Kieran said carefully. "He's been under a lot of pressure lately."

"He's always under pressure." I shot him an annoyed look. "You don't need to defend him constantly, you know?"

He let his head drop back once more so that he was staring up at the ceiling. "Am I once again going to have to play peacekeeper between you two? Because that shit was getting old before you left."

"Please," I snorted. "You loved any opportunity to be the

center of attention. It's why you love being a courtier so much."

The House Kieran was born into was one of the lower-ranking ones. Both of his parents were high-ranking courtiers and had arranged for Kieran to travel to other Houses to better represent their interests. House Harker had been the first House he'd been assigned to, and we didn't want him to leave because everyone here adored him.

Kieran felt the same, and luckily his parents had been thrilled because it would be hard to get a more prestigious House unless he landed in the Sovereign Court.

"You and Alaric have your talents, and I have mine," he said smugly.

"I wasn't aware that being able to schmooze for hours amongst boring nobility counted as a talent."

"We both know that's not true." He gave me a cocky look. "How many times have I had to rescue you before you mouthed off to some nobility creep or fell asleep face-first while listening to the ramblings of an elder?"

The corner of his lips tilted up into that stupid, mischievous grin of his that always sent my thoughts scattering when we were growing up. My eyes trailed down his body, snagging on where his shirt had ridden up, giving me a glimpse of his muscular abs.

Despite spending most of his time behind the safety of our walls, Kieran had always taken training seriously.

I could still remember Rynn and Cali dragging me off to spy on his training when we were younger. He'd been well aware of our antics and always made a show of pulling off his shirt early in his workout to give us a better view. Sometimes he'd even do some ridiculous poses and wink at us before concentrating on training.

It was during those workouts that I couldn't resist flirting back with him, much to Alaric's disapproval, but we'd never gone beyond flirting.

Kieran followed my gaze and instead of pulling his shirt down, he shifted, causing it to ride a little higher.

I swallowed as want and heat spread through me.

My marriage, as I knew it, was over. Even if we hadn't signed the paperwork yet, Demetri had made it quite clear that he didn't view monogamy as a part of our marriage.

I thought back to what I had told Rynn and Cali about my new life motto. *Want something. Take something.*

"So…" I crossed one leg over the other, causing even more skin to show. Kieran's eyes tracked the movement, and the gold threads weaving through his deep brown irises started to blaze even brighter. "Is that clever tongue of yours good for anything other than charming your way out of trouble?"

"Yes." His voice was deep as his heated gaze traveled slowly upward, taking the time to drink in every one of my curves. "It's also quite good at charming me into trouble."

CHAPTER SEVEN

—

Samara

"Is that so?" The corners of my lips curved up as I brazenly took him in.

The golden streaks in his eyes grew wider, and my heart beat a little faster every time more of the brown gave way to gold.

"As much as I enjoyed this game when we were growing up, I'm not sure I can play it now. At least, not with the same rules." His voice was still playful, but there was now an underlying edge to it.

Still, he didn't move, giving me the choice of how far I wanted to take this. I waited for the guilt to hit me. For the logical voice in my head to remind me that I was still technically married, but the voice remained silent, and the guilt never came.

My heart had never been part of my marriage, and my mind knew that it was over. All that was left were the details of ending it.

There was no reason, logical or otherwise, to deny this any longer.

"Same game." Exhilaration rushed through my body as I stood and strode over to the door to close it.

I leaned my back against the solid wood and reached my hand out to the side where the silencing spell was engraved into the wall. My fingers nimbly ran over the glyph to activate it, and then I pushed off the door, my hips swaying as I returned to the desk and perched on it once more.

I leaned back and spread my legs wide instead of crossing them. Kieran went completely still. "New rules," I cooed.

"Fuck." His eyes turned completely gold, and I laughed huskily.

"The only orgasms I've had these past three years are the ones I gave myself."

An ache pulsed from between my thighs as my heart continued its attempt to pound its way out of my chest. I'd had so many wicked dreams of Kieran over the years, but I never once thought they would become a reality.

"That's a shame." His voice took on a rough quality that had me wanting to clench my thighs together.

"Are you going to do something about it?" I arched an eyebrow at him when he continued to sit there. "Or should I see if someone else is available?"

Before the last word was out of my mouth, Kieran leapt from the chair and closed the distance between us. He nudged my knees further apart so he could slip between my legs as he braced his arms on either side of me. My pulse pounded as I held his gaze, acutely aware of the barely-there inch separating us.

"I've been dreaming about what you taste like for longer than I care to admit," he murmured as he ducked his head to kiss my neck.

A breathy sound escaped me at the touch of his warm lips against my skin, and then his hands slipped under my ass. He jerked me forward until I was flush against him. I slid my hands under his shirt, running my fingers over the taut muscles of his stomach, and he groaned against my skin, his fingers digging into me harder.

My fingers trailed up his back until I reached his hair just as I felt his fangs graze my neck. I yanked his head back, heat striking through my core when he let out a growl of irritation.

"No blood for you," I said in a breathy voice. "Not yet."

"Is that one of the rules?" He gave me a sly grin.

I tugged on his hair again. "Yes."

"Any others I should know about?" he asked lazily as one of his hands moved to graze the inside of my thigh. My thoughts scattered at the sensation, and he let out a deep, knowing chuckle. "Any other rules, Sam?"

"I'm sure,"—I gasped as his fingers brushed over my panties—"I'll think of something."

"Mmm," he hummed as he continued to trace slow patterns up and down my thighs. I could practically feel the wetness dripping out from within my core, and in the spirit of embracing my new wanton self, I widened my legs even more. Kieran growled in approval, which only further flamed my desire.

"You want to know what I taste like?" I released my hold on his hair and leaned back onto the desk. "Then find out. If you make it good, I might even let you come back for another taste."

I gave him a challenging look, and he returned it with a salacious grin before dropping to his knees.

He looked at me from between my thighs, and I almost came right then and there. I tried to maintain the haughty expression on my face, but the smirk on his told me he saw through it.

"You'll be coming to *me* after this," he said arrogantly. "And I'll make *you* beg for it."

"Unlikely," I retorted. "You think that I'll—"

I was cut off when he licked a blazing path on the inside of my thigh as he settled my legs over his shoulders and pulled me further towards him. I bit my lip to contain the wanton moan that threatened to escape, determined to hold out for as long as possible because the competitive side of me didn't want to let Kieran know just how quickly he could make me come undone.

Same game. New rules.

We weren't just flirting anymore. Touching, tasting, and fucking were now on the menu, but that didn't mean I was going to let him think that he had me wrapped around his finger. I wouldn't be begging him for anything.

Two fingers slid beneath the fabric of my panties and circled my clit. I cursed as I jerked at the new sensation, but Kieran had a strong hold on my thighs.

He laughed, and I felt the heat of his breath against my skin, which sent shivers up my spine.

"Already so wet for me."

"I was thinking about someone else," I lied. It probably would have been more convincing if my voice hadn't been so breathy.

"Oh?" He leaned back, and his nimble fingers pulled my underwear down and over my legs before he dropped them to the floor. "Tell me about this someone else. I'd *love* to know who my competition is."

He gave me a bemused look, clearly not buying my story at all, and arched an eyebrow as if daring me to lie once more. Before I could piece together another lie, he moved forward and that clever tongue of his slipped into my pussy at the same moment he ran a finger over my clit.

I was so goddamned keyed up that I let out a strangled scream as pleasure ripped through me. So much for playing hard to get. It'd taken him less than a minute to give me a better orgasm than I'd had in years.

I thought he'd pull back to gloat at making me come so quickly, but instead, it only seemed to drive Kieran mad. He devoured me like he was starving and I was the first good meal he'd had in weeks. One hand reached up, slowly trailing over every curve and dip in my body until he reached my breast, squeezing it at the same time as he sucked my clit.

A whimper tore out of me as he pushed me towards the edge again. *Fuck.* My body was still trembling from the last orgasm, yet I could already feel another one building. A fang grazed my clit as he released it, and I arched my back, trying to chase the sensation.

I started to protest when I felt him pull away, but I screamed instead when two fingers plunged into me.

He feverishly yanked the top of my dress down, freeing my breasts, and ran a thumb over one of my hard nipples. I shivered when he did it again.

My eyes closed as pleasure rippled through me with every thrust of his fingers.

"Fuck, Sam," Kieran growled, and I slowly opened my eyes to meet his blazing gold gaze as he took me in, spread out on the desk. "You taste better than I ever dreamed."

"You dreamed of this?" A playful grin spilled across my lips.

He gave me a wolfish one in return. "You gonna tell me you haven't?"

"Never crossed my mind." *Lie, lie, lie.*

"Such a liar you are."

He thrust his fingers inside me and I bucked at the sudden fullness. A mewling sound I'd never once made in my life loosened from my lips as he continued to slowly push his fingers in and out, his other hand toying with my nipple.

"I *have* dreamed about this. About what you would taste like." He drew his fingers out of my dripping pussy before sucking them clean.

There was no doubt in my mind that my eyes were pure violet right now as I watched with complete rapture as Kieran finished cleaning his fingers. A deep chuckle spilled from his lips while he reached down to teasingly graze my clit.

I raised my hips to meet his fingers, but the bastard pulled his hand away and stood up. A needy snarl ripped out of me at being denied what I so desperately wanted. I tried to shove myself up from the desk, but he leaned over and pushed me down with one hand.

"Is there something you want?" he purred, and the hand that wasn't holding me down trailed down between my breasts, past my stomach before stopping so achingly close to where I wanted those fingers again. "I'll make it easy for you."

He bent down and sucked a nipple into his mouth. I gasped at the contact, rapidly losing control over this situation and not giving one single fuck.

"Tell me what you want, Sam." Kieran moved to suck my other nipple, eliciting another whimper from me. "Fingers, tongue, or cock?"

Cock! I screamed internally but kept the word from leaping from my lips.

If Kieran was able to undo me this much with just his tongue and fingers, it would be all over once he fucked me with his cock. I had just enough of my mind left to be terrified of that and what it would mean.

"Tongue," I rasped.

He tutted, "We both know that's not what you want."

I raised my chin and met his heated stare. "Tongue," I repeated, my voice louder this time.

"No," he said with a smirk. "We'll compromise, though. I want to watch you come undone before I lick you clean." Before I could argue, two fingers thrust into me while his thumb pushed down on my clit.

"FUCK!" I screamed.

Another finger joined the other two while Kieran built up to a brutal pace. My hips ground against his hand as filthy words spilled from my lips.

"That's it, baby," Kieran groaned when my pussy tightened around his fingers. "Come for me again. I want you dripping all over my fucking hand."

I cried out as he pushed me over the edge again.

He let me ride his fingers for a few more seconds before his tongue swirled around my clit and I fucking detonated.

Thank fuck I activated the silencing spell because I'm pretty sure my screams would have shaken the entire building, and Carmilla probably didn't want to hear that. Alaric probably didn't either, but fuck him.

I laid there while panting, trying to catch my breath as Kieran slowly drew his tongue over my slick heat, and I shivered at the sensation. Then he drew himself over me and plunged his mouth into mine as he kissed me deeply. The taste of my pleasure on his tongue was fucking hot as hell, and I gasped slightly as he pulled away.

"You're welcome," he said in a satisfactory tone.

The pleased look on his face was enough to get at least some of my brain back on track.

I pushed myself up, and he backed up to give me space. Slowly, as if I didn't have a care in the world, I pulled my dress back up and got myself sorted.

"That was adequate, I suppose." I shrugged.

"Adequate?" He arched an eyebrow at me. "You're sitting in a puddle made of your own pleasure. If you stood up right now, we both know it would be running down your thighs, and that was just a warm-up."

Fuck. Me. There was no way that was just a warm-up.

My fucking clit was still twitching, and he wasn't wrong about where I was sitting. Even now, I could feel my dress sticking to my skin.

I pursed my lips. "Somehow, you're even cockier now than you were in our youth," I said breezily.

"You're just sore because I didn't show exactly how *cocky* I can be." It took a valiant effort on my part not to drop my eyes to his crotch, and based on the way his mouth twitched in amusement, I knew Kieran was perfectly aware of my inner struggle.

"This was a good show on your part. Maybe we should just leave it on a good note." I plastered a bored expression on my face. "I'm sure you would enjoy thrusting wildly over me for a few seconds before spasming and rolling over, but I think I'll pass."

He let out a low laugh and once again leaned over me to whisper in my ear, "We both know that you want my cock buried inside you at the same time my fangs pierce that lovely neck of yours. You'll be screaming my name."

"Whatever you need to tell yourself, Kier." I tapped my finger against his chest. "I think we both know that you'll be the one begging for another taste."

Heat and amusement flitted across his features at the challenge I'd just thrown down. My hand flattened against his chest as he leaned in to give me a quick kiss before turning to leave. Just as he opened the door, he glanced back at me and grinned. "I like this new game."

CHAPTER EIGHT

Kieran

I STARED at the closed door for a solid minute, convincing myself not to barge back in and toss Sam back onto that damned desk and bury myself inside her.

At the time, I'd meant every word I'd said about making her beg for it, but now as I stood here in the hallway, staring at the closed door with a raging hard-on, I realized just how much of a mistake that was.

Sam *loved* challenges.

If you told her she couldn't do something, not only would she do it, but she'd do it in the most spectacular way possible just to rub your nose in it.

She was a deliciously spiteful thing, and I had always absolutely adored that about her.

Until now.

"Fuck me," I muttered before forcing myself to step away from the door and across the hall to the study I'd claimed as my workspace.

This morning, I'd been very proud of myself for securing the study directly across from me for Sam. I had a feeling she would be drawn to it again, so I'd helped the visiting noble move and then cleaned it up. It hadn't taken long, and the delight on Sam's face had been entirely worth it, but there was no way I could now sit at my desk all day and stare at that closed door.

Or worse, knowing Sam, she would open it at some point and perch her luscious ass on the desk and continue her work just to taunt me.

I spun away from my study and headed towards the stairs, trying to get a hold on myself. I had some appointments later in the morning with some visiting courtiers, but nothing that required much preparation on my part. That meant I had a couple of hours free.

A distraction. That's what I needed. Just something to take my mind off that throaty sound Sam made just before she came that was part moan and part plea. Or the way the violet fractures of her eyes wound their way through the deep purple reminding me of how the night sky was often painted in Unseelie murals.

I sucked in a deep breath when my cock strained against my breeches as I recalled the feeling of her thighs tightening around me while my tongue devoured every inch of her.

Distraction. Right.

Normally, I didn't train until the afternoon, but there were always some off-duty rangers around. Someone who would likely spar with me.

"What are you doing?"

I turned from where I'd stopped in the middle of the hallway and saw Alaric walking out of Carmilla's study. He took in my disheveled appearance, eyes darting down to the bulge in my pants before he gave me an exasperated look.

"Really, Kier?" He shook his head and stepped around me.

I trailed after him, trying in vain to adjust my pants to make myself more comfortable.

This was far from the first time Alaric had caught me in a

compromising position. If anything, this was tame compared to the rest. Thankfully, my dick started to calm down by the time we reached his office, and I settled down in one of his chairs.

"It's too early for you to be smelling like pussy in my study," Alaric said in an annoyed tone as he stared forward.

"It's never too early for that," I scoffed as I slid a scrutinizing glance over his face and noticed him clenching and unclenching his jaw.

That was the Alaric equivalent of screaming and punching a wall. He must still be really pissed about his encounter with Samara earlier this morning, which meant I should probably avoid mentioning what I'd just done with her.

Alaric sighed. "Do I even want to know who your dalliance for the week is this time?"

Shit.

I paused, thinking about what I should tell him.

Alaric wasn't just my best friend, he was my first friend. Everyone had an agenda in the House I grew up in, including my parents. They arranged "friends" for me throughout my childhood, making sure I only associated with the children of Moroi who could provide my parents with political connections.

When I got shipped off to House Harker at fourteen years old, I was well-practiced in wearing different masks.

The dutiful son.

The charming young man.

The future heartbreaker.

A different mask for every occasion.

I excelled at determining which one would work best and continued to add more to my collection, but being myself was another matter.

I barely remembered how to do that when I was alone, and I certainly didn't know how to do it around others.

Alaric and Samara were the same age as me and both had

grown up in this house and had a bitter rivalry. They fought over literally everything. Including me.

Alaric had been the first one to get past my defenses and see the real me, something he still held over Sam's head, much to my annoyance. The only reason he'd "won" the friend card first was because Sam was my first serious crush and I struggled with how to act around her. I thought that she would like me more if I wore the charming mask all the time.

It was years before I let her start to see through the cracks and get a peek at the real me. Even then, I still held back so much.

Like how devastated I was when she left for Drudonia and how I counted the days until she would come back for various House events. The last thing I wanted was her pity over how fucked-up I really was.

But when she left for Drudonia, it was a rude awakening to the reality of my situation.

My crush had turned into something so much more than that, but I knew Sam and I couldn't be together. She'd agreed to the marriage between her and Demetri when she was fourteen years old, a month before I'd arrived, and from everything I'd observed, she was happy about it.

I knew that Sam had the option to break off the arrangement before they wed when she turned twenty-one, and I'd secretly hoped that she would.

But I'd been too scared to ever say something to her about it.

There were a lot of things I could handle in life, but a rejection from Sam wasn't one of them.

Samara had thrown herself into preparing for the marriage even as she supported Carmilla at House Harker however she could.

I knew she had a crush on me, but she never gave any hints that it was anything more than that. So I kept my true feelings to myself and pretended to only miss her as a friend and nothing more even as it shredded my fucking soul in two.

While I hoped that someday Alaric and Sam would figure out a way to hash out their differences and at least become civil towards each other, it seemed unlikely. Though, with Sam back at House Harker, and our… evolving friendship… my role as peacekeeper between the two of them was about to get a lot more complicated.

Alaric zeroed in on my silence, and he scrutinized me further. His green eyes wholly focused on me as he thought about what could possibly cause me to hesitate.

"Fuck," he ground out, crossing one arm across his stomach while the other rubbed at his face. "Tell me you didn't."

"Are you asking me to lie to you?" I asked in a teasing tone even though I couldn't hold back my wince. Shit. He was going to be so pissed.

The turquoise cracks woven through Alaric's light green eyes spread for a second as his temper flared before retreating. Apparently, he wasn't in the mood to be teased about this. Even when Samara wasn't in his presence, she *still* somehow managed to be one of the few people who could get my friend to lose control.

"Why her?" His voice was even, if a little flatter than usual. The tightness across his face still betrayed him, though. Alaric was beyond pissed about this turn of events.

He would just have to fucking deal with it.

"Don't act so surprised." I shrugged. "You know her and I have always had a complicated friendship. We couldn't do anything about it before, but now she's back, and things are different."

"She's still married to the Heir of another House!" Alaric threw his hands in the air. "You're thinking with your dick and not your head!"

"Please, we both know that marriage is over and was probably a mistake to begin with. Marvina is going to rule House Laurent until her last dying breath, and given that she's fourth generation, we have no idea when that's going to be." I arched an eyebrow, daring him to tell me I was wrong, but he just shook his head and looked away. I smiled victoriously.

The first generation of Moroi, Velesians, and Furies had burned fast and bright. Most hadn't lived more than twenty years after their transformation from being human, but every generation since then lived a little longer.

Those who belonged to the fourth generation were well over eighty years old now but still looked as if they were in their mid-to-late thirties or forties. Their aging had slowed drastically, and we assumed that our generation would be the same. How long we all would live was anyone's guess.

"Besides," I continued, "we both know that prick is probably balls deep in someone who is very much *not* his wife right now."

"It's still a complication that House Harker doesn't need," Alaric argued, refusing to let this go.

"No, it's a complication that *you* don't need right now." I gave him a flat look. "But you're just going to have to deal with it."

"Whatever," he said flippantly. "Just don't start shoving your tongue down her throat in front of me. I don't need more nightmare fuel."

"I'll be sure to protect your delicate sensibilities," I retorted in an equally flippant tone.

Although, with the challenge that Sam had laid down, it would probably be a while before my tongue was anywhere near her. Despite my raging hard-on earlier, I wouldn't be begging for shit. Sam wasn't the only one who loved a challenge.

"Thanks," he said dryly. When he rubbed his face again, I

noticed that his expression hadn't loosened. Faint dark circles were present under his eyes too.

Something was deeply troubling him.

"Has there been another attack?" I asked quietly, all thoughts about my new game with Sam forgotten.

Alaric's eyes flashed to the open door, and I got up to close it. It seemed unlikely that anyone would be eavesdropping on us from this floor, but Alaric was clearly worried about this, so I kept my thoughts to myself.

Once the door was shut and I was settled back in my chair, Alaric reached behind him and brushed his fingers against a dark red symbol that had been painted against the wall. All Moroi could perform blood magic, and a silencing spell was one of the first we learned, right after healing.

"Three more outposts have been hit," he admitted. "Two in Velesian territory, but one of them was ours."

I swallowed. "Survivors?"

He shook his head.

"That brings us to eight attacks in the last year." Only a few of them were public knowledge. The outposts that had been small and remote had been kept secret.

Technically, each House was supposed to be responsible for patrolling a section of the Moroi realm. In reality, the Sovereign House and House Harker oversaw everything. The Sovereigns commanded more rangers, but we had Vail. He was cunning and knew the wilds better than anyone. It was the reason he was put in charge of investigating the attacks.

Unfortunately for everyone, despite his skills, we were no closer to knowing what the hell was going on or how we could protect our outposts against future attacks.

Each of the Houses had taken over a Fae fortress to serve as their stronghold. The abandoned fortifications were perfect at first because they could easily house a thousand or more Moroi. The walls were not only thick but seeped with magic that we still didn't fully understand. We only knew that it kept monsters out.

On top of that, we'd added our blood wards to protect us from the wraiths. But even the largest of the fortresses had run out of space decades ago.

The Velesians were in the same situation. The Furies didn't have that problem, but nobody wanted to live with them because most of us still viewed them as potential threats. True, it had been a while since a Furie had lost control, but the last incident had resulted in over a hundred Moroi and Velesian deaths. It had taken half a dozen Furies to bring the culprit down, and only three of them had walked away from that fight.

When Furies lost themselves, they went mad… and that madness leaked to everyone around them until everyone was swimming in a sea of blood and violence.

There was a reason some within the Houses and Velesian Packs called for the extermination of all Furies. They were a brutal weapon to be wielded against the beasts that prowled the night. But that weapon could just as easily be turned on us.

Even if some were willing to take that risk and live closer to them, the Furie realm lacked the resources to support large populations because most of their territory consisted of the badlands.

The solution had been to build outposts throughout the Moroi and Velesian realms to protect trade routes, add more farmlands, and provide housing.

We'd done the best we could to make them secure, but clearly, it wasn't enough. If word spread about how fast the outposts were falling, people would panic, and we couldn't house and feed everyone within the strongholds, not indefinitely.

It was cruel, and I knew it deeply bothered Alaric. The two of us only lived in House strongholds because we were born into noble families, but the Sovereigns had decreed to keep it quiet, and the leadership of the Velesians and Furies agreed. Well, the Furies did. I'd heard that the Velesians were less than pleased about the decision but were going along with it for now.

"Is this the reason why there have been so many closed-door meetings in Carmilla's study?" I asked.

Alaric nodded and unrolled a map across his desk. I rose from the chair and leaned over the desk, watching as he crossed out each of the outposts that had been attacked recently.

"If there is a pattern, I don't see it," I admitted. Not that this was in any way my area of expertise.

As a courtier, I hosted visiting nobles and representatives from other Houses when they came here. Frequently, I traveled to other Houses to help support our alliances with them… or gossip and collect valuable information for Carmilla.

During those visits, I'd stop at outposts along the way, so I was familiar with all the ones on the main routes. But seeing patterns or weaknesses in defenses was far outside my skillset.

"I haven't been able to find one either." Alaric ran a hand over his closely shorn hair before planting both hands back on the desk and staring at the map like he could force it to give him answers. "But we have to figure out something, and soon. The wraiths have found a way to slip through our wards. We're quietly trying out new ones, but there is no way to know if they will work or not."

I swallowed past the icy dread taking root inside me. The wards around the Houses were considerably more powerful than the ones around the outposts thanks to the leftover Fae magic, so we were likely safe for now. But I had friends who lived in outposts, and all their lives were at risk. Plus, I spent a considerable amount of time traveling outside the safety of

House Harker walls and had always considered the outposts secure. That was clearly no longer the case.

"Seems like most of the attacks are in the Velesian realm, with some spilling over in ours." I ran my fingers across the southwestern portion of the map. "Only one in Furie territory?"

"Yes, but that doesn't mean much." Alaric tapped a finger on the only outpost in Furie territory that had been crossed out. "Their outposts are almost all along the coastline. Nothing can survive in badlands, so they've never bothered to build any outposts there. Their outpost that was attacked was next to the Velesian border."

It was debatable whether the Furies had the best or worst territory out of all of us. They suffered the least attacks from wraiths and the other monsters that made Lunaria their home because the badlands served as a buffer between them and the rest of Lunaria. The only way to reach where most of their population lived was to cross the badlands, which meant almost certain death, or go along the coastline, which was heavily guarded.

But they also had the least amount of livable territory, because even the Furies couldn't survive in the badlands. The terrain was too arid to grow any crops, there was no food to hunt, and the harsh landscape made it impossible to establish reliable trade routes.

Sooner or later, they would have to expand into other territories.

That political nightmare would be something people like Alaric and Samara would have to deal with someday.

Not me, though. I excelled at finding secrets and playing host to visiting nobles and courtiers, but tedious negotiation was not in my skillset, and I had no interest in learning.

"Vail is coming," Alaric said casually.

I whipped my head up from the map. "When?"

"Three days. He's currently further north dealing with a pack of howlers. Carmilla wants to talk to him in person before he goes to visit the sites of the recent attacks."

I grimaced. Vail Ferenc was the Marshal of House Harker, which meant he was in charge of all of our rangers.

Both of his parents had been rangers, and Vail had quickly risen through the ranks. No one, not even me, could deny that he was gifted. The man had survived multiple wraith ambushes that would have left anyone else in pieces, not to mention all the fights he'd survived against the other terrors that roamed these lands.

He was vicious with a short temper, which was why Carmilla rarely called him back to the House.

Vail was a monster, but he was our monster.

He also hated Samara with every drop of blood in his veins.

"Well, with any luck, he'll provide his update and then be on his way back to the wilds where he fucking belongs." I crossed my arms stiffly, trying to ignore the knot of tension that was starting to form in my chest.

Alaric gave me a pointed look. "Vail has never wavered in his support of House Harker. He deserves our thanks and respect."

I rolled my eyes. "And he has it. Doesn't mean I have to like the guy or want to be around him."

Alaric shook his head and went back to staring at the map. If I left him to it, he'd stand like this all day.

"Come on." I rolled up the map before he could stop me and held it out of his reach when he tried to snatch it back. "You need to give that crafty mind of yours a break."

"I don't have time—"

"Just a quick break, I promise." I smirked at him and tossed the map onto the desk. "It won't take me long to beat the shit out of you."

His lips pursed together, suppressing a grin, and then he deactivated the silencing spell. "I have to let you win. Your fragile ego wouldn't be able to handle constantly losing to me otherwise."

I slapped him on the back as we sauntered towards the door. "Keep telling yourself that."

CHAPTER NINE

Samara

I woke with a start, my sweat-drenched sheets sticking to my skin. Whatever I'd been dreaming slipped away, just like it had for the last two mornings.

Ever since I learned that Vail was coming here.

Alaric had been the one to tell me, no doubt enjoying seeing how much it rattled me. He was such an ass.

Trembles raced up and down my body as the aftereffects of the nightmare slowly faded. It had been years since I'd had one. They were a frequent visitor to my mind in the years after my parents had been attacked and killed in front of me, but I was nothing if not a pro at compartmentalizing.

Swallowing over the lump in my throat, I shoved that memory into its prison once more and buried it deep inside my soul. Every once in a while, it would slip free for a night of terror, but it hadn't been this bad since I'd been a teenager.

I knew it was only happening now because of Vail.

One of the few good things about living at House Laurent for the past three years was that I never had to see the Marshal of House Harker. I knew when I returned home that I'd have to see him sooner or later, but I'd really been hoping for the latter.

I'd thrown myself into perfecting the marriage dissolution these past few days. Alaric and I still traded barbs, but we managed to work surprisingly well together despite our dislike. We both agreed that the dissolution was as good as it could get for the opening volley.

I was a little surprised that neither Demetri nor Marvina had contacted me in an attempt to smooth things over and convince me to come back to at the very least discuss things there.

They had to know that I would return to House Harker where I had a support system. At House Laurent, I'd been isolated, and they would have held more power in any negotiations. I'd expected Demetri to apologize in some shallow or meaningless way and then argue that our marriage could still work since everything was out in the open now. Marvina, I had expected to simply demand my return at once, but there had only been silence from House Laurent.

I'd mentioned my confusion about this to Alaric and that it made me suspicious, and he agreed that it was odd. Then he said something rude as if he couldn't stand the idea of having a civil conversation with me. Nothing unusual there.

We'd handed over our final draft to Carmilla last night, and she promised to send it first thing in the morning, which meant they'd have it early this afternoon. The strikers were fast fliers, and they'd make the trip to House Laurent in a few hours and then wait for them to send back a response.

I doubted we'd get one today, so I was going to be a nervous wreck for the next twenty-four hours at least. I just wanted this to be done.

Maybe I could do something to break Kieran and get him to beg tonight to distract me. I smirked and stood from my bed.

He'd remained strong since declaring that he'd never beg

and that I certainly would. I'd come pretty close to getting him to give in yesterday when I'd left the door to my study open and perched on my desk to "ponder how I wanted to decorate my study."

At least, that was the excuse I'd given to Kieran when he demanded to know what the hell I was doing with my knee bent and leg propped up on the desk, causing most of my thigh to be on display. I'd slowly tapped my fingers against my leg, inching a little higher each time before dropping my hand.

The third time I did it, Kieran let out a groan and started to get up when Alaric had shown up and interrupted.

I'd been disappointed at being denied victory but had been extremely amused at Kieran trying to hide his rock-hard dick from Alaric. Given the annoyed expression on Alaric's face and the death glare he shot me, I was pretty sure Kieran's attempt had failed.

Golden sunlight warmed the hardwood floor as I padded over to the washroom. I felt my senses dull a little more with each step as night gave way to day.

Despite being used to it, I still hated feeling that loss every morning. I understood why some of the Moon Blessed chose to stay awake at night and sleep through the day. All sorts of monsters came out to play in the dark, making it far more dangerous than the day, but we were also at our strongest under the moonlight.

Besides, as long as you remained behind the walls and wards, you were safe no matter the time of day. The rangers were the only ones who spent most of their lives outside the protection of our fortifications, and they often traveled at night.

I ran my fingers across a symbol consisting of a triangle overlaid with three wavy lines on the tiled wall before stepping underneath the hot water that fell like rain from the ceiling. The shadow magic of the Furies might be impressive, but nothing beat the blood magic developed by the Moroi to get the indoor plumbing working again. Access to hot water whenever we wanted was the best magic in the world.

My thoughts drifted back to the rangers as I scrubbed my hair. Vail seemed to prefer the dangerous wilds over the Houses and outposts.

As he climbed the ranks of the rangers, he spent less and less time at House Harker. Since taking over as Marshal, he rarely came back to this House. I knew this because, as much as possible, I tracked his whereabouts. It was important to know where your enemies were, and few people were my enemy more than Vail Ferenc.

A chill ran through me despite the steam rising off my skin, and I shut the water off before wrapping myself in a towel.

Vail might want to kill me, but he was completely loyal to Carmilla and House Harker. He would never act on his desires, but he'd also never save me if I got into trouble. Not again, anyway.

While I was far from excited about Vail being here, I was admittedly interested in what he had to say about the attacks.

I'd glimpsed a map in Alaric's office and pestered him about it until he finally relented and gave me the barest amount of information to placate me. I'd then gone to Carmilla, and she'd filled me in on what was going on with the promise that I wouldn't repeat it to anyone else.

I understood why the Sovereign House wanted to keep the escalation of the attacks quiet. Panic wouldn't help anyone.

Still, I knew what it was like to be out there in the wilds, at the complete mercy of the beasts that prowled the night. The experience of those nights when Vail and I huddled in a cave together, listening to the monsters searching for us outside, had fueled my nightmares for over a decade.

We needed to figure out why the wraith attacks were increasing and also how to better safeguard our outposts. I'd been doing research these past couple of days in addition to working on my marriage dissolution, as well as catching up on general House Harker politics.

The small amount of sleep I got every night was plagued by nightmares, and today it felt like it had all caught up to me.

My fingers played with the cool, silky fabric of the sapphire blue dress I'd pulled out. With its soft, stretchy fit, it was one of my favorites. While the neckline was modest compared to a lot of my other dresses, it still clung to every rise and dip of my body.

A smirk played across my lips as I imagined Kieran's expression when I walked into a room wearing it.

Rich, black fabric snagged my attention, and my gaze flipped back and forth between it and the dress. After some thought, I hung the dress back up and reached for a pair of pants stacked neatly on a shelf.

As much as I adored wearing dresses, I was itching to go for a ride. The weather had been sunny and beautiful the last couple of days, and I'd spent all of it indoors.

Zosa would enjoy the exercise too, and I hadn't been to the beach since I'd returned home.

I pulled on the black pants, which were made of the same breathable, stretchy fabric as the blue dress. They were incredibly comfortable and made my ass look amazing.

Since the dress was still on my mind, I picked a light and airy blouse of the same sapphire-blue shade. It was slightly too large for me, so I tied a knot around my waist. Marvina would have had a conniption if she ever saw me in such casual attire, which only made me enjoy it more.

After towel-drying my hair and combing the knots out, I twisted it into a braid and stepped out of my bedroom into the sitting area of my suite.

I froze at seeing Alaric standing over the table where I'd brought some work back from my study last night. I'd had tea with Yolanthe yesterday afternoon under the pretense of catching up, which wasn't entirely a lie. I'd mentioned my concerns around House Laurent retaliating against me requesting to dissolve the marriage, and that had gotten her all fired up. Yolanthe could be a bit rough around the edges and stubborn about things, but she was incredibly loyal to House Harker.

She reassured me that all would be well and that she'd speak with Carmilla to see if there was anything she could do to help. Which was exactly the opening I needed.

I'd profusely thanked her for her assistance, even though I didn't need it since between Alaric and I we had the situation under control, and asked if I could help her with anything to repay the debt. And then coyly mentioned the negotiation she was working on with House Devereux.

I'd also mentioned that I desperately needed to take my mind off everything, and she would actually be doing me a favor by allowing me to make a few suggestions.

Floran and Nora had stopped by my suite later on to catch me up on all the gossip and had brought along a copy of Yolanthe's current draft to pass on to me. Yolanthe preferred to work in the gardens as much as possible because she enjoyed the fresh air, so Floran and Nora were used to delivering her missives. We'd spent a few hours catching up, and then I'd gotten to work on improving the draft.

"By all means," I huffed as I crossed the room to stand at the opposite side of the table, "let yourself in."

"I already did." Alaric flipped a page over, his eyes already skimming the next one. "This… isn't terrible."

Could I use the early hour and the lack of tea as an excuse to kill one of my aunt's advisors? Surely, she would understand. Tea first thing in the morning was vital to my ability to function. Everyone knew this.

"You worded this cleverly." His fingers trailed down several lines. "Hinting at the falling out between Yolanthe's sister and Severen's son without stating it outright."

Wow. *A compliment.* He must be too distracted in reviewing the document to realize what he'd just done. The corners of my mouth quirked up, and a little of the annoyance I'd been feeling faded away.

"Both Yolanthe and Severen are smart and loyal to their Houses. They know this trade agreement makes sense, but they also love their family." I shrugged. "The negotiations have stalled because they're both pissed off on the behalf of their loved ones, and that needs to be acknowledged and settled so that we can move forward."

Alaric grunted, and I had no idea what to do with that. Seriously. It was too early, and I *needed* tea.

I sighed. "Not that you're not absolutely delightful and the first thing I want to see in the morning,"—Alaric's eyes snapped from the paper he'd been reading through to mine— "but what are you doing here?"

The usual mask of arrogance and disdain slipped back onto Alaric's face.

"Carmilla has asked for your presence." The muscles of his jawline flexed. "For both of our presences, actually."

"Did she say why?" My brows pinched together.

"No." Without another word, he strode towards the door and left it open as he continued down the hallway. Rude.

I sighed. Carmilla would have tea in her office. I just had to not murder Alaric between here and there. A few servants greeted me cheerfully as I followed in Alaric's wake. None of them were the least bit upset or offended by my lack of enthusiasm in returning their greetings.

Everyone, except Alaric apparently, was well aware of how I felt about mornings.

"Ah, good," Carmilla looked up from her desk when Alaric

and I entered her study. "Vail has arrived, and I would like both of you to hear what he has to say."

"Of course." Alaric nodded and took a seat on one end of Carmilla's well-worn but cozy settee.

"Tea?" I asked hopefully.

Carmilla rolled her eyes. "Obviously. Take a seat, dear."

I plopped down on the opposite end of the settee from Alaric while Carmilla carried over a tray and set it down on the table before sitting between us. Once the tea had steeped, she poured the dark liquid it into four teacups.

Each House favored different types of teas. Laurent's was lighter and more flowery. Harker used a darker, more robust blend that resulted in a black tea with a bolder flavor. I was loathe to admit it, but I preferred the sweeter tea of Laurent over Harker's.

My aunt was well aware of my love of sweet things which was why she added several spoonfuls of honey into my cup before handing it over to me.

"Thank you." I blew on the steaming brew before taking a sip. The decadent flavors danced along my tongue, and I sighed. Delicious.

Surprise flickered through me when Carmilla put even more honey into the next cup and handed it to Alaric. I stared openly at him, but he stoically ignored me as he sipped his tea. She'd put almost *double* the amount of honey into his drink. Just how much of a sweet tooth was he, and how did I not know that?

Carmilla took a seat in one of the chairs opposite the couch and placed the last teacup down in front of the chair next to her. She took a swig of hers before setting it down on the table as well.

"I sent the paperwork off to House Laurent this morning with my seal of approval," she said kindly. "You and Alaric did an excellent job in getting that together. I think we both know that Marvina will likely not accept, at least not right away, but I do believe that we'll be able to get this resolved quickly."

"Thank you," I said, and I meant it. Carmilla had never wavered in her support of me, and I hoped to be able to repay her one day.

"Of course." She smiled gently at me. "Not only are you a member of House Harker, but you're the only family I have left. Once we have the marriage dissolution finalized, I'll officially reinstate your full status as Heir. As part of that role, I'd like you to serve as one of my advisors."

"Really?" I breathed out, setting my teacup down before I spilled the liquid in my excitement.

Her smile grew wider as she nodded back at me, and exhilaration pumped through my veins. I'd hoped that Carmilla would allow me to help her run the House, but I didn't expect her to do it this quickly or in such a major role.

"I won't let you down, I promise," I swore.

"I know you won't," Carmilla replied warmly. "Marvina was a fool to let you go. You have one of the sharpest minds of your generation, and I'm lucky to have you back."

A quick glance at Alaric told me just how excited he was about this turn of events. He was scowling deep into his teacup, which only made me grin harder.

But the grin faltered slightly when I realized that meant the two of us would likely be working closely together constantly since he was one of Carmilla's other advisors. Shit. My aunt's eyes twinkled with amusement as she saw this dawn on me.

"Given how well you and Alaric worked together this week, I trust the both of you will have no problems working together for the benefit of House Harker?"

Her no-nonsense expression made it clear this was more of a polite command than a question.

"Of course," we both answered at once.

"Excellent." She gave us a beaming smile before continuing, "Vail should be here any moment, and then we can get started."

"I'm here."

I turned towards the doorway where the low, gravelly voice had come from, and my lungs seized as I struggled to breathe.

He was exactly as I remembered, if a little broader. His dark graphite eyes latched onto mine, and I suddenly felt very much like prey. I waited for the silver fractures in his eyes to widen, but his eyes remained dark grey, not a flicker of emotion in them as he lurked in the doorway.

Carmilla spoke, breaking some of the tension between us, even though neither of us took our eyes off the other. "Come sit, Vail."

My lungs wanted to suck in a deep breath as soon as Vail tore his gaze off me, but I forced myself to breathe normally so as to not draw attention to just how much Vail's presence affected me. I could feel Alaric's curious gaze boring into me, but I ignored it.

It wasn't a secret that the Marshal of House Harker despised me. The secret was why, and I wouldn't be telling Alaric that anytime soon.

Even Kieran didn't know. Only Cali and Rynn were aware of the whole story.

And Vail.

My fingers remained steady while I wrapped them around my teacup, using the warmth of it to ground me. I sipped from it slowly and looked through my lashes as Vail sat in the chair next to Carmilla.

I'd never understood how a man so large could move so silently. Both Kieran and Alaric were tall and in good shape, although Alaric was always on the slender side, even more so than Kieran. Vail was several inches over six feet and had a body built for battle. He didn't have Kieran's carefully carved muscles and perfect flat abs. Instead, he had slabs of thick muscle layered over his body, covered in scars from fights that he'd survived, if not won.

I fought to keep my eyes off the jagged lines that ran down the right side of his face and continued down his neck but failed. The memory of hot blood running through my fingers burned through my mind, and I quickly looked away and set the teacup down, its heat no longer comforting.

"Thank you for coming," Carmilla said. "I know you wanted to head directly to the outposts that were attacked, but the Sovereign wants more updates, and I'll be traveling to discuss the attacks and other things later this week. I wanted to speak with you first."

"You're leaving?" I asked, hating how much I sounded like the scared girl I had been all those years ago.

"Not for long," my aunt assured me. "I'm overdue for a trip to the Sovereign House to visit Velika, and with the recent attacks, I can't delay any longer."

Trepidation ran through me at the thought of her being away and essentially leaving Alaric and I in charge, but I nodded anyway. "Of course."

Silver flashed from a ring on Alaric's pinkie finger as a small hidden blade snapped out and he sliced open the back of his hand. The coppery scent of blood filled the air, and all of us went still for a moment as our bloodlust flickered awake. My attention immediately went to my aunt, but as usual, she was completely unfazed.

Over half of her generation had eventually lost themselves to bloodlust and had to be put down. The ones we could catch, anyway. More than a few Strigoi had escaped to the wilds and blended in with the other monsters of the night.

Rationally, I knew that as a Harker, Carmilla was unlikely to ever completely lose herself to bloodlust. But she was the only family I had left, so rational or not, I still worried.

Every Moroi child grew up listening to bedtime stories full

of warnings about losing ourselves to bloodlust and becoming Strigoi, but so far, very few of my generation had suffered this fate. Maybe the fifth generation wouldn't have to worry about it at all.

Pressure built along my top jaw as my fangs fought to descend, but I held them back and watched as Alaric let his blood drip over the moonstone orb that rested in a cradle in the center of the table. The deep blue crystal glowed from within as the memory spell woven into it activated.

I was admittedly a little surprised that Carmilla didn't use her blood. The memories captured within the crystal could only be accessed by the Moroi who provided the blood, but they had been working together for a while, so I didn't question it. I had plenty of time to figure out the intricacies of how this group worked together.

"What have you learned recently?" Alaric asked, leaning back against the couch and wrapping a handkerchief around his hand.

Vail's eyes fell on me again, but he didn't question my presence here, instead turning his attention to Alaric, who shifted slightly under the weight of Vail's unnerving gaze.

My lips curled into a small smirk that I did nothing to hide.

It seemed I wasn't the only one who found it uncomfortable to have the attention of the Marshal on them. There was a wild edge to Vail that made everyone nervous. Except Carmilla, who had always been perfectly comfortable around him just as she was with everyone else.

"Not much," Vail said in an even, measured tone. "Wraith activity is increasing, particularly in the northwest area of our territory. I've spoken to the Velesians and Furies. They're also noticing pockets of increased activity in their territories."

"Did the Velesians have anything to share about the last two attacks on their outposts?" Carmilla asked.

"Nothing different from the other attacks," Vail replied, the barest amount of frustration slipping into his words. "Given how the bodies were found, there wasn't a single point of failure in the ward, but rather, the wards failed completely. Those on guard duty fell where they were stationed. No one had a chance to counterattack. The guards fell first, and then the wraiths swept through the outpost, killing everyone while they slept."

Horror flashed through me, but I shoved it aside. It was of no use to those already dead and wouldn't help those still alive, living in our now vulnerable outposts.

"Nothing was taken?" I asked carefully, weighing my words. "In any of the attacks?"

Dark grey eyes focused on me. "No."

"Not even any of the..." My throat bobbed, and I swallowed. "Not even any of the bodies?"

His answer was immediate. "No."

"That's weird, right?" My eyebrows bunched together as I gave Vail a puzzled look, momentarily forgetting how uncomfortable he made me while I thought about the oddness of the attack. "They went through all that trouble to kill everyone in the outposts but then left the bodies behind? Even if they did eat their fill there,"—my stomach churned at the thought— "they should have taken some of the bodies with them to feast on later."

Vail, although clearly reluctant to agree with me on anything, said, "I also thought that was odd."

"Why didn't you mention it then?" Alaric asked sharply.

The steely gaze finally left me to fall on Alaric. "I don't have to explain myself to you."

Tension built in the room, and I wished Kieran was here. He was always good at calming everyone down in situations like this, although even he might be out of his depth with this group.

"Let's just focus on what we know so far." I stared at my

teacup without really seeing it as I pieced together what I'd learned over the last few days. "I'm still catching up on all this, but there have now been eight attacks, correct?"

Vail and Alaric nodded once while Carmilla sipped her tea. I recognized the look on her face as the one she always wore while she listened to me work out problems I was stuck on. She was giving me a chance to prove myself in front of Vail and Alaric.

They didn't need to like me, but they did need to respect me if we were going to work together.

"Four in Velesian territory, one in Furie territory, and three here," I said, recalling the map I'd studied in Alaric's study.

"There's no pattern in the attacks," Alaric said. "Trust me, I've stared at that map for hours, trying to see some type of reasoning behind why those particular outposts were attacked."

Vail nodded solemnly. "Agreed. Me and my best scouts have studied the attack locations as well. The assaults appear to be random. The most recent three have all happened in the center of Lunaria. Prior to this, there were two in the far west region of Velesian territory and before that, in the south of our realm. They jump around too much to indicate any sort of pattern."

"It does seem unlikely that there is a pattern." I pursed my lips. "Vail, do you know if Rynn Valatieri has been consulted? She's a Velesian."

"I know who she is," he said, surprising me.

Rynn had been assigned to the Alpha Pack, but she hadn't officially joined them yet. She was still active in Velesian politics, but Rynn preferred to work behind the scenes as much as possible.

He continued, "I don't know if anyone has asked her."

"With your permission,"—I looked at Carmilla—"I would like to bring Rynn into this. She'll be joining the Alpha Pack later this year and will probably be told of all of it then anyway. There's no one better than Rynn at seeing patterns."

"The Velesian pack leaders have studied the attacks. Do you really think some young, unproven Velesian could see something they haven't?" Vail asked as he leaned forward slightly. There was nothing hostile in his tone. If anything, it beheld faint curiosity.

"There's no one better than Rynn at seeing patterns," I emphasized again. "There's a reason she was tapped for the Alpha Pack."

Vail stared at me for another moment before dipping his head in a small nod. Then his attention returned to Carmilla. "I brought a small group with me. We'll leave after this meeting."

"I'd like to join you," Alaric said.

Vail's gaze slid to Alaric, and his mouth tightened, but he didn't argue.

"I'd also like to come," I said firmly.

"No," Vail said instantly, causing me to stiffen at the outright rejection. "I'll already have to babysit him. I can't spare anyone else to watch you too."

I allowed myself a few seconds to appreciate the outrage on Alaric's face.

"I'm not asking you to take me with you all over Lunaria. I'm telling you to take me to the outpost that was attacked less than a three-day ride from here. I haven't seen any of the outposts that were attacked, and neither has Alaric. We need more information if we are to help in solving this problem." I didn't bother holding back my grin. "Besides, Alaric goes for a run every morning. He can just run away if we encounter any danger."

I would cherish the infuriated look Alaric gave me until the day I died. The satisfaction it provided was palpable.

"And you?" Vail gave me a flat look. "What will you do if we are attacked?"

"I'm good with knives," I said coolly.

It wasn't a lie. After my parents had died, I'd had a lot of anger, grief, and frustration to work out. One day I'd been stomping through the training courtyard and had picked up a throwing dagger before hurling it at a target. I hadn't hit the bullseye, but I'd been close and spent the rest of the day practicing.

It wasn't long before I moved on to different types of bows. Something about the blend of concentration that it took for range weapons provided peace for my wounded soul.

"Good with knives?" Vail shook his head with a scoff. "You'll be a hindrance. There is no reason for you to come."

I flushed at the reprimand, but before I could argue, Carmilla cut in.

"I agree with Samara and Alaric." She gave Vail a stern narrowing of her eyes. "There have been eight attacks thus far, and we're no closer to understanding the intentions behind them. There is an outpost between here and the one that was attacked. It's slightly out of the way, but it will give you a secure place to stay on the way there, which will limit your time in the wilds."

"It will slow us down," Vail argued.

It didn't escape my attention that the venom in his tone whenever he spoke to me was absent when speaking with my aunt.

I didn't think it was simply because she was the Head of the House; I believed that he genuinely respected her. My mouth flattened into a hard line. Unfortunately, none of that respect transferred to me.

"Speed doesn't matter as much as information," Carmilla countered.

"Fine," Vail said in a tone that made it very clear he was

still against this idea. "But she is to come to training this afternoon so we can determine just how much of a liability she will be."

I bristled at being referred to as a "liability," but Carmilla agreed on my behalf.

"Of course. It's a perfectly reasonable request for you to be aware of everyone's abilities. Alaric will attend as well." She paused until we all nodded in begrudging agreement. "Excellent. I have a few more things I wanted to discuss before I need to prepare for my own trip."

The rest of the meeting went by quickly with Carmilla just asking for clarification on a few things before going over some minor House logistic items that Alaric and I might need to attend to while she was away. She'd be here for another couple days but would likely be leaving a day before we returned.

"How long do you think you'll be gone exactly?" I asked, setting aside the scroll I'd grabbed to take notes on. Technically, it was all recorded, but I'd have to ask Alaric to replay the recording for me, so it was easier to take my own notes.

"A month," Carmilla said slowly. "Perhaps more."

Alaric's apprehensive grimace matched my own. It was rare for the head of any House to be away for that long. I knew that Carmilla and the Sovereigns were close friends, but still...

"Is there anything we should know?" I asked carefully.

She rolled her eyes. "Perhaps the two of you working together is a mistake. You both have a tendency to act like mother hens." When neither Alaric nor I disputed this, she sighed. "You know that Queen Velika and I have always been close. She has some personal things going on that she needs my help with. I'll be assisting her with that, as well as updating her on the attacks."

"Okay," I said skeptically. "But you'll tell us if you need help with anything, right?"

"Of course." She rose and made a shooing motion towards

the door. "I need to prepare for the journey to the Sovereign House and my stay there. I'll expect updates about what you find out after you visit the outpost." She gave me a pointed look. "And please inform me soon as you're back so I know you're safe."

"I will," I promised.

My eyes slid to Vail, who had been quiet since agreeing to allow me to travel to the outpost, answering any questions directed his way with the barest amount of words possible.

His wolfish gaze was on me, and I felt a shiver run through my body as I realized exactly what I had gotten myself into.

I would be out in the wilds with Vail and his rangers, with only Alaric to watch my back.

As if he was reading my mind and seeing the realization hit me, Vail did something he'd never done since that fateful night in the forest when we were kids.

He smiled.

CHAPTER TEN

—

Samara

SWEAT BEADED across my skin as I reached down and clasped my left ankle, feeling the muscles along my back and leg loosen. I had no idea what type of exercises Vail was going to put us through, but stretching beforehand seemed like a good idea.

Alaric was sitting only a few feet away from me, doing his best to ignore my existence, while Kieran hung out with some of the rangers on the other side of the training yard where he had a perfect view of everything.

This courtyard was located in the back half of House Harker and was mostly shaded by trees, yet even in the shade, the heat was damn near stifling. It was still only spring, but apparently the weather today had decided to give us a taste of summer.

I was still wearing the pants I'd put on this morning, but I'd ditched the blouse as soon as I'd got here so I didn't pass out from heat exhaustion, leaving me in only the chest band.

The feeling of sweat pooling in between my breasts where they were smooshed together thanks to the band around them wasn't great, though. The thick straps that held the band up kept slipping down, and Kieran was continuously glancing over at me in hopes I was about to have a serious wardrobe malfunction.

The third time I caught him looking, I mouthed one word back, *BEG.*

The corner of his mouth tipped up into a lopsided grin before he mouthed back, *NEVER.*

I laughed and reached for my discarded blouse to wipe the sweat from my face before promptly dropping it in disgust.

Before coming for my mandatory training session, I'd swung by the stables to apologize to Zosa for having ignored her the past few days and not being able to take her out for a ride today. I promised her that we'd be going out soon to stretch her legs, and she'd thanked me by snorting what seemed like ten gallons of snot all over my blouse, which I'd forgotten about until now.

Thankfully, none of it had gotten in my hair. I still desperately wanted to rinse off, but something told me Vail wouldn't accept horse snot as an excuse to miss this.

If anything, he'd use it as an excuse to leave me behind tomorrow.

Speak of the devil…

Vail strode into the training yard, three rangers following in his wake. My eyebrows rose in surprise as I took them all in.

As the Marshal, all House Harker rangers reported to him, but I knew that he had his own personal unit that went out with him on most missions as well. I had expected his unit to be full of copycat Vails, big and burly with matching beards. Each with a different assortment of scars to prove just how badass they were and matching scowls that they always broke out in unison.

But these rangers couldn't be more different.

The one to Vail's right was a man a few inches shorter than me. He had a stocky build but still appeared small next to Vail.

On Vail's other side was a woman who looked like she

should be on the arm of a noble at one of the House courts wearing a fine gown. Instead, she was here, wearing russet-brown leathers that looked like they had seen better days, and she had bits of what I was pretty sure was dried blood in her ashen-blonde hair.

I squinted, trying to get a clearer look. Definitely dried blood. Though, it looked too dark to be Moroi blood, so I didn't worry too much about it.

The rangers often returned with bits of monster blood and pieces on them, so it was a fairly normal sight, but if they came back with Moroi blood on them that wasn't theirs, it meant they'd had to hunt down a Strigoi. The occurrences of Moroi turning Strigoi were becoming rarer, but it still happened, and I was always worried it would one day be someone I knew.

It was one thing when the monsters that roamed the wilds were nameless beasts, but it was quite another when they wore a familiar face.

Vail and his three companions moved with a dangerous air about them as they surveyed those gathered in the courtyard. I was wondering about what type of weapons they used when my gaze fell on the third ranger who trailed behind them.

They were dressed in a way that leaned neither feminine nor masculine. Gender fluidity was common enough among the Moon Blessed, especially the Velesians.

As my gaze traveled over them, I was startled when I took in their face.

Nyx.

It had been at least five years since I'd seen them, but I'd recognize those sky-blue eyes anywhere.

Back then, they had seemed so unsure of themselves. Nyx was several years younger than me, Rynn, and Cali, and when they'd arrived to study at Drudonia, we'd done our best to take them under our wing when it was clear they didn't have any friends.

They'd never really settled in there, despite being very bright and showing an aptitude for House politics, but after years of struggling, they had simply disappeared.

I'd worried at the time and put out inquiries to find out where they'd gone. Cali and Rynn did the same. We learned that Nyx actually came from House Corvinus and was the younger sibling of the Heir. They'd been sent to Drudonia so that they could support their older sister when she eventually took over the rule of the House.

Through the process, House Corvinus confirmed that Nyx was alive and well but wouldn't give us any other information. I'd even asked Carmilla to look into it, but she'd just given me the same line.

Nyx has found a place in the world that suits them. Let them be.

With no other choice, I'd had to drop it, but now, here they were. Alive and well. With Vail.

They held my stare for another moment before dipping their head slightly in acknowledgement. I did the same but made no move to approach. We had been friends once, though I assumed their loyalty now resided with Vail, considering they hadn't reached out to me once since leaving Drudonia.

I was happy that they'd found a role in life that fit them well, but I was more than a little hurt and miffed that they hadn't told me. There was no way they didn't know that I'd been asking around about them.

I tried to subtly study them a little bit more. They seemed very at ease around Vail and the other two rangers. Nyx likely knew at least some of the history between Vail and me, although I doubted the grumpy-ass had told them everything. Maybe Nyx just felt uncomfortable telling me they had joined up with my arch-nemesis, so they'd simply avoided the conversation altogether.

More rangers came around the corner and casually leaned against the walls and buildings that surrounded the courtyard.

I didn't know if they came because Vail ordered them to, or because they heard about what was about to go down and wanted a front-row seat.

I pursed my lips into a hard line. Probably the latter.

"Nyx with Alaric," Vail ordered. "Emil with the Heir."

I held my chin high as I moved to stand in front of the male ranger. Surprise flickered through me when I noticed the fine lines around his eyes and the corners of his mouth. His black hair was pulled back into a bun, but there were some grey streaks that I had somehow missed before.

He must be a fourth generation like Carmilla, which meant he could be anywhere from sixty to a hundred years old, maybe even older.

I'd thought all the older rangers had retired to be instructors or hold positions that didn't require them to travel as much.

The ones that had survived this long anyway.

The stunningly beautiful female ranger with the dried monster blood in her hair eyed Kieran, who was still perched on a barrel on the sidelines.

Like me, she'd ditched a layer of clothes and was only wearing a tight pair of pants and a band around her chest. Her well-toned body was wrapped in lightly tanned skin that showcased her ashen-blonde hair quite well. More than a few rangers were subtly checking her out.

Hell. I was checking her out.

"You been practicing, pretty boy?" she asked Kieran with a familiarity that made me suspicious. My gaze pinged back and forth between them as jealousy spiked within me.

Before I could act on my completely irrational wave of jealousy, my feet were swept out from under me, and I crashed hard on my ass.

"Fuck!" I swore and glared up at Emil. "What the hell was that for?"

He smirked at me. "For being distracted in a training session."

"We hadn't even started yet," I grumbled.

He held his hand out and I clasped it, letting him pull me to my feet.

"When you're in the training ring, it's always an active session," he lectured, and I nodded. Despite his sneaky maneuver, his expression was kind.

"So, are we going to spar, or what exactly are we going to do?" I asked, resuming my position opposite Emil.

Alaric and Kieran regularly trained with the rangers, but I never really did. When I was younger, all my time was spent studying and preparing for life at House Laurent. The only combat skills I possessed were with range weapons, and that was something I practiced on my own because I found it relaxing.

Out of the corner of my eye, I spotted Nyx pulling the same sweeper kick on Alaric, who had been distracted by something Kieran had said.

Unlike me, however, Alaric's reaction time was on point, and he leapt over the kick and quickly took a couple of steps back to evaluate the threat.

Show-off. I bit back a scowl.

"We're going to test your instincts," Vail said quietly into my ear.

I'd like to say I handled his sudden appearance at my back well... but I did not. A shriek tore out of me, and I leapt several feet into the air.

When I landed, I whirled around to shove Vail away, but he was already gone. Kieran snickered at me while Alaric just shook his head disapprovingly.

"What?" I snapped. "He fucking snuck up on me like a—"

"Wraith," Vail cut me off from where he now stood facing me several feet away. "Like a wraith or any number of other monsters out there that are just as stealthy. You want to come with us, and for now you have Carmilla's support in this." I narrowed my eyes at his phrasing. Clearly, he was still hoping he could change her mind without me there to argue my case. "I know how all of my rangers will react in any situation, and I even know how Kieran and Alaric will react because they train regularly."

"So, you thought sneaking up behind me and scaring the shit out of me was a good idea?" I asked incredulously, taking a step towards him.

"Yes." He shrugged without a hint of remorse. "Now we know that you're not at all aware of your surroundings and that you scare easily. That scream would have attracted all kinds of things at night."

Kieran shot me a sly grin. "You are a bit of a screa—"

The pretty ranger slammed her elbow into his gut, and he dropped to the ground with a grunt of paint. "Not... nice... Adrienne," he gasped. The ranger—Adrienne, apparently—winked at me and sauntered away from Kieran.

Despite the flash of jealousy I felt earlier, I instantly liked her.

"We need to know how you'll react when you're frightened," Vail continued as if nothing had happened. "How quickly you can get out of the way so that one of us can step in and keep you from being torn to shreds or dragged off into the night."

I shifted uneasily at the predatory look in Vail's eyes.

"If we're attacked," Emil said quietly, "you need to be able to get away and run. I'll show you some basic evasive tactics once we evaluate what you're best suited towards."

"She's best suited towards lounging around and being waited on." Vail's mouth twisted in disgust.

"I have muscles," I scoffed. "Just because I'm not a trained fighter doesn't mean I can't learn enough to get out of the way and run."

"Muscles?" Vail crossed his arms and let his eyes roam over my body, his expression making it clear he wasn't impressed by my soft build.

I mirrored his position and gave him the same flat stare he was giving me. "They're sneaky muscles."

Kieran chuckled while Alaric just sighed in annoyance. "Samara, can't you take this seriously?"

"Don't be such an ass-kisser, Alaric." I rolled my eyes.

Emil took advantage of the situation and tried to knock my feet out from under me again, but this time, I was ready for him. I wouldn't call my jump over his legs smooth, but I stayed on my feet, and that's all that mattered.

"Good." He smiled at me.

"The training ring is always an active session." I returned his smile with one of my own.

Vail glared at me for another moment before waving over Emil and Nyx. The three of them conversed for a few minutes before deciding on a training course for Alaric and myself. After an hour, I was covered in sweat and dirt and sporting more than a few bruises, but at least I knew a few basic maneuvers that might save my life if we were attacked.

I wasn't delusional enough to think that I now actually stood a chance against a wraith or any of the other monsters that roamed the wilds, but maybe I'd managed to stay alive for the few seconds it took Vail or one of the rangers to get to me.

Unfortunately, my tentative confidence in my abilities to stay alive in a monster attack was short-lived.

"Don't know why you're smiling," Vail drawled. "The past hour has only made it clear how much of a liability you are."

None of the rangers voiced a differing opinion, and the grin I'd been wearing slid off my face. Kieran glared fiercely at

Vail, but Alaric was looking at me with an "*I told you so*" expression.

I didn't know why he was so cocky. He'd barely done better than me, and the layer of dirt over his clothes proved it.

"We'll be on horseback," I said defensively. "I'm a good rider."

Really, I was an amazing rider. My mother had taken me riding before I could even walk, and riding had always come naturally to me.

"And if we're attacked?" he sneered. "You'll just run away and leave us behind."

"First of all,"—I took a step towards him—"hasn't this entire exercise been about teaching Alaric and I to get out of the way so that all of you can fight? I'm not an idiot, Vail." I threw my hands in the air. "I know that I won't survive a fight, so yes, I will get out of the way if I can so that none of you have to worry about me, but I won't leave you behind."

Silver lines burst through Vail's steel-grey eyes, giving them a ghostly appearance before vanishing.

I took another step towards him. "And I wouldn't just sit there while all of you fought for your lives. I told you before, I'm excellent with a bow, and I'm good with knives too."

"Good with knives," he scoffed and sauntered over to where clean towels were hanging off the wall of a small wooden building.

Some of the rangers laughed and started to walk away. Seething, I snatched the dagger out of Emil's thigh holster, and it flew from my fingers before I could think better of it.

Vail froze as the dagger sank into the wood, directly in between his fingers.

Then, slowly, he turned to look at me.

"I told you," I said evenly. "I'm good with knives."

"You DIDN'T," Rynn said for the third time. Even with her shadowy form, I could still make out the disbelief on her face.

As soon as I'd retreated to my suite to draw a bath, I'd reached out to Rynn and Cali for a call because I needed my besties after my encounter with Vail. Rynn had appeared almost immediately in her shadow form, but Cali hadn't acknowledged my summons at all, not even to say she was busy, which caused a pit of dread in my stomach. It wasn't like Cali to not at least respond in some way.

"Okay, so, maybe antagonizing the man who very much wants to kill me right before I go off with him into the wilds wasn't my best idea." I scrunched my nose up.

"You think?" Rynn's fingers rubbed her temples in frustration.

I grinned ruefully at her. "When my rotting corpse is eventually discovered, I want it to go on record that it was totally worth it for the look of surprise on his face when that dagger slammed between his fingers."

"No dying." Rynn wagged a finger at me.

"Fiiine," I drew out the word dramatically and sunk lower into the tub, the near scalding hot water helping to soothe my abused muscles. "Ignoring my questionable actions this afternoon, what are your thoughts about everything else?"

Shadow Rynn pursed her lips. "I'm annoyed that no one has told me about all of this. Obviously, I knew about some of the attacks, but not all of them."

"They're keeping it hush-hush." I shrugged.

"Yeah, but I'm supposed to be joining the Alpha Pack in less than a year. I'm already privy to all sorts of information in preparation for that." She waved a hand. "Never mind. It doesn't matter. I need a list of all the outposts that have been attacked and the dates it happened."

"I'll send a striker with it to our usual drop-off. Do you need anything else?"

"That's enough to get me started. Ideally, I'd like to visit some of the outposts myself, but that will take time to arrange." She went predatorily still in the way she often did when she was thinking. With her soft-spoken nature, it was sometimes easy to forget that my friend was a lycanthrope and frequently shifted into a dangerous beast.

I waited silently for Rynn to think through whatever had snagged her attention.

If Cali was here, she and I would be trading amused looks right now, both of us used to Rynn's tendency to zone out mid-conversation, but she wasn't here.

A fact that still made me nervous. She usually always answered calls.

"You should reach out to Roth," Rynn said finally. "They're back at Drudonia using the library there to research more about Lunarian history. They might be able to shed some light on how the wraiths are getting past the blood wards."

"Roth?" I tilted my head back as my brows furrowed together. Why was that name so familiar?

It came to me almost instantly. A young Moroi girl, a year younger than us, arriving at Drudonia. We'd been in the grand library when she'd arrived, and I still remembered the expression of awe on her face as she took in the seemingly endless amount of books and scrolls. It'd taken her a solid five minutes to snap out of it before she saw us sitting there and introduced herself.

"I'm Astaroth Devereux." And then, a little hesitantly, she said, *"I prefer Roth."*

The rest of what Rynn had said filtered in, and I noted the use of *they*. It fit them, the same way that Roth better suited them than Astaroth. Although both names were pretty badass.

"How are they doing?" Envy crept into my voice. While I was happy with the direction my life was now headed in, part of me was jealous of Roth being able to dedicate their time to studying our history. What little we knew of it, anyway.

The spell our human ancestors had cast to turn us into monsters cost us so much more than our humanity, it also cost us our past. Entire generations' worth of wisdom that would usually have been passed down through stories, advice, song, and a myriad of other ways was simply gone. Which meant we were completely reliant on what had been written and books were painfully fragile.

We kept lists of past human settlements and noted their current state. The vast majority of them had been burnt to the ground or reduced to rubble after monsters had torn through them. Whatever knowledge they had forever lost to us. While the Fae fortresses still stood, many had been completely stripped of anything valuable, which suggested that at least some of the Fae had made it out alive. Where they had gone, we had no idea.

Any books or documents that we did manage to find were taken to Drudonia. It was the central source of all our history and knowledge now. And Roth had all that at their fingertips.

I hadn't interacted with Roth all that much while at Drudonia. They'd been Rynn's friend more than mine, but I got the impression that they were still figuring a lot of things out. Both about themselves and their place in the world.

House Devereux was a smaller House like the one Kieran was born into, which meant it was full of schemers and Moroi with scrupulous morals. Growing up in it couldn't have been fun.

"I think they're okay…"

When Rynn didn't say anything else, I leaned forward in the tub, my unruly long hair plastered along my shoulders and back. "Are they back at Drudonia because they want to be back there or because shit went down in their House after they went back?"

Roth wasn't in line to take over the House leadership. If I remembered correctly, they were a cousin to the current Moroi ruling House Devereux, but since they were still family, it was expected that they would do whatever the House asked of them. Whether they wanted to or not.

Rynn bit her lip. "I got the impression it was the latter, but you know what Roth is like. They didn't offer any personal information, and I didn't push."

No. Rynn wouldn't push. She never did. It's why Roth had always liked her, but never bothered with me or Cali. We were nosey assholes. It hadn't helped that I'd quickly become attracted to them, and my flirtation might have been a *tad* over the top. I was used to the flirty banter between me and Kieran. Roth had not been impressed with my attempts, and it'd led to a bit of awkwardness between us.

Well, awkwardness on my side. Roth had simply moved on like it'd never happened. Despite never getting particularly close to Roth, I still liked them. And I felt a sort of camaraderie with them because of our time together at Drudonia.

Not many people went there to study. There had only been a dozen of us of similar age the entire time we'd been there. I knew Cali felt the same, and if she thought House Devereux was being cruel to Roth, she would have flown straight to the House and given them a piece of her mind.

I would have been one step behind, rooting her on. I had calmed down over the years and developed a more "political mindset," as Rynn called it, but Cali… Cali still embraced her inner fire and refused all attempts by the world to snuff it out.

No matter how dangerous that was.

"I'll reach out to Roth when I get back. If House Devereux wants to throw them away, I'll snatch them up for House Harker, just like we did with Kieran. A mind like Roth's shouldn't be wasted just because they don't want to play bullshit House politics."

I rose from the tub, and Rynn quickly averted her eyes. How someone who regularly stripped down and shifted into a wolf was shy about nudity, I'd never understand. I wrapped a towel around myself before doing the same to my hair. "Alright, now that we've gotten the talk about the attacks out of the way, I think it's time we discuss Cali."

Rynn's gaze fell on me again, and she nodded, causing tendrils of shadow to drift off her. "Something's wrong."

"And she's not telling us about it." I let out a frustrated sigh.

We told each other everything. Always.

"I think she's afraid," Rynn whispered.

"Of what?" I snapped before catching myself. It wasn't Rynn's fault that I was pissed off at Cali. I sat on the edge of the tub and let my shoulders sag as I took a few deep breaths. "She is fearless. Always has been."

"Our Cali has always been fearless," Rynn agreed, "but we know what all Furies fear."

We will lose our souls to the fury.

So much history had been lost when our ancestors cast the spell to give up their humanity and become monsters instead.

We'd managed to put together bits and pieces of it, along with clawing our humanity back, but there was still so much we didn't know. Like why the Furies had been impacted worse than the rest of us.

The Velesians had been the first to gain back some of their humanity. Even their second generation had been mostly stable, and because of that, they had the greatest numbers of any of us. The Moroi had struggled, with some of our bloodlines having fared better than others. They were the ones who established the Houses and helped the others battle their bloodlust.

But the Furies… so few of them remained compared to the Velesians and Moroi, and the ones that did were always at risk of losing themselves to the never-ending fury within their souls.

Fear clamped its hands around my heart. "Do you think Cali is losing herself?"

"No," Rynn said quickly. "But I think something about her magic is scaring her. She's the most powerful Furie of her generation. Possibly ever."

She raised her hand, displaying the silver band she wore around her wrist. The shadow magic within it was what allowed Rynn to appear as her shadow self. Only Furies had the ability to wield shadow magic themselves or imbue other things with it.

Rynn explained, "It normally takes several Furies working together to craft magic like this, and Cali was able to do it on her own, on basically a whim."

"She was scared about us being apart," I murmured, remembering our last day at Drudonia and Cali clamping that band around Rynn's wrist.

But despite her power, it still hadn't worked for me. Moroi could wield blood magic but not use shadow magic. The Furies wielded shadow magic but couldn't use blood magic. The Velesians could wield neither, but they could use objects that had been spelled with either magic. No one knew why.

"You know how the other Furies are around her," Rynn said sadly. "She can't go to them with her concerns. They'll just spout more useless garbage about how she needs to tone down her emotions and not form strong bonds. Blah, blah, blah."

I snorted. The Furie elders were not pleased about how close the three of us were. More than once, they had told Cali to end our friendship. Fat chance.

"We need to go and see her. In person," I insisted. "She won't be able to brush us off so easily then."

"Agreed."

I unwrapped my hair, letting the towel drop to the floor,

and snagged my brush off the counter. "And maybe then you can tell us how you're really feeling about joining the Alpha Pack." I cocked my head knowingly.

Rynn froze. "I've already told you I'm fi—"

"If you say 'you're fine' about it, I'm going to scream." I pointed my brush at her in warning.

"Fine." She grinned at me when I arched an eyebrow at her. But after a few seconds, the grin slid off her face. "I'm getting nervous about it."

"Have they been pressuring you to come?" I asked carefully.

If she said yes, I wasn't sure what I would do, but whatever it was, it would probably be a political nightmare. My aunt had raised me after my parents died, but she was often busy ruling House Harker and supporting the Sovereign House.

Cali and Rynn had equally sad and complicated family histories. We were each other's chosen family. There was no stronger bond than that, as far as I was concerned.

"The opposite, actually." She fidgeted with her hands before catching herself.

While Cali and I didn't care about her nervous tells, we had been working with her on them. Of the three of us, Rynn managed to be both the smartest and the most inept at communicating. Given that she was supposed to join the Alpha Pack and serve as an advisor… that was a problem.

We'd come a long way from those original humans who had turned themselves into monsters, but we were still predators, and showing weakness was never wise.

"I requested some time after we left Drudonia to help my mother. Then I made another request after she passed to get her affairs in order."

"What was their response?" I asked. "The exacting wording."

"*Of course.*" She closed her eyes briefly before letting out a long breath. "Just those two words and nothing else. They haven't followed up since. What if they don't want me?"

"Then they're idiots," I growled. "You can come here and help me at House Harker. I don't care that you're a Velesian." The brush pulled on a tangle in my hair a little too hard, and I winced.

"Thank you, but we both know that won't work." Rynn gave me a sad smile that made my heart ache for my friend.

"I know," I said softly. Moroi needed blood ties. Velesians needed a pack.

Rynn's shoulders sagged, causing shadows to roll off her and twirl in the air.

"We're all doing fantastic, aren't we?" she said with a snort. "The marriage that you were destined for fell apart, the pack I'm promised to doesn't want me, and Cali is keeping secrets from us, which means something really bad is going on in her life."

I rose from where I'd been perched on the tub and stood in front of her with my fist held out. "But we still have each other, so we'll be fine."

"Yeah, we will. I'll keep harassing Cali until she answers so I can fill her in." She tapped her fist against mine. "Do us a favor and don't antagonize the big, bad Moroi Marshal over the next couple of days?"

"No promises," I said wryly.

CHAPTER ELEVEN

—

Samara

Zosa danced restlessly beneath me as we waited for the gate to be opened.

Once again, I'd slept poorly, and it had put me in a foul mood. Fortunately, after giving me one look that was dripping heavily with contempt, Vail had ignored my presence all morning. Fine by me.

We'd have to ride hard and fast to make it to the outpost before dark, which I was fine with because that meant I wouldn't have to talk to anyone on the way.

Alaric had nodded at me once in greeting, and I'd been too stunned at the almost nice gesture to respond in kind. He hadn't noticed, though, clearly too caught up in his own thoughts. As I watched him adjust himself for the third time on the saddle, I wondered how often he had been out riding.

Unlike me, he hadn't gone to Drudonia. His parents had provided his tutorage. I knew he had traveled to other Houses before, but given how uncomfortable he looked on a horse, I'm guessing it wasn't often.

While I debated teasing him about it, Kieran appeared around the corner, mounted on a tall, chestnut gelding.

He would be traveling with us to the outpost and then remaining there so he could catch up with some other courtiers and see if they had any useful information to share. His horse pranced up to us before tossing his head, his pale mane shining brightly in the morning sun.

"Did you seriously find a horse that likes to preen as much as you?" I asked in disbelief.

And may the moon bless us, but Alaric *laughed* at my joke.

"Don't be jealous," Kieran said smoothly. "Green is one of the few colors that doesn't suit you."

I glanced down at the forest-green tunic I was wearing, then back up at Kieran. He grinned at me, and I started to maneuver Zosa so I could smack him when Carmilla interrupted us.

"Children,"—she gave pointed looks to me, Kieran, and Alaric—"focus."

"Don't know why I got grouped in with them," Alaric complained. "I wasn't even doing anything."

Kieran reached out and gently punched him on the shoulder, causing Alaric's fingers to tighten around the black mane of his mare as he glared at Kieran. *Just how terrible of a rider is he?*

Carmilla walked over to me and rested a hand on my leg as she peered up at me. "Be careful, Samara. I may not have given birth to you, but you are a child of my heart, nonetheless."

"I will, I promise." I rested my hand on top of hers. "We'll be there and back in a matter of days, and hopefully, Alaric and I will be able to find something that will help us figure out why these attacks are escalating and how they're getting past our blood wards."

The portcullis clanged open in front of us, drawing Carmilla's attention. The two rangers from yesterday's training session, along with Nyx, rode out. Vail's enormous, dark bay mare shook her head as he held her back from joining them.

"Bring my niece home, Marshal," she commanded.

Vail clenched his jaw and nodded. "Of course, my liege."

Carmilla squeezed my leg once more before removing her hand. Then Zosa eagerly trotted forward, with Alaric and Kieran following me. I glanced over my shoulder and saw Carmilla speaking quietly with Vail. Whatever she was telling him, he clearly didn't like it based on his stormy expression.

"The three of you will ride in the middle," Nyx said. "Emil and Adrienne will take the lead. Vail and I will bring up the rear."

"How fast will we be going exactly?" Alaric asked nervously.

Nyx gave him an appraising look before apologetically saying, "For most of the journey, we'll be at a brisk jog, but we'll be letting the horses stretch their legs off and on. We need to make it there before dark, and all of our mounts are fit enough to be pushed a bit."

Alaric grimaced. "Great."

Kieran and I shared an amused look before his eyes dropped and snagged on my breasts, which were now bouncing around thanks to Zosa practically jogging in place. I really should have taken her out for a ride sooner. She hated being cooped up.

I cleared my throat, saying, "Have you changed your mind about green not being my color?"

His eyes snapped up, the golden fractures a little more apparent. "Not at all. Just thinking about how much better you'd look in a nice, vibrant blue."

I eyed his blue tunic and arched an eyebrow. "Really? You think blue is my color?"

The look Kieran gave me was positively wicked, causing

me to clench my legs in a way entirely unrelated to the horse dancing beneath me. "Only one way to find out."

"Kill me now," Alaric muttered.

Nyx laughed, but the other two rangers remained stoic as Vail joined us. "We'll let the horses stretch their legs for a few miles, then we'll slow the pace a bit."

My shoulders itched at Vail being at my back, but there was nothing to be done about it. Besides, I had no doubt that he would follow Carmilla's command. He was blood-sworn to her and would never disobey a direct order.

It was when we were at the outpost that had been attacked that I'd have to be careful.

He was cunning, and if he saw an opportunity to get rid of me without it being technically his fault, he would seize it.

The rangers in front of us spurred their horses forward, and a delighted laugh poured out of me as I loosened Zosa's reins and she surged into a ground-eating gallop.

I bent over Zosa's withers, urging her to go faster, my heart beating wildly in my chest.

Hooves pounded behind me as the others launched themselves after us, and I half-heartedly wondered if Alaric would be able to stay mounted, but that thought drifted away as the wind tugged at my hair, pulling strands free from my braid.

This would quite possibly be the best part of our trip, and I was going to enjoy the hell out of it.

WE ARRIVED AT FAYBELL, the outpost we'd be staying in for the night, an hour before sunset.

Since we'd made good time, we'd slowed to a walk for the last couple of miles to let the horses cool off before they got settled into the stables.

I slid out of the saddle with a spring in my step, earning a glare from both Alaric and Kieran.

"What?" I demanded.

"We've been riding nonstop all day," Kieran said. "How are you still so"—he waved a hand at me—"spry?"

I shrugged. "What can I say? I've got endurance for days, and I'm all kinds of spry." I gave Kieran a sly grin, earning a heated glance in return.

"I'm not listening to this," Alaric groaned as he handed his horse off to the stable kid and took an awkward step towards the tavern where Vail and the rangers had already disappeared to.

I couldn't help but laugh when Alaric groaned and rubbed at his thighs. "Do you seriously never ride?" I asked.

"Why would I do that?" he snapped as he stopped to glare over his shoulder at me. "I don't see what is so appealing about sitting atop a hysterical, foul-smelling beast."

Kieran patted his mare before she was led away. "All of our horses are extremely well-trained. I don't think any of them qualify as 'hysterical.'"

"Whatever." Alaric limped towards the tavern without another backwards glance at us.

Then Kieran held out an arm to me. "Shall we?"

"What do you think the chances are that they have running water here?" I asked as I looped my arm through his.

"Sorry to dash your dreams so soon, but there is no running water here," he said as we followed after Alaric. "Despite the name, Faybell wasn't built on the backbones of an old Fae town. It was built completely by us. The tavern servants can draw a bath for you, or…"

"Or…" I eyed him as he opened the door to the tavern and we stepped inside.

The large room was filled with Moroi, and the boisterous conversations almost drowned out Kieran as he leaned over to whisper in my ear, "There are natural hot springs in the back corner of the outpost. Those who run this place like me. If I requested to have sole access to them tonight… they'd probably be willing to make sure I had the springs all to myself."

"Is that so?" I whispered back. The idea of slipping into some hot water sounded positively magical right now.

"Mmm," he hummed. "Of course, if I'm to share these hot springs with you… there might need to be some begging on your part."

I slid my eyes towards him as we made our way to the table where Alaric sat. "Maybe I'll just find the person in charge of them and persuade them on my own."

"Don't be hasty," he said quickly. "Just come with me after we get something to eat, and we'll discuss it then."

Alaric eyed both of us. "I don't want to know, do I?"

I opened my mouth to respond, but Kieran beat me to it. "Probably not."

Food magically arrived in front of us moments later, and I gave Alaric a questioning look. He shrugged. "It's not like there are a lot of options on the menu, and I figured you'd be hungry."

"Thanks," I said before tucking into the spread of dried meats, roasted vegetables, and bread.

Faybell was far enough inland that fresh fish wasn't readily available the way it was at the coastal Houses like Harker and Laurent. Crops were easy to grow because none of the beasts that prowled the forest had any interest in them, but livestock was challenging.

A few outposts managed to keep around some goats and the occasional cow and used the milk from them to make cheese. Clearly, this wasn't one of them.

Some of the locals came over to talk to us as we ate. Well, they really came to talk to Kieran, but were nice enough to me and Alaric. I occasionally glanced towards where Vail and his rangers were sitting, curious about what they were talking about.

"You ready?" Kieran asked, drawing my attention away from the rangers.

I slipped my hand into his and rose from the table. Alaric's gaze flicked over us briefly before he went back to his meal.

"For you to beg?" I smirked at him. "Absolutely."

He rolled his eyes and tugged me up the stairs.

"Uhh… I thought you said the hot springs were towards the back of the outpost?" I asked in confusion as Kieran opened a door, revealing a small, tidy room with our packs from the horses stacked on the beds.

"Were you planning on putting on the same dirty clothes afterwards?" He pulled out some clean clothes for himself before digging into one of the other packs. "Or were you just going to walk back here naked? I'd vote for that option, personally."

I snatched the pair of panties he had dangling off his finger, and he smirked at me before quickly folding up a set of clean clothes.

"You're making it more and more tempting to find someone else who can show me these hot springs," I said in a mock growl.

He just grinned as he once again grabbed my hand and pulled me out of the room. I laughed as he practically dragged me to the hot springs, as if they'd disappear or I'd change my mind if we didn't get there fast enough.

"Oh," I breathed out when Kieran tugged me through the door of a simple but well-constructed building.

The wooden walls had been stained on the inside so that it was a deep reddish-brown, and dark grey stones had been stacked against the back wall, giving the room a cozy, natural feel. Fae lanterns provided a gentle blue glow that catapulted the already gorgeous space into something magical. A pool of crystal-clear steaming water awaited us.

I whispered in awe, "This is amazing."

"I know," Kieran said smugly as he placed our clothes on a bench in the corner. "There are other outposts I could visit that would be more convenient to meet people, but none of them have hot springs like this."

He moved to stand in front of me, and we stared at each other. Suddenly, I felt awkward.

Aside from that day in my office, we hadn't been intimate. I'd dreamed about it every night and thought about it when I touched myself, but this was *Kieran*.

My childhood crush who was even more gorgeous now than he was when we were teenagers. I'd been impulsive in my office earlier. It wasn't that I didn't want to move on from Demetri, because both me and my pussy were very much in agreement about moving the fuck on, but my feelings for Kieran were complicated, and I wasn't entirely sure I could handle a casual fling with him.

Yet at the same time, I wasn't ready to walk out of one long-term relationship and directly into another, assuming Kieran would even be interested in pursuing a relationship with me.

Fuck. How did I let things get so complicated so quickly?

I'd been so caught up in our flirting and teasing that I'd let myself fall into this too fast. Just because Kieran found me attractive didn't mean he felt anything beyond that. During our entire friendship, he'd always flirted back with me, and then I'd returned to House Harker and basically presented myself as a challenge.

I bit my bottom lip as I tried to contain my inner freakout. Kieran's exploits in the House courts weren't exactly a secret. Even at House Laurent, I'd heard whispers of his various bed partners.

Was I reading far too much into this when he really just thought of me as another notch on his bedpost?

Kieran started pulling off his shirt, and I stood there frozen in panic. I couldn't just leave without him asking questions, but I wasn't ready to answer them yet either.

Boundaries.

That's what I needed to do. Just set some boundaries to make sure things didn't go too far while I figured out my inner turmoil over this.

"Do you need help?" Kieran teased. "Or were you planning on getting in fully clothed?"

I gave him a breezy, confident smile to cover up the panic that had threatened to seize me moments before. Something flickered in his eyes, but it was gone before I could figure out what it meant.

"Just enjoying the show," I said in a husky voice as I very slowly perused him. His pants were untied and hanging low on his hips, allowing me a very enticing view.

He smirked as he finished pulling his clothes off until he stood there completely nude, and my mouth went dry.

Boundaries, I reminded myself firmly.

"Your turn." He winked at me and strode over to the wall to tap a glyph. Water fell from a cleverly hidden outlet in the ceiling, and he quickly washed himself off before sliding into the hot springs. "The water for rinsing off comes from the same hot springs, so it's warm. Try to get most of the grossness off you before getting in."

He leaned against the side of the pool, putting his perfectly carved chest on full display, and gestured for me to get on with it.

I casually shrugged one shoulder as if a thousand dirty thoughts hadn't just raced through my mind, and then I quickly disrobed. My plan had originally been to do it in a slow, teasing manner, but as soon as I started to unbutton my shirt, a whiff of the day's travels drifted up to my nose, and suddenly I couldn't wait to get the filth and grime off of me.

Kieran chuckled as I very unsexily tore my clothes off and chucked them onto the floor in disgust. But his laughter died off when I turned to face him and brushed my hair back over my shoulder so that I was on full display.

It was my turn to laugh as his eyes flashed gold. True to his word, the water was warm, and I scrubbed a day's worth of travel off me before languidly walking over to the pool.

"I'm ready for you to beg now." I lowered myself into the water, and a moan slipped from my lips.

Fuck. I closed my eyes. *This is heaven.*

"If you make that sound again, I just might," Kieran whispered into my ear.

My eyes snapped open to find him right in front of me with both arms braced on the pool's edge, caging me in.

"Hmm," I hummed as I ran my finger across his chest and down his well-defined abs.

He leaned into my touch, and I kept traveling southward, down past his waist before moving my hand away from the erection that was currently pressed against my leg.

He let out a frustrated groan as I dipped under his arm and moved to the other side of the pool.

"Sorry, I didn't hear any begging," I told Kieran cheekily.

Over towards the wall, several benches of varying heights had been set up so you could sit out of the water if you so desired, and I slowly swam over there.

There was nothing fancy about this building. The town residents had no doubt procured all the wood and stone from the nearby forest. Fae lanterns were easy to come by and took minimum tinkering to get working again.

If it'd been at one of the Houses, it would have tiled obsidian floors and all kinds of flourishes. But you could tell that the locals had taken pride in their work, and they'd built this place to give themselves just a little bit of peace in a dangerous world.

I sat on one of the stone benches that made the water come up to just below my chest. My long black hair was plastered to me, and I let out a contented sigh.

Kieran pushed off against the wall and slowly swam over to me before pulling himself up onto one of the taller benches. The water only covered that one by an inch, which meant he was completely on display.

I fixed my gaze on his face and kept clinging to my bored expression with everything I could. The corners of Kieran's mouth twitched as he watched me valiantly struggle not to look down.

"See anything that *you* want to beg for?" he taunted.

"Nope," I breathed out as I felt myself finally lose the battle to not look south.

My eyes widened as I took him in. I'd felt him pressed against my leg earlier, but he was even bigger than I imagined.

It took great effort not to lick my lips. "Not a single thing."

"Huh." A self-satisfied look appeared on his face as he took in my shocked expression. Then he leaned back against the pool's edge and fisted himself. My thighs snapped together, creating a splash of water. "You sure?"

"Absolutely," I said evenly. Although, my words probably would have had more impact if I wasn't staring at his dick.

With a truly heroic self-control on my part, I raised my eyes to meet his as an idea popped into my mind. My mouth curled into a sultry smile, and I bit my bottom lip, Kieran's gaze immediately snagging on the motion. Slowly, I ran my tongue across my top lip and was rewarded with his eyes turning solid gold.

The hand that had been stroking his cock froze, and I was pretty sure he stopped breathing as I maneuvered between his legs. I placed my hands on the smooth stone on either side of his legs and then leaned forward to lick his chest.

"Fuck," he ground out as his head fell back and he released himself so that he could lean back on both hands. I continued kissing and licking my way down his chest, tilting my head slightly so I could watch the muscles of his jaw flex.

I laughed huskily against his skin but stopped my downward direction before I reached his hard length.

He raised his head and stared down at me with a heat that had me wanting to climb on top of him and ride him until he screamed my name.

"Say it," I purred before licking my lips again.

"Fuck, you are evil," he growled. "And it's really fucking hot."

"Hotter than me running my tongue up your cock?" I tilted my head and sucked on my bottom lip.

"Fine!" he snapped. "Consider this me begging you to put that gorgeous mouth of yours to good use."

Fucking finally.

I held his gaze while I licked him from base to tip before swirling my tongue at the end. He let out a deep groan that sent shivers down my center. I loved hearing that sound from him and wanted to make him do it again and again.

"Shit," Kieran panted as I wrapped a hand around his thick length and sucked him into my mouth. His hips bucked as I took him in further, and he wrapped one hand around my hair.

I licked and sucked, enjoying every sound that spilled out of him. His hands tightened around my hair, but I could feel him keeping himself in check as he kept his thrusts slow and shallow.

That won't do. When he'd gone down on me in my office, I'd completely unraveled. I wanted him to do the same.

Slowly, I drew my mouth back up his cock until I swirled

my tongue around his head. More rapid swearing erupted out of Kieran as I wrapped a hand around the base before sliding it up and down. The grip on my hair tightened as my tongue and hand worked in tandem.

A salty taste spread across my tongue, and I felt myself growing wetter as I clenched my thighs together.

"Sam," Kieran ground out.

My lips released his head with a pop, and I looked up at him through my lashes, a devilish smile on my face. This time when I took him in my mouth, I swallowed him all the way down, barely managed to hold back a gag when his cock hit the back of my throat.

Kieran's control snapped.

He pulled back hard on my hair, forcing me to raise my head a few inches before he thrust back into my mouth.

My fingers dug into his thighs as he bucked beneath me. Each rise of his hips was rough and wild, and I fucking loved every second of it. Tears squeezed out of my eyes as he pumped harder and harder into my mouth, and I had to concentrate on not gagging.

His cock swelled and Kieran came hard, roaring my name. I greedily drank every drop of him down as he spilled his hot climax at the back of my throat.

Once I'd wrung every last bit out, I slowly slid him out of my mouth and licked my lips. I would definitely be thinking about this tonight while I got myself off.

I calmly pushed off against the wall and floated back to the side of the pool closest to the doors.

"Where do you think you're going?" Kieran eyed me with a hungry expression.

"It's late." I shrugged, trying very hard to come across like I was in total control of this situation and that I wasn't planning on running back to my room where I could thrust my fingers inside myself and replay this whole encounter in my mind.

Repeatedly. "We have a long day ahead of us tomorrow, so I'm going to get some rest."

Kieran let out a deep chuckle. "Do you really think I'm going to let you out of here wanting?" He slid off the bench he'd been sitting on and back into the water.

"I don't know." I swallowed. "Are you?"

I watched him swim towards me at a leisurely pace. My plan had been to walk out of here feeling like I was the one in control, but the closer Kieran got to me, the more I felt my resolve to leave fading.

Kieran reached for me and gently guided me to the edge of the pool. "Sit your ass up there and spread those gorgeous thighs of yours," he ordered.

Heat flashed through me, and I bit back a whimper. I thought about arguing or making him beg for a whole two seconds before I did exactly as he instructed.

I hopped out of the pool so that my back was towards the door before lying down with my legs still dangling in the water. Kieran wrapped his arms around my thighs, pulling me towards him before licking me straight up the center.

"My, my, my…" He let out a hot breath against my pussy. "You got off on me fucking your mouth, didn't you?"

"Hardly," I lied, even as I could feel myself growing wetter at the mere mention of it.

"Really?" He drew out the word before thrusting two fingers inside me.

My back arched, and my thighs clamped around him as need and pleasure built up in tandem. He withdrew his fingers and sucked them clean.

He drawled, "Because you're really fucking wet, love."

Any hope for coming up with a retort died when Kieran ducked his head again and sucked on my clit as he thrust those two fingers back inside, causing the orgasm I'd been racing towards to erupt. Just as a wall-shaking scream tore out of me, the door opened.

Kieran went still between my thighs, but I couldn't move because of the firm grip he had around my legs. A laugh barked out of me when I arched my back and twisted my head to look at the door behind me. Of fucking course.

Alaric stood there frozen as he stared at the both of us with his mouth gaping open.

"You here for dessert, friend?" My gaze snapped to Kieran, who was now resting his chin on my thigh with a cocky grin.

"Kieran!" I snarled and tried to tug myself free, but he just clamped down harder on my legs and laughed.

Alaric stared at us for a beat longer before spinning around and practically running out of the building, slamming the door shut behind him.

"So that's a no on dessert then?!" Kieran called after him.

"I'm going to kill you!" I hissed.

Alaric was going to be pissed about this, and I'd have to hear about it all day tomorrow.

Kieran just let out another chuckle before tugging me closer. "Guess I'll have to work hard to change your mind then."

CHAPTER TWELVE

Samara

I FROWNED at the wall surrounding the Millfell outpost and tugged my cloak closer around me despite the warm spring air. Our ride here had been uneventful, but a cloud of tension seemed to descend on everyone and only got worse when we arrived at the fallen outpost. It just looked so... normal.

All of the defenses appeared to be intact. It was a beautiful day, and there were rows of flowers blooming around the gates entering the town.

We should have been listening to the outpost residents bustling around, finishing their chores before night fell. Maybe some children running around playing. Instead, there was only silence. Stark, deafening silence.

My internal dread only increased the lower the sun sank in the sky.

It would be dark soon, and we'd be staying here tonight. I inhaled a deep breath and did my best not to think about it.

I agreed with Vail's decision for us to stay here instead of traveling back to Faybell. Traveling at night was too dangerous, especially with the horses, who would advertise our presence with every step and snort. I needed to make the trip here worth it, which meant I needed to focus and not freak out about spending the night in an outpost that had already been brushed by death.

"The wards look fine." Alaric's words jolted me out of thoughts, and my head snapped away from the wall I'd been staring at to him.

Those were the first words he'd spoken to me all day. Although he wasn't exactly talking to me, more so thinking out loud.

I'd overheard him and Kieran exchanging harsh whispers this morning, but they'd both stopped at my approach. Alaric had stalked away, and Kieran had simply planted a kiss on my lips before telling me to be careful.

I hadn't pushed Alaric to talk, mostly because I'd expected that we'd just argue, and I wouldn't apologize for what was happening between me and Kieran.

My feelings about it were complicated enough without having to deal with Alaric's shit on top of it. Although, I'd realized on the ride here that I actually *did* like working with Alaric. He was an arrogant prick, but he was also incredibly smart and often brought up flaws in my plans or thinking. Our working relationship wasn't perfect, but it was getting better, and I didn't want to lose that, so I decided to seize this opportunity and work with him on the problem at hand.

"Agreed." I crouched down next to the faint, dark red line that ran around the base of the perimeter fence.

Blood wards were some of the simplest spells, but they required a lot of blood to set up. Everyone who had lived in this outpost had donated theirs, and it had failed them.

I wanted to know why.

Alaric rose from where he was crouching and moved further down the fence before repeating the move. I did the same in the opposite direction. Emil went with Alaric, and Nyx followed me, keeping silent watch while I worked.

"There are no weak points, no broken segments," I said when Alaric and I met on the other side of the outpost. "Did you see anything?"

He shook his head. "Either whatever was done to the wards was temporary, or the wraiths have found a way to pass through them."

We were fucked either way. The blood wards had been a game changer for all of us, Velesians and Furies included. My generation had been born into relative safety as long as we stayed behind the wards. The previous generations had lived in a world where the monsters could attack at any moment, and they had.

The only reason our populations were steadily growing was because of the safety the blood wards provided.

I could tell by the deep crease between his brows that Alaric was having similar thoughts. We had to figure out a solution to this before more outposts fell and everyone started to panic.

"Let's look inside. Maybe we can find some clues there," I suggested.

The rangers followed Alaric and I back around the outpost to where Vail and Adrienne waited. I braced myself for whatever caustic comment Vail was going to make about how pointless it was to bring us, but he just looked us over and, upon seeing our frustrated expressions, moved towards the front gates.

Not before I saw the flash of disappointment across his face, though. Vail might hate me and be pissed about being ordered to bring us here, but he wanted to find out just as badly as we did why the blood wards were failing.

The silence as we entered the outpost set my nerves even further on edge. Aside from the lack of people, it looked like your typical outpost village. In front of us, a wide path led to the tavern. On either side were small shops and stalls where vendors could sell their wares.

I trailed my fingers across some sturdy dresses and tunics that were still hanging on one of the stalls, waiting for someone to buy them. Clothing, tools, and other items were displayed in the others.

This outpost was small enough that nobody was worried about theft. They'd probably been a tight-knit community that only saw the occasional visitors. This far off the main road, there wasn't much reason to come here unless you were visiting someone.

I veered off the path I was on and down one of the side streets to where the houses were.

A discarded doll lay on the steps outside of a simple but well-kept cottage, and I went still. It wore a dress that had seen better days. Even from here, I could see where the fabric had been patched.

Had the child dropped it on their way to bed? Or had they woken up during the attack and grabbed it while they ran from the house?

I squeezed my eyes shut. I hoped it was the former, and if not, then that their death had at least been quick.

It felt horrible to wish such a thing, but the alternative was that they spent their final moments in terror before getting ripped apart.

"We burned the bodies," Vail said quietly.

I jumped and slid to the side, turning to face him. He didn't comment on how badly he'd just scared me. Instead, his eyes were staring at the doll, and I didn't think he'd done it on purpose this time. Rangers survived by being able to move silently through the wilds just as much as being able to fight off attacks. It probably took more effort to make noise while he moved.

"Given the lack of smell, I figured that was the case." My words came out even but toneless.

Those who had died wouldn't even have a grave to remember them by. There were two gravestones in a small cemetery just outside House Harker that were supposed to mark my parents' final resting place.

But it was a lie. The graves were empty.

The wraiths and other monsters had ripped their bodies to shreds along with everyone else in that caravan.

Maybe burning the remains was better.

I shook my head slightly, trying to get my mind back on track. "You said the guards were attacked where they stood, but everyone else was killed while sleeping?"

Steel-grey eyes fell on me, and I fought the urge to shudder. "Yes."

I studied the houses that lined this street and then walked back to the main street. Something was bothering me about the buildings.

Vail trailed after me, a terrifying shadow in my wake, as I went to the other side of the village where more houses were packed in. They'd started adding second stories to some of the houses, but they were clearly outgrowing this outpost.

Alaric emerged from one of the houses with Emil. The crease between his brows had only deepened, and his movements were stiff. Some of that was likely from riding for the last two days, but I suspected more of it was a reaction to this place.

A few weeks ago, over two hundred people had lived here. Now, it was a solemn reminder of how quickly we could be wiped away.

"Have you looked in that one?" I pointed towards the cottage that sat at the end of the road.

Its door was closed, and there was no visible damage to the

exterior that I could see. Cheerful yellow flowers with long, delicate petals bloomed from boxes beneath the windows.

"Not yet. That's the last one." Alaric studied the house. His usually bright, sharp eyes looked haunted. "It's the last one on this side. We should check it out, just to be thorough."

Vail and Emil took the lead and entered the house first while Alaric and I waited until Emil whistled the all-clear.

I headed inside when Alaric hesitated and quickly took stock of the home. Similar to all the other ones, this one was simple but well-kept. A small, sturdy table was set against one wall with a couple rows of dried herbs hanging above it.

I reached out and gently brushed the lavender. Alaric and Vail explored the other rooms while Emil poked through the small cooking area and the cupboards above it.

"Pantry?" I waved my hand towards the door in the far corner.

Emil glanced over his shoulder. "Yes. I checked it out and didn't see anything, but help yourself."

Leaving the herbs behind, I went to investigate the pantry. I wasn't exactly sure what I was looking for, but I was determined to leave no stone unturned while we were here. Maybe the locals had found something strange in the area and didn't realize what it was or that it was dangerous, so they tossed it somewhere for storage.

Before the thought even finished forming, I dismissed it. I let out a sigh that turned into a bloodcurdling shriek as I opened the door and was knocked off my feet by snarling beast.

"Shit!" In an instant, Emil was there pulling the creature off me.

I scrambled backwards until strong hands grabbed me and yanked me off the floor. Vail thrusted me at Alaric before going to help Emil.

"Strigoi," I rasped. Not that there was any need. We all knew what it was.

Emil grunted as he was slammed back into a wall. The Strigoi slipped from his grasp and darted towards the front door only to be blocked by Vail. The monster that up until recently had been a young Moroi male let out a low hiss and backed away.

Its deep green eyes took each of us in, looking for a weakness as it flexed claws dripping with Emil's blood at its sides.

Given the opportunity, it would run. Strigoi were monsters, but they weren't mindless. They were us at our most lethal level. And like any good predator, they knew when it was better to retreat and find easier prey.

"It must be one of the townsfolk." Alaric's words were barely more than a whisper.

I tilted my head up towards him and saw the haunted look in his eyes was still there, but now it was edged with pain. His family, I realized with horror. Some of Alaric's family had turned Strigoi when we were young. It had been a few years before my parents had been killed.

"Both of you, get out!" Vail growled.

Alaric gave no indication that he'd heard the order and remained frozen in place. I gripped his hand and pulled him after me as I raced towards the door.

Out of the corner of my eye, I saw Vail's silver blade flash followed seconds later by the sound of bodies crashing into the table I'd stood beside earlier.

I didn't look back and just kept running until we were halfway down the street. Nyx and Adrienne appeared seemingly out of nowhere.

"Strigoi!" I yelled, thrusting my hand towards the house we'd just fled from.

"Stay with them!" Adrienne ordered and took off down the street."

"What happened?" Nyx asked, taking a position between us and the house.

"One of the townsfolk must have turned Strigoi during the attack and escaped." I sucked in a deep breath as I tried to calm down. "Maybe it hid here? Or snuck back in?"

Alaric swallowed. "They like to go back to their original homes if they can. Part of them still remembers."

Nyx's eyes flicked back to us and lingered on Alaric for a moment before returning to the end of the street. "That's right. Our blood wards don't keep them out because… well…"

"They're still us," I said quietly. "We may call them something different. But there is no physical or magical difference between us and them."

Humanity. That was the only difference.

None of us spoke after that. An unnerving wail came out of the house before being abruptly cut off. A couple minutes later, the rangers stepped out, blood splattered on their clothes, and Emil had a nasty cut down his right arm.

"It's done," Vail said gruffly. "Do either of you want to inspect that house any further?"

"No," I said softly. "We saw all that we needed to."

"THESE BUILDINGS…" I halted where I'd been walking down the street on the other side of the outpost and spun around in a slow circle. Something about them was different, and it was bothering me. "This was a newer outpost, right?"

"Yes and no," Nyx said hesitantly. They hadn't left my side since the Strigoi attack.

Even after a second thorough search of the outpost, we hadn't found any other creatures, but I was grateful for their comforting presence.

Nyx went on, "It was never a Fae village but rather an old

human one. The tavern and a few of the homes were from that settlement. It was the reason this was chosen as an outpost. The old human buildings were in disrepair, but it was easier to fix them up than build everything from scratch."

"Has that been the case with the other outposts?" I asked with a frown, still not sure why I felt the need to pull on this thread, but any information could prove useful.

Plus, as long as I focused on the problem at hand, I could almost forget the mind-numbing terror I'd felt when the Strigoi had pinned me down. I was lucky its claws had sunk into the floorboards above me instead of into my neck and shoulders. Having been so close to death…

Eventually, I had gone back to the house so I could examine the body. When deceased, the Strigoi looked even younger. Maybe sixteen at most. But in the home, I didn't find anything useful.

It didn't feel right, leaving him in his house, but Vail promised they'd bury the body later.

Nyx glanced at Vail before answering, "I'm not sure. The history of the outposts isn't always clear. Some of them were definitely built on top of old human towns, but the early outposts came about before we started keeping records, so we don't know as much about them other than that they're old."

"Hmm," I hummed, still staring at one of the houses that was likely originally built by a human.

"Do you think it matters?" Nyx asked.

"I don't know," I said honestly. "But any information about what could be a connection between the attacked settlements might prove important."

Alaric and I continued walking around the village, wandering in and out of houses. The three rangers trailed us, not getting in our way, but not willing to let us split up into smaller groups either.

When we found ourselves back at the front gate, I looked

up at the darkening sky. There was maybe an hour left until sunset.

"I'd like to check the surrounding area."

Vail stared at me for a long moment before opening the gate and beckoning me through. "Emil and Nyx, guard the gate," he commanded. "Adrienne, stay with Alaric. Stay close."

Everyone nodded in agreement, but I hesitated as I looked at the woods beyond the gate. I really didn't want to be alone with Vail, with no witnesses around, especially with the night creeping up on us.

"Well?" The corner of his lips tilted up ever so slightly, as if reading my thoughts. "You coming or not?"

I swallowed and stepped through the gate before Vail shut it behind us, trying to ignore the uneasy sensation of having him at my back.

My heartbeat only picked up though, feeling like it was trying to break out of my chest, and I knew that Vail could hear it. Amongst the Moon Blessed, Morois had the best sense of hearing, and rangers worked hard to hone their senses even further. He knew I was terrified of him, and the sick bastard was probably enjoying it.

The forest here was different from the ones that ran up and down the coast. The trees were shorter and more dense, thick brushes grew between them, covered in sharp thorns, and a few ravens huddled together on the upper branches, watching me with intelligent eyes.

The shadows were already starting to deepen within the woods, but I steeled my spine and continued onward.

I had no idea what I was looking for, but after ten minutes of wandering around, I felt a subtle tug. It felt like when I used blood magic and directed my power towards an object. Only, in this case, it was like my magic was being pulled forward.

Slowly, I followed the feeling as my pulse picked up. Vail moved to my side, and I felt his curious gaze on me, but thankfully he didn't question me as we wandered deeper into the woods. The tug was so faint I was worried that if I spoke, I would lose it. My foot snagged on an upraised root, and I stumbled, but Vail's hand shot out to grip my arm.

I froze as I stared down at my feet, barely noticing Vail's fingers, which were still holding tightly onto me. Then the tugging feeling within my chest faded, leaving the barest trace of satisfaction behind.

The root I had tripped over widened as it got closer to the tree, rising several feet above the ground and creating a small shelter beneath it.

Within that shallow space lay the body of a young Moroi boy.

Vail released my arm and knelt down next to him. Now that I was no longer caught up in the strange pull of my magic, the smell of death hit me. My stomach churned, and I barely managed to hold down the bread and cheese I'd eaten for lunch.

Large chunks of his body were missing. Clearly more than a few somethings had been feasting on him. I watched as Vail methodically examined each of the visible wounds before turning the body over to look at his back. His fingers briefly skimmed down the boy's neck, brushing the hair aside, and I caught a glimpse of a dark red line.

"What's that?" I dropped to my knees and leaned forward.

I'd thought the smell of decomposition couldn't be worse. I was wrong. With a grimace, I pushed back the boy's dark brown hair and looked at the symbol that had been carved into the back of his neck.

Vail shifted closer to me, his thigh pressed against mine as he studied the symbol. "Do you know what it is?"

"No." I cocked my head to the side as I puzzled over the markings for a few more seconds before pulling a folded piece of paper out of my pocket.

Carefully, I unfolded it and placed it flat against the boy's neck, then pinched the corner of the paper between my thumb and index finger where a symbol of two interlocking squares had been drawn in blood.

A tingling sensation nipped at my fingers as the blood magic sparked to life. This particular spell was one of my own creation, and I was rather proud of it. I held the paper in place as faint lines started to appear and soon the symbol on the back of the boy's neck copied over to the paper.

My head cocked to the side as I held it up and studied the lines more. "Something about it is familiar, though… I think."

"How did you know he was here?" Vail asked.

Something in his tone had me moving to create distance between us. It wasn't threatening exactly, but there was a faint accusation to it.

"I didn't." I pushed up so that I was standing and then I shifted further away from the body and Vail. "I just felt… a pull."

"A pull? Towards a dead body with a blood magic symbol carved into it?"

"Don't get pissy just because I found a major fucking clue that you missed!" I snapped.

Silver lines flared to life in Vail's eyes before vanishing, and I took a deep breath, willing myself to calm down as I refolded the paper and tucked it safely back into my pocket.

I said carefully, "Look, I'm more than a little freaked out right now. I'm not exactly used to being around dead bodies. My magic is acting weird, and you fucking scare the shit out of me. Can you just… not right now?"

"Fine, but this conversation isn't over." He glanced back at the body, lips twisting into a grimace. "I'll take you back to the village and then come back for the body. We'll have to examine it further to figure out what he died from. Most of these wounds are from scavengers."

I was grateful he didn't ask me to help him carry the Moroi corpse back. My stomach was still queasy, and if I had to touch the body again, I was fairly certain I would be vomiting up everything I'd eaten today.

We swiftly made it back to the village, where Emil and Adrienne left to help Vail fetch the body.

Alaric, Nyx, and I crowded around a table in the tavern, the paper with the symbol on it stretched out between us. Neither of them had recognized it, but I knew that I had seen it somewhere. But no matter how hard I wracked my brain, I couldn't remember.

CHAPTER THIRTEEN

—

Alaric

EXHAUSTION TUGGED at me as I stretched out on my bedroll the following morning. Nothing had bothered us during the night, but I'd had a hard time sleeping, knowing that the wraiths could get past the blood wards.

Technically, that was true of all our outposts, and probably our fortresses too, but at least in those, I was able to lie to myself about them being safer because of how many rangers patrolled the grounds and the strange Fae magic that still lingered in our perimeter walls.

It had only been the six of us last night, and the encounter with the Strigoi had unsettled me more than I had let on.

Unlike Kieran, Samara, and or even Vail, my bloodline was one of obscurity. My parents had originally been born in an outpost where they eventually fell in love and became the leaders of things when they were older. My mother was incredibly sharp, and nothing ever slipped her memory. She could remember the exact amount of wheat harvested from the previous five seasons in an instant.

And my father absolutely loved to solve problems and was

always level-headed. Their strong aptitude had eventually come to Carmilla's attention, and she in turn recruited them to be her advisors.

I was born after that, so House Harker was all I knew. My mother's family died when she was young, but my father still had family in several different outposts, and we'd occasionally go and visit them. Faolan was a cousin who was close to my age, and we'd gotten along well. The only kids my age at House Harker, before Kieran had arrived, were Samara and Vail.

Samara and I had never gotten along, a situation that hadn't much improved, and Vail was almost always gone with his parents or training with the rangers. Even from a young age, he'd been determined to be one of them.

The outpost that Faolan lived in with his parents wasn't the same one my parents had been from. It was a newer one that they were trying to build up and secure. The first few years of a new outpost's existence were always the riskiest. Most of the monsters that prowled the wilds of Lunaria had specific territories, and they didn't like it when something encroached on them.

Faolan's outpost was under frequent attacks, and it caused a lot of stress amongst the townsfolk.

My parents had pleaded with them to move back to the outpost they'd all been born in, which was older and far more secure, but Faolan's parents had been determined to make it work.

It didn't.

We'd arrived for one of our regularly scheduled visits only to find the outpost gate torn open.

Most of the residents were dead, their bodies shredded and partially eaten by whatever beast had broken through the defenses. Those who hadn't died to the monsters coming from the outside had fallen to those within.

Some of the Moroi had given into their bloodlust in an effort to survive. Their attempts to survive were successful… but they couldn't come back from it.

I still vividly remembered standing in the center of the town as my parents wept next to me and seeing Faolan peel away from the shadows of a partially collapsed house. As a Moroi, he'd always been cheerful and boisterous. But as Strigoi, he'd prowled towards us in complete silence, his eyes locked on his prey with an intensity I'd never once seen on his face.

I'd been too terrified to say anything until I saw three more dark forms moving in the house Faolan had emerged from. His parents and younger sister.

A scream tore out of my lungs, but it was too late. Faolan and the other Strigoi in town ripped into us.

We'd only survived because of pure luck. The outpost had built a secure bunker, and its door had been only a few feet away from us. It hadn't saved the residents of the town, but it had saved us. My mother shielded me as best she could while my father shoved us all towards the sanctuary.

Both of them had been severely injured, and I bore a long scar down my back where Faolan's claws had ripped into my flesh.

Eventually, the Strigoi had left to find easier prey, and we'd fled. My parents rarely left the walls of House Harker after that, and I only did so when I absolutely had to. I didn't know if Faolan was still out there somewhere, stalking in the dark forests of Lunaria, or whether he'd fallen to a ranger's blade.

It might make me a coward, but I didn't want to know. I usually preferred to deal in absolute certainties but when it came to my cousin's fate, I found an odd comfort in the ambiguity of it all. He was both alive and dead and until I knew which I preferred, I'd rather not know.

The rangers had handled keeping watch so that Samara

and I could sleep. Although, based on the way she tossed and turned, I think she got even less sleep than I did.

Vail made everyone stay in the tavern so that we were all in one location, and we all pulled down mattresses and blankets from the rooms upstairs. Eventually, I'd given up on sleeping and simply stared up at the ceiling, trying to figure out what that symbol could mean. Samara claimed to have recognized it, but I'd never seen anything like it. Granted, I hadn't studied blood magic beyond the basics that everyone knew.

Even though I didn't know what the symbol meant or what it was used for, I did know that it was made with blood magic. We could all feel it, and only Moroi used that kind of magic.

Maybe the boy's parents had used it on him in an attempt to save his life, and it was some protection spell none of us were familiar with.

If that was the case, their efforts had clearly failed.

The coldness that seeped through my bones had nothing to do with the drafty tavern. Maybe the wraiths were getting past the blood wards because a Moroi was *helping* them.

It seemed unthinkable because while the Houses bickered amongst themselves, we'd always known that sticking together was the only way we'd survive. It was the reason the Moroi were arguably the strongest of the Moon Blessed. The Velesians seemed to be getting closer and closer to outright war between their Orders, and the Furies were always on the brink of going insane and slaughtering us all. I'd thought that at least the Moroi had their shit together.

I was still trying to think of reasons why the symbol could have been on the boy that didn't mean a Moroi was betraying us when the sun fully crested over the horizon. It was an odd feeling that I'd mostly grown accustomed to but still didn't like. I could feel some of my strength flee my body. The world became… less.

Colors became less vivid. Scents less acute. At night, everything felt so alive, while during the day it felt like life slumbered.

Fatigue slammed into me, and suddenly going all night with basically no sleep seemed like a really poor choice on my part. A groan slipped out when I thought of the all-day ride ahead of us.

Samara rose from where she'd been curled up in no less than five blankets. She stretched towards the ceiling, arching her back, and the blanket she'd had wrapped around herself fell away. Every thought emptied out of my head, and certain parts of my body became concerningly hard. At some point in the night, she'd pulled her shirt off and had slept only in a tight-fitting camisole.

Every inch of her ridiculous body was on display. I mean, really. Who the fuck had curves like that?

I quickly looked away, but it was too late.

My treacherous mind took advantage of my distracted state, offering up the memories of her with Kieran the other night and the way her lips had parted when she'd moaned as he gripped her thighs and feasted on her.

I wondered what she'd feel like beneath me.

Or better yet, on top of me.

What it would feel like to run my fingers over her soft skin and dig my fingers into those luscious curves.

What it would be like to part those thick fucking thighs and taste—

"Alaric?" Samara sang from where she now stood behind the counter.

My gaze snapped back towards her. Thankfully, she'd put the rest of her clothes back on and was shaking an empty teacup at me.

She arched a brow. "Do you want tea?"

"No, I don't want fucking tea!" I snapped. "I want to get on the fucking road and back to House Harker."

"Somebody's grouchy in the morning." She smirked, and my cock twitched.

Fuck my life.

This was not happening. I did *not* like Samara. This was just the result of me seeing her with Kieran. That was all.

I repeated that thought in my head as I mentally tried to wrestle my stupid body under control and caught the tail end of a conversation among the rangers. They'd bundled up the body of the boy in several blankets and had used blood magic to prevent further decay. We'd be taking him back with us for further examination.

My brain was still sluggish, so it took me a moment to understand what the problem was.

We needed to carry the body back, and we didn't have a spare horse. Shit.

"Alaric can ride with me," Samara said loudly.

"No. Absolutely not!" I couldn't keep the edge of panic out of my voice as Nyx flashed me a knowing grin.

Samara glanced up from where she was hunting through the cupboards for something, and her eyes searched my face, but I forced my features back into my normal, bored expression. I wasn't as good as Kieran at moving between different masks, so I'd perfected this one.

"You're the worst rider of the group," she said evenly. "Someone has to give up their mount for the ride back, and you're the logical choice."

I glared at her, the muscle beneath my right eye twitching because her reasoning was perfectly logical, which only served to piss me off more. "Fine, but I'll ride with someone else."

There was no way I was riding pressed up against her all day. Not happening.

She shook her head. "The rangers shouldn't be hindered

by a second rider. If we run into trouble, we need them to protect us."

Vail's expression remained blank, but the other rangers nodded in agreement.

I wondered if Vail thought he would be struck dead if he agreed with Samara on anything. There was something between them; everyone knew that he hated her.

Since I grew up at House Harker, I'd known both of them my entire life. I still remembered the night that the news came in, that their caravan had been attacked and both of their parents had perished. Vail and Samara had been with them, both children at the time.

A search party was sent out to locate them when their bodies weren't recovered with the rest. Three days after the attack, they were both found in a nearby cave. Badly injured, but alive.

They were the only survivors.

Most people assumed that was why he hated her, but I thought there was a little more to it than that.

Vail was asshole, no doubt. But he wouldn't hate Samara the way he did simply because she had survived. She must have done something to earn the kind of hatred that burned in Vail's eyes every time he looked at her. Though, the only one who could answer that question was them.

Samara lined up four teacups on the worn wooden counter before pulling down two more, and then I watched as she poured everyone tea. She added some honey to hers and then more to another cup, which she nudged in my direction before setting the honey jar down next to the others.

I stared at the steam rising off the tea, carrying with it a tangy sweet scent. Rationally, I knew Samara was smart and observant. Her ability to read others and identify any personality traits or quirks that could be of benefit in a negotiation was unmatched. I also knew that she viewed me as an adversary, so it made sense she would study me in this way. And yet I still felt a pleasant warm tingle in my chest as I took in the tea before me.

No. I scolded myself. This is exactly what she wanted and I wouldn't fall prey to her the way Kieran had. Sooner or later, his feelings towards Samara would blow up in his face and I needed to be at my best to pick up the pieces.

All the rangers except Vail took their drinks and thanked Samara. Nyx snatched the remaining tea and thrust it at Vail, not flinching as some of the hot liquid sloshed out over their fingers. He glared at the cup, but Nyx just kept holding it out to him until he begrudgingly took it.

I caved and snatched the teacup that had been nudged towards me and took a sip. *Delicious*. Argh.

I felt Samara's smug gaze on me, and I narrowed my eyes at her. "What?"

"I'm waiting for my thanks." She arched one perfectly sculpted dark eyebrow, and the muscle beneath my eye twitched again.

"You'll keep waiting." I set the cup down with a disinterested expression even as I wanted nothing more than to wrap my fingers around the warm ceramic and savor the perfection of it for the next few minutes.

Samara sniffed and sipped her tea but otherwise kept quiet. Nyx smiled into their drink, and I wanted to smack it out of their hands. They noticed too much, and I didn't like it.

"We'll ready the horses," Adrienne said as she tugged Nyx towards the door.

"Thank you for the tea, Samara!" Nyx shouted, holding their tea up in the air in salute. Vail's annoyed expression was twin to my own.

We finished our drinks in silence before heading outside. I was beyond ready to get the hell out of here and return to the safety of my study at House Harker.

I would declare that a Samara-free zone from now on. Maybe I could make a blood ward specific to keeping her out? Pure genius.

The rangers secured the unmoving body over the back of the horse I'd originally rode on and guided it through the front gates. I followed as everyone else led their horses out, tension ratcheting up with each step.

"I really think I should ride with one of the other rangers," I said. "They have more experience, so they won't be thrown off by a second rider."

Samara snorted. "I'm just as good as them." She easily mounted her mare and flashed me a smug look. "Kieran used to ride with me all the time when we were younger."

Yeah, because he's been in love with you forever and seized any opportunity to get close to you, I thought.

Kieran would say he was in lust, but I knew it was more than that. It was one of the many reasons I could not dare to get on that horse. Samara was annoying, and I wanted nothing to do with her.

And my best friend was in love with her.

I desperately looked towards Nyx for help, but they just gave me that damn lazy grin of theirs. No help there.

The other two rangers had already moved forward, tugging the reins of the horse with the body draped over it behind them. That left only Vail, and there was no chance in hell he'd let me ride with him even if I asked, which I absolutely would not.

Shit.

"Quit being such a baby," Samara said, nudging her mare closer to me. She pulled her foot out of the stirrup and shifted in the saddle. "Mount up behind me."

Fuck.

Nyx snickered, and I gave them a death glare before

turning back towards Samara, who was just looking at me expectantly.

I didn't know if she was messing with me on purpose or if she had no idea about my body's obnoxious attraction towards her, but I was officially out of options, so I walked stiffly over towards Samara and shoved my foot into the stirrup. With an extremely ungraceful hop, I shoved myself up and swung my leg over the mare.

"Scoot closer," Samara commanded, reaching back and pulling me forward.

My jaw hardened as I did as instructed. Thankfully, the seat of the saddle curved up in the back, so my dick was nestled up against that instead of Samara's ass. It wasn't comfortable, but I didn't care.

I awkwardly tried to figure out where to put my hands, but apparently, Samara had run out of patience because she grabbed my arms and yanked them forward.

My chest pressed against her back as she wrapped my arms around her waist, and I fought back a flush.

"Hold on." I could hear the grin in her voice. Before I could snap back at her, Samara dug her heels into her horse, and we took off.

I'm not proud of the yelp that came out of me. Thank the moon, Kieran wasn't there to hear it.

A joyous laughter poured out of Samara as she urged her mare faster. The others had also spurred their mounts onward as we raced down the trail.

I squeezed my eyes shut and held onto Samara for dear life, despite everything in me screaming to let go. That this was *Samara*. I shouldn't be touching her at all.

After what seemed like forever, we finally slowed down to a more reasonable pace. Unfortunately, despite how smooth Samara's mare was in her steps, the jog was still bumpy, and I had to continue clutching onto Samara to keep from falling off.

This was going to be an excruciatingly long ride. I desperately needed a distraction. Anything.

Swallowing, I said stiffly, "Any idea where you recognize that symbol from?"

"No." Samara let out a breath of frustration. "But I *know* I've seen it before. Maybe at Drudonia? Their library is massive, and I took advantage of that while I was there. Rynn was in love with that library, so she always wanted to be there."

I could feel Samara's chuckle beneath my hands, and my heart beat a little faster.

She added with a shrug, "Cali, on the other hand, wanted to be outside all the time. She thought the library was stuffy and too confining."

"They are… very different people," I admitted.

Both Rynn and Cali had stayed at House Harker less often the last few years while Samara had been gone, but I was familiar enough with both of them to know that Rynn and Cali were exact opposites. Samara shared qualities with both of them, so it made sense that she was the middle ground between them.

I liked Rynn. She was quiet and soft-spoken, but also incredibly intelligent. Every conversation with her was fascinating.

Cali, however, scared the shit out of me. I couldn't explain why. She'd never done anything to me, had never shown any signs of losing herself to madness like so many Furies, but every time I was around her, my instincts screamed at me to get away.

Something powerful and monstrous lived inside Cali, and I didn't want to be anywhere near her when it eventually broke free.

"I've told them everything about the attacks," Samara said lightly. "Well, I told Rynn who has probably told Cali by now."

"Of course you have." I fought the urge to rub at my face

in frustration. There was no way I was letting go of Samara's waist. For safety reasons, of course.

"We all agreed to bring Rynn in on this," she said defensively. "And it's not like Rynn and I could not tell Cali. We tell each other everything."

I didn't bother arguing. Cali might freak me out, but I had no doubts of her loyalty to Rynn and Samara. She wouldn't tell anyone.

"There's someone else I would like to bring into this," Samara continued. "Roth Devereux."

I frowned. The name sounded vaguely familiar.

When I didn't say anything, Samara rushed on. "They were at Drudonia with us, but a year behind. Rynn says that Roth has continued studying the history of blood magic and that they're currently back at Drudonia. I was going to send a message to them when I get back and see if they wanted to come to House Harker, otherwise, I'll go to them."

My brow creased. "I don't know if it's a good idea for us to bring more people into this." The Sovereigns probably wouldn't like it, and I didn't know this Roth person. "The more people who know, the more of a chance there is of this getting out and causing widespread panic."

"If the attacks keep increasing, then there is just as much chance of it getting out anyway," she countered. "The last few attacks have been at outposts that are off the beaten path, but some of the early ones were main outposts. If another large outpost is attacked, people will start asking questions again."

"Alright," I sighed, weighing our options. "But I want to be involved with any conversations you have with Roth."

"Of course," she said cheerfully. "I wouldn't *dream* of keeping you out of the loop." I stared at the back of her head and debated shoving her off the horse, but I would definitely fall with her. Still… almost worth it.

Ahead of us, Adrienne veered off the road and

dismounted. We all stopped while she crouched down and studied the ground. I carefully leaned towards the side to get a glimpse of what she was looking at.

Footprints. Many large footprints.

My blood ran cold as I glanced around the tall trees surrounding us. It was daylight, so we should be fine. Most of the nasty creatures that roamed these lands only did so at night.

But still…

"Problem?" Vail asked as his beast-sized horse stopped beside us. Samara subtly nudged her mare a few steps away from him.

"Howlers," Adrienne spat. "Looks like a large pack."

"Shit," Emil and Nyx said at the same time.

Samara's body stiffened beneath me. She recognized the name too. Of course, we would run into one of the rare monsters that preferred to hunt during the day.

Howlers weren't as dangerous as wraiths or many of the other beasts that prowled the night, but they were still nasty to deal with and preferred to travel in packs, using their numbers to overwhelm their prey.

The six of us with our horses would be a very tempting meal for them. An abundance of flesh and blood.

"How old are the tracks?" I asked, fighting to keep my voice steady.

"They're fresh, probably from this morning."

Vail scanned the forest around us as we awaited his command. My heart continued to thump loudly in my chest, and I couldn't help but hold this irrational fear that it would draw the howlers to us like a dinner bell.

While I knew about the wraiths and other monsters, I'd hadn't actually seen all that many of them firsthand. My parents rarely traveled after their encounter with the Strigoi, and I'd only begun traveling again when I took over their post as an advisor.

After this fun adventure, I'd be perfectly happy to not leave House Harker again for at least another decade.

"We'll pick up the pace a little but keep it reasonable. We still have a long way to go, and we need to preserve as much of the horses' strength as we can in case we need to run later," Vail said, solemn grey eyes still on the surrounding forest. "No talking. Stay as quiet as possible. We can't do anything about the horses, but no need to draw further attention to ourselves." Vail eyed Samara then. "Does your hand-eye coordination extend to crossbows?"

"Why, Vail, are you finally acknowledging that I'm good with daggers?" Samara drawled.

I couldn't help but be a little impressed by her brazenness. I knew she was scared of Vail. Anyone with an ounce of common sense knew to be wary of him, but that fear didn't stop her from being her usual cocky self.

When Vail just continued to stare at her, Samara let out an annoyed huff. "Yes, I'm good with crossbows."

Vail grunted and reached behind him, pulling off the second crossbow that was attached to his saddle pack. He nudged his horse closer and handed it over to Samara as she wrapped the reins loosely over the front of the saddle and took it from him. After looking it over carefully, she nodded and clipped it to a ring on the front of her saddle, where it was within easy reach. Then Vail handed over half a dozen bolts, and she slid those into a pouch on the other side before picking up the reins again.

Emil and Adrienne took off at a slightly faster pace. I grimaced as Samara's mare followed after them.

This fast trot proved to be even bumpier than the steady jog had been, and my grip around Samara's waist became even tighter, but she didn't complain.

Apparently, my dick lacked all self-preservation though, because while my heart was still pounding rapidly, and my brain was thinking about all the ways the howlers could attack, my dick's only reaction was to harden at the increased contact. Great. Just perfect.

I needed to get laid when we returned. It'd been… a while. That's all this was. Just my ignored libido demanding attention.

There were bound to be some visiting nobles at the House sometime soon. I preferred to have flings with people who would be leaving at short notice, as I had no desire for a relationship and all the hassle that came with it.

We rode for hours without stopping, my thighs burning, and I knew that every part of my body would be aching tonight, but there would be no breaks today. I sighed with relief when we finally passed a sign displaying the distance to the Faybell outpost. At our current pace, we'd be there in less than an hour. Maybe I'd make use of the hot springs tonight.

Not with Samara, of course. Just on my own. She and Kieran would just have to enjoy each other's bodies somewhere else because I wanted absolutely nothing to do with their ill-fated relationship.

I was still trying to convince myself of that thirty minutes later when the attack happened. It was so fast that I didn't even process what was going on until my body jerked back as Zosa leapt into a full-fledged gallop.

"Hold on!" Samara screamed. Only her reaching back and gripping the front of my tunic kept me from falling off.

I locked my hands around her waist once more and held on for dear life. Zosa's hooves pounded into the dirt, her long strides keeping pace with the rangers in front of us. I looked over my shoulder and saw Nyx and Vail right on our heels, and behind them… Fear clamped me when I spotted howlers tearing down the trail after us.

Excited yips filled the air as they kept pace with us. Their long legs were made for running. They weren't faster than the horses, but they were just fast enough that we were barely increasing the distance between us and them.

Samara shifted the reins to one hand before unsnapping the crossbow from the saddle and carefully loaded a bolt into it. She kept it pointed down as she urged Zosa faster.

The road curved, and I saw the outpost in the distance nestled between the trees. An alarm blared as they caught sight of us.

We just had to make it to the outpost. We were so damn close.

A sleek, furry shape launched itself from the forest edge directly at Emil before I could scream a warning. Not that it would do any good. Everything was happening too fast.

Samara snapped up the crossbow and fired. The bolt pierced the beast's eye, and it jerked its head to the side before falling in a broken heap to the ground, scarcely avoiding a collision with Emil's horse.

Samara loaded another bolt, barely breaking a sweat.

I'd thought her throw the other day at Vail had been pure luck. Apparently not. Maybe I'd be more careful about pissing her off in the future.

The alarm in the outpost continued to wail as the guards raised the gate. We continued onward, not slowing down until we were within the safety of the outpost's stone walls. Then Samara steered Zosa in a wide arc to slow her as the portcullis slammed down behind us.

But not without trouble snaking its way through the gate.

Two howlers had made it inside, but the rest snarled and howled from beyond the walls, a cacophony of darkness within the forest. The rangers within the outpost were quick to dispatch the two interlopers who had made it inside and after a few arrow shots, the howlers outside melted back into the trees.

Our rides were breathing hard and dripping in sweat, and I couldn't help but feel for the beasts.

I slid off Zosa, my lip curling as sweaty horsehair clung to my skin and clothes. My knees threatened to buckle beneath me, but I forced myself to stand straight, refusing to lean against the sweaty mare for support.

Samara leapt off Zosa as if she hadn't been riding all day and nimbly landed on her feet, crossbow still in hand. I held back an eyeroll. Show-off.

The blaring alarms were finally silenced, and after a minute, the windows and doors from the buildings within the outpost started to carefully open as Moroi peered around, ensuring the danger was actually gone before they came out to greet our entourage.

Emil dismounted and walked over to the bodies of the two beasts that had made it inside before being slain. He raised his eyes, which were full of sincerity, and looked at Samara. "Thank you," he said quietly. "That was one hell of a shot."

"Don't mention it." Samara shrugged and handed him the crossbow.

Then Kieran came running and pulled me and Samara into a hug. "You two just had to make a dramatic entrance, didn't you?"

"Yep," Samara retorted, her words slightly muffled because she was pressed into his shoulder. "Didn't want to disappoint you."

"We thought about riding in here all calm-like," I said, "but then we thought, why do that when we could be chased by monsters instead?"

Kieran pulled back slightly so he could peer at me. "Did you just make a joke?"

I scowled and shoved him off me. "I'm going to clean up and get some food."

"The hot springs are real nice," Kieran said slyly, tucking

Samara into his side. "The three of us could check them out later."

It was Samara's turn to shove Kieran then. He laughed as she shook her head at him and stalked off, leading Zosa away. Vail and the other rangers followed her with the exception of Emil, who was still next to the bodies of the howlers and toeing one of them with his foot.

His lips curled. "Looks like meat is on the menu tonight."

CHAPTER FOURTEEN

—

Samara

I STARED at the box of my belongings that waited for me in my suite back at House Harker. We'd arrived in the late afternoon, the second leg of the trip home considerably less exciting than the one yesterday. Vail and the rangers had veered off to secure the body, and Alaric had gone along because he wanted to examine it again and had dragged Kieran with him.

My plan had been to rinse off and draft a letter to send to Roth, but halfway to my suite, a servant stopped me to let me know that a letter and package had arrived from House Laurent while I'd been gone.

I'd been alternating between pacing back and forth and staring at the letter I'd tossed onto my bed. Its words had yet to fully sink in.

But at the same time… they felt freeing.

House Laurent accepts the request to dissolve the marriage between Samara Harker and Demetri Laurent. Effective immediately.

I was officially a divorced woman.

The letter had been signed by Marvina. I thought for sure she would make more demands or draw this out just to be petty. I also thought Demetri might send a letter, pleading for another chance to make this work,

But there was nothing from him. Nothing at all to signify our relationship had ever meant anything.

Just the simple letter from Marvina and a signed copy of the marriage dissolution we had originally sent her. The box contained all the clothes I'd brought with me from House Harker, but none of my House Laurent possessions.

The message was clear. *You will get nothing from us, and we want nothing from you.*

I should be relieved that it was over so easily, and I was, but I was also suspicious. It seemed out of character for Marvina to give me anything I wanted. She could have easily made this process more difficult and made demands of House Harker since I was the one requesting to dissolve the marriage.

She could have gotten some very favorable trade deals. Instead, she asked for nothing, like she was as eager to have this all done as I was.

Odd.

My finger grazed the silky grey fabric of the dress I'd worn the first day I'd arrived at House Laurent.

It was one of my more modest dresses, but the look on Marvina's face had told me it wasn't modest enough. I pulled out the other dresses that I'd never worn while there because they were far too scandalous. Slowly, a smile spread across my face. I could wear whatever the hell I wanted now.

I dug through the box some more until I found a dress made of the same silky material as the grey one, but this was a rich, vibrant purple. It was a halter top style, which left the entire back open. The fitted top hugged my breasts before cascading into layers of sheer fabric.

It didn't have any high slits on the side, but the bottom half was just see-through enough to be interesting without revealing everything. It'd been years since I'd worn it.

Kieran would lose his mind when he saw me in it tomorrow.

I grinned wickedly as I gathered up all the dresses to hang them up in my closet. Once that was done, I rinsed off and tossed on a pair of comfy pants and a thin, light-weight top.

I was drying my hair when a slow, three-beat knock sounded on my door.

There was only one person who would knock on my door like that.

I swung it open, revealing Kieran leaning against the door-frame. His eyes roamed up and down, snagging on my breasts where my nipples were probably clearly visible through the thin fabric.

"Really?" I arched an eyebrow at him. "What are you, sixteen?"

He scoffed, "Please, I was much more subtle at sixteen." He breezed into my suite, and I shut the door behind him.

"I'm busy, Kieran," I said, continuing to towel dry my hair. "I need to write some letters updating Carmilla and requesting some assistance from someone at Drudonia."

"Ugh," he groaned before collapsing onto my bed. "You're just like Alaric. It's always work with you two."

"Yes," I said dryly. "Us working hard to prevent more attacks on our outposts must be a real inconvenience for you."

"Thank you for acknowledging that." He rolled over to his side and propped himself up on an elbow. "What's this?" He picked up the letter from House Laurent, where it still lay on my bed, and read it. Given that there wasn't much to read, it only took him a few seconds. His eyes flicked up to mine, both eyebrows raised. "Is this for real?"

I nodded. "It has Marvina's official seal on it. The signed marriage dissolution is over there." I pointed to the table in my sitting area. "I'm officially no longer married."

He leapt off the bed and gathered me in his arms, spinning me around. "Congratulations on the happiest day of your life!"

An embarrassing giggle bubbled out of me that I hoped no one else ever heard. Rynn and Cali would tease me about it mercilessly, and gods only knew how Alaric would react to it. He'd either ridicule me, or his lips would curl in that tiny, amused smile of his that always commanded my attention. It was rare that I'd see that smile directed at me. Usually Kieran was the recipient, but every once in a while, when the three of us were hanging out, Alaric would forget that he despised me. And I would forget every nasty word said between us as that smile sent my heart racing.

Then I would mentally slap myself and do my best not to ponder why I had such a reaction. Alaric didn't want me in that way, and I would never pursue someone who wasn't interested in my advances.

"Isn't the day you get married supposed to be the happiest day of your life?" I asked when Kieran finally put me down but didn't release me entirely. His hands were still resting on my hips, and I decided that I liked them there.

"Only for suckers."

I snorted. "Such a romantic you are."

"I can be romantic." He gave me a heated look.

"I think you're confusing romantic with horny."

"It's a personal fault of mine." His eyes twinkled for a moment before turning more serious. "Are you happy?" He gestured towards the letter. "With it being over and done?"

And that was why I adored Kieran. Even with us… taking things to the next level, he was still my friend and deeply cared about me.

Of course, that's also what terrified me about him.

Our friendship was rapidly moving toward something else, something foreign, and I didn't know what I wanted, let alone what he wanted. All I knew was that losing him as a friend would be devastating.

"Happy doesn't even begin to explain it," I said honestly. "I had resigned myself to spending the next few months arguing with Marvina and then feeling guilty about whatever demands she made of House Harker that Carmilla would have no doubt accepted. But now I'm free, and it was all pretty easy. Even got some of my favorite dresses back."

"No doubt those dresses will be tormenting me in the future," Kieran mused, but his eyes grew a little distant. "It is weird though, right? That Marvina didn't use this to her advantage?"

I chewed on the inside of my cheek. "I thought so, too."

"Maybe Demetri asked her to sign it?"

I thought about it and then shook my head. "Even if he did, which I doubt, Marvina isn't really the doting mother type. She does what's best for House Laurent. Always. No matter what that means for others."

"And signing that contract so easily was not in the best interest of her House." He frowned at where the letter still lay on my bed. "I'll be visiting House Corvinus soon. I'm friendly with one of the Heir's best friends, and she's friendly with the daughter of one of Marvina's advisors."

"She?" I stiffened before forcing the tension between my shoulders to loosen, and then I casually waved a hand to hopefully cover up my momentarily flash of irrational jealousy. "Which advisor? I've met most of their children, at least the ones that were living at House Laurent. Several of them had children at Drudonia or at other Houses." Realizing I was babbling, I snapped my mouth shut.

Kieran traced a finger down the side of my neck and across my collarbone. "Sam?" he purred as I leaned into his touch without even thinking.

"Mmhmm," I breathed as his finger continued its lazy path

back up the side of my neck and down my collarbone once more.

"Are you jealous?"

I quickly reeled back and threw my hands out to the side. "No!"

"You totally are." He grinned and matched my steps as I backpedaled across the room.

The back of my legs bumped into the bed, and Kieran neatly pinned me in so my only option was to try and shove him away or fall back onto the bed. The traitorous part of my mind that was forgetting we were annoyed at him was very excited about the second option.

"Yes, you are," he said in a satisfied tone.

"Fine." I glared at him. "But it doesn't mean anything. It turns out that maybe I'm slightly territorial when it comes to people I care about."

He went completely still, the grin slowly sliding off his face, and I realized my mistake. "You care about me?"

"Of course I do, you idiot." I shoved his chest, but he didn't budge. Damn him. "Although, I'm finding myself caring a little less right now."

A deep laugh rumbled out of his chest as his eyes sparkled. "Liar. You still like me." He grabbed my ass and lifted me up onto the bed.

I scooted back, but he moved forward, placing an arm on either side of me and pinning me against the bed with his chest. Heat pooled between my thighs, and my pulse pounded harder.

"There's no reason to be jealous. I'm not Riah's type."

"Oh?" I said breathlessly. "She doesn't like prissy courtiers?"

"She *adores* prissy courtiers." Kieran ground his hips into mine, and I swallowed back a moan. "Just ones with a nice rack instead of a hard cock." Then he leaned down to nip my bottom lip before rolling off me and snuggling into the bed.

I shot him an annoyed look. "By all means, get comfortable."

"Thanks, I think I will." He winked at me.

My heart started to pound frantically, only this time it was driven by panic and not desire. I was definitely still more than a little turned on, but Kieran being in my bed like this was exactly what I was trying to avoid. It felt like crossing a line that I wasn't ready for.

"Hey," he said softly. When I didn't turn to look at him, he gently guided my face towards his. "What's going through that chaotic mind of yours?"

"I don't know how to do this." I sat up, twisting so I was looking down at him, and then waved a hand between us. "It sounds stupid, I know. You're used to doing this type of stuff, whereas I have no idea what I'm doing."

A devilish grin flashed across his face. "Given how things went at the hot springs, I'd say you know exactly what you're doing."

"I'm serious, Kieran." I scowled at him.

"I know." He reached up to wrap a strand of my hair around his finger. "You're my friend, Sam. Whatever happens between us, wherever this goes, you will *always* be my friend."

Doubt flickered through me. Even if we stopped messing around, I couldn't go back to how things were between us. It'd been hard when we were younger, having him flirt with me and then go after other girls, but I'd dealt with it because I knew what the future had in store for me.

I looked to where the signed marriage dissolution sat on the table, my gaze hardening.

"I know that look," Kieran sighed.

"What look?" My lips thinned into a flat line. Damn Kieran and his ability to read every single emotion on my face.

"The 'Sam is overthinking everything' look." He raised an eyebrow as he studied my face. "It's reaching dangerous levels, too. There is only one thing that can fix this."

Realizing what he meant, I tried to scramble off the bed, but strong arms pulled me back. High-pitched screams tore out of me as Kieran tickled the shit out of my sides. Then he grabbed one of my legs and hauled it up so he could reach my foot.

"Don't you dare!" I shrieked. With valiant effort, I ripped out of his hold and flung myself to the side, then fell completely off the bed.

Kieran's head popped over the side, his golden hair all tousled, and laughed. "You okay down there?"

"I hate you." I crossed my arms, determined to keep my dignity intact despite how ridiculous I looked lying on the floor with half my hair covering my face.

"No, you don't." He leapt off the bed and scooped me up, propping me up on one side of the bed before he walked around my room, gathering some paperwork I'd stacked on a table along with writing supplies.

He carried it all over, setting it on the table next to the bed, then poured me some tea that he also placed on the table.

"What are you doing?"

"You said you have work to do," he said smoothly. "You're going to do it in bed. I'm going to cuddle up next to you and allow you the privilege of watching me sleep."

I choked on a laugh. "How are you so ridiculous?"

He fluffed up some of the pillows next to me before settling onto that side of the mattress.

"I know things are moving fast between us and that it's freaking you out," he said pointedly, and I bit my lip. Of course, Kieran would figure out why I was stressed out. "We'll take it as slow as you want. Whatever you need, I will give you, Sam. Minimum begging required."

I huffed. "Minimum begging?"

He shrugged. "I'm enjoying our game, and you know that you are too."

The herbal scent from the tea drifted over, and I picked up the cup, holding it in both hands over my lap. Despite my emotional turmoil, I didn't regret taking things further with Kieran, even if it probably would have been smarter to wait.

"I am," I said quietly. "Enjoying this new game of ours."

"But..." he prompted, and I flicked his forehead at the knowing look he gave me.

I sighed. "But I don't know that I'm ready to step into another serious relationship just yet. Not that you want that," I rushed on. "I know this is probably just casual fun for you and doesn't mean anything. I'm just trying to get everything out there."

I groaned inwardly at sounding like an idiot. Somehow, I could easily navigate complicated political conversations, but talking to one of my oldest friends about how I felt about him and us had me tripping over my words like some awkward, lovestruck fool.

There was nothing playful in Kieran's expression, and I swallowed at what I saw there. I was used to people looking at me with lust in their eyes, but the way he was looking at me went far beyond that.

"I promised not to freak you out earlier," he said seriously. "I'm going to hold to that promise, but don't mistake me giving you space as a lack of interest on my part, and don't *ever* presume that what happens between us doesn't mean anything."

I swallowed, carefully weighing my next words. "What if I want to... experiment with other people?"

No one but Kieran had caught my eye since I'd been back, but I'd also only been home for a few weeks. Maybe some tall, dark, and handsome prince would come strolling into my life soon. I wanted Kieran, but I wasn't ready to swear off all others just yet.

"Gonna take Alaric for a spin?" Kieran waggled his eyebrows suggestively.

"Don't start," I scolded him. "You know Alaric has always hated me. I'm trying to make things at least civil between us since we'll be working together going forward. You baiting him is not helping."

He laughed and shook his head as if he knew something I didn't. My scowl deepened, and he held up his hands in surrender.

"Okay, okay. I'll stop teasing Alaric… a little bit." I rolled my eyes, knowing that was probably the best I was going to get. Then Kieran gave me a serious look. "I don't expect you to be with me and no one else, you know?"

"Really?" I asked tentatively. "You won't get jealous if I take someone else for a ride?"

"If I do, that's my problem and not yours." He shrugged. "You just got out of a three-year marriage where you remained loyal to that stupid asshole, and before that… I know what type of training you went through to prepare for that marriage."

My cheeks heated at the way he said *training.* "You know?"

"You're not the only one I know who was destined for an arranged marriage," he said flatly.

It was expected that when you married, you'd be able to support and *please* your partner. I wasn't a virgin on my wedding night. Far from it, in fact.

A year before I married Demetri when I was twenty, the lessons began. My instructors were kind, and everything was consensual. I wasn't completely inexperienced thanks to a few casual dalliances at Drudonia, but I'd been excited to learn new things. Turns out my excitement was for naught. The lessons weren't exactly filled with passion or pleasure, and some of them were downright boring. Everything had been so mechanical.

Do this. Put your hand there. Harder. A little less hard. Pick up the pace. Dear moon in the heavens, why would you twist that?!

I snickered, and Kieran gave me a curious look.

"While I wouldn't describe the mandatory marriage training as fun, it could be entertaining sometimes." A mischievous grin played across my lips. "I'd been a little too eager to learn and a little too adventurous for my teachers more often than not."

Kieran tilted his head back and laughed. "Somehow, that doesn't surprise me at all."

The grin stayed plastered on my face as Kieran tucked in beside me and drifted off to sleep with his hand on my thigh while I got some work done. I waited for the panic of what it meant to have Kieran sleeping in my bed, but it never came.

CHAPTER FIFTEEN

—

Samara

I slipped from bed early in the morning, careful to avoid waking Kieran, which wasn't hard because that man slept like the dead. I wasn't sure I could have woken him even if I tried.

Sipping the tea I'd grabbed from the kitchen, I read over the letter for Roth one more time. I'd already packed up my update for Carmilla, which was considerably longer, and some information for Rynn. Both the messages for Carmilla and Rynn were enchanted so that the contents could only be read with a drop of their blood.

Unfortunately, I couldn't do the same for the letter to Roth because it required having prior access to the person's blood in order to spell the paper.

I had stacks of spelled paper for Carmilla, Rynn, Cali, and others for just this reason. This meant I had to keep any specifics out of the letter in case it was intercepted. Plus, I wanted to meet Roth in person before I told them everything. If Rynn thought they were trustworthy, then I was inclined to believe the same. Still… one could never be too careful.

Once I was satisfied with the letter, I folded it up and

198

secured it in an envelope addressed to Roth. My eyes drifted towards Kieran's office and the empty desk. He'd be leaving today for House Corvinus, and I already missed him.

Ugh. I was so pathetic.

I meant what I said about not leaping into another relationship and that I wanted to keep things casual between us, but I also acknowledged that the idea of anyone else touching Kieran had my bloodlust rising. It wasn't fair or rational, but no matter how much I told myself that, I didn't feel any different.

Maybe a few days apart would allow me to get my feelings under control. One could only hope.

With all three envelopes in hand, I headed up to the aviary. The strikers eyed me silently as I entered the tower, their forked tongues sliding out from a small groove in their blunt beaks, tasting the air, and their vertical pupils were thin slits against the sunlight that filtered in.

As a child, I'd been terrified of the strange creatures who hadn't been able to make up their mind whether they were reptiles or birds and instead settled on both.

I'd thought they were tiny monsters, which to be fair they absolutely were, but now I thought they were *cute* tiny monsters.

"Who's the most deadly creature in all the realms?" I cooed at one that had sky-blue and vibrant red scales down its throat marking it as male.

He stretched out his long neck and bumped his head against my hand. The scales were warm from basking in the sun, and he tilted his triangular head to give me better access to his throat.

I grinned. "You're the most vicious and prettiest one! Yes, you are!"

Another two hopped down from their perch and vied for

attention. Once I had given everyone scratches, I moved further into the tower to where the current on-duty strikers were. We rotated to give them breaks and also made sure we had some for breeding stock.

While they almost always made it to their destination safely, their life expectancy was only five to seven years.

A brilliant green striker eyed me as I approached, and I pulled a harness made of a soft rope off the wall before carefully strapping it on, making sure that it didn't rub against the wing joints.

Once I was confident that it was fitted well, I slipped the letter into a pouch on the back. The striker hopped obediently onto my arm when I held it out, its long talons flexing against my skin but not breaking it. I carried it outside, scratching the underside of its chin while I did so.

Once we were out of the tower, I thrust my arm outward, and the striker took flight, spreading its leathery wings wide as it caught an updraft and sailed away.

After it faded from sight, I went back inside towards the striker that had been trained for the route to and from Drudonia and repeated the same process. After all the messages were on their way, I spent some time cooing over the baby strikers before heading downstairs. Then I stopped by my room and saw that Kieran was gone, likely to pack for his trip.

Refusing to allow myself to dwell on my feelings around that, I decided to track down Vail and his rangers to see if they had learned anything useful about the body we'd brought back with us.

Several small groups of rangers were training in the courtyard as I skirted around the edges, heading for the small building next to the barracks where extra training supplies were kept.

As I approached, Adrienne grinned at me from where she

was guarding the door. No bits of gore decorated her hair today, but she still looked absolutely stunning in her brown leathers. I tossed her one of the spare apples I'd grabbed from the kitchen on the way here.

"Are they inside?" I asked when she bit into the fruit.

Her eyes lit up as the juices ran down her chin.

While we'd been traveling together, I paid attention to all the habits of the rangers. Adrienne absolutely loved fruit.

She'd grown up in the northwestern part of our realm where fresh fruit was scarce and lamented over the stew we'd had at the first outpost that she could go through her entire life without ever tasting another root vegetable.

The fruit-loving ranger nodded and opened the door for me. I smiled in thanks and stepped inside.

The first part of the building was a small room with various weapons neatly stored in racks or hanging on the walls. I headed further in, following the voices that came from the next room.

Vail's head snapped up as I entered a much larger room that was mostly empty save for the three tall tables that were spaced evenly down the center of the room. The first one held the body of the boy I'd found.

Vail, Nyx, and someone else I didn't recognize were crowded around it, all of whom watched as I approached.

"What are you doing here?" Vail asked as he stared at me coldly.

"Someone woke up extra grumpy today," I said cheerfully, breezing into the room as if I wasn't at all affected by the look of death Vail was sending my way.

Point of fact, it had taken every ounce of my willpower to not spin around on my heel and come back later. Nyx could probably answer all my questions, but I was here now and refused to back down just because Vail couldn't let the past go.

Nyx choked on air as they looked back and forth between me and Vail, and the unfamiliar man was staring at me wide-eyed like I was a creature he'd never seen before.

"So, have we learned anything useful?" I parked myself comfortably next to Nyx on one side of the table. Vail was still glowering at me, so I turned my attention to the man at his side. "I'm Samara Harker, and you are?"

"I know who you are," he sputtered and wiped a handkerchief over his face. "I'm… uhh… Vasili. Cormel. Vasili Cormel."

"Pleased to meet you, Vasili Cormel." I beamed at him, which seemed to only increase his panic. "I take it you're here because you can offer some insight as to what happened to this young man?"

"Yes! I mean,"—he looked frantically at Vail, who was clenching his jaw so hard I could see the muscle ticking in his cheek—"I've done advanced studies in anatomy at Drudonia. Moroi, Velesians, even some Furies.

"Although, it's much harder to get my hands on the body of a Furie since there aren't many of them to begin with, and it's kind of a weird subject for me to broach. Asking for dead bodies and all." He winced, squeezing his eyes shut and taking a deep breath. "I received a message yesterday morning requesting my presence here."

My eyes flickered to Vail. He must have sent a message from the outpost.

"I left right away and arrived early this morning," Vasili said hastily. "I was just about to go over my findings now."

"Well,"—I grinned widely at Vail—"looks like I have perfect timing."

When Vail and I just continued to stare at each other, Nyx cleared their throat. "Please continue, Vasili."

His rich brown eyes, flecked with green, darted nervously around as he shifted back and forth on his feet. I couldn't really blame him. Menace practically poured off Vail, who was still staring at me in a way that suggested he was thinking about slowly peeling off my skin.

My grin morphed into a frown. I'd been joking earlier, but he really was acting even more pissed off than usual this morning. "Did something happen?"

Vail blinked, and a mask of indifference slammed down on his face. "Nothing that concerns you," he said stiffly before turning to Vasili. "Proceed."

"Right." Vasili swallowed. "As far as I can tell, all these wounds happened after death. There are at least six distinct types of bite marks, most of which are from scavengers, but this one,"—he pointed to where a large chunk was missing from the calf—"is from a banecat. There are drag marks where the clothing he was wearing rode up, and they're quite severe. Given how far you found him from the outpost, I think he was dragged all the way there."

My eyebrows crept up as his voice gained a newfound confidence as well as a hint of excitement. Apparently, his insecurity vanished as soon as he started talking about dead bodies.

Banecats were enormous felines. Despite their size and impressive fangs, they were mostly scavengers. They liked to eat in peace, so it was the most likely culprit for moving the body to where we had found it.

"Not to be callous," Nyx said, pressing their lips into a flat line, "but why did we find the body at all? The scavengers usually pick everything clean within a couple of days, and he was out there for weeks."

"I can't say for certain," Vasili admitted. "Perhaps it's related to whatever that symbol on his neck does, but I can say that none of the scavengers seemed to take more than a few bites, which is unusual."

"So, they started to eat and then stopped?" I frowned at the body. "Odd."

"Very," Vasili agreed.

"What killed him?" Vail asked.

"The oddness continues, I'm afraid." Vasili pulled out a bowl from a shelf underneath the table, and a deep red mass sat inside it. Some type of organ?

I leaned closer, trying to get a look, but it was far too damaged for me to tell what it had been. It looked like someone had smashed it repeatedly with a hammer.

Vasili explained, "His heart exploded in his chest."

"Fuck," Nyx swore, and I nodded in agreement as I stared at the unidentifiable mass that was apparently a Moroi heart.

"That has to be magic, right?" I asked.

Vasili offered me an apologetic shrug. "I can't tell you what caused it, only that the heart was affected. All his other organs are intact."

"Maybe that's what the symbol on his neck does?" Nyx said but immediately shook their head. "No, that doesn't make sense. There are far easier ways to kill a Moroi, but there has to be some connection."

"We have to find out what that symbol means so we can hopefully figure out what type of spell it's used for," I said, nodding as I took all this in. "Thank you for coming and providing us with this information, Vasili. Please let me or Alaric know if you need anything while you're here. We have plenty of guest suites available."

"Tha–thank you," he stuttered. "I'd like to spend a little more time examining the body."

"Of course." I nodded again in thanks and then followed Vail and Nyx outside.

Before I could think better of it, I touched Vail's arm, and he went still beneath my fingers. Slowly, he turned to face me, eyes flashing in anger before he covered up whatever he was feeling again.

"Are you sure you're okay?" I murmured, keeping my voice low.

Nyx and Adrienne were close enough that they probably heard me, but they continued to converse as if they didn't. I didn't miss the slight stiffening of their shoulders, though.

"How I am," Vail said in a low, dangerous tone, "is none of your concern."

He stalked off without another word, and I watched him go, feeling a mix of anger and worry. He was right. Vail shouldn't be my concern. The man wanted me dead.

Nyx cast me an unreadable expression before following after Vail. Then Adrienne walked over and stood beside me.

"One of our scouting pairs was attacked last night," she said so quietly that I had to strain to hear the words. "Unrelated to the outpost attacks. Horned bears did it. They've expanded their territory farther than we realized. Neither of the scouts survived. Both of them had been trained by Vail."

I watched as she moved off in the direction Vail and Nyx had gone without another word.

My heart ached for them. Anyone who signed up to be a ranger knew it was a dangerous position, but that didn't make it any less painful when we lost one. Vail clearly didn't want my sympathy or condolences, but I was glad he had his own unit to lean on.

Laughter across the courtyard pulled me out of my thoughts. When I looked over, I saw three rangers taking a break from training as they watched a man practicing archery on the targets along the back wall. With their back to me, I couldn't tell who they were, but they were a terrible shot. Only one arrow had hit the target, while dozens of others lay scattered on the ground where they had bounced off of the wall.

The person swore loudly as they missed another shot, and the rangers laughed again, louder this time. The incredibly bad archer turned to glare at them.

Alaric.

I stood there in the center of the courtyard, debating whether I should leave or go and help him.

He probably wouldn't want my help because he was a stubborn asshole. Just as I started to turn around, Alaric's gaze fell on me, and I halted mid-step. He gripped the bow tighter, and his jaw was clenched equally hard. Honestly, I would be surprised if he didn't crack a tooth.

His expression said that I was the last person he wanted to see witness his absolute failure at using a bow. So, of course, I grinned widely at him and swaggered over.

"Is there any reason why you're pelting our poor wall with arrows?" I waved towards the target. "It's okay to hit the target, you know. That's actually why it's there."

"Thanks," he ground out. "I didn't realize that. I'll be sure to hit it going forward. You can leave now."

"I mean… I *could* leave…"

"Samara," he drew my name out, and I realized that I kind of liked the sound of my name on his lips. Alaric's voice was deep and smooth. It was a shame he was such a dick though, otherwise, I'd enjoy listening to him talk more.

I chuckled and held my hand out. Reluctantly, he handed over the bow, and I nudged him to the side with my hip.

"Your feet were too close together. Keep them shoulder-width apart." I adjusted my stance to show him, and then I deliberately angled my front foot slightly. "I like to shoot with an open stance, but I would suggest starting with a neutral stance and keeping your feet perpendicular to where you're aiming to start. Once you practice and get a little more comfortable, you can decide which one you prefer."

I showed him the two different stances. He watched me shift my feet back and forth before giving me a slow, deliberate nod. Then I swiped an arrow out of the half-barrel in front of me and raised the bow, nocking the arrow in one smooth motion.

"Don't grip the bow so tightly. It will throw off your aim." I drew my right arm back. "Keep your elbow slightly raised. You should be using your back muscles to draw. They're stronger than your arm muscles, and you'll need them if you need to hold the position."

"Show me again?" he asked quietly.

I nodded and went through the motion a few more times. "I was too far away to see how you were breathing, but there are a couple of different ways you can go about it. You can hold your breath as soon as you start to draw the bow and then exhale once you've released the arrow.

"Or, and this is the way I prefer, you inhale as you raise the bow, and just as you start to draw, you exhale slowly and evenly. You should be exhaling the entire time."

He frowned at me. "Shouldn't you exhale when you release the string?"

"No." I shook my head. "You're drawing across your chest and if you do that, it's going to mess with your motion and impact your aim. Everything about the draw and release should be smooth."

With a quick, practiced motion, I fired the bow without breaking eye contact with him. Alaric's eyes flicked toward the target, and he let out a sharp exhale.

The rangers who were still watching us from the sidelines let out loud whoops and clapped their hands. I dipped into a dramatic curtsy in their direction while holding the bow out to the side.

"How did you get so good at this?" Alaric murmured. I handed the bow over to him, and he accepted it gingerly.

"Practice. Lots and lots of practice." I grinned. "I've always had good hand-eye coordination. My preference will always be throwing daggers, but bows are more practical. They shoot farther and do more damage. Rynn is an excellent shot, better than me. We had a bit of a competition going while we were at Drudonia."

Alaric grunted. "You? Competitive? Shocking."

"Right?" I took a few steps back and gestured for him to take my spot, so he was aligned with the target. "What *is* shocking is that Cali is an absolutely terrible shot. Her best chance of hitting anything is to just throw the bow, and even then, she'd probably miss."

He let out a low, deep laugh that made my toes curl. Fuck, had I never heard him laugh before?

What the hell was wrong with me? I reminded myself firmly that Alaric and I were adversaries, and I was just helping him out because he had looked so pathetic.

I watched as he took up the neutral stance exactly as I'd shown him and raised the bow.

"Not too tight," I reminded him. He nodded curtly and flexed his fingers before letting them rest on the bow with a much gentler grip. "Good," I said in approval.

He started to raise the bow, and I ducked behind him, gently guiding his elbow. "Elbow up a little higher. Remember, you should be using your back muscles, not your arms. Don't fire yet. Let's practice drawing a couple of times."

I moved around him, correcting his positioning, and made him go through the motions a few times.

"This time, when you draw, brush your knuckles against your jawline and then hold just beneath your earlobe. Having anchor points is important to have a reliable aim. Those are the ones I use, but you might find you like something else."

Alaric was looking at me oddly as he held his stance and posture.

The turquoise fractures in his eyes had widened slightly, and I glanced down, realizing that I was resting my hand on his arm and standing intimately close.

Warmth rushed to my cheeks, and I let him go as I took a step back. I'd gotten so used to touching him over the past ten minutes that I didn't even think about it.

"Right," I said quickly. "Try it now and remember your breathing."

For a few seconds, he just stared at me with the same heated expression he'd held when he caught me and Kieran in the hot springs before turning his attention to the target.

I let out a breath once his attention was off me. Whatever this weird attraction thing was between us was confusing and unwelcome.

Maybe my libido was just trying to make up for lost time and, therefore, wasn't making rational decisions.

Alaric drew back slowly and carefully, just like we had practiced, and then let the arrow fly. It gave a satisfying *thunk* as it sank into the target. A wide smile spread across his face as the rangers cheered and before I could think better of it, I threw my arms around his neck in a hug.

"I knew you could do it!" He froze beneath me, and I panicked, drawing back quickly. "Sorry! Got a little too excited."

Alaric opened his mouth. "I—"

"There you both are!" Kieran said loudly as he strode across the courtyard, leading his favorite gelding behind him. "I'm just about to head out. Adrienne and Emil are going to escort me. I'll be back in a few weeks, but I'll send messages if I find out anything good. Try not to kill each other while I'm gone, eh?"

Alaric and I stared awkwardly at each other before quickly looking away. When he made no move to say anything, I finally cleared my throat. "We'll be fine. Promise."

"Of course you will!" Kieran beamed before pulling us both into a crushing hug. I was plastered against both men and found that I really didn't hate the feeling of it as much as I should.

"Well, then." I detangled myself from Kieran's embrace and backed up a couple of steps. "Safe travels!"

"Yes," Alaric said in an equally desperate tone. "That. Safe travels."

Both of us fled the courtyard in opposite directions, leaving Kieran to see himself out.

CHAPTER SIXTEEN

—

Samara

"Another dead-end," I grumbled.

Wordlessly, Alaric reached to the stack of books to his left, grabbed the dark blue one off the top, and passed it over to me. He didn't even look up from the page he was reading.

I sighed and took the book from him before leaning back in my chair.

We'd settled into a routine over the last three days. First, we met at the training courtyard every morning after breakfast and practiced archery for an hour. Then we headed to the library where we poured over every book, scroll, and scrap of paper that had anything to do with blood magic and Moroi history until dinner.

Usually, Rynn would pop in via shadow form at some point in the afternoon to update how things were going on their end.

Neither of us talked about our awkwardness from that day in the courtyard three days ago. But it felt like something had shifted between us, or was at least starting to.

Sometimes we'd go an entire hour without Alaric sending any thinly veiled hostility or cruel insults my way, which was nice.

The problem was that once he realized we were not only getting along but almost approaching friend status, he'd say something cutting to piss me off. His attitude towards me had always pissed me off… but now it hurt a little.

Every time I got him to smile at one of my asinine jokes or felt his muscles flex beneath my fingers during archery practice, I felt things shift between us a little more. Moons damn it all… I was starting to *like* Alaric. It had to be some type of temporary insanity because of the long hours I was working. Surely, that's all it was. Because there was absolutely no fucking way I was developing a crush on the impossibly arrogant Alaric Lockwood.

I was also attributing how much I missed Kieran to temporary insanity. Although, even I recognized that was a weak argument since it'd been just three days and the feeling was only getting worse.

A rather attractive courtier with teal and gold eyes had tried to strike up a flirty conversation with me the other day, and I had grown bored of him in minutes. Plus, I decided that only Kieran should have golden eyes. I made some excuse about having to leave and immediately went to the library.

So apparently, I wasn't horny for just anybody, which was troublesome.

I'd have to play hard to get when Kieran came back. I couldn't let him know just how much I'd missed him. He'd never let me live it down, and then he'd totally use it to torment me.

And I absolutely could *not* let him know about my growing feelings towards Alaric.

Kieran had already hinted about how much that idea interested him, and he would be impossible if he found out my little secret.

It was unlikely Alaric felt the same way, and it would make things weird—well, weirder—between us if he learned about it. I bit my bottom lip as I tried to focus on the book I was supposed to be reading once more.

After a few minutes, I let out a frustrated breath.

"We're not going to find anything." I tossed the book Alaric had given me onto the table after skimming the first twenty pages. "These books are all saying the same commonly known shit." We needed access to better information.

He shrugged. "Once we get through these, one of us can go to Drudonia," Alaric said in a bored tone. "A trip to the Sovereign House might be in order, too."

"You think they'll have something that they won't have at Drudonia?" I furrowed my brows, trying to think of what the library was like at the Sovereign House.

It'd been years since I'd been there and even then, I'd spent most of my time in the gardens or sitting rooms while Carmilla and Queen Velika caught up. They'd grown up together, and their friendship had only strengthened over the years. Carmilla had once confessed that she felt closer to Velika than she had her own sister, my mother. It'd been on a night after she'd had a few drinks, and she'd felt awful about saying it the next day.

I could remember the Sovereign House library being grand in appearance, but I didn't recall anything particularly impressive about the collection itself.

Drudonia was shared between the Moon Blessed. It was the second generation that was cognizant enough to want to gather knowledge and keep it somewhere safe. So early on, any books, scrolls, and artifacts recovered had been taken there. Now knowledge was a little more spread out as Houses became more independent and the Furies more distant.

"I know they have some Unseelie scrolls there that don't have copies at Drudonia." Alaric flipped another page in the book he was reading. "Who knows what else they might have?"

"Well, it's on the way to Drudonia, so I suppose it makes

sense to at least take a look." My lips quirked up into a smile. "Plus, it'd be nice to see Carmilla."

He glanced up from his book. "And why do you get to go and not me?"

I raised an eyebrow. "So eager to get back on a horse?"

He blanched and went back to reading. I snickered. Maybe another round of tea was in order. I needed something to motivate me to get through another book or two before calling it a day.

Before I could get up to make the tea, the door to the library flew open, causing both Alaric and me to jump in our chairs.

"Put them over there!" came a crisp command. The voice belonged to a Moroi with vibrant red hair that was shaved on the sides but was kept just long enough on top to be swept back.

"Damn, Roth." I grinned, rose from my seat, and walked over to stand next to the new arrival. Meanwhile, more House Harker staff entered the library, carrying boxes that they carefully stacked on one of the tables. "I see you're still as bossy as ever."

Sharp hazel eyes looked at me from a face with even sharper cheekbones and a strong jawline. The attraction I'd felt towards them at Drudonia came back full force, but I tamped it down, remembering how throughly they had rebuffed me when we were younger. After everything that had happened with Demetri and House Laurent, I didn't think my ego could handle being stepped on again. Especially by Roth and their often acerbic tongue.

"These books are centuries old, Samara," they said in that typical patronizing tone of theirs that at once felt so familiar. "Usually, I wouldn't have even entertained the idea of moving them from their safe location, but I felt it was necessary to do so."

I snorted. "Glad to see you haven't changed at all."

"On the contrary,"—Roth raised their chin as they surveyed the library, lips twisting in distaste, before finally giving me a chastising look—"I've gotten smarter, which apparently you have as well. Heard you dumped that loser Laurent boy. I honestly lost a lot of respect for you when I learned you were willingly marrying him."

They turned to fully face me while I stood there with my mouth slightly agape.

Roth tilted their head, narrowing their eyes. "Did you even talk to him before agreeing to marry him? You could have had more compelling conversations with a doorknob," they sneered, shaking their head.

Alaric made a choking noise that distinctly sounded like he was coughing to cover up his laugh. My head snapped toward him, and he ducked his face behind his hands.

Just wait. I narrowed my eyes. *Sooner or later, you'll find yourself in Roth's crosshairs too, and I'll be the one laughing then.*

I rubbed my forehead as I recalled the finer aspects of Roth's personality. Mainly that they had zero filter and often felt the need to constantly tell you how dumb you were, and then proceeded to list all the reasons why to be 'helpful' so that you could better yourself and not waste so much time in the future.

Rynn had gotten along with Roth great, but Cali and I had wanted to murder them and hide their body in the library stacks on more than one occasion. We'd even selected a couple of ideal locations that were rarely visited.

"Thank you for your commentary on my failed political marriage, Roth," I said flatly. "Really, it's super appreciated."

They flashed a serpentine smile. "You're welcome."

The choking sound from Alaric grew louder, and I prayed to the moon for patience as the staff carried in the last of the boxes.

"Mind telling me what all of this is?" I gestured towards the table that was now completely covered. "When I asked you to come and help with a research project, I didn't think you'd be moving into House Harker."

"Or stealing the entire library from Drudonia," Alaric muttered as he snagged one of the newly brought in books off the stack and started flipping through it.

"I'm not moving in," Roth snapped before stalking over to Alaric and ripping the book out of his hands.

He reached out to grab another book, and Roth smacked his hand away. Alaric glared at them murderously, but when Roth didn't back down, he crossed his arms and looked away. Ha! Not so fun when Roth has their sights on you, is it, Mr. Know-it-all?

Alaric caught me smirking at him and narrowed his eyes in response.

"I knew the books you'd have here would be a waste of time," Roth said matter-of-factly, and I couldn't help but take mild offense to that.

House Harker's library wasn't as impressive as Drudonia, but it was still one of the best ones amongst the Houses.

Roth failed to notice my frown, which wasn't all that surprising, and barreled on. "All of these books are ones that I have carefully curated for Drudonia, therefore, they did not argue with me when I said I would be borrowing them from a bit."

"Probably because you murdered them all in their sleep," I whispered, eyes wide in mock horror. Alaric caught my eye, and his lips twitched in amusement.

Roth rolled their eyes. My whisper hadn't been all that quiet. "Still think you're funny, I see."

"Yes," I said without a hint of modesty.

"Why are you so confident that we won't find anything in our books?" Alaric asked, his tone more curious than hostile.

Roth sighed impatiently. "Because that symbol you referenced is Unseelie, and all of your books are either about the Seelie Fae or were written by the Seelie Fae about the Unseelie Fae, which makes them incredibly biased." They rested a hand on top of the boxes they'd brought with them. "All of these are about the Unseelie, granted some written by the Seelie, but most are in the Unseelie language."

Alaric and I both perked up with interest.

"All of those books"—Alaric waved his hand at the table piled high with boxes behind Roth—"are about the Unseelie Fae?"

"Yes," Roth said with confidence. "And I know that I've seen that symbol in one of them." They scrunched up their nose at what had to be over a hundred books. "I just don't know which one."

The three of us peered at the table stacked to the brim.

"Looks like we have a lot of reading in our future," I said. My stomach rumbled, and I patted it. "But first, let's get some lunch." When Roth started to protest, I cut them off. "We need to fill you in on everything anyway. I had to keep that letter vague, but that blood symbol I sent you is just one of the many mysteries we're currently attempting to unravel."

They scoffed, "Obviously. I'm guessing it's connected to all the outposts that have been attacked over the past year." Roth looked around the library again. "It's really disappointing that House Harker doesn't have a grander library than this. You should work on that when you eventually take over the House."

I gaped at Roth, and I was pretty sure that Alaric had a similar expression on his face. My mouth struggled to form words, but finally, I managed to string something coherent together.

"You know?" I said in a high-pitched voice as my gaze darted to where the blood symbol on the wall beside the doors was still giving off a faint glow. The tightness between my shoulders eased a fraction when I noticed our silencing spell was still in place, so nobody heard Roth just casually mention the secret that the Sovereigns were determined to keep quiet.

Alaric snapped his mouth shut and regained his composure before giving Roth a hard stare. "How? How do you know this, Roth?"

"Because I'm not an idiot?" They glanced back and forth between us, clearly confused as to why we were surprised by this.

Alaric had that look on his face that said he was one step away from strangling somebody. It was weird to see it directed at someone besides me. I gave myself five seconds to enjoy that before turning my attention back to Roth.

"The Sovereigns are determined to keep the attacks quiet so that the outposts don't panic. We need to know how you learned about the attacks, Roth," I said carefully.

"Well, Drudonia monitors certain shipments between all the outposts and outside of the Moroi realm. Anything that contains the rarer resources is tracked. Partly to make sure nobody steals supplies, but also to study how quickly we go through certain gems and minerals so we can create comparisons." Roth paused and looked at us like we were children. "With me so far?"

"We're not idiots," Alaric growled. "We understand how supply chains work and why it would behoove us to study how our resources are being used so we can anticipate shortages in the future and have potential backup plans in place."

Roth blinked. "Sorry. I sometimes forget that other people aren't entirely useless."

Alaric turned his glare to me as if to say, *"You brought them here, therefore, this is your problem."*

I withheld an exasperated sigh. "Okay, and how did all that lead you to uncovering what was going on with the attacks?" I attempted to prod Roth along so that Alaric didn't completely lose his mind. Apparently, someone existed who frustrated him more than me.

Although, seeing as I was responsible for bringing Roth here, I suspected he'd be directing all this new frustration at me. Yay.

"There is an outpost two days from Drudonia that has a vendor who makes these delicious treats. She used some type of flakey pastry and honey." Roth's eyes momentarily glazed over at the memory before they continued. "I know the rangers who usually deliver supplies to that outpost, so I checked in with them before their next expected trip, but they said they'd been reassigned to a different outpost. So then I tried to track down who had been assigned to the outpost, but nobody had. At that point, I thought maybe it was just a mistake, so I reviewed all the schedules and trade routes."

I squeezed my eyes shut. Roth was too curious and too smart for their own good. Fortunately for all of us, they hated talking to people, so they hadn't immediately started gossiping about this.

"After some more discreet checking, I determined that the most logical explanation was that these outposts had been attacked, but since they weren't on the main road like the others, it was fairly easy to keep that secret." Roth tapped a long, slender finger on their bottom lip. "Given that at this point, about half of Moroi population lives in outposts like the ones that have been attacked, and we not only don't have space to relocate everyone to the Houses, but we also depend on these outposts for resources and securing trading routes, it made sense to keep it all quiet so we don't have a massive panic on our hands."

"And that doesn't bother you?" I bit my bottom lip. "Everyone who lives in an outpost right now is in danger, and they don't know it."

Roth just looked at me, eyebrows bunched in confusion.

"True, but they don't know that. As I previously said, there isn't space for everyone within the House fortresses. Plus, over forty percent of our crops are grown at outposts now. All the stability that we've gained over the last century would be at threat of collapsing if the outposts are abandoned."

Apparently, I was the only one struggling with the ethicalness of this decision. "I understand all that," I said with a sigh. "It still bothers me, though."

To my surprise, Alaric nodded. "It doesn't quite sit well with me either, but ultimately it's the Sovereigns' decision, so all we can do is try to figure out what's going on and how to stop it."

My stomach rumbled loudly again. "I'll have some tea and lunch brought up. We'll fill you in on all the details while we eat, and then we'll dive in."

The three of us stared at the daunting stack of books and scrolls. Maybe we'd get lucky and find the symbol right away with a detailed explanation of what it did and a map pointing to the bad guys.

I was overdue for a bit of good luck.

CHAPTER SEVENTEEN

—

Samara

THE MOON DID NOT BLESS me with good luck. It did, however, bless Rynn.

The ring I wore on my pinkie had two small, embedded gems, one blue and the other red. The dark silver band vibrated slightly, and the blue gem glowed, alerting me to Rynn wanting to chat.

It was midafternoon and I was sitting in my chair by the window reading through one of the books Roth had brought. They'd had an absolute conniption when I had placed a cup of tea down on the table with the rest of the books, so this was our compromise. I could have one book with me and sip tea while reading it while in this chair, a healthy distance away from all the other reading material.

I wasn't exactly sure what they thought I was going to do. Dump my tea over all the books while laughing manically?

But the argument hadn't been worth it. So I worked from my spot while Alaric and Roth both posted up around the table. They were both faster at skimming the books than I was; I tried to only glance at the pages looking for the symbol, but I kept getting caught up in what the book contained.

I'd read some Unseelie texts while at Drudonia, but not many. Roth had been quite busy with collecting all these books and scrolls. It was impressive what they'd managed to track down over the past few years.

"Rynn is coming," I said, putting down the book I'd been so engrossed in for the last hour.

The ring vibrated again, and I held my finger against the glyph that was engraved on the bottom of the band to let Rynn know we were ready. A few seconds later, shadows swirled in front of me until Rynn's form appeared.

"I think I found something," she said immediately, holding both hands up in earnest.

"Really?" I leaned forward in excitement.

"What did you find?" Alaric asked as both he and Roth quickly rose from their seats and came to stand closer to Rynn's shadow form.

"Sam, remember how you said the outpost you'd visited was built on top of an old human town?" she replied, and I nodded.

I'd only mentioned that detail to Rynn in passing because I'd never seen old human buildings, and it'd stuck with me.

"Well, I did some digging, and while I wasn't able to confirm this for every outpost, at least half of them were built on top of human settlements. And I wasn't able to rule it out for the others. There simply aren't enough records for me to prove it one way or another."

"Why would it matter, though?" I furrowed my brows together, trying to see where Rynn was going with this. "I mean, aren't a lot of the outposts built on top of old human settlements?"

"Yes, but when you look at the outposts that are attacked, it doesn't make any sense," Rynn said quickly and started pacing, leaving trails of shadow in her wake. "The attacks have been all over Lunaria, and there isn't a pattern that I can see, except that the outposts I know for a fact have *not* been built over human settlements haven't been touched."

"Assuming Rynn's theory is correct, and it is the old human outposts that are being targeted," Alaric said, "why are they being attacked now? And why?"

"I didn't see anything specifically targeted at the outpost we visited." I frowned, trying to think back and see if there was something I missed. "The buildings stood out to me, just because of the architectural difference, but they were just old buildings, and there wasn't anything done to them that hadn't been done to the rest of the town."

"The ritual," Roth murmured before stalking over to a box they had tucked underneath the table.

We all watched while Roth yanked out scroll after scroll and tossed them aside. I didn't think it was fair that they freaked out over me placing a cup of tea on the table, a careful distance away from any books, while they haphazardly yanked scrolls out, but Alaric and I had quickly learned over the last three days that it was best to just let Roth be Roth and not comment on any of their eccentric tendencies.

"Here!" They pulled a scroll out and held it up in the air before quickly walking across the room to where they had set up a large board.

Roth picked an empty space on the board and unrolled the scroll. As they did so, the dark red ribbons they kept wrapped around their forearms unraveled and looped around the board and its edges, pinning it in place.

I'd never encountered anyone who used blood magic the way Roth did. All Moroi were capable of blood magic, as our blood held magic, and we could use it for all types of castings. The simplest way was to use glyphs. Each glyph was a basic symbol that served as an instruction.

Heat was represented by a triangle. Water by three wavy lines. When combined, those two glyphs gave us hot water.

Such a simple trick, but damn, it practically created pure bliss.

Technically, the glyphs could be anything. We'd originally learned how to do this by studying old Fae spells, but over the years, we'd added our own. New glyphs were documented at Drudonia so that we could keep track of what they all meant and scholars could experiment with crafting more complex spells like improved wards and defenses.

Glyphs for silence and healing were the most common. We'd also learned that some of the old Fae spells could be reawakened with our blood. The wards we had around the Houses and outposts had been based off Fae wards. At first, we'd simply reactivated their wards, but over the years we'd learned to improve them even more.

Before I married Demetri and moved to House Laurent, I'd been a lot more interested in learning new blood magic castings. It didn't quite reach my obsession with training with a bow and throwing daggers, but I spent many nights reading through old books filled with Fae spells until the sun rose. I'd create small but useful castings like the one I used to protect letters I sent via strikers.

The ribbons that Roth kept wrapped around their forearms had been soaked in their blood, and Roth had enchanted them so that they could control them within a twenty-foot radius. Usually, they used them to pin scrolls in place or grab books off shelves that were out of their reach, but I was pretty sure I'd had more than one dirty dream about other things those ribbons could do.

Roth caught me looking at them a couple of times and had only smirked, which caused me to blush like crazy, and Alaric to ask what the hell was wrong with me.

But I was hardly going to explain to Alaric that I was having dirty fantasies about Roth and the ribbons that followed their demands.

Roth had also enchanted a pen that could write while they telepathically dictated to it. For some reason, that one deeply upset Alaric, so he always sat facing away from it, but I was determined to get Roth to show me how they did that. My handwriting had never been great, so maybe an enchanted pen would make it better.

"As part of my interest in the history of blood magic, I've also been collecting as much information as I can about the original ritual our human ancestors did," Roth explained as we all moved closer to look at the scroll they'd stretched out on the board. "The spell was definitely of Fae origin, but I haven't been able to determine if it was Seelie or Unseelie. However, I can say with certainty that the ritual itself was performed in their towns around this symbol."

Roth pointed to a symbol of three interconnecting crescent moons. Two of them faced away from each other, the back of each moon just barely touching, and the third crescent moon cut across the middle of the other two with its points facing up.

Alaric and I both touched the crescent moon marks on the left side of our necks while Rynn absently touched the mark on the right side of her neck. Furies bore the mark with the crescent moon facing upward in the center of their necks. I'd never seen this symbol with all three of our marks intertwined, but I supposed it made sense. We'd all been created during the same ritual.

"What if..." Roth stared harder at the scroll. "What if something was left behind in those human settlements? Something from the ritual?"

Alaric shook his head. "We would have found it."

"Not necessarily." I looked at the glyph on the wall that contained the silencing spell.

The glyph itself had been carved into a piece of wood that easily fit in the palm of my hand. It rested on top of a chunk of obsidian to power it. Something that small could easily be overlooked, especially considering the chaos that descended in the century after the ritual took place.

I added, "Most of those human settlements were abandoned for over two centuries. The Moroi who founded the Houses retreated to the Fae fortresses because they were easier to defend. We didn't expand and start building up the outposts until the third generation and by then, the priority was getting them built as fast as possible to make room for our growing population."

"Between whatever was left behind being exposed to the elements for a couple centuries and it being small," Roth said, following my line of thought, "they might have overlooked it."

I nodded. "We need to go to some outposts that were built on human settlements. Ones that haven't been attacked yet and see what we can find."

"It's going to raise a little suspicion if we do that," Alaric argued.

"We'll say it's for research." I waved a hand at Roth. "We'll bring them with us. Anyone who spends thirty seconds with Roth will just accept our reasoning so they can get away."

"I'm not leaving my books and going outside!" Roth's eyes went wide as they snatched a book up and clutched it to their chest.

The three of us started bickering then, each talking louder and louder to speak over the previous person, before a shrill whistle cut through the air, and we all slammed our hands over our ears.

"Or,"—Rynn lowered her fingers from her mouth calmly—"we can visit some human settlements that haven't been turned into outposts yet, which would actually answer two questions for us."

I glared at my friend while I rubbed at my ears. "It's bad luck to whistle inside."

She rolled her eyes. "First, that's not a thing. Second,

maybe the wraiths have been searching for whatever is left of the ritual for a long time and they just first searched the human settlements that were still abandoned."

"So even if we don't find what we're looking for, if there are signs that wraiths have already searched it, we'll at least have confirmation that it's the human settlements in particular that they're interested in." I dropped my hands to my sides, ringing eardrums now forgotten. "Based on that smirk on your face, I'm guessing you've already identified some locations for us to check out?"

"I'm not smirking!" Rynn pressed her lips into a hard, flat line, but the corners kept curling upward as she fought to keep the satisfied grin off her face.

"It's hard to tell with the shadows, but I'm gonna agree with Samara on this one," Alaric said. "You were definitely smirking."

Rynn glanced back and forth between Alaric and me. "Since when do you two agree on anything?"

Alaric stiffened, and now Roth was looking at the two of us curiously. Fantastic.

"Focus, Rynn!" I barked. "Where are the settlements?"

She gave me a pointed look that said she'd very much be bringing up the topic of what was going on between me and Alaric later. At which point, I would tell her that absolutely nothing was going on and it was just my libido going insane.

Kieran needed to get back soon so I could get laid. Once I got that taken care of, I was sure I would be thinking rationally again.

Rynn moved to where Roth had hung a map on the board, which was next to the unraveled scrolls. "I've identified three potential locations. It's hard to find information on old human settlements that haven't already been turned into outposts, but somehow we got lucky because there is one about a two-day run from me, and there's one less than a day's ride from you. There's also one for Cali to check out that is on the outskirts of the badlands. I've already spoken to her and caught her up on everything. She's on her way there now."

I looked at where Rynn had pointed on the map close to House Harker. She was right. It was less than a day's ride and was basically up the coast.

"Are you sure there was a settlement there?" I frowned. "I've ridden up and down the coast, and I don't remember ever seeing something."

She nodded. "Given how close it was to the shore, most of the town has probably been wrecked by storms with no one to repair it. If you were riding past it on the road, you probably wouldn't have noticed the leftover debris."

"Maybe." I chewed my bottom lip, still a little skeptical about missing the skeletal remains of a town, but Rynn was never wrong about these sorts of things. If she said that a human settlement used to be there, then it used to be there.

My eyes slid across the map to the general area of where she'd pointed in the Velesian territory, and alarm shot through me.

I hesitated. "Rynn, the outpost you're planning on going to belongs to the Fervis. Have you cleared it with them?"

She pursed her lips together and didn't answer my question.

I stalked towards her, wishing she was actually here so I could shake some sense into her. "Find another one."

"It's just over the border," she said dismissively. "They won't even know I'm there!"

"Rynn…" I growled in frustration. There wasn't a damn thing I could do to stop her, and she knew it.

"Why is Rynn going there a problem?" Roth asked, their gaze bouncing back and forth between me and Rynn while they tried to work out what was going on.

"Things are a little tense between the Velesian Orders these days," I said tightly.

"Understatement of the year," Alaric grunted.

Rynn glared at him, but he wasn't wrong.

While the Moroi had broken up into different Houses, each led by the strongest of our bloodlines, the Velesians were broken up into three Orders. Narchis, Avala, and Fervis. Each Order consisted of multiple packs.

Originally, each Order had primarily consisted of the same shifters. Narchis had lycanthropes, Avala had ursanthropes, and Fervis had ailuranthropes. The aetanthropes were too few in number to hold their own territory, so they had always been mixed in with all the Orders.

These days, the Orders were a little more diverse, but the dominant type of shifter in each was still what the Order was originally made up of.

Shortly after the queen and her consort rose to power in the Moroi realm, the Alpha Pack rose in the Velesian realm. Unlike the Moroi Sovereigns, however, the Alpha Pack was regularly challenged for authority.

Sure, the Moroi Houses bickered and jockeyed for power, but nobody outright revolted against the Sovereigns.

More than one bloody attack had been waged against the Alpha Pack.

Rynn had been promised to the Alpha Pack, not only because she was completely brilliant, but because she was the daughter of high-ranking members of the Order of Narchis. Just like me, Rynn's life had been given away for political reasons. While joining a pack wasn't the same thing as marriage… it was similar enough.

Only Rynn's situation with the Alpha Pack was in a weird state currently, and she couldn't just cross into Fervis territory without at least checking with them first.

I just needed to get that through her thick fucking head.

"You are not—"

"Oh, sorry! The charge is running out on the shadow spell." Rynn held her hands up helplessly. "Must be time for a new gem."

"Don't you dare!" I screamed and shoved my hand towards her shoulder. It slid through the smoke, and I dropped my clenched fist to my side. "Rynn! I forbid you from—"

She vanished, leaving behind curling shadows in her wake.

I stared at the space she'd been standing in and then at the map before returning my gaze back to where she'd been. A warm, sticky feeling slid along my fingers, and I absently noticed that my nails had hardened into claws and my fangs had jutted further out from my jaw.

Roth was staring at me, appearing mildly alarmed by my bloodlust surfacing. Alaric just held his hands out like he was about to calm down a raging beast, which I suppose was a little accurate.

I threw my head back and screamed, "THAT FUCKING BITCH!"

CHAPTER EIGHTEEN

Samara

I WAS STILL PISSED off beyond reason when I rode out of House Harker ten minutes later on Zosa.

Nyx had caught me on my way to the stables, and I'd barely managed to speak rationally for a few minutes and explain that I'd be needing an escort tomorrow. They promised to get something arranged and then slowly backed away from me with wide eyes.

I hadn't even bothered saddling up Zosa. Just grabbed a bridle and headed out. Luckily, I'd worn pants today. Riding bareback in a skirt was awkward and uncomfortable.

The rangers at the gate hadn't been thrilled about letting me out, but when I flashed my fangs, they quickly changed their minds. As a Harker, no one was concerned about me turning into a Strigoi. And sadly, it hadn't been an uncommon occurrence for me to storm out of the gates in a huff during my teenage years, usually because of something Alaric said.

But sometimes this would happen because I'd spot Kieran flirting with some gorgeous courtier and it caused me to feel things I had no right to.

My life hadn't been my own back then.

"Don't go far!" Nyx called out from behind me.

"I'll be at the beach!" I called back over my shoulder. Then I wrapped my hands around Zosa's mane and squeezed my legs.

She leapt into a ground-eating gallop, and I leaned over her shoulders for better balance while I subtly directed her with my knees. We ran straight away from House Harker before veering off to the right and down a narrow path.

But all too soon, I had to slow Zosa down as the path started to dip down and become more narrow.

The trees on either side of us became sparser before falling away altogether and the dirt became sand. Zosa trotted up a rolling hill, and I pulled her to a stop, breathing in the salty air. The beach stretched out before us with impossibly white sand.

Normally, right about now would be when I'd be calming down and getting over whatever was bothering me, but not today. Rynn was deliberately putting herself in danger, and there was fuck all I could do about it.

My eyes shifted, and suddenly everything became a little sharper.

I squeezed them shut, but that just made me more aware of the scents and sounds around me. Zosa's quick breathing from our run. The rumble of the waves crashing into the shore.

My fangs slid a little further out. Damn it.

I slid off Zosa's back and pulled my boots off, digging my toes into the sand before removing the bridle. "Go run around, but don't go too far," I told Zosa. She snorted and bumped her head against my shoulder. "I'm fine, sweet girl." I scratched her forehead and behind her ears before giving her a good shove. "Go!"

She took off like a rocket, kicking up sand all over me.

"Thanks," I grumbled, beginning to walk up the beach towards my favorite spot.

My senses were still all keyed up thanks to the bloodlust. It'd been a while since I'd had it this bad. I'd need to get a handle on it before night came because it would only get worse as my magic increased under the moonlight.

We were a week away from a full moon, so any bloodlust would be intense at night for the next couple of weeks.

I should have asked Carmilla for a drink before she left, but I hadn't been thinking about it, and it'd only been a few weeks since I drank from her last. Now I didn't have anyone to drink from. At least, no one I was comfortable asking.

While feeding from someone wasn't necessarily sexual, it was intimate. Growing up, Moroi children drank from their parents as well as from members of the House they belonged to. The bloodlines that founded the Houses were the most stable of the Moroi. We had been the first to pull away from the bloodlust, and it was almost unheard of for any House bloodline to fully lose themselves to bloodlust and become Strigoi.

When other Moroi drank our blood, it decreased the chances of them being completely overcome with bloodlust, but those feedings weren't required often, so family members were responsible for most of the blood feedings. Then, as we matured, lovers, spouses, or trusted friends usually replaced family. Emotions tended to spiral while feeding, especially when bloodlust was running high.

I went to chew on my bottom lip and felt a sharp stabbing pain as I pierced it with one of my fangs. Sweet, coppery blood filled my mouth, and I practically moaned as the pleasure of the taste quickly overshadowed the pain.

Fuck. I needed to find someone to feed from. I couldn't wait for Carmilla to get back. There was no way I was asking Alaric or Roth. Maybe Nyx? It'd be a little awkward, but they'd probably do it.

A smile tugged at my lips as my mood lightened at watching

Zosa frolic in the waves. She was literally the only good thing that came out of my time at House Laurent. I laughed softly as she ran out towards the retreating tide only to spin and haul ass back to the shore when the waves came crashing back in, her tail high up in the air as she pranced around.

"I leave you alone for one week, and you're out here grinning like an idiot with blood running down your chin."

"Kier?" I whirled around, and relief poured through me when I saw Kieran sitting on a blanket, perched on top of a grassy dune that rose above the sand, creating a nice lookout spot. "What are you doing here? I thought you wouldn't be back for a couple more weeks?"

He smirked as I scrambled up to join him and rose from where he'd been sitting. "Carmilla requested my presence at the Sovereign House. Since House Harker was more or less on the way, I decided to come back here for a night before continuing on my journey."

Just as I was about to launch myself into his arms, I forced myself to stop. He smelled achingly good. I swallowed and backed up a step.

"Umm, I actually came out here to be alone for a bit." My eyes locked onto where his throat was pulsing, and I quickly looked at the ground. "Roth is here. You should go to the library so they can fill you in. Alaric is there too."

"Sam," he drawled in a low tone that never failed to set my blood on fire.

My gaze rose from the ground as if pulled in. The way the corners of his lips curled up told me he knew exactly what he was doing by saying my name like that.

He tilted his head. "We both know you need to feed."

"I'll ask Nyx when I get back." I licked my lips and took a step forward before catching myself and forcing my feet to remain rooted. "You should go."

Every part of me wanted to sink my fangs into Kieran. The need was so intense that I was having a hard time thinking about anything else, which was exactly why I shouldn't do it. The bond I was forming with Kieran was too much, and it was happening too fast.

I needed to calm the fuck down, but instead, I took another step closer. Then another, and another, until I found myself directly in front of him.

"And if I want to stay?" Kieran's eyes were ablaze as he stared down at me.

"Things will change between us." My desire to claim him was so strong, this was so far beyond the normal bloodlust I felt. It took every ounce of my willpower, but I forced myself to take a step back. "I'm sorry. You make me want things… and I have no right to ask that of you yet."

He stepped forward, reclaiming the distance I had put between us. "Ask whatever you want of me. It's yours."

"Are you sure?" I rasped. "And think carefully, because we both know I'm a possessive bitch, and I know it's not fair because I'm not ready to commit to you and only you just yet. But if I taste your blood…" I closed my eyes and inhaled his rich and decadent scent before snapping my eyes open once more. "If I taste you, then you are *mine*."

The gold in Kieran's eyes spread, drowning out the hazel as he pressed down on the black gem that adorned his left pinkie finger, causing a blade to pop out. I watched with rapt attention when he dragged the blade down the side of his neck, leaving behind a trail of blood.

My nostrils flared as the scent hit me.

"I have always been yours, Sam."

The last of my control snapped, and I leapt forward.

Kieran caught me as I wrapped myself around him, one arm around my back holding me close while the other cupped my ass. My fangs sank into his neck, and he let out a deep groan and gripped me tighter against him.

He lowered us to the ground, settling on his back with me on top. I drank deep as I ground my hips against his, loving the way he hissed every time I did it. The rich, full taste rushed across my tongue and down my throat, and I wasn't sure if I'd ever felt this alive. Kieran's blood was the most delicious thing I'd ever tasted. It was wickedly divine.

My main source of blood these last few years had been Demetri. I'd tried to make it fun whenever we'd had to feed from each other, but it'd been nothing like this.

"Fuck, Sam," Kieran breathed out.

One hand was still gripping my ass, but the other had slipped beneath my shirt. I continued to drink deep as his hand made a blazing path up.

Just as I pulled my fangs out from his neck, Kieran ran a thumb over my pebbled nipple, and I threw my head back with a moan. My body was tight with need, and I wanted his hands on me more.

Nimble fingers unbuttoned the leather vest I'd been wearing before Kieran pulled it off me. My shirt was next, and Kieran wasted no time once my breasts were free. He pivoted up and sucked a nipple into his mouth. I shuddered and arched my back further.

When he moved to give my other breast the same attention, I pawed at his clothes, untying the various knots. He nipped at my skin before leaning back and pulling his vest and shirt off. I frantically tugged at his pants, but Kieran grabbed the back of my thighs and flipped me onto my back.

My remaining clothes were gone in a flash, and I arched my back when Kieran buried himself between my thighs and dragged his tongue up my pussy before sucking on my clit.

"Fucking hell, you're good at that," I said through panted breaths.

I licked the remnants of Kieran's blood from my lips as his fingers plunged inside me. There was nothing gentle about his movements as he pumped them hard and fast. My hands clenched the blanket beneath us, tension building in my core.

"Tell me how good I am," Kieran purred before swirling his tongue around my clit.

I whimpered as the pleasure started to become too much. Just as I was about to go over the edge, his tongue vanished, and he pulled his fingers out.

"FUCK!" I screamed and glared at him.

The asshole just laughed and plunged two fingers back in while taking up an irritatingly slow pace.

"Tell me, Sam." His golden eyes bore into mine as he demanded again, "Tell me how much you love me fucking you."

His thumb just barely grazed my clit, and a moan slipped out of me.

"I *like* you fucking me," I ground out and raised my hips to meet the thrust of his fingers, but he just pulled them back out.

"That's not what I asked," he tutted. "But maybe you just need more convincing."

"Yes," I breathed out. "That."

Warm breath brushed my inner thigh as he laughed, followed by lips kissing my skin.

"What are you—fuck!" I screamed as Kieran sank his fangs into my thigh just as he pushed two fingers deep inside my pussy again. The pleasure mixed with the brief flicker of pain immediately brought on the orgasm that Kieran had been teasing out of me for the last few minutes.

Another finger joined the other two as he pushed down with his thumb on my clit, all the while continuing to drink deeply from my thigh. My mind shattered, and I welcomed the bliss as the orgasm rippled through me.

I was only vaguely aware of Kieran withdrawing his fingers

and fangs and moving up to rest over me, a satisfied grin fixed on his lips.

"Given that look on your face," he drawled, "I suppose I don't need to ask if you loved that."

I nodded, stretching my body out languidly beneath him. His cock throbbed against me, and I reached down to stroke it.

"Sam," he groaned, thrusting into my hand. When I wrapped my legs around his waist and rested his cock at my entrance, he looked down at me with brilliant gold eyes. "Are you sure?"

In response, I thrust my hips up, and he easily slid inside. We both let out twin moans of satisfaction.

"Thank fuck," he growled.

He slid in and out slowly, letting me adjust to him, before leaning back and raising my legs up over his shoulders.

Something between a moan and a whimper poured out of me as he pushed my legs back down, bringing the top of my thighs closer to my chest and letting him thrust even deeper inside of me.

My pussy clenched around him as Kieran built up a fast and hard pace. His lips crashed against mine, and he fucked me with his tongue as he continued to relentlessly fuck me with his cock. Just as I felt another orgasm building, I gripped his hair and tore him away from my mouth so that I could sink my fangs into his neck again.

He groaned as I greedily drank his blood while he continued to pump inside me, fucking me through the orgasm. My legs eventually loosened as the aftereffects rippled through me.

Kieran was rapidly blowing past all of my best sexual experiences and setting a high bar for future encounters.

"We're not done yet, my love." Kieran pulled back and flipped me onto all fours, pushing down on my back so that my ass was up in the air. Even if I'd been capable of voicing a protest through my pleasure-addled brain, all thoughts scattered as he slammed back into me.

"Fuck, Kieran," I moaned, and he knelt to kiss my back while thrusting deep inside me.

"I fucking love hearing my name on your lips." His hips hammered against me. "Almost as much as I love you coming all over my cock."

Between his filthy words and the punishing rhythm, I was already primed for another orgasm, which I didn't think was possible. After experiencing no orgasms during sex for the last couple of years, having more than one felt greedy and impossible.

The sound of flesh slapping against flesh rang loudly around us as Kieran's pace became frantic. A mewling sound tore out of me that if I'd been rational, I probably would have been embarrassed about making. One of Kieran's hands dropped down to rub against my clit, and that was all it took to send me spiraling.

My scream was echoed seconds later by Kieran as he shuddered inside me. Both of us stayed like that, breathing heavily, scorched by bliss.

After a moment, Kieran pulled me down with him so that we were both on our sides, with me tucked against him. His cock was still buried inside me, as if he couldn't bear any level of separation between us just yet. I felt the same, so I enjoyed the feeling of his body wrapped around mine.

We lay there for some time in comfortable silence before Kieran pulled back, a low groan slipping out of both of us as he pulled his cock out and a rush of fluids followed.

He pulled me around so that I was facing him, and I rested my head on his chest with my body firmly pressed up against his side.

"So," Kieran said, "not that I'm complaining about what just happened at all, but what kicked off your bloodlust?"

"Rynn." My voice was tinged with anger, but at least my bloodlust was well-sated now. "She's putting herself in danger, and there's nothing I can do about it."

"She's a big wolf," Kieran said gently. "She can handle herself."

"I know, I know, but I still worry about her, just as I worry about Cali, even though she can definitely take care of herself."

"You know Cali is kind of terrifying, right?" Kieran's head flopped to the side to look at me, a sheepish grin on his face.

"Never to me or Rynn." I grinned back at him before it slid off my face. "I'm guessing you're aware of Rynn's situation?"

He gave me an apologetic look. "It's been making the rounds of the rumor mill for a while now. People are saying that she is refusing to join the Alpha Pack. Others are saying they are the ones refusing to let her join."

He reached out and slipped his hand into mine, and I nestled further into him. The sex was mind-blowing, but so was this.

Kieran added carefully, "I don't know Rynn all that well, but I don't believe she'd refuse to join the pack, and I see no reason why they wouldn't want her. Rynn is bloody brilliant and has that whole lithe and wild werewolf thing going on. It's super hot."

He grunted when I elbowed him hard, and then he gave me a pouty look which I ignored.

"Don't worry,"—he leaned down and kissed my neck, making me shiver—"I have a thing for a certain curvy-as-fuck Moroi."

"You'd better," I muttered.

He nipped my neck playfully, sending all my thoughts scattering until he looked at me with a self-satisfied smile.

I scowled. "Oh, get over yourself."

Kieran chuckled. "I don't know what's going on between

Rynn and the Alpha Pack, and you don't have to tell me. But there are a lot of rumors flying around about the growing tension between the three Velesian Orders and a general discontent against the Alpha Pack and how they're handling things… and Rynn's name has come up."

"Rynn and the Alpha Pack are kind of a hot mess," I admitted. "I can't go into details without checking with her first, but to answer your original question of why I was so pissed off earlier… Rynn is going to sneak onto Fervis territory to investigate an old human settlement."

Kieran jackknifed into a sitting position, jostling me to the side before his hands clamped down on my arms.

"You can't let her do that!" His eyes were wide with panic. "The last couple of attacks have been in Fervis land. They didn't even want to let the Alphas in to look at the scenes. Apparently, they've upped all patrols on their border."

"Shit!" I hissed and echoed Kieran's abrupt movement to a sitting position. "There's no way Rynn didn't know that when she announced her ridiculous plan!"

"The Fervis are still pissed that the Narchis chose to ally with Avala instead of them. Rynn wasn't the only one from Narchis chosen to join one of the Avala packs, but she was the most prominent because she's going to the moons damned Alphas!"

"I know! Why do you think I lost my shit earlier?!" I choked on the words. Now that my bloodlust had calmed down, panic was starting to override the rage.

Strong arms pulled me into a hug, and I wrapped myself around Kieran with tears streaming down my face. I hated crying, but whenever I was feeling any sort of overwhelming emotion, tears were inevitable. Especially if I couldn't scream at anything.

Kieran knew it bothered me, so he didn't comment, just silently wiped them away while holding me tightly against him.

"Are you sure you can't talk her out of it?" he asked softly.

I shook my head against his chest, not trusting myself to speak just yet.

Kieran sighed. "Rynn is stealthy and good at remaining unseen. Remember when we used to play hide-and-seek as kids? None of us could ever find her."

I sniffled. "Carmilla was so upset that one time Rynn stayed outside in the woods all night when we couldn't find her. She insisted that we put a time limit on the game after that."

Kieran maneuvered me until I was sitting in his lap and tucked me against his chest again. "I'm not any more thrilled than you are about Rynn going into Fervis territory, but we'll just have to trust that she knows what she's doing and that she'll be okay."

"And if she's not?" I whispered.

"Then we'll unleash Cali on them."

I craned my head to look at him but found his expression unreadable, which was a little unsettling. "Honestly, I can't tell if you're joking or not."

"Kidding." He kissed me softly on the corners of my mouth. "Mostly."

CHAPTER NINETEEN

Samara

THE FOLLOWING MORNING, Alaric stood with Kieran and I just inside the gate while we waited for the rangers who would be escorting us to arrive.

Alaric kept switching from giving Zosa the side eye to trying not to gawk at the matching bite marks on my neck and Kieran's. After the beach, we'd moved back to my suite and hadn't left for hours. Taking our time in exploring every inch of each other's bodies.

"If you keep glaring at Zosa like that, I'm going to let her sneeze all over you," I warned.

Zosa's ears perked forward, and Alaric took a step back, disgust tugging the corners of his lips down.

"Don't be too hard on him, love," Kieran said breezily. "He's probably just wondering how you taste." His fingers brushed across my neck, and I fought the blush that was creeping up my cheeks. Alaric fixed a glare on his best friend, but Kieran just grinned wickedly at him. "The answer, my friend, is exquisite."

"Kieran!" I stomped my foot down, and he yelped before

giving me a wounded look while rubbing his foot. "It's too early for your bullshit."

He shot me a pouty look, and I rolled my eyes. I was proud of myself for being civil to Alaric all week and ignoring the growing attraction I was feeling towards him.

Alaric might have sent me some heated looks, but those all happened in the spur of the moment. He probably would have reacted that way to anybody. He clearly did not want *me* in that way, and I didn't want to ruin our working relationship, especially since we were just starting to work so well together.

I don't know why Kieran had decided to tease Alaric so much about me, but I was determined to put a stop to it. Before I could apologize to Alaric for Kieran's obnoxious behavior, the rangers came around the corner leading three horses.

Surprise flickered through me when I saw that Nyx wasn't among those present. It was Vail and two other rangers I recognized from the training yard. Raoul and Aerin. They'd been part of the group that had laughed at Alaric that first day he'd been practicing with the bow.

Despite their behavior that day, they'd actually stepped in to help give Alaric advice in the days that followed when they saw he was determined to learn how to shoot. He nodded at them in greeting before he gave me an uneasy look, which I returned. I'd assumed that Nyx would be coming with me today since Emil and Adrienne weren't available. While Raoul and Aerin were nice enough, and probably trustworthy since they reported to Vail, I wasn't sure if it was a good idea for them to escort me today. They would no doubt have questions about why the Heir of House Harker was traipsing around in an old human settlement.

"Raoul and Aerin will be escorting you to the Sovereign House, Kieran," Vail said, causing my brows to furrow.

Who was going to escort me then? I stood on my tiptoes, trying to see if Nyx or someone else was coming behind Vail.

He finished, "I'll be escorting Samara for her trip today."

I froze, my eyes darting to Vail before I slowly lowered myself back onto my heels just as Kieran slid closer to me and eyed the marshal.

His gaze narrowed. "Surely, you're needed here? Isn't there someone else who can escort Samara?"

Cold, grey eyes locked onto Kieran. "Are you saying that I am inadequate to keep the Heir safe in broad daylight?"

"I'm sure Kieran meant no offense," Alaric said smoothly. "We simply wouldn't want to monopolize your time with such a trivial errand."

I gave Alaric a thankful nod, appreciating that he was standing up for me despite Kieran being an ass earlier. While it was unlikely that Vail would try anything today, I was still stressed out about Rynn, and the idea of being stuck with him all day was less than appealing. At least I didn't have to worry about my bloodlust rising so soon after drinking from Kieran yesterday and giving Vail an excuse to get rid of me once and for all.

Vail studied Alaric before looking at Kieran, then he let out a disgusted sound and curled his lip up at me. "Well, it didn't take you long to sink your claws into them. Or I suppose, in this case, spread your legs."

"Shut the fuck up, Vail," Kieran growled and took a step forward.

I slapped my hand across his chest, and he halted immediately. Vail pointedly looked at my hand on his chest and gave Kieran a lazy smile. I felt a growl rumble out of Kieran's chest and swiftly moved to stand between them.

"Enough! Who I fuck"—my eyes flicked briefly over to Alaric's—"or don't fuck, is none of your damn business, Vail, and stop acting like it's irrational for my friends to be concerned about my well-being just because you don't have anyone in your life who gives a shit about you."

The rangers standing near Vail stiffened and shot me murderous looks, but I ignored them.

I spun and placed my hands on either side of Kieran's face, forcing him to take his attention off Vail and set it on me. His hazel eyes were bright in the morning sun, and I gave myself a second to appreciate them before brushing a kiss against his lips.

"I'll be fine," I murmured. "We're only riding a few hours from here. We'll be back well before sundown. Vail is an asshole, but he won't do anything."

The asshole in question muttered something behind me, but I couldn't make out the words, which was probably for the best. I was trying hard to be the bigger person here, mostly to keep Kieran from doing something stupid, but if Vail called me a whore again, I was likely to punch the marshal myself—and then run away as quickly as possible.

"Alright." He tenderly kissed me back, resting his forehead against mine. "Let me know what you find?"

"Of course." I nodded and stepped away from him, immediately missing his body heat in the brisk morning air. "Make sure Roth eats today, will you?" I asked Alaric and clarified when he just arched an eyebrow at me. "They tend to get caught up in their research and forget to do silly things like eat or drink. That's why I've been bringing food up to the library all week and risking their wrath at the books being damaged."

He cringed a little. Roth hated the idea of food, or worse drinks, being brought into the library, but it was significantly easier to bring the food to Roth than it was to get them out of the library and bring them to the food.

"Fine, but you owe me one," Alaric agreed.

I immediately thought of ways I could return the favor and

had to slam the door down on all those thoughts. Apparently, even though Kieran had quite satisfied me last night, I was still doomed to have dirty thoughts about Alaric.

Given the way the gold fractures in Kieran's eyes were glowing brightly and that the corners of his lips had tipped up ever so slightly, I figured he'd caught my blush before I had crushed it and had a very good idea of every dirty thought that had just gone through my head.

Damn it. Now he was going to be even worse at teasing Alaric about me.

"Let's go." I quickly mounted Zosa, and the rangers and Kieran did the same as the gate was raised in front of us.

Kieran steered his horse next to mine and leaned over to kiss me, and when he pulled back, he whispered, "Don't have too much fun while I'm away." Then his eyes slid to Alaric and back to me. "But do have a little fun."

The blush I'd just barely managed to force into retreat came flaring back to life. "I hate you," I muttered and urged Zosa forward, leaving Vail to catch up, Kieran's laugh chasing me the whole way out.

***

THREE HOURS LATER, Vail pulled up his horse, and I slowed Zosa down to a walk. We'd rode the entire way here in complete silence.

If I hadn't been so stressed out about Rynn, I would have enjoyed the ride. It was a beautiful sunny day, and the road we took was along the coast, so I was able to view the ocean for most of it.

I only had a general idea of where the human outpost was based on the map, but Vail seemed to know exactly where he was going which, for some reason, I found really annoying. Maybe it was because he seemed overly confident about everything, and I'd never seen him be wrong about anything.

For once, I wanted him to be wrong. *It's probably for the best that he's right in this instance though*, I thought begrudgingly.

The quicker we found and searched the human settlement, the sooner we could get back to House Harker and its fortified walls. Away from the monsters lurking in the woods, awaiting their next meal.

Vail dismounted and looped his horse's reins over the saddle, and I did the same, giving Zosa a good pat before joining Vail. Both were well-trained enough to not go far unless we were attacked, in which case it was better to give the horses at least a chance to run for their lives and possibly serve as a distraction. Hopefully, with it still being daylight, we wouldn't have to worry about that.

"I can see why I never noticed it before." My eyes scanned the area, spotting a few pieces of well-weathered wood and some crumbling brickwork. "There really isn't much left."

Vail grunted and began walking around, studying the ground as he moved while I surveyed the area a little more.

The human village had been built very close to the beach. We were on higher ground, but the beginning of the shoreline was directly below us. Based on where the seaweed had piled up, there was less than a quarter mile between the edge of the town and where the water came in at high tide.

Because of how high up the village had been, they would have been fine… until there was a storm.

I wondered what had driven them to build a town here. It didn't seem safe. Then again, the world hadn't been a safe place for humans even when the Fae were still around to keep the monsters under control.

The coastlines had always been safer than living in the forests because the monsters preferred the coverage provided by the trees and thick ground cover. There were more prey options in the forest, as well.

We might be a favorite food source for the monsters, but we were hardly the only one.

My foot slipped on some loose rocks, and I stumbled forward towards the edge. I waved my arms as I tried to backpedal but only succeeded in tripping over another loose rock. Just as I was about to pitch forward, Vail grabbed my arm and yanked me back.

The movement sent me spinning around, and I fell right into his broad chest. "Thanks," I breathed out, placing my hands on his shoulders to steady myself.

"Despite your low opinion of me, you are House Harker's Heir, and therefore, I am bound to keep you safe," he said coldly before stepping away and putting several feet of space between us. "I'm simply not under the spell of that cunt of yours like those two peacocks."

I bit back the retort that tried to burst free. Almost tumbling over the cliff had left me unsettled, and being saved by Vail only to have him throw his cruel vitriol at me had my emotions all over the place, but I absolutely *refused* to let him know he'd hurt me.

I shoved away the anger and lingering fear and planted a sultry smirk on my face while batting my eyelashes at him.

"Well, my cunt doesn't have any interest in you, so that works out for both of us." I tapped a finger against my bottom lip and fixed my features into a thoughtful expression. "I can see how Kieran would qualify as a peacock. Alaric, not so much."

Vail stared at me, uncertainty flashing across his face. He probably thought I'd be mad about his rude comment, but it didn't really bother me all that much.

I enjoyed sex and wasn't going to feel bad about that. Marvina constantly belittling me and dismissing my intelligence had pissed me off far more than any crude insult about my sex life. It was Vail's unwarranted hatred towards me that hurt. But I'd never let him know that.

His mouth flattened into a hard line, annoyance etched in his features at me brushing off his cutting remarks so easily.

I laughed even as a flicker of pain sliced across my heart and set about searching the area, this time further from the edge. "You'll have to work harder to get under my skin, Vail. Also, I'm not sleeping with Alaric."

"Yeah, I give that a week," he said with a slight edge to his voice. "We have two hours to search, and then we need to head back to make sure we make it before night falls."

A shiver ran through me at the idea of being caught out in the wilds at night with Vail. I couldn't help but remember that night when we'd both lost our parents and this animosity between us had started. Before then, we'd been friends in a way. He was three years older than me and was often busy training with rangers or traveling outside House Harker with his parents. But we'd always gotten along, and I'd often sought out his company when possible.

Whenever my parents traveled outside of House Harker, it was Vail's parents who always escorted them. When Vail was old enough, he started going as well because his parents thought it would be a good experience for him. My parents often brought me along too, which I never could understand because I was too young to gain anything from their political conversations, but they rarely left me alone in House Harker.

Most of the time that Vail and I spent together was on those trips. We were usually the only two children, and despite our age difference, we got along really well.

I'd loved picking Vail's brain about what it was like to train to be a ranger and asked him about what types of monsters he'd seen. He was more than happy to show off his knowledge and keep me entertained. Every time we'd stop to rest, he'd show me different animal tracks or point out plants that were edible. Some of my best childhood memories were those trips, solely because of Vail.

I studied his face. With the jagged scars running down the right side across his eye and his long beard, he looked so much older than me when only three years separated us.

I remembered what he was like when we were kids. Even then he carried so much responsibility on his shoulders, determined to live up to the expectations placed on him by his parents who had been the previous marshals of House Harker. It was hard to reconcile the boy I remembered with the man standing before me.

"Will you ever stop hating me?" The words slipped out before I could think better of it.

Vail flinched. It happened so fast that I almost missed it, and part of me still doubted that I'd even seen it to begin with.

"I could have saved them," he said, turning away from me. "Your selfishness cost me my parents."

"Bullshit," I hissed.

"Excuse me?" He whirled to face me, the silver fractures in his eyes widening, making him look more than a little terrifying, but I didn't back down.

"I understand why you felt that way when we were kids." I closed the distance between us until only inches separated my chest from his. "But you are a grown-ass adult now! Our caravan was attacked by over a dozen wraiths! And only the moon knows what else!

"Your parents ordered you to protect me because they wanted you to get away! They knew that they wouldn't be walking away that night, but they wanted to give you a chance!"

"I COULD HAVE SAVED THEM!" Vail roared in my face.

"No! You couldn't have!" I yelled back, leaning forward

even more until my chest bumped into his and I had to tilt my head back further to continue holding his pissed-off gaze. "If your well-trained and experienced parents couldn't fight their way out of that night, there was no way in hell their thirteen-year-old kid was going to make a difference. You need someone to blame for that night, and you chose me because I'm a convenient target, but my parents died too, you asshole!" I shoved him with every ounce of strength I had and still only managed to push him back a step.

Vail's nostrils flared, and his eyes turned solid silver, giving them a ghostly appearance. My eyes flicked briefly to his hands, which were clenching and unclenching at his sides like he was imagining wrapping them around my throat.

The small voice that I'm pretty sure was my survival instinct was screaming in one corner of my mind to back away with my hands held up and try to look as small and harmless as possible, but the voice that was full of rage was louder and it was telling me to hold my fucking ground. So I did.

"I guess we'll never know," Vail said in an eerily calm tone. "Because you took that choice from me when you knocked me out."

He stared at me for another moment before taking a step back and walking to the other side of the settlement, where he started angrily sifting through the remains. The tension bled out of me, and I felt so tired all of a sudden. I don't know why I bothered trying to fix things between me and Vail. He was the only one besides me who had survived that night, and I just wanted to have someone to talk to about it.

I wanted to know if he had nightmares. If he still heard the screams and terrified commands of our parents telling us to run and protect each other.

I looked down at my palm and the jagged scar that ran across it. At some point in the attack, I'd cut it deeply, and then when Vail said he was going back to help his parents after we'd gotten away, I'd panicked. I'd screamed at him to stay, not wanting to lose him too. He'd frozen for a moment at my command, but I didn't think he would actually stay, so I'd grabbed a chunk of branch off the ground and hit him with every ounce of my ten-year-old strength.

Normally, it probably would have just annoyed him, but he already had a bunch of wounds at that point and had dropped like a stone.

When he woke hours later, his eyes burned with hatred at what I'd done. He'd looked at me the same ever since. I let out a long breath, trying to expel the last of my anger with it. Vail would have to deal with his issues towards me at some point because I was back at House Harker, and I wasn't going anywhere.

Not wanting to push Vail anymore, I stayed away from him for the next hour while I searched through what was left of the human settlement. A dull pain throbbed within my chest from a wound that had never healed.

My parents had been my entire world. They'd both ruled House Harker and that had kept them incredibly busy. But they'd always made time for me, always making sure that at least one of them was always there to tuck me in at night. It was my father who had instilled my love of riding. And my mother a love of reading.

When they died, it shattered me. I didn't know how to handle the grief and I'd wanted to be strong for Carmilla and everyone else at House Harker. So I had gathered all the jagged pieces and shoved them into a box that I then tucked away into the farthest depths of my soul.

And Vail had just reached in to grab that box and rattle it.

I was debating if I could shove him over the cliff and down onto the beach below when the glint of steel caught my eye. All of the buildings had long since been wiped away but their foundations remained.

Dropping to my knees, I pushed away bits of dried grass and dirt, revealing a locked cellar door. The metal lock remained strong, as did the thick bars stretching between the doorframe like a grate. Some slabs of wood were bolted to the bars, but most of the boards had decayed, allowing me to see a little bit of the room beneath the door.

"I think I found something," I called out.

Vail ambled over and eyed the door, then motioned for me to stand back.

Taking the hint, I moved a few steps away as he stomped down on the door. The wood cracked and buckled immediately, leaving behind only the metal bars. Then he pulled on the frame, but it didn't budge.

"This was probably the safe hideout for the village," he said. "We've encountered them before. They have steel beams that run across the ceiling, and that's what the doorframe is attached to. Some of the outposts have managed to melt away the locks and repurpose them, but I didn't bring anything with me to get through it. We'll have to come back to search it."

My nose scrunched up as I stared at the door. Coming back tomorrow wasn't the end of the world, but patience wasn't my strong suit, and I wanted to know now. We were already here, and I'd be annoyed if we came all the way back tomorrow only to find out that it was empty.

Once again dropping down to my knees, I skimmed my fingers over the joint where one of the steel bars running across the door was connected to the frame. "I think this one is loose? If you kick it a couple of times, it might snap free."

I looked up at Vail just as he shook his head. "Still not enough space for me to get through."

"It will be for me though," I pointed out.

Emotionless eyes looked at me, scrutinizing my body before catching on my full breasts.

I smirked at him and put my hands flat on my breasts and pushed them down. "They're squishy, Vail. I'm pretty sure I can squeeze through, and if I can't, we'll come back tomorrow."

"Fine," he said flatly, still clearly not believing I'd be able to manage this.

To be honest, I wasn't sure I'd be able to squeeze through the bars, either. I was far from dainty, but unlike Vail, who was all slabs of hard muscle, I was soft and there was some give to my body.

It might take some wiggling on my part, but there was a decent chance I could get in. Getting out might be more difficult, but I'd deal with that later.

Hopefully, Vail wouldn't just leave me here. Hmm… maybe this *wasn't* a good idea.

A few stomps and a loud clang later, the bar snapped away, leaving a gap in the door. I knelt down and did my best to peer into the space below, but it was hard to see anything from this angle. But there were no sounds, so I decided to call that good enough.

I maneuvered so that I was sitting across the door with my feet dangling down. Shit, this was really narrow.

"You'll have to hold my arms and lower me down." I scooted forward as far as I could until it would only take a tilt of my hips to have me sliding down and held my arms straight up.

Vail let out a long sigh and then moved so that he was standing directly in front of me with his legs in a wide stance across the door.

If I tilted my head up, I'd basically be staring directly at his crotch.

I did not tilt my head up.

Strong hands grasped my wrists and once I was sure he had a secure grip, I let myself slide forward and wiggled my hips through the gap. Then I sucked in my stomach as much as I could while he lowered me through.

My breasts did indeed get a little stuck, and it was uncomfortable for a few seconds, but then I was past the bars.

Vail held on for a few more seconds before letting me drop to the ground.

"Yes!" I called out in victory while I brushed off my clothes. It wasn't the most pleasant experience, but I made it through and proved Vail wrong, so… worth it.

"We don't have all day," Vail said gruffly. "Take a look around and see if you can find anything. Then we'll have to get you out of there and head back."

"You can just admit I was right about being able to fit through, you know?"

He didn't bother answering, but I suspected he was wearing an annoyed expression and was probably debating the merits of leaving me here for the night. I didn't think he actually would leave me entirely, but I wouldn't put it past him to post up in one of the trees for the night and keep watch while I bunkered down here, cold and terrified.

I moved further into the underground bunker and then stopped until my eyes adjusted to the dark.

It was a big, open space. I was a little surprised that the ground above hadn't caved in, but there were steel beams running across the ceiling. Maybe the townsfolk had strengthened them with magic.

Back then, the Fae had been somewhat willing to share their magic with the humans to help keep them safe. Roth might be interested in visiting this place in the future to figure out how they'd managed to build this underground area. I walked around, scanning the space, trying to find anything of interest.

At first glance, it appeared to be empty, and my hopes sank at finding something useful. I forced myself to slow down and looked over the area again steadily, focusing on different areas. Nothing stood out on the ceiling or walls besides the impressive support structure they'd built, but something caught my attention in the center of the room.

I walked over and studied the ground, finding it was the same dirt flooring as the rest of the room, but parts of the floor were darker here.

My breath caught in my throat as I knelt down and swept dirt away from a jet-black piece of stone.

"Holy shit," I breathed out.

It looked like obsidian, but there were threads of gold running through it, and in the center of it was a crescent moon outlined in blood-red. I dug with my fingers until I could lift up the flat piece of obsidian-like stone. It was oddly heavy in my hands despite its relatively small size and fit neatly inside my two hands cupped together.

"I found something!" I raced back over to Vail and carefully handed it over to him.

I had to stand on my tippy-toes, and he had to get on his stomach and reach down to get it. In the back of my mind, I realized that this meant getting out of here was not going to be fun, but I was way too excited about finding something to care all that much.

"It still contains magic," Vail murmured where he knelt over the grate. "I can feel it."

"This must have been part of the ritual," I said. "Roth and Rynn were right in their speculation!"

"We still don't know if this is why the wraiths are targeting the outposts," Vail retorted flatly.

I rolled my eyes. He was such a downer.

"Let me see if I can find more." I hurried back over to where I'd found the first piece and started moving the dirt around.

Soon, I discovered two more segments, each with a lunar

symbol on them. We now had three parts of this strange obsidian stone that corresponded to our three species.

This had to be something. I didn't know what yet, but I was excited to get this back to Roth so we could start figuring it out.

After spending another ten minutes looking around, I was satisfied that there wasn't anything else here to find, so I went back over to the opening where Vail waited patiently above. Apparently, me finding something was enough to buy a little bit of goodwill from him.

"I think that's it," I said, peering up with a frown at the door.

There must have been stairs or a ladder down here at one point, but now there was nothing to help me close the distance.

It'd been a stretch to just pass the pieces I'd found back to Vail. How the hell were we going to do this?

As I was trying to figure this out, Vail moved so that he was squatting over the opening, bent over so that one hand was braced on the other side, and reached down with his other hand. Even with him crouching as low as he could, it was still a good two feet between me and that hand.

"You'll have to jump," he said.

"Sure, no problem," I said wryly. "Are you sure you can hold my weight with one hand?"

In my head, I pictured myself performing a magnificent leap and latching onto his hand, only for him to slam forward into the metal grate and knock himself out, leaving me trapped down here and him bleeding up top with a head wound. I really hated my overly active imagination sometimes.

"I'll be fine. Concern yourself with making the jump," he said gruffly.

"Okay, but if this goes poorly, it's not my fault," I grumbled and then backed up a few paces before running forward and jumping up… and missing by at least half a foot.

"Samara, you're a damn Moroi. This jump should be nothing," Vail said in an annoyed tone. "You should be training more."

"If it was nighttime, I could make this jump no problem," I said, moving back further this time to give myself even more of a running start.

"You shouldn't be dependent on the extra power you get during the night," he said disapprovingly.

"I'm not one of your rangers, Vail," I reminded him.

"Thank the moon for that," he muttered.

I scowled up at him. "Ready?"

"Waiting on you."

Argh.

I eyed his dangling hand and took off at a run. This time, I waited until the last possible second and then pushed up off the ground with every ounce of strength I could muster.

My fingers brushed against his wrist, and his large hand locked onto my right forearm. After awkwardly swinging for another moment, and feeling like my arm was going to get wrenched out of its socket, I managed to grab onto his arm with my left hand.

Once Vail was confident my grip was secure, he started pulling me up. Holy shit, he was strong. He pulled me up like I weighed nothing at all. It was a little uncomfortable wiggling through the small opening, but we managed to get me out a lot easier than I thought.

"Thanks," I mumbled, taking a step back as soon as my feet were on the ground.

Vail clearly didn't like touching me or having me around, so the least I could do was not press him on it. Unless, of course, I lost my temper. Then rational thinking went right out the window.

Vail didn't acknowledge my thanks and instead swiped the three obsidian pieces off the ground and headed over to the horses where he secured them in the saddlebags. I sighed and walked over to Zosa, who butted me gently with her head, and then I prepared myself for another silent ride back.

I hoped Rynn's excursion had gone as smoothly as ours. Even if she didn't find anything, I didn't care as long as she made it back safely.

Without waiting for Vail, I spurred Zosa forward and headed home, to where hopefully Roth could provide us with some answers once they looked over what we had found.

CHAPTER TWENTY

—

Alaric

"IF YOU TAP that thing one more time, I'm going to stab you with it," Roth said in a voice so calm that it took me a moment to register their threat.

I dropped the pencil that I'd been methodically drumming against the table, and it rolled before coming to a rest against a stack of scrolls.

"Sorry," I grunted. "Just a little keyed up today."

Roth glared at me for another second before returning their focus to the book in front of them.

The book had the symbol we'd been looking for, and they were working on translating the text now, but it took time. I was eager to look at it, but Roth was likely faster at translating than me, so I let them have it. Plus, I wasn't ashamed to admit that Roth terrified me a little.

I couldn't exactly explain why. Physically, they were no threat to me, but Roth was just so intense about everything. Plus, they used blood magic with ease more than any other person I'd ever met.

Sure, it was mostly to help them navigate around the library and be more productive with their research, but those

261

ribbons they had wrapped around their forearms could easily be used to restrain someone.

And I was pretty sure their enchanted quill could at the very least gouge out some eyes.

"Is it Samara who has you worried or Kieran?" they asked, not taking their eyes off the page they were reading.

The familiar thread of tension that formed every time Kieran left tugged a little. But now it felt like that thread was split in two, and I was trying very hard not to think about who was at the end of the second one.

"I'm always concerned about Kieran when he leaves House Harker," I admitted. "But he travels fairly often to visit the other Houses and occasionally the Velesians. It doesn't mean I don't worry about him, but he's traveling on well-known roads and stopping at outposts along the way."

The Sovereign House was probably the safest place to be in all of Lunaria. Aside from the impressive blood wards, they had the highest number of rangers out of the Houses. Kieran would be fine… once he made it there.

Absently, I picked the pencil up and started to tap it before a growl rumbled out of Roth and I hastily put it down again. I glanced at the nearest window.

The sun hadn't even started to set yet. There was plenty of time for Samara and Vail to make it back safely.

"And Samara?" Roth prompted.

I stared at the pencil, unsure how to answer that question. Samara confused the hell out of me, and I didn't like it. It was why I always sniped at her in a desperate attempt to maintain some distance between us.

"Samara is the Heir of House Harker," I hedged. "Her safety will always be of concern to me."

That got Roth to raise their head and arch an eyebrow at me. "You are so full of shit."

I bit the inside of my cheek as I forced my expression to

remain neutral. I really was. To make matters worse, Kieran had definitely picked up on my increasingly conflicted feelings about Samara.

I thought he would be jealous or upset about it. Instead, he seemed *intrigued* by the idea of me being with Samara.

I'd heard his comment to Samara when he was leaving about her having a little fun while he was gone. I'd also caught her blushing like crazy when she looked at me.

Samara had always been funny like that. She was obnoxiously bold with her flirting, wasn't the least bit shy when it came to sex, and had become even more so since returning to House Harker. Yet relatively tame words or suggestions could get her to blush from head to toe.

I wondered what she'd been thinking about when she looked at me and blushed earlier. The bite marks on her and Kieran's neck had thrown me off, although it made sense. They both trusted each other, and anyone who had eyes knew that they'd been more than a little in love with each other growing up, and with Samara no longer married, there was no reason for them not to be together.

Though, Kieran seemed to think that Samara wanted me too… and that we could *share*.

Fuck. I shifted in my seat as my cock hardened, glad that the table blocked Roth's view. Was I seriously considering sharing Samara with Kieran? How would that even work?

The Velesians usually had multiple partners in a relationship, but the Moroi were always just a couple. There was also the complication of Samara being the House Harker Heir. Carmilla loved her niece and wouldn't push for another marriage anytime soon, but it would still be expected of her to marry another high-ranking House member someday.

Neither Kieran nor I qualified as high-ranking. What would Kieran do if he were forced to give her up again?

Shit. What would I do?

This was exactly why it would be foolish for me to get involved with Samara as anything beyond friends. There was no happy ending here, and if I went down this path with Samara, I wasn't entirely sure I'd be able to let her walk away.

The rational choice was to be friends and nothing more so that I could support Kieran when my friend's heart was shattered at losing her.

I could do that. I just needed to ignore the throbbing hard cock in my pants.

Something smacked me in the forehead, and I blinked at the balled-up piece of paper before realizing Roth was staring at me expectantly.

"What?"

They sighed and shook their head. "I asked you *twice* what the deal was with Samara and Vail?"

"Oh." I pursed my lips.

The history between those two was a bit of a mystery to everyone, and I really didn't like sharing other people's business. Definitely not those I considered my friends.

I didn't know what was going to happen between me and Samara, but I did know that at the very least, things had changed between us enough that I no longer thought of her as an adversary.

Samara trusted Roth, and if Roth asked around, they could uncover at least some information about what had happened that night.

They might as well hear it from me.

"Samara was traveling with her parents to Velesian territory when she was ten years old for some type of diplomatic meeting. Vail's parents were the previous marshals of House Harker and were in charge of escorting them.

"They brought the best rangers under their command with them, and also brought Vail, who was thirteen at the time," I explained. "A storm hit that day and slowed their travel down significantly. They didn't make it to the outpost before nightfall and were attacked by wraiths."

"Her nightmares," Roth murmured. When I looked at them questioningly, they just shook their head and waved for me to carry on.

I swallowed. "Only Samara and Vail truly know what happened next because they were the only ones who survived." I could still remember what they both looked like that day when the rangers had brought them home.

Samara had been so broken, her eyes red and puffy from crying, and there was such a defeated look to her. Vail had been silent, his rage practically scorching the air around him. He'd learned how to harness that anger over the years, but it still burned.

I added, "Both of them were questioned about the attack after they were found, and I've read the reports. Samara didn't see much, but Vail claimed that there were over a dozen wraiths that attacked the caravan, along with several other monsters."

"Is it normal for that many wraiths to attack at once? And with other monsters?" Roth asked, suspicion brewing in their eyes.

"No." I shook my head. That part of the story had always bothered me too. "That information concerned everyone, and many claimed that Vail simply misremembered what happened. He was only a young boy, and he'd been traumatized. His parents and Samara's were mauled in front of him, along with the rest of the rangers."

"No wonder he is the way he is." Roth's eyebrows stretched to their hairline, their words marred with sympathy.

"Vail says his parents told him to take care of Samara. He grabbed her and ran. A wraith followed them and attacked. Vail managed to kill it, but not before it severely injured him. That's... that's how he got his scars." I let out a breath. "They made it to a small cave where they stayed hidden until rangers found them three days later when a search party was sent out to look for the missing caravan."

"Okay," Roth drawled. "They both share a fucked-up childhood trauma. Doesn't explain why Vail always stares at Samara like he's thinking about slitting her throat and chucking her body off a cliff."

I thought over their words, recalling all the times Vail looked at Samara. "That really is the look he gives her, isn't it?"

"Yes." Roth nodded. "I cycled through quite a few options before settling on that one."

"No one knows why Vail hates Samara the way he does, besides the two of them." I suspected Samara had told Rynn and Cali, but they'd take that secret to their graves.

"Hmm," Roth hummed out loud. "I get why you're worried about the two of them being out in the wilds with no one else around them. I'll still kill the shit out of you if you tap that fucking pencil again, though."

"Noted," I said dryly. "How is the translation coming?"

Roth flipped through several pages of notes before answering me. "Almost done. Still trying to make sense of it. Whoever wrote this used obnoxiously flowery language and a lot of vague allegories, but... I have a theory, and it's not good."

"Really? Because I really expected good news to explain how the wraiths have been getting past our blood wards," I responded flippantly.

If Samara or Kieran were here, they would have called me on my bullshit, and I found myself missing the banter we would have exchanged when Roth just dismissed me entirely and went back to reading.

"Sorry." I leaned back and pinched the bridge of my nose. "I haven't found anything useful, and it's frustrating, so I'm acting like an ass." Serious, hazel eyes just stared at me, and my lips twitched as I put my hand back down onto the table. "More of an ass than usual," I amended.

Roth nodded in what I assumed was acceptance. It was hard to tell because their face seemed to be perpetually locked in this bored expression with just a hint of haughtiness.

Okay. Maybe more than a hint.

"The symbol that was carved into that boy's neck means *'draw unto.'*" I took the book that Roth passed over to me and looked at the symbol on the opened page.

"The boy was drawing magic into himself?" I asked with a frown. "Have we been wrong in thinking that he was a victim? Was he trying to work some type of spell and it backfired?"

"It confused me at first too," Roth admitted. "But the more I read, the more it became clear that this symbol is often used in spells of transference." They paused for a moment before asking. "What do *you* think wraiths are?"

I shrugged, caught off-guard by the question. "The Unseelie always fucked around with shadow magic. The theory that they created the wraiths and then lost control seems plausible enough. The Seelie were pushing back against them, and they didn't want to lose, so the Unseelie tried to make their own shadow monsters stronger and fucked it up for everyone."

Whatever had happened to the Fae happened fast because we'd never found any written records of what went down.

There were some writings in the years before about a growing divide between the Unseelie and Seelie, but that was it. There were no mentions of wraiths in any of the writings we'd located, which implied the wraiths were something new that came about when whatever shit went down with the Fae occurred.

"I don't think that's what happened," Roth said slowly. "Not exactly. I do think that the Unseelie are responsible, though."

"What are you saying, Roth?" I asked, really not liking where this was going.

"Isn't it strange that all the Fae disappeared when the wraiths appeared?"

"I know where you're going with this." I shook my head. "The wraiths are different than the Fae. I've read the texts about the Unseelie and how they used their shadows to spy. Their shadows were an extension of them, but they weren't separate beings, and the Fae themselves didn't turn into shadows."

"We were humans and became monsters," Roth pushed. "I think the Unseelie tried to make it so they could turn themselves into shadows and became trapped in that form. The first humans that turned themselves into the Moon Blessed lost their humanity. What if the Unseelie lost themselves too? And they're just now starting to come back to themselves?"

The crease between my brows only deepened. "And you think that's why their attack strategies have changed from going after whoever they could find to being more concentrated on the outposts?"

Chills ran down my spine. Wraiths were always the worst of the monsters to roam these lands, but they'd still been beasts. The idea that they could be intelligent and capable of using magic… no, that didn't make sense.

I shook my head. "Wraiths are nothing but shadows," I replied, unable to accept this. "They can only become corporeal for a few seconds at a time." Enough to slash open a throat or disembowel a body.

"That's where the symbol comes in," Roth said. "I think it's being used to draw the twisted magic within the wraiths into whoever bears the mark."

"Draw unto," I murmured.

But why? What would be the reason for doing such a thing?

I stopped breathing for a few seconds when I connected the dots.

Slowly, I said, "If your theory about the wraiths is correct, and they're actually Unseelie trapped in their shadow forms… then they'd likely want their original forms back. They'd want to undo their magic."

Roth shrugged. "Or at least fix it enough that they can easily move between forms, which was likely their primary goal when they worked whatever spell they'd crafted."

"This is all still speculation. Absolutely *terrifying* speculation," I added. "But still speculation. We don't have enough proof to take this to Carmilla yet, let alone the queen and her consort."

"I know," Roth said begrudgingly. "But I *also* know that I'm right about this. We just have to keep researching and fill in the gaps."

"Maybe Samara and Vail will find something that will help." Assuming they didn't murder each other.

But I instantly dismissed the thought. Samara never returned Vail's hatred. She went back and forth between acting like she couldn't care less about him to being annoyed by his very existence, but there was never any hatred on her end.

If anything, I thought it was the opposite. Samara cared about Vail, and his hatred hurt her.

"Did y'all miss me?" Samara asked as she pushed the double doors wide open, a triumphant grin spread across her face.

"You found something," I said hopefully.

If the trip had been a bust, she likely would have stalked back in here with a pissed-off expression. Samara could control her emotions when necessary—usually, anyway—but it cost her.

Outside of delicate conversations and negotiations, she wore her emotions plainly for all to see.

"Whatever you found better not be covered in grime the way you are," Roth snarled. "And your ass better not take one step further in my library until you've cleaned up."

Samara shot Roth a playful look before dramatically raising one foot in the air and taking a step forward. One of the dark ribbons that Roth wore around their forearm shot forward like a whip and slapped Samara across the thigh before drawing back and preparing to strike again.

I laughed as Samara yelped and jumped back… straight into Vail, who had just crossed the threshold.

She bounced off his chest and stumbled forward, but he instinctively grabbed her around the waist to steady her before dropping his hands as if he'd been burned, a hard expression on his face.

I thought I'd seen something else there, but whatever it had been was gone before I could tell what it was.

The amused expression that had been on Samara's face from Roth's ribbons instantly fell, and I found myself hating Vail for it.

I shook my head, trying to focus on what mattered. "What did you find?"

Vail held out a leather satchel, and I rose to take it from him. The instant I did, I felt the pull of magic. As if in a trance, I untied the bag and lifted out a smooth stone the size of my palm with an etching of the lunar moon.

The same symbol that marked the left side of my neck.

"There are two other stones inside," Samara said from where she still stood at the entrance to the library. "They bear the markings of the Velesians and the Furies."

I stared down in wonder at the stone before walking over to the table where Roth waited and set it down in front of them. They immediately snatched it off the table and clutched it in their hands with their eyes closed, no doubt trying to understand the potent magic dripping off of it.

I reached into the bag and pulled out another stone, admiring the glossy black exterior.

If these were used for the ritual the humans had performed to make us all Moon Blessed—and I didn't know what else it could be—then they were centuries old. Yet the stones still gleamed brightly, and the lunar symbol remained a vibrant red, as if the blood had just been painted on it. My brows furrowed.

"How have we never found these before?" Roth said, eyes still closed in concentration.

"The first and second generations were concerned with surviving," Vail said with a shrug. "The Velesians might have regained their humanity before the rest of us, but they've always felt the pull of the wild in their souls. Most of their time was spent hunting down monsters in their territory and carving out a safe place to live."

"Maybe the wraiths have been hunting for these ritual stones longer than we thought," Samara mused. "There have to be countless human settlements that have been abandoned for one reason or another. We only started really building the outpost towns in the last few decades, and when possible, we use old Fae towns."

"Leaving all the ritual stones at the human towns ripe for the taking," I finished with a thoughtful nod.

"We just need to figure out why the wraiths would be interested in these stones to begin with," Samara said, fatigue touching her features. I could only imagine how exhausting the trip had been.

"Why don't you go and get cleaned up, and then Roth and I can tell you what we found?" I suggested.

"That sounds nice," she said, flashing me a relieved smile.

I fought to keep from showing what that smile did to me as I nodded curtly. "I'll have some food brought up as well."

"Thank you, Alaric," Samara said before shooting an amused glance at Roth, who was still doing their weird communion with the ritual stone. "Make sure to set up the food away from the books, lest our dear Roth get upset over their books being in danger."

"If you keep up that sass," Roth replied casually, "I'll show you just what my blood ribbons can do."

"Promises, promises," Samara sang as she exited the library.

My lips quirked up into a smile that froze in place when I caught Vail's glare. I didn't see Vail all that often since he was gone for months at a time, but we'd always had a good working relationship. Though, I suspected that might change with Samara being back and my working closely with her.

I added it to the list of reasons why Samara was a complication in my life and why things had been far simpler at House Harker before her return.

CHAPTER TWENTY-ONE

—

Samara

I STRETCHED my arms up and arched my back as I tried to loosen my body after hours of sitting in the hard wooden chair. The nice cushy lounger by the window was calling to me, but after staying up until almost sunrise pouring over books after getting home yesterday, I suspected I would fall asleep for a late afternoon nap if I settled in that chair.

Just because Moroi could operate on very little sleep didn't mean I enjoyed only getting a few hours of it.

Alaric was attending to some House Harker business today. We'd discussed it this morning over tea, and we'd both agreed that since he had more knowledge and experience with the current day-to-day workings of the House, it made sense for him to handle it and me to continue helping Roth.

It bothered me a little, though. I wanted to be able to help run the House in every aspect, and I felt like I was failing by not being able to do everything.

I knew it was foolish of me to think like that, but I couldn't help it. After failing so spectacularly at House Laurent, I wanted to prove to Carmilla that I was worthy of being her Heir and remaining at House Harker.

I sighed, desperately craving more tea and a cushier seat, but all the books had been laid out on the table and Roth kept snatching them randomly while mumbling to themself. When I'd attempted to take one book that they hadn't looked at once all morning, I'd received a look that froze me in place and made me immediately drop back down in my seat.

Just as I was about to take a break and go chug an entire pot of tea in the kitchen, away from Roth's judging eyes, the blue gem on my ring glowed.

Rynn. Relief flowed out of me, and the tension I'd been carrying since she'd announced her insane plan finally eased. I held my finger over the glyph on the ring and spun to face the center of the room. A second later, her shadowy form appeared.

"Rynn!" I bolted upright, startling Roth, who hadn't even noticed Rynn appear. "Are you okay?"

"I'm fine," she said in a clipped tone. "I told you I would be fine. The trip was a bust. I didn't find anything."

I eyed her carefully. It was hard to tell, given that she was nothing more than a shadow, but her shoulders seemed hunched inward. I glanced down at her hands and saw that her fingers were constantly curling in and out, like they did when she was fighting off a shift.

Something had happened, and she was lying to me about it. First Cali, now Rynn. My temper flared.

"Rynn—" I started, but she cut me off with a wave of her hand.

"I can't talk right now. I just wanted to let you know that I was okay and that I hadn't found anything. We'll catch up soon, I promise."

With that, she vanished from sight, and anger and concern warred within me.

This behavior was something that I'd expect from Cali, but

not from Rynn. What the hell had happened to rattle her so much? And why was she hiding it from me?

I sucked in a breath, ignoring the stab of pain in my chest.

"Are you going to detonate again?" Roth asked in a bored tone. "Because I could do without the screaming you did last time."

"No." I forced myself to exhale before calmly returning to my chair. "I'm still pissed off, but at least I know she's safe. Last time, I flipped out because I was both pissed off and scared out of my mind that my friend was going to land herself in serious trouble."

Roth nodded. "Understandable. Still, I appreciate you not losing your shit in my library this time."

"*Your* library?" I smirked at them.

"Any library I'm in is my library."

"Of course it is." I rolled my eyes. "Do you want tea or anything? I'm going to take a break and head to the kitchen."

They waved me off, and I headed downstairs.

After drinking what was probably an unhealthy amount of tea and devouring at least half a dozen honey rolls, I headed back up to the library with a much clearer head.

I'd figure out sometime in the next month to get my two besties here in person. They'd find it a lot more challenging to lie to my face, and if they tried it, I'd just tackle them to the ground and beat it out of them.

Well, I'd do that to Rynn. Cali could kick my ass, so I'd have to figure out a different approach.

Roth was leaning over the table when I walked in, a fierce scowl in place and a few stray hairs broken away from where the rest had been swept back, falling around their face. The deep red was such a striking contrast to Roth's pale skin. They really were striking, even when they did have such a murderous look on their face.

I barely managed to hold in my laugh because I did not want that look redirected at me.

Instead of taking a seat, I stepped around the table to peer over their shoulder. *"Bâm m ḅâchà qe qâ dam,"* I read the phrase out loud. "The flowers remind us of home."

Roth went rigid before slowly twisting around and gazing up at me. "What did you just say?"

I looked at them in confusion. "I was just reading the phrase you were pointing at?" I had no idea why I phrased it like a question, but I didn't understand why Roth was looking at me the way they were. Like I was interesting. Roth never looked at anything or anyone like that. Well, other than books.

They narrowed their eyes. "You said the Unseelie part, and then you said the translation. Did you already know it?"

"No?" I said slowly, still so confused.

"Then how did you know what it meant?" they pushed, leaning further into my space. I swallowed as the green in their hazel eyes started to spread.

"Because I can read and speak Unseelie?" Why the hell was I saying everything like it was a question?

"Since when?" they asked with something in their tone I couldn't quite figure out.

"Since I was a kid." I moved to stand next to Roth, leaning back against the table. "My mom used to always read me bedtime stories in Unseelie. Whenever we were alone, we'd usually speak in Unseelie, too. She thought it was a fun game. I can read and speak both of them, although I'm a little better with Seelie." I frowned at Roth. "I don't understand why you're so surprised by this. We've been reading through all these books for days, so you had to know what I was doing. And you haven't had any problem reading the Unseelie texts."

They shook their head. "I'm not fluent. I'd been stuck on that damn phrase you just read for over an hour. I've had to use translators for the past few days, which is why it's taking forever. You always spent so much time on one book, I thought you were just slow at translating."

My cheeks flamed red. "I would get distracted sometimes and read the books cover to cover. It's not my fault!" I said quickly, flinging my hands up in defense. "You dropped a bunch of Unseelie books that I'd never read before in front of me. I tried to just scan them, looking to see if they had any relevant information, but sometimes they'd be really interesting, and I'd get drawn in!"

"I can't believe you never told me you could read or speak Unseelie!" they yelled back.

"I used to read Unseelie poetry next to you in the library at Drudonia! I'd even say the poems out loud sometimes as I read along! How could you never notice?"

"Well, I never paid you any attention back then because I thought you were just a pretty face! I didn't know you actually had a brain!"

"Rude." I crossed my arms and glared at them before repeating Roth's words in my head. My expression softened before I asked tentatively, "You think I have a pretty face?"

Roth looked at me like I was an idiot.

"I'm not blind, Samara." They tilted their head to the side, causing the light to glint off the dangly earring they always wore. "Can you still recite the poetry from memory?"

"Yes." I gave Roth a curious look as they rose from their chair and moved to stand in front of me, their thighs brushing against mine. "I picked up some new ones this week," I offered.

"Tell me."

"Kov bâm reb qâ qa." The words rolled off my tongue and Roth's hazel eyes darkened, making the dark umber-orange fractures of their eyes stand out like fire in the night.

"Say it again," they breathed out.

"Kov bâm reb qâ qa," I repeated, not taking my eyes off Roth as heat spread through me.

The dark red ribbons on Roth's forearms slowly unwound, and I watched as they brushed against me with fascination, remembering what it felt like in my dreams when they'd touched me.

While I was distracted, Roth seized the opportunity to shove me down onto the table, the ribbons barely managing to push the books to the side.

"Careful with the books!" I cried out as one slipped off the table, only to be caught by one of Roth's blood ribbons.

My concern quickly faded as one of the ribbons brushed the side of my face before sliding down to graze the top of my breasts, and I let out a surprised exhale. Wherever the ribbons touched me, I could feel the warm, lingering traces of blood magic.

And I desperately wanted to feel more.

"Don't worry about the books," Roth said smoothly as they ran a hand down my thigh, causing my flesh to shudder with anticipation. "Just worry about reciting that poetry."

"What exactly are you going to be doing while I do that?" I asked, arching an eyebrow at them in challenge.

The ribbons snapped to wrap around my arms and pulled them to the side, pinning me down on the table. More slipped around my thighs and pulled them apart as Roth bunched up my dress. Excited, breathy pants slipped from my lips as elation filled me. This was already so much better than my dreams.

"I'm going to play with myself while eating out this lovely cunt of yours." They spoke in such a matter-of-fact way that it took my mind a second to process what they'd said.

"Fucking hell, Roth." My thighs quivered as I felt myself get even wetter.

When Roth paused upon lifting my dress, I raised my head to meet their gaze. "Are you good, Samara?" they asked.

"Yeah, Roth," I breathed out. "I'm good, about to be really fucking good."

"Your flirting at Drudonia would have gone a lot better if you'd revealed this talent of yours back then instead of using all those ridiculous pickup lines." They smirked and then tossed my dress up before tugging at my panties. A silver knife flashed, and I felt them pull the fabric away. "Let's hear that poetry, Heir."

"Kov—" A cry tore out of me, cutting me off as Roth brazenly licked straight up my pussy before sucking on my clit. There was such a demand in their movement that I came within seconds. Then they teased my clit while I trembled beneath them before pulling away.

"I can just as easily use these ribbons for punishment," Roth warned as the end of one ribbon rose and snapped against my thigh.

I swore at the stinging sensation and pulled at the ribbons pinning my arms to the table, but then Roth ran one finger across my dripping center before circling my clit again.

My swears turned into whimpers as pleasure quickly overtook the pain.

"Be a good girl," they said soothingly.

Fuck me. I was never going to look at Roth or those damned ribbons the same way again. I licked my lips and started again. *"Kov bâm reb qâ qa."*

Roth's tongue slipped into my pussy, and their finger continued to play with my clit. My thighs strained, causing the ribbons to dig into my skin, and my pulse quickened at the pressure.

I'd never really played with being restrained, only dreamed about it. The real version was turning out to be quite fun.

"Bâm beduv challs ḅà dov," I breathed out, fumbling over some of the words as Roth slipped two fingers inside of me, dragging them in and out. The wet sounds of my pleasure accentuated my words. Roth moaned against my core, and I

wondered if they were fucking themselves as well. The thought made me burn even hotter.

A whimper slipped from me when they pulled their fingers out and tauntingly traced them around my inner thighs.

I raised my hips as much as I could, but the ribbons only tightened and pulled my thighs further apart. Another ribbon ran across my throat, squeezing it for a few seconds, and I gasped when it released me before I pushed out the next verse.

"Hom àlche d ḫà medm," I moaned out the last word as Roth thrust their fingers back inside me and bit down on my swollen clit.

Their movements became harder and faster, and I knew they were building towards their own orgasm.

"Hom bab' m̀ùl—" A scream tore from my throat as one of Roth's fangs pierced me and they sucked hard. I'd never been bitten down there before, but the pain and pleasure wrapping together was one of the best things I'd ever experienced in my life.

The orgasm ripped through me, and I felt Roth scream out theirs at the same time.

My body strained against the ribbons as delicious trembles ran through my muscles. Then Roth moved until they were perched on the desk next to me, gazing down at me with blazing eyes.

"The last line, Heir," they demanded as they lazily swirled one finger around my poor, oversensitive clit while their other hand was still buried between their own legs.

"Hom bab' m̀ùl ḫà ḫâm gàtdi," I said in a husky tone.

"Good girl," they murmured and pulled their hand from their thighs to trace my lips. I opened my mouth and Roth slipped their fingers in as I greedily sucked them clean, enjoying the taste of their pleasure on my tongue.

It was at that exact moment that the library doors burst open. The silencing spell had been in place, but we'd never bothered locking the doors because nobody ever came in here except for us… and Alaric. Whoops.

"I think I have an ide—"

Alaric froze as he took in the sight of me sprawled out across the table full of books, Roth's ribbons still holding me in place and their fingers still in my mouth and between my legs.

"Damn it, Sam!" Alaric yelled. "Why can't you ever lock the fucking door?!"

CHAPTER TWENTY-TWO

—

Samara

ALARIC AVOIDED the library for two whole days. When he did eventually return, he very dramatically knocked before entering.

I briefly pondered letting out some fake moans to mess with him but decided against it, only because we truly needed the help.

Now that Roth knew I could read Unseelie, they snapped at me whenever it became clear I was caught up in what I was reading and forced me to scan the text instead. We'd gotten through all the books on the table and were now going through the ones that we'd pulled out as potentially helpful again.

Roth's previous lamenting about the flowery language used in the texts was spot on. I often had to read passages over and over again, not because I didn't know what the words meant, but because I had no idea if what I was reading was actually poetry or if they were just wrapping up the potentially horrifying usage of a spell in pretty words. It was exhausting.

On the plus side, I'd found more poetry books, and Roth had been very enthusiastic to show me their appreciation.

Those fucking ribbons of theirs were really useful for

getting into some fun positions. I'd even distracted them this morning with my fingers and, based on the breathy moans as I finger-fucked their pussy, I'd done a good job.

It was my first time playing with a pussy that wasn't mine, and I'd been a little nervous that I wouldn't do it right.

I knew what made mine happy, but I had no idea what Roth liked. Given Roth's to-the-point attitude about everything though, I assumed they would have been quick to give me commands if I was doing it wrong.

I bit my bottom lip as a smile blossomed across my cheeks. Kieran had told me that he wanted me to have fun and explore what made me happy, and Roth made me happy.

They were absolutely not a cuddler, though.

When I'd asked in my best flirty coy voice if they wanted to come to my room last night, they'd just looked at me puzzled and said, "Why? You can fuck me here well enough."

I missed Kieran. He'd cuddle the shit out of me.

"Why do you have that stupid look on your face?" Alaric snapped.

"Not everyone is determined to be as pissy all the time as you," I snapped back, and then, because I was a goddamn adult, I stuck my tongue out at him.

The corners of Roth's mouth tilted up the tiniest amount, which for them was like a full-blown smile.

I'd decided that we were keeping Roth, even after all this was over. Which, hopefully, it would be soon. I was fairly confident that if I just kept bringing in new books and read Unseelie poetry out loud while they devoured my pussy, they'd be content to stay here.

Maybe I could convince Carmilla to build a bigger library with a dedicated poetry section...

The red gem on my ring glowed brightly, pulling me out of my lust-filled mind. Cali. Finally. The old human settlement she'd gone to inspect had been much more remote than either of the ones Rynn and I had visited.

A mix of concern and annoyance flickered through me as I held a finger over the ring's glyph.

I hadn't heard anything from Rynn since she'd dropped in a couple of days ago. It was unlikely, but maybe Cali would have some idea as to what was going on with our furry friend.

I blinked when Cali appeared in the library. She was still made of nothing but shadows, but there was more detail visible than usual. Normally, her wings were wispy shadows behind her, but now they were fully visible. Even the strands of her hair were more defined.

"Did you improve the shadow projection spell?" I rose and stepped closer as my eyes continued to scan her and pick out more details. "This is incredible…"

"Hi, Cali! It's so nice to see you! I'm glad you made it to the middle of nowhere in the freaking badlands okay!" Cali said in a deep voice with an exaggerated, husky tone that I assumed was supposed to be me. I narrowed my eyes at her as she continued. "Why, thank so much for asking about my welfare and greeting me so nicely, Sam!"

Roth sighed. "So, Cali hasn't changed at all then?"

I snickered as Cali leaned to the side to peer around me at where Roth was still seated at the table. They'd never hated each other the way Alaric and I had, but it was hard to find people who were more polar opposites than Cali and Roth.

"Oh." Cali's wings deflated a little. "Hi, Roth."

I rolled my eyes "Hi. I'm glad you're okay. Sorry for not saying that right away, but your fancy new shadows threw me off."

Cali shrugged, and I marveled at how well I could see the movement right down to the muscles flexing in her arms. "Just been practicing and fine-tuning a bit is all."

My brows started to furrow, but I forced them to smooth out. There was something Cali wasn't saying.

I didn't know if it was because Roth was here or because she wasn't ready to talk about it yet. All I knew was that even though this seemed harmless, it would be yet another thing that made Cali terrifying to everyone else. Especially to the other Furies.

"Did you find anything useful?" I asked, trying to focus on the problem at hand. Cali could explain her upgraded shadow form when we were alone, and damn it, she *would* explain it to me.

"Not at the human settlement. There was very little left of it, and with how exposed it was to the elements, it's hard to say if the wraiths had been there and picked it over or not." She glanced over her shoulder, eyes focusing on something I couldn't see before turning back to me. "But I found something else. While I was flying back, I passed an old temple that had been built into the side of a mesa. I've seen it before and explored it a little when I was a kid. Pretty sure it was built by the Unseelie."

"You know of an Unseelie temple?" Roth suddenly came to life like a monster smelling blood in the night. "And you didn't tell anyone?!"

"It's in the badlands." Cali rolled her eyes. "If I told someone, they would have made me lead an expedition there, and I checked it out. There's nothing there. Or... at least... I didn't think there was anything there..."

Roth looked like they were contemplating how one would go about murdering a shadow, so I quickly asked, "Did you see something there this time?"

Cali dipped her head slowly in a deep nod. "There are wraiths there, but not like any wraiths I've ever seen before. They're more solid and they look..." She paused, again looking over her shoulder. "Sam, they looked like Fae. At least like the sketches I've seen of them in books."

"Holy shit," I breathed out as my eyes snapped to Roth. "You were right."

"Right about what?" Cali said quietly but urgently.

"Cali," I said slowly. "Where are you right now?"

"On top of the mesa."

"Get the fuck away from there!" I snarled. "We don't know what they're capable of! You can't be there by yourself!"

"They can't fly," she said dismissively before tilting her head. "I don't think they can, anyway. The wraiths only glide. Could the Fae fly?"

"I'm going to slap the shit out of you next time I see you," I growled. What the fuck was with all my friends taking unnecessary risks all of a sudden?

Seeing that I was genuinely freaked out and pissed off, Cali reached out and placed her hand on my arm, and I felt it. She yanked her hand away, but it was too late.

"What the fuck?" I whispered in shock.

Cali's shadow form could never physically interact with anything or anyone, but I'd felt her hand on me just now. It'd only been for a second... just like how wraiths could only become corporeal for a few seconds at a time.

"Something's happening to me," Cali said quietly. "It's been happening for a while, but being around these wraiths... or Fae... whatever they are... my magic is changing."

"How?" I asked, trying to stay calm and not have the proper freak-out like I wanted to. "How is it changing? Are you..."

Losing yourself? I couldn't say the words out loud. As if saying it would make it real.

Cali moved closer to me, her hands hovering over mine. "I'm not losing myself," she promised. "Like I promised you and Rynn all those years ago. You both hold my heart, and I will never leave you."

My throat was too tight for me to say anything, so I jerked my head in a nod.

"Whatever is happening to me, we can sort that out later," she said calmly. "Right now, I think we need to figure out what the hell these wraiths are up to and why they look the way they do."

"How many are there?" Alaric asked, coming to stand beside me. "Does it look like they're just passing through?"

"Three of them," she said. "And I think they live here. I kept an eye on them all night. They spent most of it in the front part of the temple, but I couldn't get close enough to hear them."

"They were speaking?" Alaric exclaimed, and I shared his surprise. The wraiths didn't really speak, they only let out strange whispering sounds and occasional shrieks.

Cali nodded. "I couldn't tell what language, but given that they look Fae, I'm assuming it was Unseelie or Seelie." Her gaze flicked back and forth between the three of us. "None of you seem that surprised that they're Fae. I was sure as fuck surprised."

I looked at the map that we'd hung up and did some mental calculations before clearing my throat and turning my attention to Roth and Alaric. "Fill Cali in on what we found. I'm going to find Vail."

Alaric's upper lip curled in distaste. "There's another horse ride in my future, isn't there?"

"You can stay here if you want," I tossed over my shoulder as I headed for the hallway. "But I'm going to that temple and getting some damn answers."

An hour later, we were riding hard on our way to Cali. She promised to let me know right away if the wraiths went on the move.

The temple wasn't far from the border between Furie and Moroi territory. Unfortunately, we basically had to ride all the way across our land to get there. We had no idea whether the wraiths truly lived at the temple or if they would be leaving soon, so time was of the essence, which was also why we wouldn't be stopping except to change horses at some of the outposts.

Zosa hadn't been happy about me leaving her behind, but I wasn't going to leave her behind at an outpost, even if I could pick her up on the way back. I also selfishly didn't want to risk her life.

We'd be traveling through the night, and the horses were primary targets for most of the monsters that prowled the forests.

I squinted against the setting sun that was currently blinding me. There was less than an hour until sunset. It'd be dipping behind the trees soon enough, and then I'd at least be able to see better.

The black gelding I was riding skittered to the side, and Alaric's grip around my waist tightened.

My brows furrowed. "You okay back there?"

I urged the gelding to move a little faster but didn't let him break out of the canter he currently maintained. He wouldn't last long at a full gallop, and we still had a ways to go before we could swap out for fresh horses.

Hopefully, my next one wouldn't be so skittish, because things were only going to get hairier as night fell.

"I don't understand why I couldn't have my own horse," Alaric griped even as he started to lean to the left and I had to reach back and shove him upright.

"Kieran would be really mad at me if I let you get hurt," I

said over my shoulder. "And we both know you would get hurt if you had your own horse. We should rotate riding into our archery practice."

"*Our* archery practice? You're the one who crashed my training. You don't get to dictate what I do."

I resisted the urge to shove my elbow back and knock him off the horse. He wouldn't be that seriously injured from falling off, but it would slow us down, and he'd no doubt tell Kieran… who wouldn't be happy with me.

I silently regretted not convincing Alaric to stay behind and watch over the House while I was gone, but he'd been adamant that he'd taken care of all urgent matters and that everything else could wait until we were back.

If I'd known he was going to be this pissy on the ride, I would have found a way to leave him behind and just deal with his anger when we got back.

Vail pulled his horse back to a trot, and I did the same, maneuvering the gelding until we were riding side by side as Nyx joined us.

"Something wrong?" I asked, keeping my voice low. Not that it really mattered with how loud the horses were.

"No," Vail said, "but we have another twenty miles to go before we reach the next outpost, which means we'll be in the dark for the last portion of that. I want to reserve as much of the horses' energy as possible so that if we have to run later, they won't falter."

"Right," I said, barely managing to keep the tremor out of my voice.

If we rode round the clock with minimal resting, we should be able to reach Cali in three days, but that meant two nights out in the forest. We'd hopefully reach the temple on the afternoon of the third day, so we'd have at least daylight to our advantage then.

"It'll be fine, Samara," Nyx reassured me. "Vail and I have

spent plenty of time out at night. The horses can outrun almost anything."

"*Almost* anything?" Alaric asked.

With his chest plastered against my back, I could practically feel him vibrating with tension. I shot Nyx a look. They damn well knew they could have phrased that better.

They gave me an unrepentant look and urged their mount forward. "I'm going to scout up ahead while we still have some daylight left."

"We'll be fine, Alaric," I said with a confidence I didn't entirely feel. "Vail knows what he's doing."

This seemed to relax Alaric enough that he no longer had a death grip around my stomach. Small victories.

I didn't miss Vail stiffening slightly at my words, as if he was surprised that I had such confidence in him, but despite our problems, I didn't doubt Vail's skills at all. He'd spent most of his life traveling these lands, and he was still alive to tell the tale.

"What do you think Kieran is doing?" I asked, trying to keep Alaric's mind off the ever-darkening sky.

"Don't you mean *who* he's doing?"

His words struck a sharp blow just as he intended, and I clenched my jaw against the pain. I'd forgotten with all the camaraderie we'd built up over the last couple of weeks that no one was as capable of wounding me with his words as Alaric.

He had the advantage of knowing me well enough to strike at my weak points, and Kieran was very much my weak point.

I concentrated on the feeling of the horse moving beneath me and the reins made of braided rope in my hands, and gradually, the pain ebbed.

The doubt remained, though. Was it selfish of me to want both Roth and Kieran but not want to share them with anyone else? I hadn't even broached the topic with Roth, but I was fairly confident that, unless someone else walked into that library sprouting Unseelie poetry, I had them to myself for now.

But Kieran was… well… he was gorgeous and well-liked by everyone. I knew that he had lovers in basically every House across Moroi territory. Moons damn him. He probably had lovers in Furie and Velesian territory, too.

He said he only wanted me, but what if he changed his mind while he was away? Would he really turn down an invitation to someone else's bed?

I continued to stew in my self-doubt as we traveled on in silence, only vaguely aware of the rising tension between Vail and Alaric.

"I'm sorry," Alaric blurted out. "That was a cruel thing to say."

"It's fine," I said stiffly, still too absorbed in my own fucked-up head to say anything else.

"Alaric was being a dick," Vail said sharply. "Everyone knows how Kieran feels about you. That boy is stupidly loyal. Even to those who don't deserve it." I inwardly flinched but before I could respond, Vail kicked his horse into a canter, leaving us behind.

"Are you sure you're okay with traveling with him at night?" Alaric asked quietly. "I realize that you and I have our problems, but I'm pretty sure that Vail would be happy to see you dead."

I stared after Vail's retreating form, mulling over Alaric's words. "At least I know where I stand with him so I can watch for his knife in the dark."

CHAPTER TWENTY-THREE

—

Samara

"Easy, boy," I quietly soothed the dark bay gelding as he danced nervously beneath me.

He'd been fine when we'd left the outpost hours ago after swapping out our mounts, but something had been unsettling him for the last few miles. Vail's and Nyx's mounts were also tense, but they were both large draft horses who weren't as inclined to panic.

Still, the horses were clearly sensing something we weren't. When I voiced my concerns to Nyx, they didn't seem all that worried.

"All kinds of beasties prowl the forests at night," they said simply. "Most of them aren't a threat to us, but they would happily snack on the horses if they could. As long as we don't leave the horses unattended, the less dangerous predators will leave them alone to find easier prey elsewhere."

"Unfortunately, the horses tend to draw in the more lethal monsters," Vail said. "They've learned that horses usually have riders." He eyed my gelding when it snorted loudly again. "I'd been hoping we'd procure quieter horses for this portion of the ride."

"Is there another outpost we can go to and switch to a quieter mount?" Alaric asked.

He'd been holding on so tightly around my waist that I was pretty sure I'd have bruises tomorrow. I couldn't bring myself to say anything though because I knew he was just nervous about our situation… plus, I kind of liked having his grip on me like that.

Vail shook his head. "Not without going far out of our way. There's not much in this area; all of our strongholds are either further north or along the coast. No reason to have outposts where nobody travels, and it's too dangerous to grow crops."

"Why don't we pick up the pace for a bit?" I suggested. "This boy is wasting energy prancing around. Might as well let him run."

Alaric let out a low groan but didn't disagree.

"We'll let them canter for the next few miles and then pull back," Vail said as he scanned the woods around us. "Make sure to keep them under control. We can't afford for anyone's mount to get spooked and take off from the group. I'll lead. Nyx will take the rear." His eyes fell on me then. "Stay between us, Samara."

"Will do." I looked over my shoulder. "Ready?"

Alaric adjusted his grip, and I winced as his fingers dug into my hips. "Yes."

Vail's dapple grey mare broke into a canter, and I loosened the reins enough for my gelding to follow after them. He tugged at the reins and tried to break out into a gallop, but I firmly held him back.

The echoes of Nyx's horse came behind us, and my heart started to race as we continued our fast pace down the trail. The horses had been loud before, but now every time their hooves struck the ground, it sounded like thunder to my ears.

The miles flew by, and gradually my tension eased. It didn't completely disappear—that wouldn't happen until we were safely behind some well-fortified walls—but my heart no longer beat like it was trying to break out of my chest.

Alaric maintained his death grip around me, though. Clearly, he wasn't feeling any less stressed out.

Ahead of us, Vail pulled up his mount, and I halted mine next to him as I looked at what had caused him to stop. Several large trees had fallen across the road, their trunks far too wide for the horses to jump over. We'd have to go around.

Vail hopped off of his horse and handed his reins over to Nyx before going to investigate the trees. My eyes scoured the surrounding forest, and I could see more than a few creatures prowling around in the trees, but most of them were small and harmless. At least to us.

The trees here grew tall and thick, their gnarled roots running along the surface, making the ground uneven. Several large flowers bloomed from where they perched atop their thorn covered stems. A sweet, enticing nectar dripped from their wide, brightly colored petals. I watched as a small furry beast with thick hindquarters and long arms that ended in three curved talons leapt to a branch that stretched over a flower with bright orange petals. A black tongue unfurled from its mouth and swiped at the nectar.

A thick green vine with red-tipped barbs slid up behind the small creature. It sensed the danger at the last possible second and leapt away as the vine struck the branch where it had been sitting. An angry chitter erupted from the trees as it took off to find an easier meal.

Good luck, little fella. Everything in this forest wants to eat you. Including the pretty flowers.

I refocused on the blocked road that Vail was still studying. Something wasn't right about this. The positioning of the trees seemed almost intentional. I forced myself to remain calm even as I wanted to spin my mount around and run in the opposite direction.

"These trees weren't here when we passed this way a month ago," Vail said from where he was crouching at the base of the trunk. "Something chewed through the base at just the right angle to ensure they fell onto the road."

"Kùsu?" Nyx guessed. "We saw signs of them last time, and they're clever fuckers."

Vail grunted in agreement as he rose and walked back to us. He took the reins from Nyx and led his horse over to the side. "We'll have to dismount to lead the horses around. The ground is too rough to ride them through it."

"If this is a trap, shouldn't we turn back?" I asked. "I want to get to Cali as soon as possible, but this seems risky."

"They likely set traps like this throughout their territory," Vail said. "The cut in the tree isn't that fresh, at least a week old. Chances are pretty good that they moved on to a different part of the road to set another trap."

I chewed my bottom lip as Nyx and Alaric dismounted, then slid out of the saddle myself. My thighs and butt ached from riding so hard for the last day. I'd probably be barely capable of walking by the time we finally made it to our destination if we kept up this pace.

The three of us followed after Vail and led our horses through the forest. Nyx took up their post behind us once more.

With our keen night vision, it wasn't too difficult to pick out the best path. I understood why Vail had insisted we lead the horses through on foot. There were several spots that easily could have resulted in broken legs and would have been hard to see from the saddle. Even with our careful pace, the horses still stumbled a few times.

The trees and roots were the densest by the road, so we had to venture deep into the forest to work our way around. It would have been nerve-wracking during the day, but at night, with all of our senses and instincts keyed up… it was an odd mix of exhilarating and terrifying.

The faint heartbeats of dozens of small animals reached my ears, and I knew that if I looked, I would see all kinds of creatures in the night.

Our sense of smell wasn't as good as the Velesians unless blood was spilt. We could sense blood from miles away at night. I felt the call of the night, just as all Moroi, Velesians, and Furies did. Our ancestors had remade themselves beneath the moonlit night sky, and that was where we truly belonged.

Unfortunately, while we were all monsters, we were far from the biggest and baddest, and those apex predators claimed the night as well.

Everyone in our party froze when a loud pop sounded from beneath Vail's horse, causing it to shy to the side a few steps before he got it under control.

"What was that?" I asked, keeping my voice as low as possible.

Vail maneuvered around his horse and picked up its right hoof. I squinted, trying to make out what he pulled off of it.

All I could gather was that whatever it had been was a mossy-green color with bright orange speckles. When he started scanning the forest floor close to where his horse had walked, I handed the reins to Alaric and wordlessly moved a little closer to look as well.

"There," I whispered and pointed towards a large, bulbous mushroom that had the same green and orange pattern from whatever Vail had pulled off of his horse's hoof.

"Shit. Poppers," Vail said gravely. "Clever fucks."

"Damn it, I told you," Nyx cursed. "Their traps have been getting more elaborate. They probably chose that section of the road to block off because they knew these things grew here."

"There are more ahead of us," I said. Now that I knew

what to look for, I could see the brightly colored mushrooms all over the ground ahead of us. There was no way we could avoid them. "Do we need to turn around?"

We waited as Vail stared at the path before us, thinking through all the options. I returned to my mount, who was growing increasingly more restless, and took the reins from Alaric. Horses were very sensitive to our own moods, so I did my best to repress my panic as I soothed him. We were deep in the woods, in the territory of the kùsu, and I very much suspected we had just rung the dinner bell.

"There is a river ahead, less than five miles away," Vail said. "We get to the road as fast as we can, mount up, and run like hell. The kùsu can't swim."

"Alaric, get on," I commanded quickly. "I'll guide the horse, but it will be too slow for us both to mount up once we reach the road. I'll either sit behind you or ride with one of the others."

He stared at me for a moment, clearly not liking this idea, but finally jerked his head in agreement when neither Vail nor Nyx countered my command. I helped him get into the saddle and handed him the reins.

"Grip tightly with your legs. Grab onto the mane if you have to, but *don't* drop the reins," I instructed. "You fall, you die."

Alaric swallowed but did as ordered. I didn't tell him that I wasn't loving this either.

Alaric wasn't a strong rider, and the horse was nervous as hell, but it would run fast and follow whichever horse was in front of it. All Alaric had to do was hang on. Hopefully, I'd be able to mount behind him, but I was pretty sure our horse was on the verge of bolting, so I wasn't willing to bet on it.

I untied the crossbow from the saddle and strapped it to my back. Then I checked to make sure the dagger at my thigh was secure. The chances of either being useful against a kùsu were slim, but I still felt better being armed.

"Everyone ready?" Vail asked, making eye contact with each of us.

We all nodded before Vail pulled his horse forward, and then we picked up the pace as we weaved our way through the forest back towards the road.

It wasn't long before another loud pop sounded, then another. I kept my hands on the reins of Alaric's horse as it began to shy off the path, refusing to let it and Alaric out of my sight. Vail broke out into a jog, and I did the same, pulling the stupid panicking horse along with me.

Just as the road came into sight again, my foot snagged on a piece of root, and I stumbled. The horse yanked its head up, and the reins slipped through my fingers as I fell.

"Sam!" Alaric called out in alarm.

"I'm fine!" I reached back to pull my foot free from the two roots it slipped between. "Go!"

Even if he wanted to stop, Alaric's horse had decided it was done with all of this bullshit and surged forward towards the road. Alaric yelped as he held on, and I prayed the damn horse didn't break a leg in the remaining distance it needed to clear.

My ears picked up the sound of something very large crashing through the underbrush towards us, and terror-fueled adrenaline flooded my system as I frantically tried to pull myself loose.

With one final yank, my foot finally slipped free just as Nyx grabbed me and hoisted me up. We raced towards the road, but I was too late to stop Alaric's horse from leaping into a full-on gallop and sprinting away from us.

"Go!" I screamed at Nyx. "Make sure they reach the river!"

They nodded and smoothly leapt onto their mount and tore off after them. I took one step towards where Vail waited before stumbling back as a massive black form scuttled onto the road between me and him.

Mindless words and whimpers poured out of me at the sight.

I'd seen drawings of kùsu, but that was nothing compared to seeing the enormous insectoid creature in person.

Its body had to be over fifteen feet long, and there were so many fucking legs. There was a reason we named them after the Unseelie word for *death*. If I survived this, I had no doubt this would be the star of my nightmares for years to come.

The kùsu turned in my direction and raised the upper part of its body until it towered over me.

Large black eyes looked at me above foot-long pinchers that could easily snap my body in half. Even if I could reach the crossbow on my back, it would be useless. The bolts would never penetrate the hard carapace that covered its entire body including its underside.

The best I could do would be to shoot out its eyes, but it would be on me too fast. Plus, they could sense vibrations, so even without its eyes it would still hunt me down.

Vail's horse snorted and danced beneath him as his steely grey eyes met mine.

I let out a sharp exhale at the death I saw in them. This was the exact scenario I'd always feared. He didn't have to kill me. All he had to do was not save me.

No one was here to witness it, and the kùsu would probably chase after him and the others once it was done with me. Alaric and Nyx would be witnesses to the fact that we'd wandered into the monster's territory.

"Don't," I pleaded. The reins tightened as Vail pulled the mare back. Away from me. "Please" I tried again, terror overriding my pride about begging Vail for anything.

Despite knowing that he'd craved my death since the night our parents died, I was a little surprised at the sharp pain that echoed through my chest. Part of me always wanted to believe that he wouldn't do it. That he'd be able to get past what I had done that night to save his life.

Something faltered in his cold expression, but I didn't have time to figure out what that meant before the kùsu dove towards me with its pinchers wide open. Instead of running to the side, I lunged forward and tucked myself into a roll.

During the day, I would have been too slow to pull such a move, but beneath the full moon, with my magic running at full speed, I was fast as hell. The kùsu passed over me, its pinchers slamming into the earth where I'd been standing a second ago. I was on my feet and running before it even realized where I'd gone.

Its large body still blocked the path to Vail, and I didn't trust him anyway. So I ran towards the opposite side of the road from the forest we'd traipsed through, where a ridge bordered the road. My feet slid out from under me as I frantically made my way up the slope.

The kùsu let out a high-pitched scream behind me, and I pushed myself to run faster.

"Sam!" Vail shouted.

I ignored him. For all I knew, he could be calling after me to distract me.

The sound of a hundred legs racing over the ground came from behind me. The damn thing was closing the distance between us.

I needed to slow it down. I scanned the area as I kept running as fast as I could. Several trees had fallen up ahead and landed on top of each other. That would have to do.

My muscles burned as I pushed my body to its limit. I could hear the kùsu as it chittered in excitement at closing in on its prey. I dove forward into the fallen tangle of trees, hissing as rocks and branches cut into my skin. The tangy smell of blood filled the air, and I felt a warm line of it running down my arm where a deep gash had been torn open.

I didn't allow myself to stop as I scrambled deeper into the pile of downed tree trunks.

The kùsu crashed in after me, its long body jostling the trees loose and causing them to collapse on top of it. I barely made it out the other side and was scrambling away on my butt as I watched it struggle to get free.

Pinchers snapped closed, barely six inches away from my foot, and I yelped. Everything hurt as I climbed to my feet and ran. I was bleeding from at least a dozen cuts now, some of them quite deep, and a mind-numbing pain struck me every time my left foot hit the ground.

I'd done something to that knee in my mad dash through those logs, and it really wasn't happy about having any weight on it.

I shoved the pain aside as best I could and kept running. The forest sprawled out to my right, but there was nowhere for me to run in there. The kùsu would be faster than me over the uneven footing, and who knew what other monsters were prowling about?

Vail had said there was a river up ahead. I just had to hope I could reach it from this ridge or find somewhere to slide back down to the road.

A loud crash came from behind me as the kùsu finally broke free of the fallen logs.

Because luck never seemed to be on my side, as the ridge abruptly ended.

I skidded to a halt and looked down. It wasn't that far of a drop, maybe twenty feet. I'd never jumped from anywhere this high before, but theoretically, I was pretty sure I would be fine.

A quick glance over my shoulder told me I didn't have much time to debate this. The kùsu would be on me in less than thirty seconds.

I studied the incline. It was steep, but there might be enough of an angle to it that I could run down it? I'd have to either jump far enough to clear the steep slope entirely and risk breaking something on landing, or run down it and just hope I didn't stumble.

The kùsu let out another ear-piercing shriek… and was answered by a second one.

"Are you fucking kidding me?" I looked on in horror as a second kùsu burst out of the woods just ahead of the other one.

"Samara!"

I looked down to the ground beneath me and found Vail there with a foreign expression on his face. Panic.

"Vail!" Surprise slammed into me. He came back for me after all.

You're only in this mess because he left you, the warning whispered in my mind.

I shook my head. It didn't matter. He was here now, and survival came first. Carefully, I inched closer to the ledge while he maneuvered his large horse as close to the ridge as he could.

"Jump!"

With the monsters bearing down on me, I didn't hesitate. I stepped off the ledge and skidded down the incline in a controlled fall, trying to stay on my butt as much as possible.

More jagged cuts tore through my flesh from the sharp rocks and debris, and I hissed in pain but focused only on my descent. As the distance shrank between us, Vail stretched his arm out. I leapt off the incline, grabbing his arm and letting him pull me the rest of the way. I landed hard behind him, the saddle digging into me, and wrapped my arms around his waist.

He urged his mount forward, and the horse clearly needed no further encouragement to get the hell out of here.

The horse leapt forward, and my grip around Vail tightened. I looked over my shoulder just in time to see the long, dark shape of the kùsu skitter down the side of the ridge. Their legs were moving so fast that they were a blur as they tore off down the road after us.

Shit. I'd really been hoping they would decide the chase wasn't worth it once they saw the horse, but the idea of a larger meal seemed to only excite them more.

We were keeping our distance from them, but Vail's mount wasn't built to maintain this type of speed for long. I could already hear his breathing become more labored.

If we didn't get to the river soon, Vail deciding to not be an asshole and come back for me wouldn't matter, and that really pissed me off because I wanted to survive this so I could beat the shit out of him myself.

"They're gaining on us!" I warned Vail.

"It's not much further!"

With every passing second, fear clamped onto me as the distance between us and the kùsu shrank.

We weren't going to make it.

"Hold on!" Vail clamped one large hand over where both of mine were clasped together.

I felt our horse slow its mad dash and it hesitated before the excited twin shrieks of the kùsu closing in on their prey made it leap forward. My stomach flipped as we plummeted through the air, the wind whipping at my face before freezing-cold water surrounded us.

Letting go of Vail, I kicked with my legs and broke the surface, only to dive back under as one of the kùsu came barreling over the cliff, unable to stop in time. I swam away towards the opposite side of the river as fast as I could. When I couldn't hold my breath any longer, I surfaced again.

Vail had managed to get his horse to land and was currently swimming back for me. The kùsu had apparently latched onto the side of the cliff and was desperately trying to pull itself out of the water.

I snapped my head back towards where Vail had left his horse, and relief coursed through me when I saw Alaric and Nyx. They were both soaking wet and shivering, but unharmed.

Vail reached for me, but I slapped his hand away and swam to where the others waited. Alaric ran towards me and helped me out of the water. Now that I wasn't running for my life, the pain from my knee and the cuts covering my body became agonizing.

I gritted my teeth and leaned on him. My teeth immediately started chattering, which somehow made the pain even worse.

"What happened?" Alaric asked as he set me down carefully on the shore, the sand a welcome relief.

"Vail is a piece of shit is what happened!" I spat. "He left me to die."

Nyx shifted uncomfortably as they looked back and forth between me and a glowering Vail. We'd rekindled our friendship, but they'd served Vail, and I knew they looked up to him. The rangers of House Harker would always be loyal to Vail, not me. I'd have to remember that.

"I did no such thing," Vail said coldly. "I was figuring out how to get to you when you stupidly ran off."

"Bullshit!" I hissed.

Alaric held me back when I tried to struggle to my feet, which was probably for the best, because I'm pretty sure I would have fallen flat on my face.

"Figures you'd be ungrateful for me saving your life," he sneered. "Maybe I should have let you die after you ran off like that." We glared at each other for a moment before Vail stalked off, tossing over his shoulder, "I'm going to check on the horses. We'll rest here for an hour, then continue on our way."

Nyx trailed after Vail, and my lip curled in a silent snarl. Fucking Vail. I didn't care what he claimed. I saw the look in his eyes when that kùsu got between us. He was absolutely going to leave me to die.

But he did come back for me. Why?

The pain in my knee ached, drawing my attention away from his retreating form. I'd have to dwell on Vail's odd decision later.

"What do you need?" Alaric knelt next to me, genuine concern in his eyes.

"Nothing at the moment." I winced as I dipped my fingers into the large cut on my arm and then drew a symbol on my knee with the blood.

I chanted the words for a simple healing spell and fought the urge to scratch my knee as the torn tendons and skin pieced themselves back together. This spell might be a life-saving one at times, but I still hated how itchy it made me feel.

Alaric kept a close watch on me as I slowly healed my injuries. Ideally, I could use a top-off of blood after this, but I wasn't going to ask Alaric for that, and I wasn't willing to ask Vail or Nyx either.

"What do you want to do about Vail?" he asked.

"Nothing for now. We still need him." I pursed my lips. "I'll just have to be extra careful to not be in a situation like that again. Vail may not come back next time."

CHAPTER TWENTY-FOUR

—

Vail

I COULD FEEL Nyx's eyes on me as we approached the boundary of Moroi and Furie territory.

They hadn't brought up Samara's accusation at all over the last two days. Not even when we stopped to rest for a few hours at an outpost. Technically, we could all go a week without sleep, but even getting a few hours would help keep us more focused. It was worth the loss of time.

Plus, I needed to set my head straight.

I'd been waiting for an opportunity like that with the kùsu for over a decade.

The few times my sleep wasn't plagued by nightmares, it was filled with wonderful dreams of watching Samara get torn apart by monsters. She'd stopped me from saving my parents. I didn't care what she thought. I *knew* I could have saved them. I should have let her fucking die.

But that look on her face when the kùsu got between us? The moment she knew that I was going to walk away and leave her there?

I'd expected anger, but that wasn't what I saw.

Instead, Samara was hurt by the betrayal.

Despite everything between us and her knowing that I would seize an opportunity like that, part of her still trusted me.

It was that look that had me racing along the ridge, trying to find a way to get to her. I'd left her to die, only to save her minutes later.

That small amount of trust she still had in me was gone now, and I knew I'd never get it back. I told myself that it didn't matter. That next time I got an opportunity like that, I'd take it and leave her to fucking rot.

The more I repeated it in my head, the closer I came to believing it.

I hated the way Nyx looked at me now. They were still loyal, I knew that, but they liked Samara, and I knew they'd looked up to me since joining the rangers. They were a couple years younger than Samara and the youngest of the rangers that made up my usual crew.

Nyx was like a younger sibling to all of us, and like a younger sibling, they put all of us up on high pedestals. And now they had to reconcile the fact that I'd pulled some shady shit, and I felt bad for putting them in that position.

I'd really fucked this up. As soon as we figured out what was going on with these wraiths, I'd head north for a bit. Maybe get permission from the Velesians to run around in their territory. Tensions were high between them and the majority of the Moroi, but I'd always gotten along with most of them fine. Probably because I spent my time in their territory hunting down monsters and never looked down my nose at them the way many of the other Moroi did.

"What's the plan, Marshal?" Nyx asked tightly.

My jaw hardened until my teeth hurt from clenching them together. I couldn't even remember the last time Nyx had referred to me by my title. Only the rangers who didn't normally work with me did that.

This was Samara's fault. She fucked up everything in my life.

"Cali reached out to me while we were staying at the outpost," Samara said from behind us. "She's going to meet us up ahead. She can guide us the rest of the way to the temple."

I heard her mount pick up its pace until it was on the other side of Nyx. This one was calmer than the frantic one she'd been riding the night we were attacked, but it was solid white and painfully stood out, even here where the forest had given way to scrub lands. I was surprised the damn thing hadn't been eaten the first time someone had taken it for a ride outside of the outpost.

"That information would have been nice to know before now, Heir," I growled.

Samara gave me a cool look. "It wouldn't have mattered before. If we started to veer off course, I would have said something, *Marshal*."

"Did she have any updates about the wraiths?" Nyx asked stiffly before I could say anything else.

"You're leaning to the left again," Samara murmured to Alaric. He really was a terrible rider, and after his horse had run away with him the other night, he was even more nervous around them. Samara helped him center his weight again before focusing on Nyx once more. "The wraiths are still in the temple. They haven't left."

"Is she sure they're still there?" Nyx frowned.

"Yeah," she said uncomfortably. "She can feel them."

My eyebrows crept up. "How far inside the temple are they?"

Samara didn't look at me when she answered, but I saw the strain running through her body. Something about Cali's abilities bothered her. "I'm not sure," she said evenly.

Furies were the most sensitive to wraiths and shadow magic, but they usually had to be fairly close to feel them. Cali had been perched on top of a mesa, and the temple was far below. They should have been too far out of her range to sense.

Unease ran through me. I didn't like Samara, but I respected both of her friends. Rynn was smart as hell and would be a huge asset to the Alpha Pack if they could ever figure their shit out, and Cali was an incredible warrior who had saved some of my rangers' asses on more than one occasion.

Most Furies eventually gave into the rage they all carried inside of them and had to be put down, and killing a Furie who had lost themself was no easy feat.

The current generation seemed to be doing the best. They had strict rules in place to keep themselves level.

But Cali had never followed the rules.

She'd seemed fine every time I met her, but now that I thought about it… when was the last time I'd seen her in person? The idea of fighting any Furie made me nervous.

For one, they were our allies. Fighting one of them was similar to fighting a Moroi who had given into bloodlust and become a Strigoi. You weren't fighting some random monster, you were fighting one of your own, and that was not something I ever enjoyed. The last time I'd had to take down a rogue Furie, I'd brought twenty rangers with me and less than half of us walked away from that encounter.

Cali was the most powerful Furie in existence, possibly ever. Between that and the wild cards that were Samara and Rynn, it would be better for everyone if she stayed sane.

A shadow passed over us, causing the horses to skitter to the side. A few seconds later, Cali landed in front of us with silent wings.

In a heartbeat, Samara threw her leg over her horse's neck and practically leapt out of the saddle, leaving poor Alaric to slide forward while frantically grabbing the reins. The Furie grunted as Samara threw herself at her and wrapped her in a tight hug.

"Fuck you for making me worry so much," Samara grumbled into Cali's shoulder, where she was still tightly nestled.

The Furie's leathery black wings stretched around Samara as if they could shield her from the world.

"Missed you too, bestie," Cali murmured.

As Samara untangled herself, the Furie turned her glowing golden eyes on me, and I tensed at the death I saw in them. I guess that answered the question of whether or not Samara had told Cali about what had happened that night.

I gave her a lazy grin as if to say, *"Gonna do something about it?"*

Cali stared at me for a second, and I forced myself to remain calm and not reach for the sword strapped across my back. Not that it would do me a lot of good against Calpyso fucking Rayne.

The Furie was a few inches taller than Samara and had considerably more muscle, but she was still a fraction of my size. But size didn't matter against someone who could wield shadow magic, was wickedly fast with a blade, and could shred your mind if she really cut loose.

Seconds ticked by before the Furie slowly blinked and the burning light in her eyes dimmed a little.

That told me two things. Cali wasn't that far gone if she could rein in her fury so easily, and I would definitely have to watch my back around her from now on. Samara, Rynn, and Cali were as different as three people could be, but the one thing they all shared in common, besides their love for each other, was coldhearted pragmatism.

Death would come for me on silent wings someday, but not while I was still needed. For now.

"Whatever the wraiths are doing, they've moved much further into the temple," Cali said, tossing the long braid of her hair back over her shoulder. The red color was so dark it looked black at night; only in the day could you make out its true deep red tones. "You should be fine to take the horses and leave them out front without alerting them to our presence."

I looked up at the sun arcing across the sky. We still had at least four hours of daylight left, and there weren't nearly as many creatures that called the badlands home the way they did the forests.

"Alright," I agreed. "Lead the way."

After one more pointed glare at me, Cali shot up into the sky. The horses startled at the sudden movement, but luckily—if not surprisingly—Alaric managed to keep his under control until Samara could reach him.

"You want to ride up front this time?" she asked.

He shook his head quickly. "I'd rather you drive."

"Funny." She shot him a teasing smile. "Kieran says the same thing."

"I somehow doubt that," Alaric retorted dryly, the corners of his lips twitching as if he was fighting off a smile.

My mouth twisted in distaste. "Enough messing around," I said sharply. "Let's go."

Alaric awkwardly shifted back so that Samara could mount. As soon as she was in the saddle, I nudged the horse forward, and she broke out into a steady canter. Cali was slightly ahead of us so that we could easily keep her in sight as we made our way across the badlands. After a couple of miles, she veered off the road, and we had to slow our horses as we traversed the deeper sand.

I wiped the sweat from my brow with a grimace. If I never had to come back to the badlands again, it would be too soon. Between the oppressive heat and being out in the open, I hated everything about it. Luckily, we rarely had to come out this way because most of the badlands were in Furie territory, and there was little out here.

It was probably why the wraiths were able to settle in at the temple for so long without being noticed. We were lucky Cali had spotted them.

I'd have to speak with her or one of the Furie elders later about setting up some type of regular scouting party here. I didn't like the idea of wraiths being able to operate underneath our noses like this.

Cali led us a few more miles in, and I had to squint against the sun reflecting off the white sand. It wasn't long before I spotted the enormous mesa rising out of the ground. I'd never been to this one before, but there were dozens of mesas like this throughout the badlands. They also felt strange to me, like they weren't entirely natural.

"Think that's it?" Nyx asked. They'd draped their extra long-sleeve shirt over the back of their head to keep the sun off their neck and shoulders.

"Must be," I remarked. "The mesas are always spread out, so there won't be another one for at least twenty miles."

"Stay away from that prickly-looking tree up ahead," Samara warned.

"Why?" Nyx asked as they guided their lanky chestnut mare a safe distance away from said tree.

I did the same as I eyed it. It was small, only around six feet, but instead of bark, it was covered in short spines that curved downwards. Three short, stocky branches protruded near the top of the trunk, each ending in a bright red, bulbous flower. More thorns surrounded the base of the flower, but these had vivid orange tips.

"Most of the thorns are just to keep animals from climbing up it," Samara explained, "but the ones near the flower with the orange tips? Those ones can shoot out when it feels threatened."

Nyx gave the tree a wary look and then nodded at Samara. "Thanks for the tip."

I wondered if she would have said anything had Nyx not been riding next to me. Probably not.

"How much time have you spent out here?" Alaric looked at Samara curiously. "As far as I know, even the rangers avoid this place."

"We do," I agreed. "There are enough threats in the forests in Moroi and Velesian territory to keep us busy."

Samara casually shrugged a shoulder. "Rynn, Cali, and I have actually spent a lot of time not too far from this exact spot, just a little further north. It wasn't far from Drudonia, and it gave us a place to be away from prying eyes… and high expectations while we studied there."

I remained facing forward even as my eyes slid to the side to glance at Samara. She was riding tall in the saddle, her shoulders relaxed and a serene expression on her face.

It was a lie.

Samara told everyone that she'd agreed to the marriage with House Laurent, and she'd worn that same expression whenever her aunt or best friends had asked about it. Her response had always been the same: "*I am happy to support House Harker in any way that I can.*"

As she got older and more confident, she would crack jokes about how attractive Demetri was and that it wasn't actually a hardship at all. But I remembered coming across a young girl, crying over the graves of her parents and whispering words she'd never utter to a living soul.

"*I don't want to marry him. I want to be more.*"

She hadn't seen me that day, and I'd never once mentioned that I knew her secret.

Not that it mattered anymore. She'd probably sabotaged her marriage in such a way that she knew her aunt would side with her. Samara was nothing if not a long-term strategist.

My lips curled and I slid my eyes back to the temple, which was drawing closer.

She's such a pretty little liar.

"So do you know about the trees from experience?" Nyx asked.

Samara let out a delicate laugh. "You could say that. The three of us used to dare each other to race up the tree and tap the flower and avoid getting a bunch of thorns in the ass."

"That doesn't surprise me in the least." Alaric snorted. "This also explains why you came home that one time and refused to sit down. Carmilla had put on a welcome home dinner for you, and you stood the whole time."

"I remember that," Samara replied with a cringe. "I got cocky and tried to tap two flowers in a row and got an ass full of thorns for my arrogance."

Nyx cackled and even I couldn't keep the barest of smiles off my lips. That was the true danger of Samara. In moments like this, I could almost forget how much I hated her.

CHAPTER TWENTY-FIVE

—

Samara

I POINTED out a few more plants and animals as we made our way towards the mesa where the temple was located. While the badlands weren't my favorite place, there was something about this place that I loved. In moderation, that is. I loved this place in moderation.

Sweat dripped down the back of my neck, and I swiped some of my hair that was stuck to the side of my face away. The sun here was unrelenting. It didn't help that Alaric was plastered to my back, so I had his body heat to deal with as well, but if I asked him to move back a little, he would no doubt lose his balance and fall off. Cali swerved a little more to the west, leading us to the side of the mesa.

"Oh," I breathed out, my eyes widening as I took in the sight. "I've never seen one like this before."

Up close, I could see the veins of amethyst and serpentine running up the side of the mesa walls. The purple and green minerals created mesmerizing patterns against the nearly white stone. I waited for Alaric to dismount and then I did the same before stepping closer to the stone and tracing my fingers along a spiral of eye-catching crystal.

"Maybe this is why they selected this mesa to build a temple," Alaric mused from next to me.

"Perhaps." I tilted my head back so that I could see more of the patterns. "I've seen some of the other mesas and while they're pretty and often have minerals running up them, they're more rugged. This looks too flat and shiny to be totally natural."

"Wait till you see the temple entrance," Cali said as she landed quietly behind us. "The Fae must have used a ridiculous amount of magic to build all of this."

"Why, though?" I asked. "And why here, of all places?"

"Hopefully, we'll find more answers inside," Cali said. "The entrance is around the corner."

We secured our horses using some metal spikes that we shoved into the earth and looped their reins around, and then I fastened the crossbow to the saddle once more. It would be too slow against wraiths, and my aim was just as good if not better with the dagger strapped to my thigh.

Although, if I threw it, I'd be giving up my only weapon.

I frowned. Once we made it back home, I should ask Roth more about the blood magic they used for their ribbons. A dagger that responded to my mental commands could be handy…

"No talking once we're inside," Vail said once the horses were secure. It was still hard to look at him without my blood-lust rising.

The fucker had left me for dead, and now he was acting like nothing happened. I schooled my features into a bland expression while he went through some basic hand signals with us. As long as I focused on the task at hand, I could handle being in Vail's company without attempting to rip his throat out.

Probably. If I stayed *very* focused.

"Remember, our goal is to figure out what the wraiths are

up to," Vail said firmly. "We should avoid confronting them if we can. Even if we outnumber them, wraiths are nasty in a fight."

"And if they don't detect us, we can continue to monitor them and gather information," I added.

Something told me we weren't going to get lucky and just walk in on the wraiths carefully explaining all the details of their evil plan. The longer we could watch them without detection, the more information we could potentially gather.

Cali took point since she was the best among us at detecting wraiths, and Vail followed after her. Alaric and I were next, with Nyx once again taking up the rear.

I exhaled sharply when we turned the corner and I saw the front of the temple. Cali wasn't kidding. It was one of the most beautiful things I'd ever seen. The lower half of the white stone had been cut away, creating an overhang that functioned as a roof for the open space below. A dozen pillars sprung down from the ceiling and spiraled towards the earth.

My fingers quietly ran across one. It was smooth and cool beneath my touch. Lines of jade wound around this one, almost as if they had been coaxed toward the surface. There were no signs of any tools being used to create these, making me wonder if they were all done by magic.

Roth would love this place if I could ever convince them to leave the library and traipse into the badlands.

A few yards behind the columns stood an enormous arched entrance. The sun hung low enough in the sky that it hit the other side of the mesa, leaving this side in shadow.

Trepidation ran through my blood as we took in the darkness that awaited us inside.

We'd be able to see just fine in the dark, but we were entering an unknown space where there was likely only one exit, and at least three wraiths waited for us inside.

As much as it annoyed me to do so, I looked to Vail for

what to do next. If anyone could get us in and out of here alive, it was him.

Silently, he moved forward, and we all fell into step behind him. Once we'd cleared the entrance and taken a few steps into the dark room, he stopped, allowing our eyes time to adjust. A vast open space greeted us, full of more spiraling columns and tables and chairs carved out of the same stone.

Despite how beautiful everything was, the wonder that I felt outside failed to overcome me now. The wraiths were all I could think about. Our sharp night vision would help us navigate, but it couldn't see the wraiths hiding in the shadows. Only Cali would be able to sense them, though most wraiths had encountered Furies before, and they could sometimes trick their senses.

Cautiously, we continued through the room until we reached another doorway. Then Vail raised a fist in the air, the signal for us to stop, and we all immediately halted. Another signal came, this one to wait, before he jerked his head towards Cali, and the two of them proceeded into the next room.

I remained completely still but studied the area while we waited, trusting Nyx to keep an eye on things. There wasn't much to the room, aside from the doorway where Vail and Cali had disappeared through, but I did spot a set of stairs in each corner opposite the entrance.

Curiosity flickered through me, wondering where they led, but I forced myself to stay put.

After what felt like hours but was probably only a few minutes, Vail and Cali returned, both wearing troubled expressions.

I tapped Vail's shoulder, and once his attention was on me, I pointed out both of the stairwells.

He looked at Cali, and some sort of silent conversation happened between them before she shrugged. Vail gave her a pointed look, and she returned a sharp smile.

My eyes bounced back and forth between them, not really having any idea what was going on but taking away some enjoyment at my friend getting under Vail's skin.

Finally, Vail made a decision and gestured for us to follow him as he moved towards the stairs, which, as it turned out, led to balconies running along each side of the room he and Cali had explored. The walls were lined with empty shelves and narrow, arched bridges periodically stretched across the room to connect the balconies.

What had this place been used for? I carefully looked around the walls and the ceiling for clues.

The first room we'd entered had been pitch-black, but this one was dimly lit. Thick lines of what appeared to be gold ran up the walls and across the ceiling, giving off a faint warm light.

I looked around but I didn't see any other lanterns hanging anywhere. Maybe the golden light used to be brighter? Or perhaps there had been lanterns at one point?

I couldn't tell if this had been built by the Seelie or Unseelie, which I thought was a little strange. The fortresses they'd left behind had very distinct styles based on who built them. But here, there were no distinguishing features anywhere. Everything from the shelves to the bridges had been carved out of the plain white stone of the mesa as if it were all one gigantic piece.

Even in the dim lighting, it was magnificent.

Faint voices came from up ahead, and all of us froze. I tried to make out what they were saying, but they were talking too low, and we were too far away. Vail made us move away from the railing so that we hugged the shelves along the wall as we crept forward.

Vail, Nyx, and Cali all remained calm, but I could hear Alaric's and my heart beating loudly. I did my best to soothe myself, trusting the instincts of Cali and the rangers.

As we closed the distance between us and whoever was speaking, it became clear they were using one of the Fae languages. But their voices were too low and raspy for me to understand any of it or tell if it was Seelie or Unseelie.

When it sounded like we were directly above them, Vail halted, and we all stood still with our backs to the wall. He slowly stepped forward until he could see over the railing and then glanced over his shoulder, motioning us forward. I held my breath as I moved towards the railing and peered down.

My heart threatened to leap up in my throat at what I saw. Normally, wraiths were amorphous shadows. They could contort themselves into various shapes and for a split second take corporeal form. In that small window of time, they would rake their claws down our sides or tear out our throats with long, curved fangs.

Fighting them was almost impossible because you couldn't injure them when they were shadows. Only for that split second they were solid.

The wraiths below were nothing like the ones I'd seen before. Even though Cali had told us that these were corporeal, or close to it, I still hadn't really believed it until now. Three figures stood facing each other, deep in conversation. Dark shadows dripped off their forms and contorted their features, but they were unmistakably Fae.

We were right. The Unseelie *had* fucked up and cursed themselves into shadow monsters. But how? And what were they doing here now? Were they waiting for someone?

A tap on my shoulder got my attention, and I turned to face Vail. He gestured for me to get down, and I noticed that everyone else was crouching. I quickly glanced back at the wraiths below. If I knelt down, I'd still be able to hear them, but I wouldn't be able to see them. Though, if they looked up, it was possible they'd see me.

Reluctantly, I silently sank to my knees with my feet flexed on their toes beneath me. It wasn't super comfortable, but it meant I'd be able to spring to my feet in a hurry.

Time ticked onward, and the wraiths continued with their conversation. No matter how hard I strained, I couldn't make out what they were saying. My damn ears felt like they were bleeding from the effort, but the raspy voices were just low enough to be out of my range.

Alaric shifted beside me, nervously looking back towards the stairwell. I desperately wanted to know what he made of all this, but we couldn't risk speaking. I shared his concern, though. We were running out of time. Sunset couldn't be too far off, and we couldn't chance being here at night.

Cali shifted, drawing my attention. Her black wings were wrapped around her shoulders like a cloak, and shadows began to swirl around her. Vail's hand snapped forward to grab her, but he was too slow. On liquid joints, Cali slipped through the darkness until she was perched on the railing in a shadowy corner. The only reason I could even make out her form was because I knew she was there.

She blended into the shadows perfectly as if she was a wraith herself.

Looking at her scared the shit out of me. Not because I was scared of her, but because I was scared *for* her.

Whatever was happening to Cali, I knew frightened her too, because she was watching the wraiths below with a quiet intensity, like they held all the answers she sought.

Which they likely did. They held all our answers, and we couldn't understand a moons-damned word they were saying. While we'd been listening to them the past hour in vain, I realized what was bothering me about their words.

They seemed to be twisted somehow and reminded me of the sounds they made when in their pure shadow forms.

What the fuck are you saying? I thought in frustration. We'd risked our lives coming in here, and aside from seeing with our own eyes what Cali had already told us, we'd gotten no new information.

Suddenly, the wraiths stopped talking. I couldn't see anything from my vantage point, and Vail cut a glare at me which clearly stated to not move. As much as I wanted to see what was going on and further piss off Vail, I didn't move an inch. My preference was to not die, and that was more pressing than anything else.

"Apologies for the delay," a strong, masculine voice announced in our common tongue.

It felt like my heart froze for a moment before painfully starting to beat again. I knew that voice, but it couldn't be him. There was no fucking way someone that important would be meeting with the wraiths.

Vail and Alaric seemed rooted in place before they both swung their heads to look at me and I saw the shock in their eyes. They recognized the voice, too.

The footsteps slowed, and we all very quietly moved forward enough so that we could confirm with our eyes what our ears had already told us. That the son of the Moroi Sovereign had betrayed us all.

CHAPTER TWENTY-SIX

—

Samara

Prince Draven Nacht looked exactly as I remembered him. Sinfully gorgeous. Which, considering how many attractive Moroi I had surrounding me these days, was saying something. But Draven always held a presence about him. Even the dark, loose-fitting clothes he wore tonight did nothing to diminish his tall, muscular build. His black hair with its unusual silver streaks was contained in a tight braid that fell midway down his back.

My fingers tightened around the railing from where I now peered down as Draven closed the distance between him and the wraiths with languid strides. He was even wearing the same easy, confident grin that he always had when he greeted me, as if meeting wraiths in a forgotten Fae temple was just another day in the life of a Moroi prince.

Because of how close my aunt was to the Sovereigns, I'd grown up knowing Prince Draven my entire life.

While I didn't know him as well as I knew those I'd grown up with in House Harker, I never would have suspected him as the Moroi working with the wraiths. He'd always reminded me of Kieran and seemed content to spend his life socializing and being a flirt.

The wraiths' whispery language filled the room, and the charming grin slid off his face.

"You know I can't understand you when you speak like that," he snapped.

I held my breath as the three wraiths stopped talking and stepped back. A fourth wraith, one we hadn't even known about stepped further into the room and I had to swallow the gasp that tried to escape.

While the other three had form, they still seemed to be at least partly made of shadow. This one only had a few wisps of shadow swirling around him.

Everything about him was bright and golden, completely at odds with the shadows trailing in his wake. The wraiths bowed their heads as he walked past them. I committed everything about his appearance to memory. Deep, golden-blond hair. Bronze skin. Tall and powerful build. From my viewpoint, I could only see his face in profile, but he seemed to have strong masculine features and tapered ears.

Definitely Fae, which wasn't surprising since we already knew the other three wraiths were as well. I assumed Unseelie, given what we knew so far.

"Careful, Princeling," the Fae said in a dangerous, low tone. "The shadows pull to us still, and they are not yet strong enough to speak without the shadows intertwining with their words."

"My apologies, Erendriel," Prince Draven said stiffly, the confident mask he wore slipping slightly. "The ride here was long and arduous."

The Fae, Erendriel apparently, studied Prince Draven the way a predator would study passing prey and debate whether they were hungry enough to go for a hunt.

"Of course. The forests are treacherous these days," he said with a sly smile.

Prince Draven's shoulders loosened just a fraction. These two clearly knew each other, but Draven was definitely wary of whoever this Fae was.

Not that I blamed him. I was terrified of him, and he didn't even know I was here. The only things we knew about the Fae were what we had been able to piece together in the books and scrolls that we found, along with what we were able to reverse engineer from the spell castings they'd left behind.

I was intimately familiar with what wraiths could do, though. A shiver ran through me. Did Erendriel possess his Fae magic or wraith magic? With our shitty luck, he had both now.

"Did you bring me what I asked for?"

"Yes," Draven said before quickly adding, "Mostly."

The golden Fae stared at him with a cold, expressionless look, and the Moroi prince swallowed.

"I brought you a dozen Moroi. They think they're guarding the caravan a short distance away. It was all I could bring without raising suspicion among the rangers."

I glanced at Vail and saw nothing but cold fury as he stared at Draven. Technically, Vail had sworn his oath to House Harker, but all the rangers supported the Sovereign House with undying loyalty. I couldn't imagine what he was feeling at this betrayal. Despite our differences, I felt sorry for him. He had placed his faith in the wrong person.

The question was, did the queen and her consort know what their son was up to?

I needed to warn Carmilla as soon as possible. There was no way she was involved in this. My mother had been the only family she'd had left, and the wraiths had killed her.

No matter her friendship with the queen, Carmilla would never agree to helping the wraiths.

"That is not enough."

Shadows rippled from the three Fae, contorting their appearance and making them more wraith-like.

I leaned forward slightly to get a better view. Earlier, the golden Fae said that the shadows still pulled at them. So whatever they were doing to regain their Fae forms wasn't permanent, and these three definitely had a more tenuous grasp on it.

"I can get you more," Draven promised, keeping a close eye on the three Fae. "But we can't keep this up forever. There are only so many Moroi we can sacrifice before we begin to lose power. The Velesians are already sniffing around, and there are some amongst the Moroi who are taking notice as well."

"You assured me that you could handle it. Perhaps I chose my allies poorly." The Fae's expression remained one of icy arrogance but there was no mistaking the threat interlaced with his words.

"It will be handled," Draven said in a clipped tone. "The Alpha Pack is a problem, but soon they'll be too busy dealing with infighting amongst the Velesian packs to do anything else, and I already have plans in motion for the Moroi who are asking questions."

"Good." A chilling smile spread across Erendriel's face. "Let's go see what you brought me."

"They're camped a few miles from here near the border," Prince Draven said. "The guards wearing red sashes are mine. You can take the others."

Rage seethed out of me, and I could practically feel Vail's anger rippling off of him. Alaric and Nyx both wore matching disgusted expressions. I thought of the boy I'd found outside that outpost and wondered if he'd been someone who the wraiths had found themselves, or whether Prince Draven had handed him over like cattle.

We'd suspected that a Moroi was helping the wraiths, but

this was so far beyond what I'd thought was happening. How could Prince Draven turn on his own people like this?

Erendriel turned to face the other three then. "Prepare the ritual. We'll use half to finish your transformations and then bring the rest north."

They whispered their agreements and slipped away.

"How is your supply of the ritual stones?" Prince Draven asked as they headed towards the exit. "We might need to come up with a different strategy for the outpost attacks. Questions are starting to be asked. I was thinking we…"

His words became too faint to hear, and I twisted on my feet as I started to head after them before Vail clasped a firm hand over my arm. I jerked away at his touch, and he gave me a flat look before pointing three fingers at Cali and then gesturing them towards where the prince and Erendriel had gone.

Shadows rippled around her as she shot forward on silent wings after them. My lips twisted into a hard line as I watched her fly away. Rationally, I knew she would be fine, but I didn't like the idea of my best friend going after a Fae with unknown magic.

Once she was gone from my sight, I turned my attention back to Vail, who was gesturing firmly at Nyx while pointing at me and Alaric.

They kept firmly shaking their head at him while their fingers flew through different movements. I only knew the very basic signs that the rangers used, but I suspected that Vail was telling Nyx to get us out of here while he went after the wraiths.

Fuck. That.

The prince said the guards were miles away. This was our chance to see what type of ritual the wraiths were doing to turn themselves back into Fae. While Vail was arguing with Nyx, I slipped towards the rail and leapt over it. A jolt shot through me when my feet hit the floor, but not a sound echoed across the room.

A low growl came from above before Vail swallowed it, and a tiny smirk played across my lips. *Suck on that, Marshal.*

Seconds later, Vail and Nyx joined me, both landing quietly as well. We looked up at Alaric, who peered down at us with a frown. I waved for him to come down, and he glared at me before leaping over the rail into a flip and landing in a kneeling position with one hand raised behind his back.

I rolled my eyes at the showy move even as a part of me found it kind of hot. What other tricks did Alaric have up his sleeve?

Vail headed towards the back of the room, and I shook the dirty thoughts out of my head while I focused on the task at hand. We needed to learn what we could about the ritual and then get out before Erendriel returned.

Another archway appeared along the back wall, this one smaller and more simple in design than the previous ones. Carefully, we crept underneath it and down the hallway as I tried to ignore the growing tension between my shoulder blades. There was no sign of the wraiths anywhere.

It was possible they'd just traveled further into the temple and we couldn't hear them, but I couldn't shake the bad feeling that sunk further into my mind with every step.

The hallway abruptly ended, and Vail stopped. I couldn't see anything past his bulky frame, and when Alaric halted just behind me, I leaned against him slightly, needing something to ground me. As if he felt the same way, he rested one steady hand on my shoulder and the other on my hip. I couldn't pinpoint the exact moment it happened, but somewhere along this journey, our relationship had shifted from rivals and reluctant peers to friends.

I looked over my shoulder as Alaric met my gaze, and I saw trust in his eyes… and maybe something more.

A sound from somewhere ahead of us drew our attention away from each other, and we both leaned to the side, trying to peer around Vail.

From what I could see, there was a small square room. Unlike the previous rooms, however, this one didn't have any columns or seating, but I smelled the stench of blood. Moroi blood. A lot of it.

We need to leave, I thought frantically, but as I reached for Vail's shoulder, Alaric slammed into me, and we tumbled into the room. Two wraiths dropped from where they'd been hovering on the ceiling, and the third hurled Nyx into the wall.

Their body crunched and fell into a still heap as a scream tore out of my throat, and a chilling sound came from the wraiths as they backed us into a corner. Laughter.

We were so fucked.

BEFORE I COULD REACT, Vail pulled his sword free and slashed across the abdomen of the wraith closest to us. I didn't know if was because Vail was so fast or because the wraiths were closer to their Fae form, but his blade bit into flesh. The wraith shrieked as blood and intestine leaked from its stomach.

Bile rose in my throat, but I swallowed it down as I continued backing up towards where Nyx had fallen, Alaric urgently following in my steps.

The wraith Vail had wounded collapsed to the floor and twitched a few times before going still. The remaining two focused cold, black eyes on him. One snapped into shadow and disappeared while the other took a swipe at Vail with elongated claws. He leaned back, narrowly avoiding the strike, and went on the offensive.

I drew the blade from my thigh and stood guard over Nyx, trying to figure out where the other wraith had disappeared to.

I didn't know why they both hadn't turned into shadows. The one fighting Vail was holding its own, but all of their tactical advantage came from being incorporeal most of the time, which it seemed to be refusing to do.

"Grab Nyx," I commanded Alaric. "We need to get out of here."

Alaric didn't question me as he quickly but carefully picked Nyx up off the floor. The ranger didn't so much as stir, but I could still hear their heart beating. They still stood a chance. But there was nothing we could do for them in here; we needed to get the hell out.

Shadows streamed from the ceiling and slammed into Vail, who flew backward and through the hallway before crashing into the other room. Alaric and I darted after him but just as we reached the fallen ranger, he leapt to his feet and started back towards the wraiths. I wrapped my fingers around his arm and pulled, stopping him in his tracks.

Vail snarled and shoved me against the wall next to the hallway entrance. His dark grey eyes had turned completely silver, and his fangs were on display. *Hello, bloodlust.*

"Samara!" Alaric screamed.

"GO!" I ordered. Alaric hesitated, clearly torn between getting Nyx to safety and helping me. "He won't hurt me," I said with a confidence I absolutely did not feel, but I needed Alaric to get out of here. "Save Nyx, Alaric! Please!"

He let loose a pissed-off snarl but did as I asked and took off running towards the exit with Nyx gripped tightly in his arms.

Vail's claws dug into my shoulders, and I heard the wraiths whispering excitedly as the scent of my blood filled the air. Hopefully, that meant they would focus on me and not Alaric fleeing with Nyx.

Fuck. On second thought, wraiths being completely focused on me sounded really, really bad.

Vail tilted his head, mesmerized by the blood pooling in the pocket of my collarbone. I had to snap him out of it, and then we needed to hightail our asses out of here to where the sun was still shining outside.

Erendriel didn't seem to be bound by shadows, but hopefully these ones weren't far enough along in their transformation to withstand sunlight.

"Vail," I warned when I felt him adjust his grip.

Before I could do anything, he yanked me against him and ran a rough tongue against my skin.

Of all the times for his bloodlust to rise, of course it had to be now.

Thin tendrils of shadows leaked from the ceiling and brushed against the blood gushing from where Vail still had a brutal hold on me. Whispers swam through my mind, making me shudder until one word floated to the surface.

Delicious.

"FUCK!" I screamed and threw all of my weight to the side. Agony tore through me as Vail's clawed fingers ripped from my flesh.

Blood that had been steadily streaming now gushed from my wounds, and the wraith that Vail had been fighting earlier laughed and took a step into the hallway. The chittering sound of excited whispers filled the space as shadows slid down the wall.

I slipped the dagger free from my thigh sheath and threw it at the wraith, who was still mostly corporeal. It sank into his throat, cutting off his laughter.

I slapped a hand over my wound and then shoved it into Vail's face.

"You want it? Come and get it!" I dropped my hand and whirled around, running as fast as I could, pissed-off snarls and angry whispers screaming in my wake.

I made it halfway through the large cavern of a room

where the prince had met with the Fae before a shadowy figure snapped into existence in front of me and swiped for my chest. My feet slid as I tried to stop, but I wasn't fast enough. Pain flared as claws pierced my skin just above my heart before vanishing, and then I crashed to the floor on my already wounded shoulder.

Blood seeped out of my injuries and formed a pool around me as the shadows swirled; both wraiths had fully retreated to their shadow forms now. I could sense their excitement as they circled, occasionally snapping into physical forms to take another strike at me or graze my skin with their razor-sharp talons.

Stand up. I needed to get off the damn floor and run. But when I tried to rise, my body instantly gave out, and I sank back into my own blood. My thoughts grew hazier, but I forced myself to think.

Why aren't they killing me?

More whispers in my ear, and I was starting to get good at picking out words. *Delicious. Power. Mine.*

Something about their whispered language tickled the back of my mind, but I couldn't figure out what it was. Just when I started to realize why it was bothering me, a loud crash punctuated with snarls came from above me.

Vail was still alive then.

A sharp hiss tore out of me when one of the wraiths gripped my wrist and yanked me forward. It could only hold on for a few seconds, so it had to keep repeating the process. The third time it pulled, I screamed as something in my arm tore and my vision darkened.

My eyelids fluttered as I clung to consciousness. I tried to pull myself away, but I'd lost too much blood. *The ritual.* They must be dragging me back for the ritual.

Well, I'd wanted to know what it was they were doing. I guess this was one way to find out.

Something slammed into the floor next to me, causing my eyes to fly open. I stared stupidly at the huge piece of white stone that had shattered the floor before realizing there was sunshine beaming down on it.

It took me several more seconds to realize the wraiths had released me to get away from the light that now bathed my mutilated body.

"Pretty," I slurred, winding my fingers around the golden light. The wraiths shrieked and backed further away, and then Vail appeared over me. "You're pretty too," I said weakly.

Vail cursed, that predatory gleam still in his silver eyes before he bit down hard on his wrist.

"Sam!" he growled into my face.

I blinked, realizing I must have blacked out. I was practically in his lap now, and he was holding his bloody wrist in front of me.

His blood called to me, and my fangs snapped down to tear into his flesh.

Rich, decadent blood spilled down my throat, and I greedily swallowed as much as I could. A moan slipped from my lips as power flooded me and still, I drank more. A deep rumble came from Vail's chest as he held me tightly against him.

Another piece of the ceiling collapsed, landing with a solid thud a few feet from us. The haze that had been encircling my mind lifted as my body recovered from blood loss.

I instantly released Vail and tried to push out of his arms, but he just clamped me to him as he rose to his feet.

"Nice of you to finally get your head back in the game." His voice had an odd raspy quality to it, and he was looking at me with something akin to need.

I was so used to seeing nothing but hate in his eyes when they fell on me that I didn't know how to process this. It must be some leftover feeling from the bloodlust. Which reminded me…

"Oh, I'm sorry that I almost died from getting clawed up by the wraiths *and* you," I growled back.

His lips pursed together in a flat line. Maybe he was hoping I wouldn't have remembered that part. I frowned. There was something else I was forgetting. Something after I ran away from Vail. I racked my brain, trying to remember, but the last few minutes were such a blur.

A dark shape flashed by our haven of light, followed soon by another. The second one got a little too close to the light, and it let out an ear-splitting shriek before diving back into the shadows.

My eyes roved around the room, but I didn't see the third one anywhere. Maybe it was still recovering from the wound Vail had given it.

"Can you run?" Vail asked quietly.

"Only one way to find out."

He stared at me, and I could tell he was debating trying to carry me out. At least, I hoped he was thinking that and not chucking me off into the shadows and getting himself out while the wraiths were distracted.

But given that he'd just given me blood and probably saved my life, I was inclined to believe that he wanted to save us both.

Which confused the hell out of me given his previous actions, but I wasn't going to question it now.

At least I wasn't dead.

"I'm fine," I murmured. "Set me down quickly and then we make a break for it, okay?"

Vail looked at me with silver and dark grey eyes that reminded me of a storm cloud. When he made no move to set me down, I pushed against him until he finally relented and set me on my feet. I wobbled for a second, but with Vail's blood coursing through me, I wasn't in pain at all. If anything, I felt fucking amazing.

I quickly took stock of my injuries and found that the worst of them had already healed. Vail also looked no worse for wear despite the fights he'd been in with the wraiths and whatever the hell he had done to break down part of the ceiling.

Before I could think better of it, I slipped my hand into his and gave him a questioning look.

Fathomless eyes looked at our hands clasped together before slowly trailing up to my face. He stared at me for a long moment before slowly nodding.

When the wraiths circling us passed by, leaving a wide-open path to the front room, we both bolted forward. Despite the boost of Vail's blood, it only took him a few seconds to outpace me. His fingers clamped down harder around my hand as he pulled me with him.

A scream ripped out of me as I stumbled when one of the wraiths swiped its claws down my back, but Vail only tightened his grip and refused to let me fall.

Finally, we passed the archway that led to the front room, and I could see the sunlit exit ahead of us. Without warning, a wall of shadows slammed into existence between us and it, and Vail yanked me to the side. We raced between the columns, weaving in and out as the wraiths kept trying to slow our progress.

They were clearly trying to keep us alive because they kept going for our legs and arms in an attempt to maim, probably so they could drag us back for that moons-damned ritual.

But their tactics changed when we got closer to the exit and they saw us slipping from their grasp.

I barked out a warning when I saw one of them snap towards Vail, talons solidifying at the last second to rip out his throat. He swerved to the side and swiped at the arm with his dagger. Shadows dripped to the floor like blood as the wraith shrieked in pain.

Alaric appeared in the archway but stayed within the light as he watched in horror as we did our best to outrun our deaths.

The wounds down my back felt like liquid fire, but I was too hopped up on adrenaline to let it slow me down. Anticipation coursed through me as the exit drew nearer, and I could practically feel the sunlight on my skin as we closed the distance between us and salvation.

Vail made it through the exit first, and just as I passed Alaric and felt the sun hit my skin, something wrapped around my throat and ripped me out of Vail's grasp.

"Samara!" Alaric screamed and grabbed my arm with both hands.

Vail reached back for me, but a slash of shadow shot out and knocked him back, far past the columns that decorated the outside of the temple.

The pressure around my throat vanished, only to immediately be replaced by another as the wraiths worked together to pull me back into the darkness. I felt claws pierce my skin where Alaric was holding on, pulling on me with all his strength.

The wraiths were relentless and for a second, I thought I was going to know what it felt like to have my arm torn off.

Vail's pissed-off expression filled my view as he raced back towards us with his dagger raised. The wraiths doubled their efforts to claim me as both theirs and an agonized scream erupted from my throat when my shoulder dislocated.

The cold realization that Vail was going to be too slow slammed into me.

"Don't let go," I pleaded as I stared directly into Alaric's panicked but determined eyes.

"I won't!" Alaric swore, even as his grip on me started to slip.

An outraged roar shook me to my core, and suddenly Cali was there. She reached into the darkness behind me and yanked one of the wraiths out into the daylight.

Its screams were like nothing I'd ever heard as the sun slowly began to burn its existence away. Without another wraith to alternate grabbing me, Alaric was able to pull me free as soon as the wraith still in the shadows lost its grip on its corporeal form.

I crashed into Alaric and we both tumbled, with me landing on top of him and letting out a hiss of pain at jostling my shoulder.

We both turned our heads to where the wraith was still writhing and screaming in agony as it was burned. Every time it tried to run towards the safety of the temple, Cali would coat her hand with her own shadow magic and pull it back.

After one final shriek, the shadow dissolved into nothing.

Cali let out a pained grunt, exhausted. I immediately rushed over to her, shoving aside Vail, who was also going to check on the Furie.

"Are you okay?" I asked frantically, using my one good arm to check her for injuries.

"Fine," she said through clenched teeth. "It's hard to use my shadow magic against the wraiths, and whatever magic they're using on themselves to become Fae again makes it worse."

"Where is the prince and the other Fae?" Alaric asked, scanning the area around us as if he expected them to appear at any moment.

Which, given our shitty luck lately, seemed like a distinct possibility.

"That Fae prick threw up some kind of barrier when they reached the rangers that the prince brought with them," Cali said with a grimace. "I couldn't get through it, so I came back here to see if you needed help."

Vail sighed. "We need to deal with the remaining wraith. Even if he didn't catch our names, he'll be able to describe us, and the prince will figure it out."

Fear washed over me. Both at the idea of walking back into that temple and at the prince learning that we knew about whatever deal he had going on with the wraiths. Cali patted my knee before rising to her feet, a soothing gesture.

"I'll go with you," Cali told Vail. "You two stay here and watch over Nyx."

I wanted to protest as I watched the two of them walk back into the shadowed temple, but Vail was right. We couldn't let the prince learn that we were aware of his betrayal, and with Cali by his side, they should be able to take on the remaining wraith.

Unable to stop myself, I let out a hoarse giggle. Sharp pain barked from my shoulder at the movement and I hissed, clutching my arm tighter. I half stumbled over to a pillar, its top half broken off and lying in large chunks around us. A wheezing sound somewhere between a pained gasp and laugh bubbled out of me, each one hurt but I couldn't seem to make myself stop.

Ugh. This was going to hurt. I should have asked Cali to help me before she flew off. After lining up as best I could, I slammed my shoulder against the hard stone, popping it back into place.

The fiery agony was rapidly replaced by blessed cool relief. I leaned against the broken pillar and let myself slide to the floor as more hysterical laughter erupted out of me

"Samara?" Alaric shot me a concerned look. "Exactly how hard did you hit your head while struggling to get free?"

It took a few attempts, but finally I got out, "Vail saved my life again. He's going to be so pissed when he has time to think about it later."

CHAPTER TWENTY-SEVEN

—

Samara

Alaric groaned as he sat down at the table we'd claimed at the tavern of the outpost we'd been holed up in for the last few days.

Hybell was one of the older outposts that was close to both the Furie and Velesian borders. There were closer outposts to where we'd been in the Furie realm, but we all agreed that we wanted to put as much distance between us and the temple as possible.

Hybell wasn't on any of the trade routes, so the locals were used to keeping to themselves. Our arrival three nights ago had surprised them, but it was when Cali landed behind us, wreathed in shadows, that they'd all screamed and ran to hide in their homes while the few rangers in town called out the alarm. Not that any of us could really blame them.

I'd shot Cali a look, but she'd merely shrugged and let the shadows dissipate.

I didn't know if she'd simply forgotten to pull her shadows away before landing or if she was still shaken up from the fight with the wraiths. Knowing Cali, it could go either way, and she'd never admit to which one.

I didn't like the way Vail was looking at her these days, like he was trying to find weak spots to use when Cali inevitably lost her way.

Every time I caught him studying her, I stepped in between them. I'd cut out his fucking heart before I let him go after my friend.

"How are you still sore?" Nyx eyed Alaric in disbelief.

"Because he's too stubborn to drink from anyone," I muttered, earning me a glare from Alaric. "It's true! Everyone else topped off. I don't know why you're being so ridiculous about it."

We'd all taken turns feeding Nyx on our way to the outpost. It'd taken them hours to regain consciousness enough to be coherent after the hit they'd taken. If I closed my eyes, I could still remember the sound of their bones snapping as they collided with the wall.

Alaric had managed to control his mount enough to ride back even at our fast pace, which allowed me to carry Nyx in front of me as we raced to Hybell.

Thanks to the amount of blood we pumped into them at every break, they looked almost as good as new. I'd also forced Vail to drink from my wrist when I realized he still had broken ribs from the hit he'd taken towards the end of our fight with the wraiths.

It'd been awkward as hell, but he couldn't drink from Nyx in their condition, and neither Cali nor Alaric offered.

But Alaric's stubborn-ass had refused to drink from any of us. He hadn't been injured much in the fighting, but clearly, it'd been a while since he'd partaken in any blood because the days of travel to and from the temple had taken a lot out of him.

"I'm fine," Alaric grumbled as he reached for one of the rolls at the center of the table and stuffed it with a few slices of cheese. "Everyone good to head back today?"

Vail grunted, which I took as a yes. He'd been extra moody

all morning. Maybe he was just realizing that he'd missed an opportunity to get rid of me once and for all. Instead, he'd ripped open a hole in a stone ceiling to save my life.

"Cali left this morning," I said, twisting the ring around my finger. "She's going to check on Rynn."

Rynn hadn't reached out for the last few days, which was unlike her. She knew we were going to the temple and should have been harassing me for an update. Instead, there was nothing but silence from her.

"I'm sure she's fine," Nyx said.

"Of course." I gave them a smile that I knew didn't reach my eyes.

"Let's eat and get going," Vail finally said. "We should be able to reach one of the outposts halfway back to House Harker by nightfall if we keep a decent pace."

Alaric grimaced but didn't argue. We were all more than ready to be home and safe.

Two days later, relief swept through me as the gate of House Harker was opened in front of us. Rangers called out greetings as we passed under them and hurried over to take our mounts from us.

It had taken us a little longer than we thought because of some howler activity on the way back. Thankfully, we hadn't run into them, but we'd taken shelter at an outpost earlier than we'd anticipated after leaving Hybell.

"I'm going to help get the horses sorted and then collapse into bed," Nyx announced. "Don't bother me for the next twenty-four hours unless it's an emergency."

The corner of Vail's lips twitched in the closest thing to a smile I'd seen on his face in the last week. But his expression was hard again when his eyes fell on me. We both stared at each other with thinly veiled hostility. Vail confused the hell out of me, but despite him saving my life at the temple, I still didn't come close to trusting him.

I didn't know why he'd done it, and I was pretty sure he didn't know why either. He'd already left me to die once, and I had no doubt that he'd do it again.

But even if I could convince Carmilla to get rid of Vail, it would leave House Harker in a weak position, and we couldn't afford that right now. Vail was an excellent marshal, and all the rangers looked up to him. If we kicked him out of the House, a large number of them would probably leave with him.

We needed Vail. So I'd just have to make sure to watch my back around him.

"Samara?" Kieran called out.

I looked up at the stairs that led to the main house to see Kieran waiting on the landing for me.

My lips broke out into a grin, and I took a step towards him, about to run up the stairs and throw myself into his arms before I noted the strained look on his face and halted.

"What is it, Kier?" I asked as my eyes searched his face, trying to find the answer as to what had upset him.

I got my answer a second later when Prince Draven strolled through the doorway and out into the afternoon sun to stand by Kieran's side.

I felt Alaric stiffen at my side, and out of the corner of my eye I saw Vail go predatory still as he took in the enemy who had so easily waltzed into our home. Thoughts rapidly shot through my mind as to why the prince would be here.

We'd killed all the remaining wraiths. There was no one to tell the prince that we knew he was the one betraying us.

It was possible that there was one hiding in the shadows that we missed, but if he knew what had happened, why not attack us on the way back when we were isolated from the rest of House Harker? Maybe he wanted to find out if we had told anyone else? Or maybe he was here for something completely unrelated, and this was just an unnerving coincidence?

"Prince Draven," I said smoothly and resumed my walk up the stairs to greet him. "Apologies for our greeting. We've been traveling for the past few days to check in on some outposts and reassure them that they're safe. I'm afraid we're all a little tired, and your presence here took us by surprise."

"No need to apologize, Samara." A charming smile spread across his handsome face.

His long hair was loose and fell in waves over his shoulder. In the darkness of the temple, the silver streaks in his inky black hair had almost blended in.

But out here in the sunlight, they gleamed brightly. Intense blue eyes that always reminded me of the color of lapis lazuli stones found along the riverbanks in the Velesian realm sparked with interest as they ran down my body.

He remarked with a knowing look, "Looks like you've had quite the ride."

A muscle in Kieran's jaw ticked before he smoothed out his expression. "The prince is here on official business," he said. "Carmilla asked me to escort him personally since she'll be at the Sovereign House for the foreseeable future."

"Is she okay?" I asked quickly, trying to keep the panic off my face. Did the prince target my aunt as a way to keep me compliant?

"She's fine." Draven gave Kieran a chastising look. "My mother just has a lot on her plate right now, and your aunt is helping her work through it." He offered me a sheepish smile. "Both me and my father have tried to help, but Carmilla is way more qualified."

I laughed politely, fighting back the cringe of how fake it sounded to my ears. "She's a force to be reckoned with, for sure."

Unease coursed through my body as I fought to keep my

breathing even. Draven's polite, interested gaze never wavered as I frantically attempted to calm myself enough to speak rationally, causing the moment to stretch.

I cleared my throat, attempting to break the uncomfortable silence. "What brings you to House Harker, Prince Draven?"

It was Kieran who cut in, his frustration and anger slipping through his calm mask. "He's here to court you, Samara. Carmilla and Queen Velika think it's time for House Harker and the Sovereign House to be joined, and as the Heir of House Harker, it's been proposed that you should marry Prince Draven."

I snapped my jaw shut and gave the prince a bewildered look that I didn't have to fake at all as he offered me a salacious smile in return.

Well. Shit.

Want to Read More?

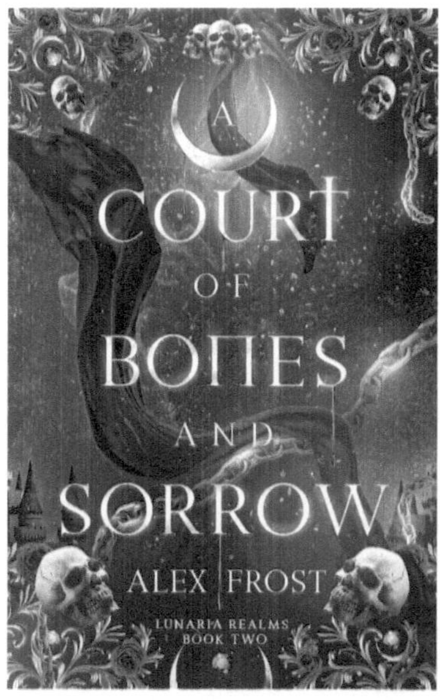

The next book in the series, A Court of Bones & Sorrow is out now!

Want to know what Kieran was thinking on that beach?

Signup for the Alex Frost newsletter at <u>alexfrostauthor.com</u> to read some of the emotional and spicy scenes from an alternative character's point of view!

If you enjoy fantasy romance with morally grey characters and slow burn angst you may like this series...

Lost Legacies

A Shift in Darkness*

A Shift in Shadows

A Shift in Fate

A Shift in Fortune

A Shift in Ashes

A Shift in Wings

A Shift in Death

*A Shift in Darkness is available for free download at maddoxgreyauthor.com.

About the Author

Alex Frost is… actually Maddox Grey. Dun dun duuuuun!

Okay probably not that dramatic of a reveal since it isn't exactly a closely guarded secret. The pen name Alex Frost was created to publish the spicier fantasy series that fall under the "Why Choose" genre.

Why Alex Frost? Because Maddox is a freaking nerd. After being trained by local baristas to respond to the name "Alex" instead of Maddox, it seemed like the perfect pen name. Half of it anyway.

Since Maddox already shares their last name with Jean Grey of the X-Men, it seemed fitting to borrow Emma Frost's last name for their other persona. If you know, you know. (insert smirking face)

To get regular email updates about new releases and other announcements, be sure to sign up for the newsletter on alexfrostauthor.com

facebook.com/alexfrost.author

instagram.com/alexfrost.author

tiktok.com/@greymalkinpress